"WHAT WOMAN DOESN'T LIKE CHOCOLATE?"

She picked up a dark chocolate truffle. *Nirvana,* she thought as it melted in her mouth. "What do you like?"

"I like you," he said quietly. "Far more than I should. Far more than is good for you."

Megan stared at him, suddenly reminded that she knew almost nothing about this man. That they were alone in an empty building. That no one would hear her if she screamed for help. An innate sense of self-preservation had her taking a step backward, even though there was no place to go.

"I'm sorry," he said. "I didn't mean to frighten you."

She searched her mind for some flip reply to ease the tension that stretched between them, but nothing came to mind. Why was she suddenly so afraid?

"Megan." Putting his glass aside, he ran a hand through his hair. He had known bringing her to his lair had been a bad idea from the start. Having her here, so close, was proving to be even more of a temptation than he had expected. If only her eyes weren't as soft and brown as sun-warmed earth, her skin so incredibly smooth, her lips so pink and inviting. If only her blood didn't sing to him. . . .

Other titles available by Amanda Ashley

A Whisper of Eternity

After Sundown

Dead Perfect

Dead Sexy

Desire After Dark

Night's Kiss

Night's Master

Night's Pleasure

Night's Touch

Immortal Sins

Everlasting Kiss

Published by Kensington Publishing Corporation

EVERLASTING DESIRE

Amanda Ashley

ZEBRA BOOKS are published by

Kensington Publishing Corp.
119 West 40th Street
New York, NY 10018

All Kensington titles, imprints and distributed lines are available at special quantity discounts for bulk purchases for sales promotion, premiums, fund-raising, educational or institutional use.

Special book excerpts or customized printings can also be created to fit specific needs. For details, write or phone the office of the Kensington Special Sales Manager: Attn. Special Sales Department. Kensington Publishing Corp., 119 West 40th Street, New York, NY 10018. Phone: 1-800-221-2647.

ISBN-13: 978-1-4201-0444-8
ISBN-10: 1-4201-0444-6

First Printing: October 2010

10 9 8 7 6 5 4 3 2 1

Printed in the United States of America

For Brandon

and

Skylynn

May the Good Lord bless you

with health and happiness

I love you!

In fond memory of
Elizabeth Camp.
Reader, friend, and poet.

Prologue

Standing at the helm of his eighty-foot Ferretti, Tomás Villagrande stared out at the vast ocean, his thoughts turned inward. He had been a vampire for a very long time. Some believed he had been turned by Dracula, but Tomás had been made long before the notorious count arrived on the scene. Ah, yes, if the truth were to be known, it was Tomás who had bequeathed the Dark Trick to the world's most infamous vampire.

Tomás grinned at the memory. Vlad Dracula had been born to be a vampire. Tomás had turned many people in his time, but none had embraced the Dark Gift as fully or as eagerly as the Transylvanian warlord.

Tomás blew out a sigh. In his long existence, he had traveled the world countless times, seen and done all there was to see and do. And now, after more than fifteen hundred years of existence, he was bored with life as he knew it.

As a mortal man, he had been born to be a warrior, though he had always had a love for the sea. When he wasn't at war, he could be found out on the ocean. But it seemed there was always another war, and another.

When he turned vampire, being a warrior became a

whole new adventure, and, for a time, he had put his love of the ocean behind him. Impervious to death, he had stalked the night, instilling terror in the hearts of his enemies even as he turned the land red with their blood—what blood he didn't consume. He grinned into the darkness. Ah, in those days, he had glutted himself on the warm, rich red elixir, sated himself until he could hold no more. Drank until he was drunk with it, and in so doing, he became stronger than any other vampire who walked the face of the earth.

Gradually, ground warfare had lost its appeal, and he had gone to sea where, once again, he instilled terror into the hearts of his enemies. Sailing under a black pirate flag, he had terrorized English ports and ships, robbing wealthy Englishmen of their riches and their lives until that, too, lost its allure, and he had come to the New World seeking peace.

Tomás drew in a deep breath, his nostrils filling with the scent of surf and sand. He'd had enough of peace. It was time to fight again, time to rally the ranks of the Undead and spread a little terror among the masses.

His lip curled with pleasure at the mere idea. It was time to stir things up, to remind mankind that there really were monsters hiding under the bed and in the closet.

Chapter 1

Reclining on a chaise longue on the balcony of his penthouse, a snifter of imported red wine in one hand, Rhys Costain stared out over the city of Los Angeles and contemplated the events of the last few months.

Mariah, the treacherous vampiress who had offered a sizable reward for his head, had been destroyed, sent to hell by Rhys's own hand.

Erik Delacourt, the only being—man or vampire—Rhys had ever called friend, had moved to Boston with his new bride, the delectable Daisy O'Donnell. It was an odd match, Rhys mused, the vampire and the Blood Thief. Former Blood Thief, he amended, since she had given up that line of work when Delacourt turned her.

Ah, Daisy, Rhys thought. A tasty morsel, indeed. But she was a female, and, as a sex, they were more treacherous than the male and not to be trusted, a truth he had learned firsthand centuries ago.

He rarely let himself think of the fair Josette, but tonight, feeling maudlin and a little lonely, he unlocked the gates of the past and stepped inside.

He had met Josette Rousseau in the summer of 1575 in Warwickshire. He remembered the year well because

Robert Dudley had thrown a lavish party for Queen Elizabeth I at his castle in Kenilworth. The gathering had lasted three weeks. Of course, Rhys hadn't been invited. Commoners, whether vampire or mortal, didn't mingle with royalty, but everyone, highborn or low, talked about the gala event for weeks afterward.

Josette had been a young widow and a woman of means, with an estate in the country and a small townhouse in London. Rhys had been a young vampire back then, bold and impetuous. One look at Josette's clear porcelain skin and sparkling blue eyes and he had been hopelessly smitten. He could have mesmerized her and made her want him, but it hadn't been necessary. The attraction between them had been instantaneous and impossible to ignore.

He had met her on a Saturday night and taken her to his bed the following Friday. Because he had been young and proud, he had refused to move into her lavish estate. Instead, he had insisted they meet at his flat, humble as it was. Fearing that he might hurt her, or worse, turn her in a moment of weakness, he had been careful to feed each night before she came to him.

He had never known a woman like her, as elegant and proud as a queen when they were with the ton, as wanton as any common courtesan when they were alone.

Several months passed, and Rhys had been happier than he had ever been, either as a mortal man or a vampire, so in love that he no longer cared that she was wealthy, or that he was far beneath her socially. So in love that he had decided to put their differences aside and ask her to marry him. It was a bold move for a man whose mother had been a prostitute, a man who had once stolen from the rich to keep body and soul together.

He'd had marriage on his mind the night he went, unexpected and unannounced, to her estate. It was a night he would never forget. Expecting to find his lady love in her bedroom dressing for dinner, he had floated up to her second-floor window, thinking how surprised she would be to see him at such an early hour.

The surprise had been his. He had found Josette in bed with a young duke, and in that instant, reality had come rushing in, and with it the certainty that she had never loved him. She had merely been using him for her own amusement. The lady and the commoner. Fueled by rage and a sense of betrayal beyond words, he had killed the young man. Deaf to Josette's cries for forgiveness, unmoved by her incoherent pleas for mercy, Rhys had let her see him for the monster that he was. Her terror had driven him over the edge. Taking her in his embrace, he had buried his fangs in her throat and taken what he had denied himself for so long. Took it all, until she lay limp and unmoving in his arms. Horrified by what he had done, he fled the house.

In the four hundred and thirty-five years since that night, he had never let himself care for another woman. He had seduced them. He had made love to them. He drank from them, but he had guarded his heart like a fortress. Four hundred and thirty-five years, he mused, sipping his wine. It was a long time to be alone and unloved.

He thought again of Delacourt and his Daisy. Despite the fact that Delacourt was a vampire and Daisy had been a blood thief when they met, the two of them had fallen in love.

Rhys grinned inwardly. Knowing Daisy, it was hard to believe that she had once crept up on sleeping vampires, stolen a pint of their blood, and sold it on the Internet. But then, looks could be deceiving.

Rhys ran a hand through his hair. If Delacourt and Daisy could overcome obstacles like that, maybe it was time for him to try again.

Rhys snorted softly. What the hell was he thinking? If he had learned anything in the last five hundred and twelve years, it was never to make the same mistake twice.

Chapter 2

Megan DeLacey sighed when she glanced at her watch and saw that it was only a few minutes after midnight. Two hours until closing and, except for the owner, Shore's was empty. She didn't really like working nights and, if the pay and the perks hadn't been so good, she would have gone looking for a new job long ago.

Shore's was an exclusive men's shop that catered to wealthy clients—mainly eccentric rock stars and theater and movie people who preferred to shop late at night, thereby avoiding those who were less rich and famous.

Robert Parker had taken his knowledge of menswear and his friendship with a well-known actor and parlayed that combination into a tidy little business. Shore's opened at ten A.M. and closed at four P.M. to accommodate those who preferred to shop during the day, and then reopened its doors at eight P.M. and stayed open until two in the morning. Megan and Mr. Parker worked the late shift.

Parker stocked only the finest men's apparel—Shore's most inexpensive shirt sold for $375. Megan thought it was an outrageous price to pay for a short-sleeved cotton shirt, but then, she had been raised by a frugal mother and a father who was frequently out of work.

Parker also kept an assortment of spirits and black caviar on hand for his exclusive customers, as well as imported chocolates for the ladies. The chocolates were one of the perks Megan enjoyed the most, as Mr. Parker let her take home whatever was left at the end of the week.

Megan had worked at Shore's for just over a year, and, in that time, she had become a favorite of several of Mr. Parker's clients, including a well-known Hollywood producer, an Oscar-winning actor, and a famous country singer, all of whom had become regulars and insisted that she cater to their needs. In return, they showered her with expensive gifts—jewelry, tickets to gala movie premieres, passes to concerts. She had felt guilty at first, accepting such costly gifts, but Mr. Parker had laughed at her reluctance.

"Honey, to guys like these, a hundred bucks, heck, even a thousand, doesn't mean a thing."

Looking at it like that soothed her conscience. Mr. Parker was right. To an actor making fifteen or twenty million a picture, a few hundred dollars was just chump change.

A handful of her regular customers wanted more from her than her fashion expertise, but she refused to mix business with pleasure. One of her customers, an up-and-coming rock star, proposed to her every time he came into the store. He was cute and rich and very appealing, and she might have at least dated him except for one thing—Drexel was only nineteen years old.

Of course, there were nights like tonight when the store was empty. Hopefully, Mr. Parker would decide to close early since his last appointment had left an hour ago and her midnight appointment had called earlier to say he had missed his flight from New York and wouldn't be able to make it.

Megan was rearranging a display of imported French silk ties when a young man entered the store, bringing a blast of wind and a rush of cold air in with him. One look, and she knew he had never been in the store before, just as she knew she would never forget him.

A quick glance showed that his tan slacks were Armani, his boots were Gucci, and his dark brown leather jacket was top of the line Hugo Boss. It was said that clothes made the man, but this man didn't need any help. He looked young, in his early twenties, but he exuded the confidence and authority of a much older man. His dark blond hair was short, though it had a slightly shaggy look, as if he were letting it grow out.

He moved toward her on silent feet, every movement somehow sensual yet dangerous, as if he was a predator and she was his prey.

Where on earth had that thought come from?

Thrusting the foolish notion from her mind, she forced a smile. "May I help you?"

As he drew closer, Megan saw that his eyes were a deep dark brown, world-weary eyes that should have belonged to a much older man. She shivered when he turned the full force of his gaze on her.

"I was just passing by." His voice, low and innately sensual, seemed to resonate within every fiber of her being.

She couldn't stop staring at him. He was incredibly handsome, but it was more than that. She was used to being in the company of handsome men, but there was something about this man that had every nerve and cell in her body tingling and on edge. A part of her wanted to throw herself into his arms, to beg him to stay with her forever, while another part of her wanted to run away and hide while she still had the chance.

"It's kind of late for an evening stroll, isn't it?" she asked, somewhat flippantly.

"Not if one enjoys the quiet of a cool winter night."

Something in his tone had her shivering again. "I prefer

warm summer days myself." She made a broad gesture with her hand. "Please, look around. Let me know if I can be of any help."

She was keenly aware of his gaze on her back as she walked toward the rear of the store. Suddenly nervous without knowing why, she began to set up a new display of cologne and aftershave. Even with her back to him, she sensed his presence as he moved up and down the aisles. There was something almost otherworldly about him, she thought, though she had no idea where that thought came from. He dressed as well, if not better, than most of her clients. He exuded an aura of power, but so did most of the men who frequented Shore's. After all, money *was* power. But it was more than that.

"Miss?"

Megan's hand flew to her throat at the sound of his voice so close behind her. Closing her eyes, she took a deep breath. "Yes?"

"I'll take these."

Pasting a smile on her face, Megan turned and found herself gazing up into his eyes. He was close. Too close. She couldn't think, could scarcely breathe. She glanced around the store, relieved to see Mr. Parker emerge from the back room.

"Miss?" The stranger was watching her, a faint smile curving his lips, as if he knew just how much his nearness flustered her.

He liked Armani, she mused, as he held out a pair of black slacks and a black silk shirt, along with a black coat that cost more than she made in three months.

"Will this be all?" she asked, striving to keep her voice steady.

"For now."

She quickly rang up the sale, noting, as she swiped his

credit card, that his name was Rhys Costain. His signature was a bold scrawl across the bottom of the receipt.

Willing her hands not to shake, she slipped his purchases into one of the dark blue garment bags inscribed with the silver Shore's logo.

When she handed him the bag, she was careful not to touch him. "Thank you, Mr. Costain. Please come again."

His gaze, as potent as a shot of Irish whiskey, bored into hers. "Count on it," he said, and whistling softly, he turned and headed for the door.

Taking a deep breath, Megan held onto the edge of the counter as she watched him walk away. Lordy, she didn't know who Rhys Costain was, but that voice, those eyes . . . She fanned herself with her hand as she willed her heartbeat to slow down, and fervently hoped never to see him again.

Standing in the shadows outside the store, Rhys watched the woman as she straightened a shelf here, rearranged a display of silk ties there, answered the phone. She was a remarkably pretty woman, probably thirtyish, with hair the bright reddish gold of autumn leaves and warm brown eyes. He usually preferred blondes in their early twenties, but in this case, he was willing to make an exception.

Was it luck, coincidence, or fate that had sent him into the store that night? Most likely it had been fate, now having a good laugh at his expense due to the fact that not more than twenty-four hours ago he had renewed his vow never to get involved with a mortal woman again; like it or not, he had become involved the minute he laid eyes on her.

Whistling softly, he headed for home. Time to clean out his closet, he mused, since he suspected he would be buying a whole new wardrobe in the next few weeks.

* * *

Megan was ringing up a sale for the lead guitarist in a popular rock band when she felt an odd sensation skitter down her spine. Looking up, she felt a nervous flurry in the pit of her stomach when she saw the young man who had come into the shop late last night. Rhys Costain.

Her smile was forced as she bid good night to her customer, then quickly turned away, pretending to check something on the computer, all the while hoping Mr. Parker would come forward to assist their customer.

But Mr. Parker remained in his office, with the door closed.

Megan didn't hear Costain's footsteps come up behind her, but she knew he was there. She could sense his presence, feel the intensity of his gaze on her back as he waited for her to acknowledge him.

Megan took a deep breath, counted to three, and turned around. "Good evening, Mr. Costain," she said coolly. "How may I help you?"

"How, indeed?" he murmured.

His voice was smooth and soft, yet she detected a sharp edge underneath, like satin over steel. "Excuse me?"

"I'm looking for a black leather jacket."

"What length?"

He shrugged, a graceful, unhurried movement. "Mid-thigh?"

"We have a few back here you might like." Without waiting to see if he followed, she walked toward the back of the store. Pulling their most expensive coat from the rack, she held it up. "How about this one?"

He ran his hand lightly over the supple leather.

Watching him, Megan couldn't help imagining that pale, graceful hand stroking her bare skin.

"Do you like it?" he asked.

"Y . . . yes, very much."

"Do you mind if I try it on?"

"Of course not."

His hand brushed hers as he took the coat from the hanger. His skin was cool, yet a rush of heat flowed through her at his touch.

The coat fit as if it had been made for him, emphasizing his fair hair and broad shoulders.

"What do you think?" he asked.

Not trusting herself to speak, she nodded. What was there about this man that made her feel like a tongue-tied teenager?

She felt her cheeks grow hot when he looked at her and smiled, as if he knew exactly what she was thinking.

"So, you like it?"

Striving for calm, she said, "It looks very nice. There's a mirror over there. See for yourself."

"No need." Still smiling, he turned away, heading for the other side of the store.

Megan felt her blush deepen when he picked up several pairs of silk briefs, all black. Why was she acting so foolish? Men came in here and bought underwear all the time.

Frowning, she watched him pick up a dozen wife-beater T-shirts before moving to the checkout counter.

Regaining her senses, Megan stepped up to the register. "Are you going to wear the coat?"

With a nod, he removed the price tag and handed it to her.

She quickly rang up the sale, dropped his briefs and T-shirts in a bag, and offered it to him, careful, once again, to avoid his touch.

Again, his lips curved in that knowing smile.

"Good night, Mr. Costain," she said, her voice tight.

"Good night, Miss DeLacey."

The way he said her name made her insides curl with pleasure.

And then she frowned. "How did you know my name?"

He shrugged. "You must have mentioned it."

She stared after him as he left the store. She was certain she hadn't told him her name. The fact that he knew it left her feeling violated somehow.

He returned to the store every night just after midnight for the next week, and he always bought something: a dark pinstriped suit; a dozen dress shirts—black, brown, navy, and dark gray—all silk. He bought four pairs of Armani slacks in varying shades of brown, as well as three pairs of black slacks, two belts, three ties, a pair of black slippers, a black silk dressing gown.

Tonight he picked out a Trafalgar American Alligator wallet priced at $550.

He gave her a long, lingering look that made her insides curl with pleasure before he left the store.

"He's a big spender, that one," Parker said, coming up behind Megan. "I wonder what he does for a living."

"I have no idea."

"Well, I hope he sticks around. We haven't had a week like this since Bono came in to do his Christmas shopping."

Megan nodded, though secretly she hoped that Mr. Rhys Costain would go back to wherever he had come from. His mere presence flustered her, and she didn't like it. She was far past the age to come unglued in the presence of a handsome man, especially when that man was at least ten years younger than she was.

It was close to three A.M. when Megan arrived at the small, two-story house she shared with her best friend, Shirley Mansfield. Shirl was a fashion model, which sounded a lot more glamorous than it was. Being a model involved dedication and self-denial, especially for Shirl, who was older than most of the popular models and had to work harder to keep fit. Of course, as far as anyone in the business knew, she was seven years younger than her actual twenty-eight years. Shirl rose every weekday at six and headed to the gym for a thirty-minute workout. Then she came home, took a shower, and ate a calorie-controlled breakfast. Then she was off to casting appointments and fittings, and, because she was extremely popular, more often than not she had a fashion shoot in the afternoon. She didn't usually make it home before five. Of course, the pay was excellent.

Megan didn't see much of Shirl during the week, since Shirl was usually in bed long before Megan got home from work.

After taking a quick shower, Megan slipped into a pair of comfy pj's and curled up in her favorite chair, determined to read for a few minutes before she went to bed. But she couldn't seem to concentrate on the words. Instead, Rhys Costain's image drifted through her mind. She told herself to forget him. For one thing, he was much too young for her; for another, there was an air of danger about him that scared her on some deep inner level she didn't understand.

With a sigh of resignation, Megan closed the book and set it aside. Tomorrow was Saturday. She didn't have to work Sunday or Monday. If Shirl didn't have anything scheduled for Sunday night, maybe they could get together for dinner and a movie.

Later, lying in bed waiting for sleep to find her, Megan was irritated to find her thoughts again turning toward Rhys Costain. How did he spend his weekends? Was he buying all those new clothes to impress a new girlfriend? Or a new wife?

The thought of him with another woman was oddly disconcerting, and she shook it away. She didn't like him. Didn't like the way he made her feel, or the dark thoughts that flitted through her mind whenever he was near.

Flopping over onto her stomach, she pounded her fist against the pillow. She had been spending far too much time thinking about the man.

Yet even as she tried to convince herself that she didn't care if she ever saw him again, a little voice in the back of her mind whispered that she was a liar.

Chapter 3

It was late Saturday night, his favorite night to hunt. Finding prey was never a problem, but it was always easier on the weekend, especially if you were hunting young males. They tended to party too much, drink too much, making them easy targets. But it was the tasty young women with them that Rhys generally preferred. Female blood tended to be warmer, sweeter on the tongue. And even when they were high, they smelled better than their male companions.

At midnight, Rhys lingered outside one of the more fashionable nightclubs, waiting. He intended to pay a visit to Shore's again, and it would be better for him, and for the woman, if he fed before he saw her. He didn't need to feed as often as he once had, but he was addicted to the hunt. He feared he was also becoming addicted to the woman. Megan. He had plucked her name from her mind on a recent visit. Megan DeLacey. He liked the sound of it, the way it rolled off his tongue, like poetry.

He liked her.

And he intended to have her.

All of her.

But not just yet.

Moments later, a man and a woman in their midtwenties emerged from the bar, their arms wrapped around each other as they staggered down the street.

Pushing away from the side of the building, Rhys followed the couple to the parking lot, his fangs extending as he quickened his pace.

Taking them was all too easy.

Megan was somewhat surprised when Rhys Costain arrived at Shore's half an hour or so before closing. Since he usually arrived just after midnight, she had assumed he wouldn't be coming, and had even managed to convince herself she was relieved, though her foolish heart had skipped a beat in nervous anticipation every time the door opened.

Each time a client had walked in, she had swallowed her disappointment and told herself she didn't care if ever she saw Rhys Costain again or not, even though she knew it was a lie. She had never been one to deceive herself, and it annoyed her to no end that she was doing it now. She didn't know the man. She wasn't even sure she liked him, so how to explain her illogical desire to see him again, or the way her heart seemed to skip a beat whenever he stepped through the door?

He was dressed all in black tonight. The color suited him perfectly. She watched him walk toward her, although *walk* didn't come close to describing the way he moved. He moved so lightly, so fluidly, she wondered if he studied ballet. Mikhail Baryshnikov meets Bela Lugosi, she thought, with a rueful grin.

"Good evening," he murmured.

"Your closet must be full to bursting by now," Megan remarked. "I've never known anyone to buy as many clothes as you do."

He smiled a slow, crooked smile that made her insides turn to jelly. "Surely you realize that I only come here to see you."

"A date would be less expensive," she muttered, and then clapped her hand over her mouth. Where had that idea come from? And why on earth had she voiced it aloud?

"I should like that very much," he said. "Shall I pick you up after work?"

"I don't think so. You're a little too young for me."

"I'm older than I look."

"How old are you?" It was an impertinent thing to ask a customer, but her curiosity refused to be stilled. He looked young, except for his eyes.

"What does it matter? Age is only a number."

"Well, you look to be about twenty, and since I'm pushing thirty, I'm afraid I'll have to pass."

"Are you sure I can't change your mind? There's a little club not far from here where we can share a bottle of Cabernet Sauvignon and get to know each other better."

Megan shook her head, though she couldn't help being flattered. He wasn't the first young guy who had asked her out, but, until now, she had never been tempted to accept. She found the idea of getting to know Rhys Costain quite intriguing, and scary as hell. "Thank you, but I don't think so. It's against company policy to date customers."

"Indeed?"

Megan nodded, certain he knew she was lying.

"Then I guess I'll just have to buy something." He glanced around the store, then moved toward a display of Italian driving gloves.

He picked out a pair of black leather ones by Forzieri that sold for one hundred and twenty dollars, a pair of dark brown Bentleys that cost over three hundred, and a pair of gray wool Cavallis that went for a mere eighty-nine bucks.

"New socks, too, I suppose," he mused. Making his way to the far side of the store, he plucked a dozen pairs of black socks from the shelf, then added six pairs of dark brown, six pairs of navy, and three pairs of dark gray. "I guess that will do it for tonight," he remarked, heading toward the checkout counter. "Have to save something for next time."

Megan shook her head. "I can't imagine what else you could possibly need. Honestly, if you live to be a hundred, you'll never wear all the clothes you've bought in the last week!" She frowned when he burst out laughing. "Did I say something funny?"

"You have no idea." He slid his credit card across the counter, signed the receipt, and bid her good night as he scooped up his bag.

He was still chuckling when he left the store.

As had become his habit, Rhys lingered in the shadows, watching her. What was there about Megan DeLacey that intrigued him so? True, she was lovely, but he had known a lot of lovely women in the last five hundred and twelve years. Maybe it was the way her eyes met his, a faint challenge in their depths. Maybe it was the tone of her voice, the smell of her skin, or the way her heart beat a little faster when he entered the store. Maybe it was the way she filled out that green wool dress, or the way her legs looked in those three-inch heels. Hell, maybe it was all of those things—or none of them.

Of one thing he was certain. She was afraid of him.

Smart girl, he mused, as he turned away from the window and strolled down the sidewalk, still thinking of his undeniable attraction to Megan.

He hadn't gone far when two young men clad in dark jeans and leather jackets, their heads covered with black knit caps pulled down to their eyebrows, hurried past him. They reeked of cheap alcohol and cigarettes. The added scents of potassium nitrate, sulphur, and carbon told him one of them carried a gun.

A quick brush of his mind against theirs and Rhys tossed his packages in a Dumpster and turned to follow them.

Megan was getting ready to tally the night's receipts when the front door opened, admitting a pair of young men. One look and she knew trouble had just entered the store. The taller of the two remained near the door, one hand tucked inside his faded black leather jacket.

A thin white scar bisected the left cheek of the other young man. He swaggered toward her, a smirk on his swarthy face.

"Let's make this short and sweet," he said. "Just give me all the money in the drawer, and we'll be gone."

Megan had always thought people who put their lives in danger to protect large sums of cash were idiots, and she had no intention of doing so now. Mr. Parker was well insured, and he could always earn more money. She had only one life.

She had just opened the cash drawer when Mr. Parker emerged from his office.

"What's this?" he exclaimed. "What's going on?"

"None of your business, old man," Scar Face said. "So shut your mouth before I shut it for you."

"See here, you young punk!" Parker retorted indignantly. "Get the hell out of my shop before I call the police!"

"You ain't callin' nobody, old man."

Parker's face turned a deep red as he pulled his cell phone from his pants pocket. "We'll see about that!"

Megan let out a shriek as the thug near the entrance pulled a gun and leveled it at Mr. Parker.

What happened next happened so fast, Megan wasn't sure how much was real and how much she imagined. The front door opened, and a blur of black leather flew into the store seconds before the man fired the gun. In the space of a heartbeat, Mr. Parker had been pushed out of harm's way, the two would-be robbers were unconscious on the floor, and Rhys Costain stood in front of her, the robber's pistol in his hand.

"Are you all right?" he asked.

She blinked at him. "How . . . ? Where . . . ?" She glanced at the front door, still swinging, at the two young men, both out cold. At Mr. Parker's ashen face. At the ominous red stain spreading down Rhys's left arm.

"I think you'd better sit down," he said, slipping the pistol into his coat pocket. "You look a little pale. You, too, buddy."

Mr. Parker looked offended at being called "buddy," but he didn't argue. Sitting down in one of the store's padded chairs, he folded his arms over his chest, then, shoulders slumped, he cradled his head in his hands.

Megan looked up at Rhys. "I should call the police." She started to touch his arm, then drew back. "And an ambulance."

"I'm fine. Sit down before you faint."

"I'm not going to faint!" she exclaimed. Her knees were as weak as a newborn kitten's, and she felt light-headed. "I'm not going to faint," she repeated, and hoped it was true.

"Uh-huh." Taking her lightly by the forearm, Rhys guided her to a chair and gently pushed her down. "Just rest a minute. These guys aren't going anywhere."

Megan took several deep breaths. Had she been alone, she would have put her head between her knees and sobbed, but she wasn't alone. She could feel Rhys Costain watching her, knew he was just waiting for her to faint or go into hysterics like some spineless female.

"Hey." His voice was soft and low as he laid a gentle hand on her shoulder. "Are you sure you're all right?"

His voice, his touch, went through her like an electric shock. Startled, she looked up, her earlier fear momentarily forgotten. Who was this man, that he should affect her so profoundly?

"I'm . . . I'm fine." She glanced at the two hoodlums who had come in to rob the store. They were still sprawled on the floor. Were they dead? She was vaguely aware that Mr. Parker was on the phone.

A short time later, two police officers arrived. Polite, but all business, they took her statement, then Mr. Parker's, then Costain's. One of the officers offered to drive Rhys to the hospital, but he refused, insisting he wasn't badly hurt. Megan didn't believe him. Neither did the police, but when Rhys removed his coat and shirt, there was little more than a shallow gash on his arm.

"But there was so much blood . . ." Megan murmured, frowning.

"Just a flesh wound," Rhys said with a grin.

When the police were satisfied that they had all the information they needed, they handcuffed the two suspects, who had regained consciousness as soon as the police finished interrogating Rhys.

"We'll be in touch, Mr. Parker," one of the officers said, and then they marched the suspects out of the store.

Mr. Parker locked the front door behind the police, then walked back to where Rhys was standing. "Mr. Costain, I don't know how we can ever repay you."

"No need."

"Please," Mr. Parker said, pulling his checkbook from the inside pocket of his suit coat. "I'd be happy to give you a reward."

"If you insist," Rhys said. "How about a new shirt?"

Mr. Parker blinked at him. "A new shirt? That's all you want?"

"That's it."

Shaking his head, Mr. Parker fetched the most expensive shirt the store had to offer. Handing it to Rhys, he said, "How about a new coat? That one's ruined."

Rhys shrugged. "Sure." He didn't really need another coat, but what the hell? It would give him an excuse to see Megan again. "I'll stop in and look around next time I'm in the neighborhood."

"Very well," Mr. Parker said. "Megan, if you're ready, I'll take you home."

"I'll see her home," Rhys said.

Mr. Parker looked doubtful, but there was no arguing with Costain's expression or the implacable tone of his voice.

Taking Megan by the hand, Rhys lifted her to her feet. "Ready?"

"Yes, but . . ."

Before she quite knew how it happened, they were in her car, with Rhys behind the wheel.

"I can drive," she protested.

"Not tonight." He slid the key into the ignition.

Megan frowned. She didn't remember giving him her keys.

After a glance in the rearview mirror, he pulled away from the curb.

"What made you come back to the shop?" Megan asked. "And what happened to all the things you bought earlier?"

"I dropped them off at my place."

"You must live close by."

He shrugged. "Close enough."

She gave him the directions to her house, then wrapped

her arms around her middle, suddenly chilled. Nerves, she thought, but that was to be expected. She had just been through a traumatic experience. She and Mr. Parker could have been hurt, killed. If Rhys hadn't come along when he did . . .

She shook her head. He had been shot because of her. She couldn't explain it, but she knew in the deepest part of her being that he had come back to the store because she had been in danger, which begged the question: how had he known?

Rhys slid a glance in her direction. "You doing okay?"

She nodded, but she couldn't stop trembling. "You came back because of me, didn't you?"

He hesitated a moment before he said, "I was hoping to change your mind about that drink."

"I could sure use one." She didn't believe for a minute that was why he had returned to Shore's. She was tempted to pursue the matter, but she just didn't have the energy.

They drove in silence for a few moments, and then she frowned. "Where are we going?"

"You said you needed a drink. I know just the place."

"It's late. I don't think . . ."

"One drink," he said, "and I'll take you home."

Looking at him, at the gleam in his fathomless dark eyes, she knew without a doubt that Rhys Costain was more dangerous than a dozen armed thugs.

Ten minutes later, he pulled up in front of a brick building. The name BLUE MOON flashed in turquoise neon above the entrance.

Rhys came around the front of the car and opened the door for her. She hesitated when he offered her his hand, reluctant to touch him without knowing why. When he continued to stand there, his arm outstretched, she heaved a sigh, then placed her hand in his. His fingers were cool as they closed over her own.

He handed her out of the car, then stripped off his ruined coat and bloody shirt and dropped them into the gutter. Opening the Camry's rear door, he pulled out the shirt Mr. Parker had given him. After removing it from the wrapper, he shook it out and slipped it on.

"Nice," he said, running his hand over the navy blue silk. He gestured toward the club. "Shall we?"

Megan gestured at the gutter. "What about your clothes?"

"I'll have someone from the club dispose of them."

"Oh."

"Shall we?"

Still somewhat dazed, Megan nodded.

The Blue Moon was a small club that catered to jazz enthusiasts. Old black-and-white photos of famous, and not-so-famous, musicians lined the walls, interspersed with pages of sheet music autographed by singers and songwriters.

Rhys guided Megan to a vacant booth and slid in beside her. He could sense the tension rolling off her in waves. A part of it was due to the incident at Shore's, but Rhys knew his presence caused the majority of her nervousness. She was afraid of him without knowing why.

He smiled inwardly. He knew why. Some mortals were sensitive to the presence of his kind. On some instinctive level, they recognized the danger he represented. Most dismissed it, overwhelmed by his vampire glamour.

He ordered a bottle of vintage red wine, then settled back against the seat. His gaze trapped hers as, ever so gently, he whispered peace to her mind, his words easing away some of the tension that gripped her.

When she relaxed, he said, "So, tell me about yourself."

"There's nothing much to tell. I was married, but it didn't work out. . . ."

"Why not?" It was a silly question. Few marriages lasted

any length of time these days, but any man who let Megan get away was crazy.

"Oh, a lot of reasons. He was too young, not really ready to settle down. I wanted a home and a family. He didn't. He liked partying and riding motorcycles with his friends on the weekends." She lifted one shoulder and let it fall. "It was years ago. He's married now. They just had a baby. I guess I should have waited for him to grow up."

He didn't miss the wistful note in her voice. "You never married again?"

"No. Once was enough."

"Once burned, twice shy?" he asked with a rueful grin.

"Something like that. How about you? Have you ever been married?"

He shook his head.

"I'm surprised."

"Oh? Why?"

"You're young, rich, handsome. . . ." She shrugged. "It just seems like someone would have snatched you up by now."

"You think I'm handsome?"

"In a dark, devilish sort of way, yes."

Devilish. He laughed softly. If she only knew. "Go on," he coaxed. "Tell me more."

"There's not a lot to tell. I live with a friend of mine. I work." She shrugged. "Sounds boring, doesn't it?"

"If you don't like it, change it."

"I didn't say I didn't like it. I've always enjoyed my job and the people. At least until tonight."

"The friend you live with . . . ?" He waited, jaw clenched, afraid of what he might do if her roommate was a man. Just because she hadn't married again didn't mean she wasn't involved.

"Shirley. We've been friends since college. She's a high fashion model, very pretty. You'd like her."

"I like you."

The words, the tone of his voice, the sultry look in his eyes, sent a shiver down her spine. She took a sip of her wine, hoping it would calm her. His thigh brushed against hers, but it was more than his nearness that unsettled her.

She eased her leg away from his. "What about you? What do you do for a living?"

A smile flitted across his face before he said, "I own a little nightclub on the other side of town."

"Oh? What's it called? Maybe I've been there."

He laughed softly. "I doubt it."

"Why? What kind of club is it?"

"It's a Goth hangout."

"Goth?" she asked, frowning. "You mean those weird people who dress all in black and pretend to be vampires, that kind of thing?"

"Exactly."

"Are they into the blood thing?"

"Some of them are."

"Shirl dated a guy who was a Goth a year or so ago. She was really into that kind of thing for a while. You know, the whole vampire mythology, but I can tell you, she broke it off with him pretty darn quick when he said he wanted to drink her blood." Megan grimaced. "I'm not sure vampires really exist. I mean, I've never met one. Have you?"

"Who can say? They don't advertise it, you know."

"No, I guess not."

Rhys refilled his glass, then looked at her, eyebrows raised. "More?"

"Yes, please."

He refilled her glass, wondering what she would say, what she would think, if she knew a five-hundred-year-old vampire was sitting beside her, contemplating how he might steal a taste of her blood.

When the band broke into something soft and slow, Rhys set his glass aside. "Care to dance?"

"Are you sure you want to?" She gestured at his arm. "Doesn't it hurt?"

"I'm a quick healer. So, what do you say?"

She considered it a moment, then nodded.

On the dance floor, he took her into his arms without hesitation. Her body fit against his perfectly, as he had known it would. She was warm with the juices of life, supple in his embrace. He took a deep breath, his nostrils filling with the clean scent of jasmine, the musky scent of a young female. And blood.

Her gaze met his. He knew what she was going to ask even before she spoke. "I have to know," she said, almost apologetically. "Just how old are you?"

"Twenty-five." The lie slid easily past his lips. He was too young for her at twenty, too old at five hundred and twelve. "Relieved?"

"Yes. You look younger."

"A blessing, don't you think?"

"Some people never seem to age. Sometimes I hate to look in the mirror, you know? The other day, I found a gray hair." Shirl was even more afraid of growing old than Megan was, since when Shirl's looks went, so did her career.

"Not to worry," he said with a faint smile. "You'll always be beautiful."

"Flatterer."

"I call 'em the way I see 'em." He regarded her a moment before asking, "If you could stay young forever, would you?"

She considered it a moment, then shook her head. "I don't know. Growing up, growing old, it's what life is all about."

"Yes," he remarked. "Life."

The song ended, and he escorted her back to the table.

Life, Rhys thought as he drove her home a short time later. Its flame burned bright within her, drawing him in, warming the cold, desolate places in his soul.

If he drank from her, he knew he would never be cold again.

Megan stood at the window, watching Rhys walk away. She had suggested he drive home in her car or call a cab, but he had dismissed her suggestions with a wave of his hand, saying the walk would do him good.

She had been a bundle of nerves during the drive home, wondering if Rhys would try to kiss her good night, wondering if she should let him. The knowledge that she had even considered it still astonished her. Maybe he wasn't as young as she had thought, but she hardly knew the man. Still, a hero deserved a reward, and after what he had done tonight, he was definitely a hero.

Awfully full of yourself, aren't you, Megan? Thinking one of your kisses would be ample reward for saving your life!

As it turned out, she needn't have worried. When they reached her house, Rhys walked her to the door, made sure she was safely inside, and bid her a chaste good night.

She watched him until he was swallowed up in the darkness; then, after double-locking the front door, she went through the rest of the house, making sure all the windows were closed and locked, drawing the drapes to shut out what was left of the night. Funny, that while sitting in the club with Rhys, the events at the store had seemed distant, almost as if they had happened to someone else, but here, in her own home, she was suddenly afraid. She knew there was evil and violence in the world. She saw it in living color on the nightly news, but, until this evening, she had never experienced it firsthand.

She could have been killed tonight. They could all have been killed.

Folding her arms over her chest, she rubbed her hands up and down her arms. Maybe it was time to buy a gun, or at least a canister of pepper spray.

After changing into a T-shirt and a pair of pajama bottoms, she went into the kitchen and fixed a cup of hot cocoa. She was sitting at the table, waiting for the chocolate to cool, when Shirl shuffled into the room. Even without makeup, her blue eyes puffy from too little sleep, and her long, silver-blond hair mussed, Shirl was gorgeous.

"I'm sorry," Megan said. "Did I wake you?"

"It's all right," Shirl replied, smothering a yawn with her hand. "I have to be up in a couple of hours anyway." She dropped into the chair across from Megan's. "What are you doing up so late? Or so early? Did you just get home?"

"Yes." Megan wrapped her hands around the mug. "We had some trouble at the store tonight."

"Oh?" Shirl stared at her, suddenly wide awake. "What happened? Did anyone get hurt?"

"No."

"Well, come on, girl, I want details."

With a sigh, Megan quickly told her about Shore's newest client and how he had come to the rescue. "Just like Batman," she finished, "but without the mask, of course."

"Too bad," Shirl said with a grin. "I like men in masks."

Megan had to laugh at that. It was one of things they had in common, liking masked heroes. Batman, Spiderman, the Lone Ranger. They all wore masks.

"Did he at least have a cape?" Shirl asked hopefully.

"'Fraid not," Megan said, smothering a yawn. "I think I'm ready for bed. Do you want to go out tomorrow night?"

"I can't. I have a date."

"You do?" Megan exclaimed. "With who?"

"Geez, don't look so surprised."

"Well, it has been a long time. For both of us."

"His name is Greg, and he's a patrol sergeant with the LAPD. Six-foot three, brown hair, brown eyes. Divorced. No children."

"When do I get to meet him?"

"I don't know. We'll see how it goes tomorrow night. So, what about this guy, Rhys? Any vibes there?"

"It doesn't matter," Megan replied, shaking her head. "He's only twenty-five."

"So you're four years older than he is. So what?"

Megan shrugged. "I don't believe him."

"You think he's older?"

"No, younger. A lot younger. But it's more than that. He's . . ." She bit down on her lower lip as she tried to find the words to describe Rhys Costain. "Different."

"Different how? Two heads? Three arms? One eye in the middle of his forehead?"

"No, nothing like that. I don't know how to explain it. He scares me, and I don't know why." She ran her fingertip around the edge of her cup. "You're going to think I'm crazy, but . . . he changed his shirt after he was shot . . ."

"What's so crazy about that?"

"Hush. I saw his arm when he changed his shirt and I swear—I swear!—the wound in his arm was gone. I mean, gone like it was never there."

"Are you sure?"

"Yes! Well, I could be wrong. It was dark, but . . ."

"You've had a rough night, girlfriend. Maybe your eyes were playing tricks on you."

"Maybe." Megan blew out a sigh. "Sometimes, when

I'm with him, I get the feeling he's hiding something. Something dark and dangerous."

"Hey, if you're having scary thoughts about this guy, then I'd say follow your instincts and stay away from him."

Good advice, Megan thought as she rinsed out her cup and made her way upstairs. Good advice, indeed.

Chapter 4

Although Rhys had little to do with the affairs of mortals in general, he made it a point to keep abreast of what was happening around the world, especially in the United States. Especially now, when he was no longer just Master of the City, but Master of the West Coast Vampires.

He grunted softly as he recalled the battle that had increased his territory. It hadn't been a battle he had sought, but he had never run from a fight. He had destroyed the other vampire without a qualm, and now his domain included Oregon, Washington, and Idaho as well as California, Arizona, New Mexico, and Montana.

He was always amazed at the violence humans were capable of. His kind were supposed to be the monsters, yet man's cruelty to his fellow beings made vampires seem benevolent by comparison.

Someone had once said there was nothing new under the sun. It was proved nightly, on the news. This evening was no different. Gang killings. Teachers having affairs with underage students. Congressmen being arrested for nefarious dealings. The rich preying on the poor. War in the Middle East. The price of gas going up and down like a yo-yo on steroids.

Rhys was about to turn off the set when the perfectly coiffed female anchorwoman said, "This just in from our sister station in New York City. The bodies of a man and a woman were discovered near the Hudson River only moments ago. According to undisclosed sources, both victims appear to have been drained of blood."

It was the last three words that caught his attention. They seemed to echo off the walls.

Drained of blood.

Rhys leaned forward, his gaze focused on the screen. In his gut, he knew those three words could mean only one thing. There was a vampire on the rampage somewhere in the city of New York.

Switching off the screen, Rhys opened the French doors and stepped out onto the balcony. The cops would never catch the vampire responsible for the killings, just as they would never solve the crime. It would take another vampire to bring the rogue down. Or a damn good hunter.

He grinned faintly, thinking it was too bad for the NYPD that Daisy and her family had given up hunting.

Thoughts of Daisy brought Megan to mind, not that he needed help to think of her. Megan had been uppermost in his mind since that first night. He wondered what she was doing this evening, since Shore's was closed on Sundays and Mondays.

Curious, he went into his bedroom to change clothes. Before he'd met Megan DeLacey, his wardrobe had been sparse—a few pairs of good slacks, a dozen shirts. But now . . . He shook his head. His closet held enough outfits to clothe three or four men for a year.

Until Megan, he had never given much thought to what he wore. Now, he found himself wondering what she would find most appealing.

Exasperated, he pulled on a pair of black slacks and a dark gray shirt, stepped into a pair of black boots, and made his way to the underground garage and his private parking place. Being the owner of the building definitely had its compensations, he thought, as he slid behind the wheel of the Jag and backed out of the garage.

Moments later, he pulled up in front of Megan's house.

Lifting his head, he expanded his senses, swore softly when he realized the place was empty. After rolling down the window, he sniffed the air, sorting through the myriad scents that swirled through it for the one he sought.

It didn't take long. With a wry grin, he put the Jag in gear and followed her scent across town to the multiplex.

He parked next to her car, then hurried inside, only to come to an abrupt halt when he entered the darkened theater. He hadn't detected the scent of anyone else in her car, but what if she had come here to meet another man? Hands clenched, he searched for her. With his preternatural vision and enhanced sense of smell, it took only moments to locate her.

On silent feet, he slid into the empty seat beside her.

Megan didn't have to see Costain's face to know he was there. She didn't even wonder why he had come, or how he had known where she was. Quite the contrary. It seemed perfectly natural that he should appear, seemingly out of thin air. One minute she had been thinking of him, and the next he was there beside her, as if her thoughts had summoned him.

"Did I miss much?" he whispered, leaning toward her.

"Only the first hour," she whispered back, and suddenly the depression that had sent her to the movies was gone as if it had never been, and all because of a man she hardly knew. "How's your arm?"

"What? Oh, it's fine. Don't worry about it."

"Would you like some popcorn?"

He wrinkled his nose at the smell of butter and salt. "No, thanks."

She wondered what he would say if she suggested they leave. The only reason she had come to the theater was because she hadn't wanted to stay home alone. She hadn't wanted to interact with anyone, either, so coming to the movies had seemed the ideal solution. She could sit in the dark, surrounded by people, without having to say a word. And hopefully forget about last night. But now Rhys was here, and everything had changed.

She was thinking about asking him if he wanted to leave when he beat her to the punch.

Leaning toward her, he whispered, "What do you say we get out of here?"

"Let's."

She dumped her popcorn in a trash can on the way out.

"Where would you like to go?" Rhys asked when they were out on the sidewalk.

"I don't know."

"Let's go to my place."

"I don't think so."

He grinned at her. His teeth were very white, even in the darkness. "I didn't mean my house. I meant my club."

"Oh. All right."

He smiled inwardly as they walked to the parking lot. Although she didn't know it, she wouldn't be any safer in his club than in his lair.

"Nice car," Megan murmured as he opened the passenger door for her.

"Yeah, it's not bad."

"Not bad?" The Jag was beautiful. Smoke gray in color, it seemed to glow in the moonlight. When she slid into the seat, the soft leather seemed to enfold her. "Oh! What about my car?"

"We can pick it up later."

Megan was wondering if she had made a mistake as Rhys pulled onto the highway. In minutes, they had left the city behind. Hands clenched in her lap, she looked out the window, her tension growing as the miles slid by. She had expected his club to be located closer to home, not out on some deserted stretch of road. Her uneasiness increased when he pulled up in front of a place called La Morte Rouge.

"The Red Death?" she murmured.

"I told you, it's a Goth hangout."

She nodded, not at all reassured by his explanation.

He turned to face her, his dark eyes glittering in the light of the dash. "Have you changed your mind?"

She swallowed hard. "I . . ."

"Hey, it's okay. I'll take you home if that's what you want."

She knew that would be the smart thing to do, but she didn't seem to have much sense when it came to Rhys. Besides, she was suddenly curious to see the inside of the club. "Let's have a drink first."

Smiling, he switched off the engine.

As she watched him walk around the front of the car to open her door, she couldn't shake off the feeling that she was Little Red Riding Hood and he was the Big Bad Wolf.

A tall man clad in a black suit, an impeccable white tie, and a long black cloak opened the door. Inclining his head, he murmured, "Good evening, Mr. Costain," and bowed them through the doorway.

Megan took a deep breath before following Rhys inside. A narrow hallway illuminated by candlelight opened onto the club's main floor. Megan glanced around, noting a long bar at the far end of the room. High-backed booths lined one wall. A grand piano stood on a raised platform in the far corner.

As was to be expected, the lighting in the club was subdued. Music filtered through the sound system; though it was low, it had a dark, sensual beat. Several couples sat at the small tables located at intervals around the room. Each table was covered with a black damask cloth; each held a blood-red rose in an ebony vase. Dark red paper covered the walls. She noticed several numbered doors, but hesitated to ask what lay behind them.

The women she passed as she followed Rhys were all beautiful, and they all wore provocative clothing, mostly black, which she supposed wasn't all that unusual considering this was a Goth club. Megan thought it was odd that the women all wore broaches inscribed with their names, and that all the names were French—Monique, Angelique, Capucine. The men, too, wore mostly black. She noted they also sported tags with French names. Maybe they were all into role-playing, she thought, and the names were those of the characters they played.

"So, what do you think?" Rhys asked as he led her to a booth in the back corner that she suspected was reserved for his use only.

"It's . . . I don't know. I've never been in a Goth club before."

She slid into the booth, and Rhys slid in beside her. The high, curved back provided them with a good deal of privacy.

A waitress arrived at their table almost before they were seated. "What can I get for you tonight, Mr. Costain?" she asked in a deep, throaty voice.

Rhys looked at Megan. "What'll you have?"

"Whatever you're having."

Megan didn't miss the subtle shake of Costain's head as he ordered a glass of red wine for her and one for himself. She wondered what it meant. Was he telling the waitress to put something in her drink?

Megan tapped her fingernails on the tabletop. If she asked him to take her home, would he still be agreeable?

Why had she wanted to come here? Across the way, a couple rose and went into room number six.

"Megan?"

She jumped at the sound of his voice.

"Are you all right?"

"I . . . Yes, of course."

"You look a little pale."

"Do I?" She lifted a hand to her forehead. Of course, she could plead a headache. Wasn't that the excuse women always fell back on? "Now that you mention it, I am feeling a little under the weather all of a sudden."

"Maybe the wine will make you feel better," he suggested. "If it doesn't, I'll take you home."

The waitress arrived with their drinks a short time later. Megan stared at the glass the woman placed before her. Was it drugged?

Rhys didn't miss the worried look in Megan's eyes. A quick brush of her mind with his explained everything. She had seen the look he'd given Lena and assumed it was some silent order to drug her drink. As if he would have to resort to drugs if he had anything nefarious in mind. His unspoken communication to Lena had merely been to alert her to the fact that he also wanted wine and not his usual. Now, how to assure Megan she had nothing to worry about without arousing her suspicion?

Before he could decide, Megan reached for her drink. And knocked it over.

"Oh, how clumsy of me!" Grabbing her napkin, Megan dabbed at the dark stain spreading over the tablecloth.

"Nothing to worry about," Rhys said. "Here, have mine."

He slid his glass across the table before she could object.

She looked up, her eyes narrowed.

Rhys smiled benignly, curious to see if she would pull the same stunt twice.

Megan hesitated a moment, and then, with a murmured, "Thank you," she picked up his glass and took a sip. She wasn't much of a wine connoisseur, but she thought she tasted a hint of cherries and cinnamon.

At his signal, the waitress arrived with a fresh tablecloth and another glass of Pinot Noir.

Rhys leaned back in his chair. She was as nervous as a kitten in a den of coyotes. Bringing her here probably hadn't been the best idea he'd ever had. But it wasn't just her surroundings. She was still upset over what had happened at the store last night, although she didn't want to admit it, even to herself.

With his preternatural power, he reached out to her, willing her to relax.

Megan didn't know if it was the wine or the heat in Costain's eyes, but after a few sips, she suddenly felt lethargic.

"Maybe I should take you home so you can get some sleep," Rhys said, and taking the glass from her hand, he led her outside to the car, buckled her seat belt, and drove her home.

A light burned in the window. Inside, Shirl had left a note saying she wouldn't be home until morning.

"Are you going to be all right, here alone?" Rhys asked.

"Yes, of course," Megan replied.

"Would you feel better if I stayed a while?"

She hesitated a moment before asking, "Would you mind?"

"No. Go on up to bed. I'll stay until first light." He couldn't blame her for not wanting to be alone. After all, she'd had a hell of a scare last night.

"Thank you."

"Don't worry, I'll keep the bogeyman away."

With a nod, Megan went upstairs and, after a moment's indecision, locked her bedroom door. Better to err on the side of caution, she thought, and then shook her head, certain that, if he wanted in, no locked door would keep him out. She still couldn't believe she had asked a man she scarcely knew to spend the night.

She brushed her teeth, combed out her hair, slipped into a pair of pj's, and crawled into bed, asleep as soon as her head hit the pillow.

Rhys made himself comfortable on the sofa. With his preternatural hearing, he could track Megan's movements as she went from bathroom to bedroom. He heard the rustle of sheets as she slid under the covers. For a moment, he considered going upstairs, mesmerizing her with a look, sliding into bed beside her, taking her in his arms, and making love to her, but it was only wishful thinking. When he took Megan DeLacey to bed, he wanted it to be her idea. A short burst of preternatural energy brought the TV to life. He surfed through the channels—game shows, reality shows, world news. Muttering an oath, he switched it off. He sat there a moment, fingers drumming restlessly on the arm of the sofa.

Getting to his feet, he wandered around the room. It was totally feminine, from the pale yellow walls, flowered sofa, and colorful throw pillows, to the knickknacks on the mantel and the fancy curtains at the window. He stopped in front of a bookshelf and spent a few minutes perusing the titles. Her taste ran to mysteries and romances, neither of which appealed to him.

He was about to turn the TV on again when a muffled cry reached his ears. Megan!

A thought carried him up the stairs to her room. The door was locked, but he had yet to come across a lock that could keep him out when he wanted in.

A whisper of preternatural power opened the door, and

he stepped into her room. A quick glance showed it was just as feminine as the living room. The walls were pink, the carpet a deep mauve. Flowered curtains hung at the single window. A matching quilt in colors of pink, mauve, and forest green lay folded over the foot of the bed. An antique dresser stood against the wall opposite the bed; a small desk occupied one corner, the seat cushion on the chair covered in the same material as the curtains.

On silent feet, he made his way to Megan's bedside. She looked incredibly young and innocent lying there, her hair like a splash of reddish gold silk across the flowered pillowcase, the blankets pulled up to her chin. Of course, everyone seemed young and innocent when compared to him and the life he had led, he mused ruefully. No one could do the things he had done, see the carnage he had seen, and remain innocent.

Megan moaned softly. Caught in the throes of a bad dream, her body moved restlessly beneath the covers.

"Megan." He whispered her name as he toed off his boots. After stretching out beside her, he drew her body against his, one arm holding her close while he lightly stroked her hair. "It's all right, darlin'. I'm here. No one will hurt you," he promised. Not even me.

Still asleep, she quieted at the sound of his voice, and then she snuggled against him, her body warm and soft and oh, so alive. And in that moment, as her scent enveloped him, he knew that, for better or worse, he wanted more from Megan DeLacey than her life's blood.

He stayed at her side until a familiar tingling along his spine warned him of dawn's approach.

Rising, he pulled on his boots, then rained featherlight kisses along the alluring curve of her slender throat. A thought took him to the theater parking lot where they had left her car the night before.

Taking time to drive her car home was cutting it close,

he mused. He parked her car in the driveway, left her keys on the kitchen table, then slid behind the wheel of the Jag and put the pedal to the metal.

She was sweet, he thought, as he sped toward his penthouse. So sweet. And one day soon, she would be his in every way that mattered.

Chapter 5

It was near midnight when Rhys transported himself to his second lair. The house was little more than an empty shell. Except for three large, tan leather sofas and a couple of overstuffed chairs, there was no furniture in the room. No pictures on the walls. No lights save for a large wrought-iron candelabra. A medieval sword hung over the fireplace. The grip was made of wood covered in shagreen leather. It wasn't merely for decoration. Rhys had used it on more than one occasion. He had, in fact, used it to take the head of the vampire who had recently betrayed him. Rhys used the house as a meeting place to conduct vampire business; on occasion, he took his rest in the walk-in pantry that had been converted to serve that purpose, but not often. There'd been a time when he'd kept a Mastiff to guard the house, but someone had poisoned the dog and he hadn't gotten around to finding another one.

Tonight, he had called a meeting of the West Coast Vampire Council to see if any of the members had information on the killings in the East. A rogue vampire was bad news for all of them. He didn't summon the Council to LA unless there was trouble of one sort or another brewing. And the killings in the East smelled like trouble. Big trouble.

While waiting for the Council to arrive, he let himself think of the night past. He had held Megan in his arms until just before dawn. It was a testament to his self-control that all he did was hold her when his body had urged him to take her while she slept, while his hunger had urged him to feed. Monster he might be, but to take advantage of Megan while she slept was unthinkable. Tempting as she was, he wouldn't defile her in such a despicable way.

He tucked thoughts of Megan safely away as the members of the Council arrived.

Five members of the Council had been destroyed not long ago. Damon had been killed by Erik Delacourt. Saul had been destroyed by Daisy. Tina and Craig had been terminated by Daisy's brother, Alex. Rhys had destroyed Mariah for her betrayal. News of her destruction, which had been slow and painful, had spread quickly through the vampire community, a warning to others who thought to betray him.

Rhys surveyed the remaining members of the original Council. The handsome vampire with dark, slicked-back hair and a thin mustache was Rupert Moss. He reminded Rhys of a young Valentino. Rupert kept his lair in Idaho.

The tall, angular vampire with wispy gray hair and pale blue eyes was Nicholas. He had been turned when he was in his late seventies, something Rhys had always found a little creepy. He could understand why humans didn't want to die, but to be immortal at seventy? What was the point? Nicholas spent most of his time in Arizona.

Julius Romano was a California boy who had started dealing drugs in high school. Of medium height, with brown eyes and short brown hair, he had been turned when he was twenty-three. A red-and-black snake tattoo ran the length of his left arm.

Rhys had appointed four new members of the Council shortly after he'd destroyed Mariah.

Adrianna made her home in New Mexico. She was fire and ice, that one, with her flaming red hair and cold blue eyes. She had a penchant for diamonds and furs and was rarely seen without one or the other. She had been a vampire for one hundred and fifty years, and she reveled in it. Rhys didn't like her and he didn't trust her, which was why he had brought her into the Council where he could keep an eye on her. If there was one thing about women he was certain of—it was that the female was always deadlier and more cunning than the male. Mariah had been proof of that.

Mark Winchester resided in Montana. He was a good-looking kid, with his wheat-blond hair and dark brown eyes. Winchester had been a year younger than Rhys when he was turned. Built like a Mack truck, Winchester had been a college quarterback in mortality. He had been turned by an admirer after a football game. Fifteen years later, he was still bitter about having to give up football, but there was no help for it. After all was said and done, there were only so many excuses he could use for constantly missing practice and day games.

Stuart Hastings made his lair in Medford, Oregon, where he had once been a renowned surgeon. He hated what he had become. Rhys couldn't blame him. For a man whose sole reason for living had been saving lives, becoming one of the Undead seemed like a cruel trick.

Seth Adams had been a Union soldier during the Civil War. He would have died at Gettysburg if a hungry vampire hadn't found him, bleeding and near death, on the battlefield. Adams resided in Washington.

"So," Adrianna said, looking bored, "why have you called us here?"

Rhys told them as succinctly as possible about the killings in the East. "Have any of you heard anything?" he asked, glancing around the room. "Winchester?"

"What?"

Rhys shook his head. "Stop texting, and pay attention. I asked if you've heard anything about the killings in New York."

The kid shrugged one big, burly shoulder. "Nah."

"What about you, Adrianna?"

"Nothing. How do you know it's a vampire?"

"I know.

"I had an e-mail from an old friend who lives in New York," Rupert said. "He heard the report on a police scanner and went to the scene. It was definitely the work of a vampire. Neat. Clean. He was positive that an old one was responsible."

Rhys nodded. An old one. There were a number of aged vampires on the East Coast. Of course, that didn't prove anything. Few vampires stayed long in one place. "What about you, Julius?"

"I haven't heard anything, but I say we stop sneaking around and join up with whoever it is."

"I'm not looking for a war," Rhys retorted. "I've had enough of that. Nick?"

"I haven't heard anything other than what was said on the news, but to my way of thinking, there's no point in worrying about it now. Unless the rogue comes here, I don't see how it concerns us."

Rhys swept his gaze over the Council. "We've lived under the radar for quite a while. I'm older than any of you. I remember what it was like to be hunted by hysterical mobs wielding scythes and torches. It isn't something I want to experience again."

"Sounds dreadful," Nicholas said. "What do you want us to do?"

"For now, just keep your eyes and ears open. If you hear of anything the least bit suspicious, tell me immediately. The last thing I want is a bunch of humans running scared. They might be weak and sometimes stupid, but they're persistent when they get their tails in a knot. One more thing, there's a new hunter here in LA."

"Anyone we know?" Nicholas asked, and then frowned. "It's not that Blood Thief, is it?"

"No," Rhys said, grinning, "it's not her." Those who knew Daisy had good reason to fear her. In spite of being young and a woman, she had been a force to be reckoned with.

Rhys remembered Daisy well. He had been at rest here, in the pantry of the meeting house, minding his own business, when her brother, Alex, had attacked him. The two of them had been locked in a life-and-death battle when Daisy burst into the room and hurled a bottle of holy water at his head. Rhys had howled in pain and fury as the water burned his skin. With murder on his mind, he had whirled around to face her. He could only imagine how frightful he must have looked, with his eyes glowing like hell's own flames and his fangs dripping with her brother's blood. But it hadn't slowed her down. With a wild cry, she had pulled a stake from her pocket, lunged forward, and driven the damn thing into his chest. Had her hand been steadier, her aim true, she would have destroyed him on the spot.

Funny, how things never turned out the way you expected. He had fully intended to avenge himself on the Blood Thief and her brother; instead, they had become reluctant allies. But that was all in the past.

His gaze rested briefly on each member of the Council. "All right, you all know what to do. Now get out of here."

Chapter 6

Tomás Villagrande strolled through the streets of New Orleans admiring the lacy iron balconies that fronted so many of the buildings, the Spanish moss that hung from the branches of the trees, giving them a somewhat gothic look that appealed to him.

In the old days, the city, founded in 1718 under the direction of Jean Baptiste Le Moyne de Bienville, had been known as *La Nouvelle-Orléans.* Tomás had walked its streets then, too.

The city had changed much in 292 years.

He had not.

A thought took him to the French Quarter, his favorite part of the city. He strolled down Bourbon Street, which was virtually unchanged from days gone by and was still the center of town. Rows of townhouses and cottages lined the sidewalks, many with elaborate wrought-iron balconies, flagstone courtyards, and bubbling fountains.

The first floors of many houses had been turned into commercial enterprises, with living quarters upstairs.

No matter the time of day or night, the streets in the Quarter were always crowded. Tourists quickly learned three things about this part of the city—the bars never closed, the food was spicy, and there was music everywhere. Jackson Square was another area that bustled with activity, a place where fortune tellers, jugglers, musicians, and artists gathered to perform and sell their wares.

A thought took him to the Garden District, which remained one of the city's most popular and picturesque areas. The houses, done in magnificent Victorian, Greek Revival, and Italianate styles, were beautiful, timeless. The Garden District had originally been the site of a plantation, but later it had been sold and subdivided into lots for wealthy Americans.

Leaving the Garden District behind, Tomás thought briefly about the young man he had dined on earlier. He had left the body of his victim atop a stone angel in St. Louis Cemetery #1 where it was sure to be found. By morning, the citizens of New Orleans would be in a state of frenzy, as were the sheep in New York and Chicago and a few other cities where Tomás had left evidence of his presence with the bodies he had left behind. The word "vampire" would travel the length of New Orleans before dawn.

Thanks to Anne Rice, New Orleans knew all about vampires, he thought with a grin. Some of the most popular tourist attractions were the vampire tours, including a stop at something called the Vampire Tavern. Tomás had, in years past, appeared to one tour group or another. He had let them see him as he truly was, with his eyes glowing red and his fangs extended, and then vanished from their sight. It was always good for a laugh. Yes, it was entertaining to stir up the masses from time to time, though he had changed his mind about urging those of his clan to come out of hiding and prey openly upon the populace. It had been an idea born out of the dreariness of his life.

A full-scale war, once started, was difficult to curtail, even for one as old and powerful as he.

He thought of the body he had left behind in St. Louis

Cemetery #1. The cemetery, located eight blocks from the Mississippi River on the north side of Basin Street, and one block from the inland border of the French Quarter, was the city's oldest and most famous burial ground.

Tomás grinned ruefully. Only in New Orleans would graveyards be considered places of interest. Since the city itself was built on a swamp, the deceased were buried in above-ground tombs. The cemeteries had come to be known as "cities of the dead" due to the elaborate sculptures and decorative artwork that adorned the crypts and mausoleums. Many of the tombs were well maintained; some were surrounded by decorative wrought-iron fences, others were little more than piles of crumbling red brick. The tomb of the fictional vampire, Louis, from *Interview With a Vampire* had been located here. It was rumored that Anne Rice had purchased a tomb in #1 for her eventual use.

There were those who considered the cemetery to be located in a bad part of town, since it bordered the Iberville housing projects. On the plus side, the New Orleans Police Department was practically right next door. Still, wise tourists didn't visit the place alone, didn't stay after dark, and certainly didn't carry anything of value with them.

Marie Laveau, the legendary "voodoo queen," was buried in the cemetery. Even now, long after her death, believers and nonbelievers came to visit her tomb, where they performed an act most thought odd. First, they left a gift—either of food, money, or flowers—for her spirit. After that, they turned around three times, and then inscribed an *X* on her tomb in hopes of receiving blessings in the future.

Tomás had met Marie on several occasions. Both of them. Few people knew that when the first Marie Laveau retired, her daughter, who had also been named Marie, took over. Both had been tall, statuesque women, with curly black hair, flashing eyes, and reddish skin. Back in the 1800s, people of all colors and classes had sought Marie's help, whether with ordinary, everyday problems, or affairs of the heart.

Marie wasn't the only famous person buried in the cemetery. It also held the remains of Bernard de Marigny, a French-Creole playboy who had introduced the game of craps to the United States.

He paused on Bourbon Street to listen to a little Dixieland, his foot tapping to the music as he scanned the crowd. He wasn't looking for prey now, at least not the kind he dined on. His gaze came to rest on a raven-haired beauty with bright blue eyes and the kind of complexion that used to be described as peaches and cream.

When her gaze met his, he inclined his head. Unable to resist the compulsion in his eyes, she walked toward him, slim hips swaying. He assured her she had nothing to fear as he slipped his arm around her waist. Young men were for relieving one's hunger, and he took them quietly, quickly. But young women. Ah, how he loved the taste and smell of young females. Before killing them, he often made love to them, giving them pleasure before he thrust into them one last time, before he drank the last drop.

A thought took them to the Ferretti, which was moored in the harbor. He gave her a tour of the yacht, and she was suitably impressed, and then he took her into his bed, where he impressed her several times before the sun came up.

Chapter 7

Rhys stood hipshot against the end of the bar as he listened to the idle chatter of the well-dressed men and women around him. Outwardly, he seemed much the same as the other men. He wore the same expensive clothes, drove a flashy car, owned real estate in the city, including the building where he kept his primary lair. But inside, he was still the bastard son of a prostitute. The world changed. Kings and queens and presidents came and went. People were born, grew up, grew old, and passed on, but he remained always and forever the same, never quite able to shake off the feeling that he was inferior to those around him, never able to forget the scared little boy who had become a thief to survive.

He was still stealing, he mused somewhat bitterly, but instead of gold and silver and fancy baubles, he stole the life's blood of his victims.

He snorted softly. The humans in the room were no better than he was. He could hear their innermost thoughts—the middle-aged man to his left had just embezzled three million dollars from his employer; the brunette at the other end of the bar was having an affair with her husband's brother; the well-dressed black man standing near the entrance was checking the crowd, looking for an easy mark. The balding man on his right had just lost his job and was contemplating suicide.

Straightening, Rhys closed his mind to those standing nearby. He had no interest in their mundane lives, didn't care a lick whether they solved their problems or not. What mattered was that it was almost midnight. Time to visit Shore's and the ever so lovely Megan DeLacey.

Megan paused in the act of hanging a new pair of slacks on the circular rack in the center of the store. Rhys was coming. She knew it by the sudden, rapid increase of her heartbeat, by the way her skin grew warm all over.

She was trying to figure out the how and the why of her reaction when he walked into the store.

Tall and blond and wearing clothes she had sold him, he looked like he had just stepped off the cover of *GQ*. She couldn't help wondering if he had spent as many minutes as she had deciding what to wear.

He smiled his hypnotic smile as he closed the distance between them. For a moment, she forgot where she was, forgot everything but the incredible attraction that flowed between them. What was there about him that left her feeling weak and shivery inside, that made her want to give him anything he desired?

"Megan, how pretty you look this evening."

"As do you."

His dark eyes reflected his pleasure at her words.

His nearness made her nervous on several levels. She folded her hands to keep from fidgeting. "Did you come for the other half of your reward?"

"Reward?"

"The new coat Mr. Parker offered you. To replace the

ruined one, remember?" She forced a smile. She hated being reminded of that dreadful night.

"Oh, that."

"Yes, that." He couldn't possibly have come to buy more clothes. He had already purchased enough shirts, pants, ties, and socks to keep three men clothed for a year. What would she do when he tired of coming into the shop? The nights would be unbearably dull when he no longer stopped by.

Before he could reply, the front door opened and Drexel swept inside, followed by his entourage. The young rock star was dressed as flamboyantly as always, from his fluorescent green shirt to his mustard-colored slacks. He wore his long brown hair slicked back. A diamond stud sparkled in the lobe of one ear. His hazel eyes lit up when he saw Megan. Grinning, he swaggered toward her.

She didn't know what other stores he frequented when he was in town, but one thing was certain; he hadn't bought that garish outfit at Shore's.

"Hey, babe, what's shakin'?" His exuberance faded a bit when he noticed Rhys. "Who's this guy?"

"Drexel, this is Mr. Costain. He's a new client of mine."

"Yeah, well, nice to meet ya, dude, but I'm gonna need Megan for an hour or two. I've got a happenin' gig tomorrow night, and I need to look smokin' hot."

"You should have called in advance," Megan quietly reminded him.

"It's a last minute thing. I just found out about it this morning, babe. I need something fresh, and I need it now."

Megan looked up at Rhys. "Do you mind?"

Rhys shrugged. Had Drexel been a grown man, he would have quickly put him in his place, but what the hell, he had all night, and the kid couldn't be more than eighteen or nineteen. "Go ahead, I'll wait."

Megan smiled at Rhys as she led Drexel away.

Rhys grinned as he heard Drexel say, "So, babe, when are you gonna marry me?"

As Megan helped Drexel put together an outfit guaranteed to get him noticed, she was ever aware that Rhys's gaze followed her every move. Drexel never stopped flirting with her, never stopped complimenting her. Once, when he used a line she recognized from a recent movie, she saw Rhys smile. Had he overheard what Drexel said? But that was impossible. Drexel had spoken to her in a whisper, and Rhys had been at the other end of the store.

Megan breathed a sigh of relief when, after a grueling two hours, Drexel finally rounded up his entourage and left the store. In those two hours, he had proposed three times and tried to kiss her twice. On his way out, he had given her two tickets to his upcoming concert and told her he would send a limo to pick her up. Megan would have refused the tickets, but it had been easier, and quicker, just to smile and accept. Besides, it might be fun.

Megan smiled at Rhys, surprised he had waited so long. "He's like a tornado, that one," she remarked.

"If he lays a hand on you, he'll answer to me."

"Oh, for goodness sake. He's just a kid."

"He's old enough."

"I don't believe what I'm hearing," Megan exclaimed. "Not to mention the fact that it's none of your business."

"You think not?"

Megan glared at him, momentarily speechless. And then her temper kicked in. "I don't have to answer to you, Mr. Costain, or to anyone else, for that matter. Just because we shared a glass of wine doesn't make you my keeper. Good night."

With a toss of her head, she pivoted on her heel and stalked into Mr. Parker's office, where she slammed the door so hard, the glass rattled.

Rhys stared after her, one brow raised in wry amusement.

His kitten wasn't as tame as she appeared. But that was all right, he thought with a grin. He liked a woman with a little fire in her blood.

Mr. Parker looked up from the papers scattered across his desk when Megan stormed into his office. "What'd Drexel do now?"

"Nothing," Megan said quickly.

Mr. Parker regarded her quizzically for a moment, then shrugged. "I'm ready to lock up." He gathered the papers on his desk and dropped them into a drawer. "You ready to call it a night?"

"More than ready."

"He's like a whirling dervish, that boy," Mr. Parker remarked, fishing his keys out of his pocket. "But he's sure good for our bottom line."

No doubt about that, Megan thought. Drexel had spent enough tonight to pay the rent on the building.

Stifling a yawn, she grabbed her handbag from the storeroom and followed Mr. Parker out the back door to the parking lot.

And found Rhys Costain waiting for her beside her car.

Startled, she pressed a hand to her heart. "What are you doing here?"

"I thought we'd go out for a drink so you could apologize for your little tantrum."

"Excuse me?"

Rhys held up one hand. "I'm kidding about the apology, but not the drink. What do you say?"

She studied him while she tried to make up her mind. Dressed all in black, he blended into the darkness. No. He *was* the darkness. She didn't know where that thought had come from, but it raised the hair on her arms. For all that he seemed to be a gentleman, she really didn't know anything about him other than his name and the fact that he owned a nightclub and had a great deal of money. He looked normal enough, and yet . . .

"It was an easy question," he remarked.

Quite the contrary. There was nothing easy about this man.

"Yes or no, Megan?"

Her common sense said no, but her curious heart said, "Yes."

A slow smile spread across his face. In the darkness, his teeth looked very white. And sharp.

The better to eat you with, my dear.

Megan took a step backward. Had she heard those words in her head, or had Rhys spoken them aloud?

"My car, or yours?" he asked.

"I . . ." She bit down on her lower lip as she recalled Shirl's advice. *Follow your instincts.* And right now, her instincts were screaming for her to get in her car and drive away just as fast as she could. Which was odd, since she had felt completely safe when he'd stayed with her the other night. Why was she so conflicted?

As though sensing her change of heart, Rhys took a step backward. "Another night, maybe?"

"Maybe." Wrenching open the car door, she slid behind the wheel and shoved the key in the ignition as he thoughtfully shut the door for her.

When she glanced into the rearview mirror, he was gone.

Megan blinked and looked again. How could he have vanished so quickly? She told herself he was still there, she just couldn't see him because he was dressed all in black. Like the night.

Because he was the night.

Suddenly chilled, she turned on the heater, hit the door locks, and drove out of the parking lot, tires squealing.

Shirl always left a lamp burning in the window for her, and tonight was no exception. Never before had that light looked so welcoming or been more appreciated.

There's nothing in the dark that isn't there in the light, her mother had always said. But tonight, in the dark with Rhys Costain, Megan might have argued with her.

Once inside, Megan double-locked the door, then laughed at her own foolishness. She was lucky she hadn't gotten a ticket for speeding on the way home. Standing in her own living room, with the door locked and the lights on, she wondered what she had been so afraid of.

After making sure Megan got safely home, Rhys went to his club to ponder whether he should continue to pursue the delectable Miss DeLacey. She was beautiful, and he wanted her more than he had ever wanted any woman, living or Undead. She was attracted to him, as well, but tonight she had shown that she possessed a strong sense of self-preservation. He couldn't remember the last time a woman had recognized the darkness within him and fled from his presence.

He raised the glass in his hand. "Here's to you, Megan, my sweet. May you have a long and happy life."

Rhys didn't show up at Shore's the next night, or any night that week, or the next. On the one hand, Megan told herself she was relieved, and it was partly true. He frightened her on a level she didn't fully understand, nor could she put her finger on what it was about him that troubled her. On the other hand, he was the most fascinating man she had ever known. Not to mention the sexiest. His touch, his voice, his very presence, enflamed her senses. Had he hypnotized her? Drugged her?

Megan fretted over him on her two days off, two days that seemed even longer because Shirl had gone to San Francisco to visit her folks. Megan cleaned the house from top to bottom, did the laundry, washed the windows, and even waxed the kitchen floor, but all the mindless chores in the world couldn't keep her from thinking about Rhys, or wondering what he was doing, and whether he was thinking of her.

She arrived at Shore's half an hour early Tuesday night, eager to get out of the house and back to work.

Her ten o'clock appointment arrived right on time. Shelby Brooks was a big-name Hollywood producer. In his midsixties, he had thick gray hair, blue eyes, and a no-nonsense attitude about shopping. He always brought a list, then sat in an empty dressing room, reading over a script, while she gathered the items he needed. He never tried anything on and rarely returned anything. She often wondered why he didn't just phone in his order and have his chauffeur pick it up.

Time and again, as she moved through the store, Megan found herself glancing at the front door. Even though Rhys rarely arrived before midnight, she kept hoping to see him striding toward her.

When she finished filling the order for Mr. Brooks, he thanked her profusely, handed her a small black velvet box, waved to Mr. Parker, and left the store.

"Well, it's been a good night," Mr. Parker said, coming to stand beside her. "What with Brooks and that agent who was here earlier . . . yes, a good night, indeed." He jerked his chin at the box. "What did he bring you this time?"

"I don't know yet." Mr. Brooks always brought her a gift—a watch from Cartier, a silk scarf by Forzieri, a bracelet from Tiffany's. Megan opened the box, revealing a jeweled comb for her hair.

"Nice," Parker said.

Megan nodded. Mr. Brooks had impeccable taste.

Mr. Parker glanced at his watch. "Well, what do you say we close up early?"

Megan couldn't stifle a wave of disappointment. It was only a little after eleven. If Rhys should decide to come by, she wouldn't be here. But she could hardly argue with the boss.

Pasting a smile on her face, she tucked the velvet box into her handbag, grabbed her coat, and followed Mr. Parker out the back door.

Her heartbeat accelerated when she saw a dark shadow by her car but, to her disappointment, there was no one there.

Rhys watched Megan from the shadows. In spite of his good intentions, he couldn't stay away from her. Like a moth to a flame, he was drawn to her humanity, her warmth.

Would she destroy him if he flew too close?

After five hundred and twelve years of living alone, would he even care?

Chapter 8

When Megan got home from work, she found Shirl stretched out on the sofa, a folded washcloth draped over her forehead.

"Another migraine?" Megan asked, dropping her handbag and coat on a chair.

Shirl nodded.

"You've been having them more often lately. Maybe you should go to the doctor."

"Never."

Sitting on the love seat, Megan kicked off her heels. Shirl hated doctors and hospitals, probably because she had spent so much time in one during her father's illness last year. "Can I get you anything?"

"Another head?"

"I'll call Frankenstein and see if he has a spare."

"Very funny."

"Who are the flowers from?" Megan asked, noticing the huge bouquet on the mantel.

"I don't know. They're for you. They arrived a few minutes ago."

"For me?" Tired as she was, Megan jumped to her feet. Who would be sending her flowers? And where on earth had whoever it was found a florist who delivered at this time of the night?

"What's the card say?" Shirl asked. "It was all I could do to keep from reading it."

Megan opened the envelope and withdrew the small white card. "It says, 'I'm sorry for being such a cad. Can we start over? RC.'"

"Who's RC?"

"The guy I told you about."

Sitting up, Shirl folded her arms under her breasts. "You mean the one who scares you?"

"The very same." Megan ran her fingertips over the roses. There must have been three dozen flowers, each one a perfect, blood red bud.

"I thought he hadn't been coming around?"

"He hasn't."

"And that's a good thing, right? Right?"

"What? Oh, right." Megan plucked a bud from the vase, then sat down on the end of the sofa.

"You don't sound convinced."

"Well . . ."

"Go on."

"I miss him."

"Apparently he misses you, too. I'll bet those roses cost a good three hundred dollars, not to mention an extra couple of bucks for that vase. It looks like real crystal. And I'll bet it cost him a pretty penny to get the florist to make a delivery this late, too. So, what is it about Mr. RC that scares you?"

"I don't know."

"Something he did? Something he didn't do? Something he said?"

"No, nothing like that. I think I'm just, I don't know, letting my imagination run away with me. How's your headache?"

"Better," Shirl said with a yawn. "I think I'm gonna try to get a few hours' sleep. And as for that RC guy, maybe you ought to give him another chance."

"I thought you said to trust my instincts?"

"I did, didn't I?" Shirl yawned again. "I don't know, Meggie," she said as she headed for the stairs. "He's young, rich, and thoughtful. Doesn't sound that bad to me. Maybe we can double date some time."

Megan shook her head. So much for Shirl's advice about following her instincts. She glanced at the roses on the mantel. Should she give Rhys another chance? Even if she didn't want to see him again, the least she could do was thank him for the flowers. She could look up his number at the store tomorrow.

She felt a bubble of excitement at the thought of hearing his voice again.

Smiling, she replaced the rose in the vase, then went up to bed. The sooner she went to sleep, the sooner tomorrow would come.

She dreamed of him that night, a strange dream unlike any she had ever had before. It was so vivid, so real, it didn't seem like a dream at all. She heard his voice in her mind, entreating her to let him in, and because it was what she wanted, she bid him come to her, and in an instant, he was there, inside her bedroom, kneeling on the foot of her bed, a strange reddish glow in his devil-dark eyes. When he held out his arms, she went to him gladly, only then realizing just how much she had missed him.

He cradled her to his chest as his hand stroked her hair. "You should tell me to go, now, before it's too late."

"But you just got here."

"I'm no good for you."

She looked into his eyes; such deep, dark eyes. Hypnotic eyes.

"Megan. I don't want to hurt you, but I can't stay away."

"Then don't."

"Foolish girl." His hand stroked her neck, slid over her shoulder and down her arm. "If you only knew . . ."

"Knew what?"

"Who I am." His hand cupped her breast. "What I am."

Her eyelids fluttered down as he caressed her. "It doesn't matter." She moaned softly as he feathered kisses over her cheeks, the curve of her throat. His mouth was hot, so hot it sent waves of heat spiraling through her. Trembling with need, she clung to him.

He groaned deep in his throat. Drawing her down on the bed, he stretched out beside her, his arms holding her body close to his, their legs intimately entwined. He kissed her again and yet again, kissed her until she was aware of nothing but his touch, his voice. Her need.

He sobbed her name, his body tensing, and then she felt his teeth at her throat. There was a sharp pinprick of pain followed by a wave of intense sensual pleasure.

The pain startled her. You didn't feel pain in a dream.

Reaching for the bedside light, she switched it on, expecting to see Rhys lying beside her.

But no one was there.

Rhys cursed himself as he fled Megan's house. He hadn't gone there with the intention of drinking from her. He had only wanted to be near her again, to bask in the warmth of her presence. Damn! As for the flowers, he had sent them in a moment of weakness. Weakness! Damn her. What was there about Megan DeLacey that made him think of settling down? He swore a vile oath. He was a vampire, not some puny mortal. Even if he desired a wife and a family, which he didn't, that life was impossible for such as he. And yet Megan . . . ah, Megan with her sweet lips and her luscious body, she made him long for the kind of life that was forever denied him.

A thought took him to his club. Several of the regulars were sitting at the bar, sipping drinks. He grabbed the nearest female and took her to his private room. He was a single, white male, the Master of the West Coast Vampires, one of the most powerful creatures in the world. Why was he mooning over one mortal female?

The woman, Monique, smiled up at him when he closed the door, obviously pleased that he had chosen her.

When she started to speak, he held up his hand, silencing her. He didn't want conversation. Didn't want anything from her but relief from the twin talons of thirst and desire that he couldn't satisfy in Megan's arms.

Frightened and confused, Megan sat up in bed, the blankets tucked under her arms. What had just happened? Had it all been a dream? Of course, she thought, what else could it have been? And yet it had seemed so real. Her skin still tingled from the memory of his touch.

Rising, she padded into the bathroom and turned on the light, then stood in front of the mirror, turning her head from side to side. There! Were those bite marks on her neck?

She ran her fingers over the bites. They were definitely real. And strangely hot to the touch, as if she had a fever. Spider bites? Of course. She shook her head. Vampires, indeed!

After filling a paper cup with water, she took two aspirin and went back to bed. It was hours until dawn.

* * *

In the clear light of day, it was easy to convince herself it had been nothing but some weird dream. Besides, the proof was right in front of her eyes. Standing in front of the bathroom mirror, she ran her fingertips over her neck, relieved to find that the bite marks were gone.

After taking a quick shower, she went downstairs to fix something to eat. Shirl, of course, had already left for work and, as usual, she had left her dirty dishes in the sink, but that was all right. They had an agreement. Megan did the dishes, dusted, vacuumed, and did the shopping. Shirl did the laundry, watered the plants, and took out the trash. They took turns cooking dinner.

With several hours to kill, Megan slipped a DVD into the player, then curled up on the sofa, planning to lose herself in the movie Shirl had rented the night before.

She grimaced when she realized it wasn't the love story she had been expecting but a horror movie. She should have known. Shirl had a thing for vampires, werewolves, and other creepy things that went bump in the night. Megan had a feeling that, deep down, Shirl hoped vampires really existed.

In spite of herself, Megan soon found herself caught up in the story of a young vampire who was in love with a mortal woman. Of course, it ended badly, but then, how else could it end?

When the movie was over, she sat back with a shake of her head. It hadn't been a bad story, but what woman in her right mind would fall in love with a vampire, if such things actually existed, and let him drink her blood?

And even as the thought crossed her mind, she lifted a hand to her neck as the memory of the last night's dream rose, unbidden, in her mind. She knew it had only been a dream but now, with the memory of the movie she had just seen fresh in her mind, she couldn't help thinking how vampire-like her dream had been, with Rhys bending over her, his teeth grazing her throat. . . .

"Stop that right now, Megan! It was just a dream, that's all. There's no such thing as vampires!"

After switching off the TV, she went into the kitchen. Shirl was doing a night shoot, so she wouldn't be home until late. Megan ate soup and a toasted cheese sandwich for dinner, then went into her bedroom to get ready for work.

Megan rang up her fifth sale of the evening. They had been busy all right, thank goodness. At home, she had done a fair job of keeping thoughts of Rhys Costain at bay, but the minute she had walked into Shore's, he was all she could think about. She had hoped to distract herself with work, but everything reminded her of Rhys.

She was straightening one of the shelves when a sudden ripple in the air sent a shiver down her spine. Lifting a hand to her neck, she went suddenly still. He was here. She knew it. Hardly daring to believe, she glanced over her shoulder. And he was there, as tall and handsome as she remembered. All her foolish imaginings and ridiculous fears took flight as he glided toward her. She couldn't take her eyes off of him. Everything about him appealed to her—the red silk shirt that clung to his broad shoulders, the black slacks that emphasized his long legs, the dark blond of his hair. His eyes, so brown they were almost black.

"Megan." As he murmured her name, he offered her a single blood-red rose.

She looked up at him. Every female on the planet knew a single red rose meant "I love you." Had that been his intent, or was he just partial to red roses?

"It's beautiful."

His gaze moved over her face. "Your beauty puts it to shame."

"Thank you."

"I hope you'll forgive me."

"For what?"

"For acting like a jealous fool."

"I think we both acted like a couple of idiots," Megan allowed. "Let's just forget it, shall we?"

"Would you like to go out for a drink after work?"

"Yes, very much."

"I'll see you then," he said, and taking her hand in his, he kissed her palm.

His lips were cool against her skin, yet they sent a shaft of heat straight to the core of her being.

"Till then," he murmured.

Too stunned to reply, Megan could only nod. Oh Lord, the effect that man had on her senses was almost hypnotic.

He was waiting by the back door when she got off work. "Where would you like to go?"

"I don't care." She had been counting the hours until this moment, when she would see him again, hear his voice. Whatever magic he possessed, she was helpless to resist it. Nor did she want to. Their separation, though brief, had made her realize she never wanted to be without him again.

He walked her to his car, opened the passenger side door, then went around to the driver's side and slid behind the wheel. She had never known a man who moved with such innate power, or such effortless grace.

"Where are we going?" she asked as he pulled out of the parking lot.

"How would you feel about going to my place?"

"The club?"

"No. My apartment."

Her common sense told her it probably wasn't a good idea to go to a man's apartment, alone, at two in the morning, but her curiosity about seeing where he lived kicked her common sense under the rug. Smiling, she said, "Let's go."

In minutes, they were on the 101 Freeway heading toward Hollywood. Forty minutes later he pulled into the driveway of a tall, glass-fronted building.

"You live here?" she asked, staring out the window.

He nodded. "On the top floor."

Her heart was racing a mile a minute when he pulled into a space marked PRIVATE in the underground garage.

After opening the car door, he took her by the hand. Her heels echoed loudly off the cement floor as he led her to an iron-barred door. He unlocked it and ushered her inside. Overhead lights came on when she crossed the threshold.

Giving her hand a squeeze, he led her down a wide corridor inlaid with black and white tiles to a bank of elevators. It was creepy, being in such a large building when everything was closed. Her heartbeat kicked up a notch when they stepped into the elevator. What was she doing here? No one even knew where she was.

When they reached the tenth floor, they took a private elevator up to the eleventh floor. Moments later, the elevator opened, revealing yet another door, this one made of what looked like solid steel.

Flashing a reassuring smile, Rhys unlocked the door and bowed her inside. Megan looked around in wonder as her feet sank in dark blue-gray carpet that must have been two inches deep. Twin sofas made of black leather faced each other in front of a white marble fireplace. Megan wasn't well versed in the art of the Old Masters, but she thought the painting over the fireplace might be a Botticelli.

As she turned in a slow circle, her gaze came to rest on a statue of a golden-haired Madonna. "She's lovely." Funny, Megan thought, it had never occurred to her that Rhys might be a religious man.

Rhys nodded. "She's very old." He ran a hand over the

statue's shoulder. He had stolen her from a Catholic church soon after he had been turned. For a time, she had been his only companion.

Moving to a covered table located against the wall, Rhys lifted the cloth, revealing a bottle of vintage wine and an assortment of fruit, cheese, crackers, and chocolates. "I thought you might be hungry."

He filled two glasses and handed her one.

"What shall we drink to?" she asked.

"To forgetting the past," he murmured, and wished it were possible.

Smiling, Megan touched her glass to his. "And starting over."

"Starting over," he repeated.

For a moment, it seemed as though his eyes glowed red, but then she realized it was probably just the reflection of the wine.

It was while she was filling her plate that she noticed there was only service for one. "Aren't you having anything?"

"I'm not much for fruit and cheese."

"Or chocolate?"

"Or chocolate. But I thought you might like it."

"What woman doesn't like chocolate?" She glanced at the sweets. Light, milk, and dark chocolates of every variety filled a large crystal bowl. "You don't expect me to eat all of that, do you?" she asked, although she didn't think it would be much of a hardship.

He shrugged. "I didn't know what kind you liked, so I got a little of everything."

"Good choice," she said, grinning. "Since I like a little of everything." She picked up a dark chocolate truffle. *Nirvana,* she thought as it melted in her mouth. "What do you like?"

"I like you," he said quietly. "Far more than I should. Far more than is good for you."

Megan stared at him, suddenly reminded that she knew almost nothing about this man. That they were alone in an empty building. That no one would hear her if she screamed for help. An innate sense of self-preservation had her taking a step backward, even though there was no place to go.

"I'm sorry," he said. "I didn't mean to frighten you."

She searched her mind for some flip reply to ease the tension that stretched between them, but nothing came to mind. Why was she suddenly so afraid?

"Megan." Putting his glass aside, he ran a hand through his hair. He had known bringing her to his lair had been a bad idea from the start. Having her here, so close, was proving to be even more of a temptation than he had expected. If only her eyes weren't as soft and brown as sun-warmed earth, her skin so incredibly smooth, her lips so pink and inviting. If only her blood didn't sing to him. "I should take you home."

She nodded, but she made no move toward the door, and neither did he.

Muttering an oath, he took a step toward her. She was here, and he wanted her.

The next move was hers. Only she didn't move.

As though frozen in place, Megan stared up at him.

With a sigh, he closed the distance between them, took the plate from her hand, and set it on the table.

Megan's heartbeat shifted into overdrive when he reached for her. Like a rabbit hypnotized by a hawk, she could only stand there, waiting, wondering what would happen next. Would he carry her into his bedroom and ravish her? Would she care?

Rhys inhaled deeply as he took her in his arms. The scent of her blood, her fear, enticed him. He fought the urge to taste her; instead, he lowered his head and claimed her lips with his.

The sweet warmth of her lips was more intoxicating than the wine that lingered on her tongue. She pleased him in every way. Her scent enflamed his hunger, her lush curves aroused his lust.

She moaned softly, and Rhys drew back, not certain if her muffled cry was a whimper of pleasure or a plea for him to stop.

"Megan." Hoping for enlightenment, his mind brushed hers as he murmured her name. As he had feared, her thoughts were indecisive. Her body wanted him; her mind was advising caution; her instincts were screaming for her to back away before it was too late.

She looked up at him, her gaze confused, her lips slightly parted.

Rhys swore softly. He could easily bend her will to his, but he didn't want to take her by force, didn't want to take her to his bed until it was her own idea. Blowing out a sigh of frustration, he lightly stroked her back.

"Relax. We won't do anything you don't want to do." Taking her by the hand, he led her to one of the sofas and urged her to sit down, then he went back to the table for her plate, hoping that doing something as ordinary as eating would calm her nerves.

"Please, eat," he said as he offered her the plate.

"Thank you." She was relieved that her hands barely shook at all as she licked the rich, dark chocolate off a plump red strawberry.

While Rhys sat at the other end of the sofa, thinking how lucky that strawberry was.

Chapter 9

It was early morning when Rhys drove her home. It wasn't until they were standing outside her door that Megan realized her car was still at Shore's.

"What time should I pick you up for work tomorrow night?" Rhys asked. "Seven thirty?"

"That would be great. You must have been reading my mind," Megan said with a smile. "Since I forgot all about my car."

He winked at her. "I'll see you then."

She nodded, a flurry of anticipation rising in her stomach as she waited for him to kiss her good night.

She didn't have to wait long.

"Megan?"

She looked up, her gaze meeting his, felt herself falling into the depths of his deep brown eyes as he drew her into his embrace. His lips were cool against her skin as he lightly kissed her brow, her cheeks, the curve of her throat. She moaned softly as his teeth grazed her neck, only for a moment, and then his mouth covered hers and he kissed her again. Kissed her until she was dizzy with the heat of it.

Moments later—or was it longer?—she was standing in the doorway watching him drive away.

Megan frowned. Had she missed something? She didn't remember going into the house, or telling him good night.

Lifting a hand to her neck, she went inside and closed the door, wondering how she could still be hungry after all the fruit and cheese—and chocolate—she had eaten earlier.

She wobbled a little as she went into the kitchen. Had she had too much to drink? Was that why she felt so woozy?

Shaking her head, she filled a glass with orange juice. Maybe she was drunk, she thought with a faint grin. Oh, yeah. Drunk on Rhys Costain's kisses.

"I have tickets to Drexel's concert this coming Saturday night," Megan said. "Would you like to go? I already asked Mr. Parker for the night off."

Rhys had driven her to work earlier and was now in the process of trying on three-quarter-length Armani coats to replace the one that had been ruined in the attempted robbery.

"Drexel? Is he the kid that was in here the other night? The one who wants to marry you?"

"That's him. By the way, Mr. Parker's been telling all of our customers what a hero you are. One of them is a reporter for the *Times*. He'd like to interview you for a human interest story."

"No, thanks."

"Don't you want your fifteen minutes of fame?"

"Not even five minutes."

"Most people these days will do almost anything to get their names or pictures in the news."

"True enough," he agreed. "But I'm not like most people."

She couldn't argue with that. Lifting her hand, she

smoothed the collar of his coat. "This one fits like it was made for you. Check it out in the mirror."

"No need." He smiled at her. "I can see myself in your eyes."

It occurred to her that, in all the times he had been in the shop, she had never once seen him look in a mirror.

Shrugging out of the coat, he handed it to her. "Do you want to meet me when you get off work?"

"I don't think so." Megan yawned behind her hand. "All these late nights are starting to catch up with me."

"Maybe I could come over before you go to work tomorrow night?"

"All right. Shirl's dying to meet you."

"Shirl? She's your roommate?"

Megan nodded. "She's been seeing a cop pretty regularly and suggested the four of us go out for dinner and a movie sometime, if you want to."

"Sure," Rhys said agreeably, although dinner might present a problem. But he'd worry about that later.

"I told her about your nightclub. She said she'd like to see it."

"As I recall, you mentioned she was into the Goth scene at one time."

"Right. Do you want to try on anything else?"

"No, I'll take this one."

"Okay, just let me wrap it up."

He followed her to the counter, content to stand there, watching her, as she slipped one of Shore's distinctive vinyl garment bags over the Armani.

"What time tomorrow night?" he asked, taking the coat from her hand.

"Well, I have to be at work at eight. How about five? It's my night to fix dinner."

The hour wasn't a problem. He could endure the sunlight for brief periods of time. But the food. Short of planting the thought in her head that he was eating, there was no way to get around it, so he said, "Go ahead and eat without me. I've got a meeting with some associates in the evening. I'll try to be at your place around six thirty."

"We can always eat later."

"Don't worry about me. I'll grab something on my way over."

"All right. Too bad about dinner, though. I'm a pretty good cook when I want to be."

"I'm sure you are," he said, kissing her on the cheek. "I'll see you tomorrow night."

Megan nodded. "Associates," she murmured as she watched him leave the store. What kind of associates? Business? Or pleasure?

Adrianna brushed a lock of hair from her brow as she settled onto the sofa. "So, we're all here," she said impatiently. "Now what?"

"You have something better to do?" Rhys asked.

"Yes, as a matter of fact. I haven't fed yet, and I'm hungry. Why are we meeting so early?"

"Because I've got a date," Rhys said, which got everyone's attention. "That rogue vamp has left New Orleans and seems to be heading our way. There have been several killings reported in Houston. Bodies all drained of blood. No clues left behind. Have any of you heard anything?"

"Just what's been on the news," Nicholas said, shrugging. "I still don't think it's anything for us to worry about."

"Unless he comes here, you idiot," Seth Adams said. "One rogue vamp is all it takes to stir up the sheep."

"If he comes here, it'll be Costain's problem," Adrianna said, looking bored as she examined her fingernails. "After all, he's the Master of the West Coast Vampires."

Rhys turned his gaze on Adrianna. "If it comes to a fight, I'm sure we're all hoping I'll win," he said, his voice harsh.

"Of course," Adrianna replied smoothly. "Besides, there's nothing for you to worry about. After all, there aren't many vampires around who are older than you."

Rhys grunted thoughtfully. He could count those older than himself on one hand—first and easily the most dangerous was Tomás Villagrande, the oldest vampire in existence. Tomás ruled the East Coast. After Tomás came Gregor McCarthy, an eight-hundred-year-old vampire who laid claim to both England and Ireland. Next came Baiba. Tall and svelte and seven centuries old, she made her home in Russia. Lastly, there was six-hundred-year-old Sandoval, who kept his primary lair in Madrid.

The ancient ones might defeat him, but Rhys had no fear of any of the other vampires who might come against him. He knew most of those who resided in the United States who might pose a threat. Volger ruled the states in the Midwest; a cocky vampire known as Tristan claimed the North; the South belonged to Morag, one of the oldest female vampires in existence, though not so old as Baiba.

Rhys dismissed the Council with a wave of his hand, and then he smiled. It had been a long time since he'd fought another vampire to the death. He discounted the fight with Mariah. That hadn't been a battle so much as an execution.

But tonight, he had a date with Megan DeLacey.

A knock at the door had Megan's heart racing like a runaway train. He was here.

"You okay, girlfriend?" Shirl called as Megan went to answer the door. "You're looking a little frazzled."

Frazzled didn't begin to cover it, Megan thought. Just thinking about Rhys sent her hormones into overdrive.

"Don't worry," Shirl said, a smile in her voice. "As soon as I get a look at him, I'll make myself scarce."

Megan nodded. She paused to take a deep breath before she opened the door. "Hi."

Lord, the man was gorgeous. Tonight, he wore a gray-and-black–striped shirt with the sleeves rolled up over a black T-shirt, black jeans, and boots. When he smiled at her, she thought she might melt.

"Hi." He arched one brow at her. "You gonna invite me in?"

"What? Oh, yes." She took a step back, thinking how good he smelled as he moved past her into the living room where Shirl waited.

Megan quickly introduced Rhys to her roommate, and then, true to her word, Shirl excused herself and went upstairs, but not before giving Megan a wide-eyed nod of approval.

"So," Megan said, gesturing for Rhys to sit down, "what did you do today?"

He lifted one shoulder in a graceful shrug. "Nothing much. Worked on the books. Ordered some new stock for the bar, that kind of thing."

"Oh. How did your business meeting go?"

"About as I expected."

"Have you owned the nightclub very long?"

"A few years. It keeps me busy."

"So, what do you think of Shirl?"

"She's a knockout."

It was the response Megan had expected, but she couldn't help feeling a little jealous just the same. Men rarely paid any attention to her when she and Shirley were in the same room.

"But not as pretty as you."

"That's nice of you to say, but it isn't necessary. Or true."

"Hey, beauty is in the eye of the beholder. And to me, you're beautiful."

She felt her cheeks warm at the compliment. "Thank you."

"Okay if I kiss you?"

She laughed softly. "You've never asked before, but, yes, it's okay."

She closed her eyes as his arm slid around her shoulders, drawing her closer. His lips were cool, yet, at their touch, heat flowed through her, turning her blood to liquid fire. She had been kissed by other men, but never with such intensity. If kissing were an art form, he would surely be the master, she thought dreamily. The Michelangelo of osculatory delights. The Picasso of kissers.

Somehow, they were lying on the sofa, with Rhys's body covering hers, his mouth trailing fire as he rained kisses on her forehead, the tip of her nose, her eyelids, and her cheeks before returning to her lips. She moaned softly, every nerve and cell in her body straining toward him. It had been years since her divorce, years since she had taken a man to her bed. Or wanted to.

She felt bereft when he took his mouth from hers and gained his feet.

A rush of heat flooded her cheeks when she looked past Rhys and saw Shirl standing in the doorway, a smirk on her face. "I hate to interrupt you, but Mr. Parker just called."

"He did?" Sitting up, Megan smoothed a hand over her hair. "I didn't hear the phone."

"I'm not surprised. Anyway, he said he's going to be late tonight and wants to know if you can go in a little early and open up."

"Is he still on the phone?"

"No. He said to call back if you can't make it."

Megan glanced at her watch. It was seven fifteen. "I guess I'd better get ready."

"Sorry for the intrusion," Shirl said, looking at Rhys. "It was nice to meet you, Mr. Costain."

He grinned at her as he raked a hand through his hair. "Just Rhys."

"Rhys it is," she said, returning his grin. "See you tomorrow, Meggie. Good night, Rhys."

He waited until Shirl left the room before taking Megan by the hand and pulling her to her feet. "Meggie?"

"I hate that name."

"Would you like me to drive you to work?" he asked.

"That isn't necessary."

He was about to say he would be glad to do it when his cell phone rang. "Excuse me." Turning his back to Megan, he flipped open the phone. "What is it?"

"There've been three more murders," Rupert said. "Bodies all drained of blood."

"Where?"

"Fort Worth."

"Thanks for letting me know," Rhys said, and ended the call.

"Is something wrong?" Megan asked.

"Some business at the club I need to take care of," he replied. "I'll see you tomorrow night."

A quick kiss, and he was gone.

"He's a hottie, that one," Shirl said, coming up behind her.

"What? Oh, yes, he is."

"He sure left in a hurry."

"Some business at his club. I'll have to take you there some time. You'll love it."

"He's gorgeous, but I can see why he scares you. There's an edge about him, something . . . I don't know."

"You sensed it, too?"

"How could anyone miss it?"

"I thought maybe it was just me."

"Another thing, he seems really, I don't know, really worldly wise and self-assured for someone so young. You know what I mean?"

Megan nodded. She had noticed that, too. "He doesn't act his age, that's for sure."

"Be careful, girlfriend," Shirl admonished. "I think this one plays for keeps."

Rhys swore softly as he drove to the club. He didn't want to have to worry about some rogue vamp, or what it might mean if the renegade decided to come to LA. As Master of the West Coast Vampires, Rhys had only one rule for those in his territory—don't leave any bodies drained of blood where they could be found. Most vampires were smart enough not to call attention to their kind. They preyed on transients or the homeless—people who wouldn't be missed. But this rogue, he was killing indiscriminately, and that boded ill for all of them.

Chapter 10

Tomás strolled through the Log Cabin Village located in a woodsy section of Trinity Park in Fort Worth. Seven fully restored cabins occupied the settlement. All had been built sometime in the 1850s. During the day, volunteers gave visitors a taste of what life had been like in days gone by, demonstrating things like grinding corn, spinning, weaving, and the art of making candles. The botanical gardens were another of his favorite sites. The gardens featured over two thousand acres of trails and garden exhibits in what was one of the oldest and largest natural settings in North Texas. In addition, there was a large conservatory filled with tropical plants and exotic birds.

Another place he visited whenever he was in town was the Kimball Art Museum. At one time or another, the museum had showcased the work of such noted artists as Rubens, Picasso, Renoir, and Rembrandt, as well as the works of contemporary artists from around the world.

One of the advantages of being a vampire was that he didn't have to endure the crowds of tourists who descended on Trinity Park or roamed through the museum during the day. Visiting the museum late at night, he could study his favorite paintings without being bothered by impudent teens or noisy toddlers.

Leaving the museum, he moved swiftly to Sundance Square. Located in the heart of downtown, the square gave him the feeling of walking the streets at the turn of the century, with its renovated storefronts and red brick streets. He had walked here when the city was new, when the streets were dirt and the stink of cowboys, horses, and cattle filled the air. But now his nostrils filled with a different scent.

The scent of prey.

He found them parked in a car on a side street, the windows covered with steam. Young lovers, he thought, as he wrenched the driver's side door open. He broke the boy's neck with a quick twist and had the girl in his arms and out of the car before she realized what was happening.

His hand stifled her cries as he carried her away from the car, away from the city, to a place where her screams wouldn't be heard, and then he let her scream to her heart's content as he buried his fangs in her neck. She fought him as best she could, but her fists were puny weapons; he hardly noticed them striking his back as her warm red blood trickled down his throat.

Chapter 11

On the night of the concert, Rhys arrived at Megan's house a few minutes after eight. He looked drop-dead gorgeous, as always. Clad all in black and wearing a pair of trendy dark glasses, he could easily have passed for a rock star himself.

There was a line around the building when they arrived at the venue, but Megan had a pass so she and Rhys didn't have to wait. There were hoots and hollers of protest when they bypassed the crowd and ducked through a side door reserved for VIPs.

"Have you ever been to a rock concert?" Megan asked as they took their seats in a roped-off section in the front of the hall.

"One or two," Rhys answered. In his time, he had seen them all. He had to admit, being in close quarters with thousands of screaming fans wasn't his favorite way to spend an evening. It wasn't easy to keep his hunger under control when every indrawn breath carried the scent of blood, when his ears were assaulted by the sound of so many beating hearts. If not for the lovely woman beside him, he wouldn't be here now. He supposed it was a sign of how smitten he was with Megan DeLacey that he had agreed to come to the concert at all.

Excitement flooded the stadium and screams bounced off the walls when Drexel appeared. He wore a pair of black spandex pants, a white shirt reminiscent of the kind pirates had once worn, and knee-high black boots.

Colored lights flashed as he swaggered to center stage. He looked out over the crowd and then, as if reaching for a woman, his hand curled around the microphone, and he began to sing.

Rhys shook his head. He doubted if anyone could actually hear Drexel's voice over the earsplitting music and the near-hysterical screams of thousands of crazed female fans. White vapor rose from the stage floor and curled around Drexel's ankles. Cameras flashed. Girls fainted. Yellow-shirted security guards prowled the front of the stage and the edges of the crowd, leaping into action now and again to prevent overeager fans from jumping up on the stage.

Rhys glanced at Megan when she tugged on his arm. "What do you think of him?" she asked, shouting to be heard over the roar of the crowd.

"He's good." The kid might be young, but he knew how to play to the audience. They had fallen under his spell the minute he walked out on the stage, and he never let them go. Rhys had to admire that.

The band had been playing for about an hour when Rhys detected the acrid scent of smoke. Lifting his head, he sniffed the air. The smell was coming from backstage, and getting thicker and stronger by the minute.

"Come on," he said, grabbing Megan by the hand. "We're getting out of here."

"Why? What's wrong?"

"No time to talk about it now." He slid his hand up until he had a firm grip on her forearm.

"Rhys!" She twisted, trying to break his hold. "I'm not ready to go."

"Yes, you are." He pulled her along behind him until they reached the aisle.

A security guard stepped out in front of Rhys. He glanced at Megan, who was still trying to wriggle free of Rhys's grasp. "Something wrong here?"

"There's a fire," Rhys said curtly. "Backstage. You'd better get these people out of here before it's too late."

The guard's eyes narrowed. "Fire?"

"Can't you smell it?" Rhys glanced back at Megan. She had stopped fighting him, her gaze riveted on the stage where long, yellow tongues of flame were eating their way up the backdrop.

Drexel and the band seemed unaware of what was going on until shouts of "fire!" grew so loud, they drowned out the band. The music came to an abrupt halt when Drexel glanced behind him. The drummer jumped to his feet when the backdrop dissolved in a shower of rainbow sparks. Without the barrier, the acrid stink of burning wood and fabric grew stronger, heavier. Panic erupted on the stage and spread through the audience as thousands of people blindly fought their way through the smoke toward the exits, tripping over each other in their haste.

Muttering an oath, Rhys swept Megan into his arms and transported the two of them out of the building to the sidewalk across the street.

Megan stared up at him, her eyes wide. "What happened? How did you do that?"

"Do what?"

"Get us out of there so fast. I don't even remember leaving the building."

"That's understandable. You were afraid. The mind can play funny tricks on you when you're scared."

Frowning, she shook her head. "No." One minute they

had been inside; the next, they were here. She had no memory of what had happened in between.

Rhys set Megan on her feet, then folded his hands over her shoulders. Gazing deeply into her eyes, he spoke to her, his voice low and hypnotic. "I carried you through the crowd and out of the building. We were lucky to escape so quickly."

"Yes," she murmured. "Lucky."

When he was certain she believed what he wanted her to believe, he released his hold on her mind and turned his attention to the people still running out of the building, which was now engulfed in flames. The screams of those trapped inside, the sobs of those who had escaped, the sickly sweet smell of burning flesh rode the night air. And over all, the wail of sirens as fire trucks, police cars, and ambulances rolled to the scene.

Freed of his spell, Megan blinked up at Rhys. "Drexel? Do you think he's . . . ?"

She couldn't say the word, couldn't bear to think of the enthusiastic young man who had proposed to her so many times being burned alive in the inferno.

"I don't know." Rhys stared at the fire. It was like a scene out of hell, with the flames shooting skyward and sparks falling in the streets and landing on the crowd. Men and women, some with their clothing on fire, ran out of the building, trampling each other in their panic. Rhys shook his head. There wasn't much in his existence he feared, but fire . . . It was one of the few things that could destroy him.

Megan watched in morbid fascination as the firemen went to work. A few of them dashed into the burning building while others manned the fire hoses. The air crackled as thick streams of cold water met the hot, hungry flames.

It wasn't long until the reporters arrived, shoving their microphones in the faces of spectators, asking people who had just survived a horrible ordeal the same stupid questions reporters always asked at scenes of death and destruction.

Rhys glanced at Megan. “Are you ready to go?”

Megan shook her head. She couldn’t leave, not until she knew whether or not Drexel had survived. And then she saw him, sitting on the curb across the way. His pants were singed, his face and hands were smeared with soot, his right arm looked badly burned. But he was alive.

The reporters saw him, too. Like vultures on a fresh kill, they swarmed around him, all asking questions at once.

“Why can’t they just leave him alone?” Megan exclaimed. “Can’t they see he’s hurt?”

“Do you want me to get rid of them?”

“Can you?” she asked hopefully.

“Watch me.” Flexing his shoulders, Rhys pushed his way through the crowd of reporters. “Drexel, do you want to talk to these clowns?”

Drexel shook his head, then started coughing.

Standing in front of the boy, Rhys fixed his gaze on each reporter in turn. “You heard him, ladies and gentlemen, he wants to be left alone. Now get the hell out of here.”

As though pulled by the same string, the reporters all turned and walked away.

“Come on, kid,” Rhys said, “let’s get you out of here.” And so saying, he swung the young man into his arms and carried him toward an ambulance that had just arrived at the end of the block.

When one of the attendants started to protest that there were others more in need of immediate care, Rhys forced his will on the EMT, then opened the ambulance doors, jumped inside, and lowered Drexel onto the bench that ran along one side of the vehicle.

The EMT came in behind Rhys and began examining the burn on Drexel’s right arm.

Drexel stared up at Rhys. "You," he said, his voice gruff from all the smoke he had inhaled. "I know you. . . ."

"We met at Shore's."

"Young man," the EMT admonished, "You shouldn't try to talk right now."

"The medic's right," Rhys said. "Save your breath."

"Megan . . . I saw her. . . ." Drexel broke into a paroxysm of coughing. "Is she . . . ?"

"She's fine. You'll be proposing to her again in no time."

Drexel smiled faintly; then, with a pain-filled sigh, he closed his eyes.

Rhys stared down at the kid for a moment. Had he ever been that young? With a shake of his head, he jumped out of the ambulance and returned to Megan.

"Is he all right?" she asked anxiously.

"He'll be fine. He's got a bad burn on one arm, and he inhaled some smoke. Nothing too serious."

Rhys glanced at the six covered bodies lying in the street. He could have told the firemen there were two more inside, but the dead were beyond help, beyond caring.

The fire was under control now. Cops were directing traffic away from the scene. The scream of sirens pierced the night as ambulances pulled away from the stadium. Reporters, their cameramen in tow, prowled the edges of the crowd like wolves on the scent of prey, hoping to chase down a good story.

"Come on," Rhys said, "let's get out of here."

She didn't argue this time.

Wrapping his arm around her shoulders, Rhys led her to his car, helped her inside, fastened her seat belt.

"Do you want to talk about it?" he asked.

She shook her head. She didn't want to talk about what had happened, didn't want to think about it, but she couldn't get the images out of her mind—the relentless flames, the firemen rushing into the inferno, putting their own lives at risk to try to save others. It was frightening, the way the fire had spread so quickly. She thought of all the people who had gone to the concert looking to have a good time and had lost their lives. Images of the covered bodies lying in the street flashed through her mind. If not for Rhys's quick thinking, one of those bodies could have been hers. It was the first time she had ever seriously considered her own mortality. She was young and healthy. Dying was something that happened to other people.

Rhys slid a glance at Megan. She was trembling now. After removing his jacket, Rhys tucked it around her. He needed to get her home, warm her up with some hot tea, and put her to bed before she collapsed.

He had no sooner pulled up in front of Megan's place when Shirl came running out the front door, her bathrobe flying behind her. She yanked open the car door, then dropped to her knees. "Megan! Are you all right? I saw the fire on the news. I was so worried!"

"I'm fine, just a little shaky." Clutching Rhys's jacket closer, she got out of the car. Rhys was instantly at her side, his arm sliding around her waist to steady her.

Shirl glanced up at him and realized there had been nothing to worry about. On some innate level, she knew this man would never let anything happen to Megan.

"Why don't you make us some tea?" Rhys suggested. "And add a little brandy to Megan's, if you've got it."

With a nod, Shirl hurried back into the house.

"I'm fine," Megan said, seeing his worried expression. "Really."

"Uh-huh." Swinging her into his arms, he carried her inside. He knew it wasn't necessary. She could have walked, but he needed to hold her. He knew even better than she did how quickly a life could be snuffed out. He had been responsible for dispatching a few himself.

In the living room, he lowered her to the sofa. Taking his

coat from her, he slipped it on, then covered her with the afghan folded over the back of the couch. Sitting beside her, he took her hands in his. "You're cold."

"So are you."

"Yeah." He needed to feed, something he had been doing more of since meeting Megan. It was the only way to keep his skin from feeling abnormally cool.

"Here we go." Shirl glanced at Rhys as she placed a tray on the coffee table. "I brought sugar, milk, and honey, since I don't know how you like your tea."

He grinned up at her. "I don't like tea."

"Oh. Can I get you anything else?"

His gaze moved to the pulse throbbing in her throat, and then he shook his head. "No, thanks."

She stared at him a moment; then, with a shrug, she picked up the teapot and filled two cups. She added a spoonful of honey to one of them, and handed the other to Megan.

"Did they say anything on the news about how the fire started?" Rhys asked.

"Something about the wiring backstage. I don't know what that backdrop was made of, but it went up like flash paper. The band was lucky to make it off the stage. I saw Drexel on the news. They said he's going to be all right." Shirl grinned at Rhys. "They interviewed one of the EMTs. He said some really intense guy insisted he take care of Drexel right away, even though he wasn't that badly hurt. I'm guessing that was you."

"You'd be right," Rhys said, chuckling.

"I thought so. I'm just glad you're both all right." Shirl glanced at Megan, who was yawning. "I think it's time I put you to bed."

Megan nodded. The tea, heavily laced with brandy, must have been doing its work. She was suddenly very sleepy.

"Come on," Rhys said, gaining his feet, "I'll carry you upstairs."

"I can walk," Megan said, smothering another yawn.

"I know you can," he agreed, lifting her into his arms, "but why should you?"

She couldn't think of a single reason. Instead, she rested her head against his shoulder and closed her eyes.

"Look at that," Shirl said. "She's asleep already."

Rhys brushed a lock of hair from Megan's cheek, then bent his head to kiss her brow. Thanks to his preternatural power, she would sleep through what was left of the night and wake up feeling glad to be alive.

He looked up to find Shirl watching him, an inquisitive expression on her face. "Something wrong?"

"Who are you?"

He lifted one brow. "What do you mean?" It was an inane question. He knew exactly what she meant.

"There's something about you. Something . . ." She shook her head. "I can't put my finger on it, but there's something not quite right."

"I'm going to take Megan up to bed."

"You're not going to tell me who you are, or what you are, are you?"

"No. All you need to know is that I'm in love with Megan, and I would never hurt her."

Shirl nodded. She didn't know much about this man, but she could see the truth of his words in his eyes.

She led the way up to Megan's room and turned down the covers on the bed. After Rhys lowered Megan onto the mattress, Shirl shooed him out of the room and shut the door. She undressed Megan, eased a nightgown over her head, then pulled the covers over her before allowing Rhys back into the room.

"I'll wait for you downstairs," Shirl said, and left the room.

Rhys sat on the edge of the bed, one hand lightly

stroking Megan's cheek. She might have perished in the fire if he hadn't been there tonight. The thought cut like a knife. Even though she wasn't hurt, he was hesitant to leave her, but Shirl was waiting downstairs to lock up after him. It was the only thing keeping him from leaving by the window. Using his supernatural powers would only add to her suspicions. Rising, he kissed Megan's cheek before going downstairs.

He found Shirl by the front door.

"Good night, Mr. Costain."

Stifling a grin, he murmured, "Good night, Miss Mansfield," and left the house.

She stared after him. Megan had been right to be wary of Rhys Costain, Shirl decided as she turned off the lights in the living room. He was remarkably handsome. He was polite. He dressed well and drove a great car, but . . . She shook her head. Something about him definitely wasn't right.

"Mr. Costain," she murmured. "Who are you?"

Feeling a sudden chill, she closed and locked the door. Maybe that double-date she and Megan had talked about wasn't such a good idea, after all.

Chapter 12

In the morning, Megan woke feeling wonderful. Smiling, she sat up and stretched her arms over her head. It was a beautiful day.

Rising, she took a long, hot shower, washed her hair, brushed her teeth, wrapped up in her favorite fluffy robe, and went downstairs to get the Sunday paper.

Humming softly, she fixed a cup of hot chocolate, then sat down and spread the paper on the kitchen table.

She frowned when she read the headlines:

INFERNO AT DOWNTOWN ROCK CONCERT
EIGHT DEAD, TWO HUNDRED INJURED

How could she have forgotten about the fire? She quickly read the article, which gave a brief review of the concert, then went on to say that the cause of the fire was still under investigation, although the preliminary report pointed to defective wiring and faulty smoke detectors.

Reading the paper brought all the unbelievable horror of the evening rushing back—the terror that had engulfed her, the almost hypnotic glow of the flames as they licked at the building, the bodies of the dead being put into shiny black body bags.

How could she have forgotten such a horrible ordeal?

And then there was the way Rhys had spirited them out of the stadium. How had he done that? And why couldn't she remember? She drummed her fingertips on the edge of the table. One minute she had been inside the burning building and the next she had been across the street with no memory of how they had gotten there. Had Rhys been right? Had she been so afraid she had blocked it from her mind?

One thing she did know. If it hadn't been for Rhys, she probably wouldn't have made it out of the building alive. She read the names of the deceased again. Six of them had been teenagers. One had been a young mother. The last fatality had been a member of the band. Four firemen had suffered smoke inhalation; three had been hospitalized with severe burns. The building was a total loss.

Megan was trying to work up an appetite when Shirl entered the kitchen, looking gorgeous in a pair of snowflake pj's and pink bunny slippers. "Hey, girlfriend, I didn't expect you to be up so early."

"It's almost noon."

"Well, after the night you had . . ." Shirl lifted one shoulder and let it fall. "I thought you'd be out most of the day."

Megan frowned. She had expected to have nightmares last night, or at least to have trouble sleeping, but she had slept like a baby. There had been no bad dreams, and when she woke this morning, she hadn't even thought of the fire until she read about it in the paper. How could she have forgotten something so traumatic, she wondered again. She pondered that a moment, trying to wrap her mind around the strangeness of it.

"Have you eaten?" Shirl asked.

"Not yet."

"What are you in the mood for?"

"Nothing really."

"Well, you need to eat." Moving to the fridge, Shirl opened the door. "How about French toast? Waffles? Pancakes? Scrambled eggs, hash browns, and bacon?" She glanced over her shoulder. "Well?"

"Pancakes and bacon sounds good."

When Megan started to get up, Shirl waved her off. "I'll do it. You just relax."

"Shirl . . ."

"What?"

Megan ran her finger around the rim of her cup, and then, taking a deep breath, she told Shirl what was bothering her.

"Don't you think it's odd?" Megan asked when she finished. "I mean . . ." She shrugged. "It's like I completely forgot about the fire and everything that happened last night."

After mixing the pancake batter, Shirl pulled a frying pan from under the stove for the bacon. "It does seem odd, but maybe it's not uncommon. I mean, it was a horrible experience. Maybe your subconscious just wasn't ready to handle it when you woke up."

"Maybe, but I can't help thinking there's more to it . . . something I can't put my finger on. It's like, I don't know, somebody wiped it from my memory. I guess that sounds really strange."

"Yeah, it does."

"And then . . . you know, I don't remember getting out of the building. It's like, one minute we were inside, and the next we were across the street. Rhys said the reason I don't remember is because I was so scared."

"Well, that makes sense, I guess."

"I guess. It just seems so, I don't know, weird."

Shirl sighed heavily. "Girlfriend, the whole world is

weird these days. I mean, have you read about all those deaths back East? Bodies drained of blood. It's like we're living in the twilight zone." She turned the bacon, then began ladling batter onto the griddle. "One of the news channels mentioned vampires."

"Vampires! Are you serious?" Megan tilted her head to one side. "You're loving this, aren't you?"

"Of course not, but it is kind of exciting. Get the syrup and the butter, will you?"

Vampires, Megan thought, as she set the syrup and the butter on the table, along with a couple of knives and forks. There were rumors of creatures of the night from time to time. It seemed that whenever there was a mysterious death, some reporter attributed it to werewolves or vampires. She had even heard that you could buy vampire blood on the Internet, but she had laughed it off, certain it was either a joke or just some kind of fake blood for the Goth crowd.

Megan sat down at the table across from Shirl. "Looks great, thanks," she said, and then did a double take when Shirl actually put a pancake and a strip of bacon on her own plate. "I don't believe it. You're eating real food?"

Shirl blew out an aggrieved sigh. "I deserve it. Besides, I'm on vacation for a week."

"I didn't know that. What are you going to do?"

"Greg has a cabin up in the mountains. He wants to go up there, but I don't know. . . ."

"You should go. It'll be good for you to get away for a while."

"I don't think I should leave you alone."

"Don't be silly. I'm fine. Really."

"Are you sure? I mean, Greg and I can find plenty to do here in town."

"Shirl, I'm a big girl, remember? I think I can get along without you for a few days."

"Well, I really would like to go," Shirl admitted with a dreamy smile.

"Then it's settled." Megan slapped her palms on the table. "When are you leaving?"

"Tomorrow morning. Early. And we'll be back next Sunday, not too late, since I have a shoot on Monday."

Megan nodded. "I think it's just what you need. You've been working way too hard lately. I'll help you pack."

The rest of the day passed quickly. Megan dusted and vacuumed. Shirl did the laundry. Since they'd had such a late breakfast, they skipped lunch and splurged on hot fudge sundaes instead.

After packing Shirl's suitcase, they went out to their favorite Italian restaurant for dinner.

"So," Shirl said, reaching for a bread stick still warm from the oven, "what are you going to do about Rhys Costain?"

"I don't know." Megan propped her elbows on the table and rested her chin on her folded hands. "When I'm with him, he makes me feel wonderful, beautiful. Special. Safe."

"And when you're not with him?"

"I know he's hiding something," Megan said. "I just don't know what it is."

"Well, you be careful. I'll call you from the cabin tomorrow night. And I'll keep my phone on in case you need me."

Shirl hadn't been kidding when she'd said Greg was picking her up early in the morning. Greg arrived at six, bid a sleepy-eyed Megan a quick hello and good-bye, and whisked Shirl away.

Megan waved as the car pulled out of the driveway, and then went back to bed, only to get up an hour later. She made her bed, fixed breakfast, did the dishes, and got dressed, and it was only eight thirty.

She had expected to enjoy having the place all to herself for a few days; instead, she was overcome with a feeling of depression. Even though there were days when Megan didn't see Shirl at all, it was comforting to know that, sooner or later, Shirl would come home from work and there would be another warm body in the house.

The day stretched before her. At loose ends, Megan went to the local day spa and indulged herself—she had a facial and a full body massage, swam in the heated pool, spent some time in the meditation garden before leaving for home. On the way, she stopped and picked up some Chinese takeout for dinner.

When she reached home, it was only six o'clock. Would this day never end?

The house seemed incredibly empty without Shirl. After eating, Megan went upstairs to take a shower, donned her favorite pj's, and then went downstairs. Curling up on the sofa, hugging a pillow to her chest, she surfed through the channels.

"Five hundred channels," she muttered, "and there's nothing worth watching."

As always, she eventually found her thoughts turning toward Rhys. How did she really feel about him? She had told Shirl she thought he was hiding something, but what? The most likely secret would be a wife. Or worse, a wife and a couple of kids. Maybe it was something even more damning. Lord, what if he was a sex offender or a felon? He certainly knew how to take care of himself. He had taken those two would-be robbers at Shore's down in the blink of an eye. And then there was his quick thinking at the concert. She still didn't know how he had gotten the two of them out of that burning building without a scratch.

She drummed her fingertips on the arm of the sofa.

Where had he learned to react to danger with such blinding speed? Maybe he belonged to some Special Ops organization, or the CIA, or maybe the DEA. Maybe he taught martial arts. She blew out a sigh. Maybe she'd never know.

She was thinking about going to bed when the doorbell rang. Her heartbeat immediately jumped into overdrive.

It was Rhys. She knew it with every fiber of her being. She wished fleetingly that she was wearing something more alluring than pj's and a tank top, but there was no help for it now.

She forced herself to take three slow, deep breaths before she opened the door. And he was there. Dressed all in black, he blended with the shadows, a part of the night and the darkness.

"Megan." His voice, soft and low, yet filled with heat and desire. It wrapped around her, seeping into her very being. "I thought you might like some company."

"What makes you think I'm alone?"

"Didn't Shirl leave town this morning?"

"Yes, but how did you know that?"

"She must have mentioned it the other night, after you fell asleep." The lie rolled easily off his tongue.

"Oh. Well, come on in. To tell you the truth, I was feeling a little lonely."

He followed her into the living room, sat beside her on the sofa. Not too close. He was well aware of her ambivalent feelings toward him. It was time to reestablish trust, assure her that she had nothing to fear. He jerked his chin toward the TV. "What are you watching?"

"Nothing, really. I was about to turn it off."

"Why not put some music on?"

"All right." She found an all-music channel that played soft rock.

"Would you care to dance?"

"What? Here, now?"

"Why not here?" Rising, he reached for her hand.

Why not, indeed, Megan thought. Putting her hand in his, she let him pull her to her feet.

Dancing with Rhys wasn't like dancing with anyone else. He moved effortlessly, fluidly. She wasn't any great shakes as a dancer, but he held her so close, it didn't matter. Her body moved with his as though they had danced together for years instead of only once before. But dancing at the club hadn't been anything like this. They were alone now, just the two of them. It was exhilarating, being in his arms, feeling his breath against her cheek, seeing the heat in his eyes. She had once heard someone describe dancing as vertical sex. With Rhys, it was definitely true. Her hormones sat up and took notice every time his body brushed against hers.

"You're trembling," he remarked.

"Am I?"

"Are you cold?"

"No." How could she be when he was looking at her with such blatant desire?

"Afraid?"

She blinked up at him. She was afraid, afraid she would wake up in her bed and discover that this was only a dream. Afraid that when the music stopped, he would disappear. But she couldn't tell him that.

The music changed to something slow and sensual. His arms tightened around her, drawing her even closer. "Megan?"

"Kiss me, Rhys."

If her request surprised him, it didn't show.

She closed her eyes as he bent his head toward her. Her heart slammed against her rib cage when his lips met hers. Heat flowed through every nerve and cell, turning her blood to fire, threatening to melt her bones.

"Ah, Megan, do you know what you do to me?" His gaze moved to the pulse throbbing wildly in the hollow of her throat. The rapid pounding of her heart was like the beat of a drum only he could hear. "Do you have any idea how difficult it is not to . . ." Muttering an oath, he released her and stepped away.

Confused, she wrapped her arms around her waist to keep from reaching for him. Had she done something wrong? Displeased him in some way? Disappointed him?

Seeing her bewildered expression, Rhys drew her back into his embrace. If he was smart, he would leave now and never see her again. The longer he was with her, the harder it would be to let her go. Even though he cared deeply for her, he knew, realistically, that there was no future for the two of them.

There was no denying that she was attracted to him, but then, most women were. He had no way of knowing how much of that attraction was due to the inherent allure all vampires possessed, and how much was genuine affection.

For his part, he hadn't felt this way about a woman since Josette. Closing his eyes, he opened his senses, basking in the feel of the woman in his arms, the flowery perfume of her hair, the musky scent of her skin.

She wanted him.

But no more than he wanted her. "Megan?"

He liked it that she didn't pretend she didn't know what he was asking.

A flush crept up her neck and into her cheeks as she took his hand in hers and led him up the stairs to her bedroom.

Once in her room, Megan was overcome with uncertainty. What was she doing? Did she really want to hop into bed with a man she had known for such a short time? A man she had been having serious doubts about only yesterday? Even thinking about taking him to bed was totally out of character for her. Still, she was a big girl, and it had been a long time since she'd had this particular itch scratched.

"Megan?" His voice surrounded her, winding around her like a silken web from which there was no escape.

She shivered with pleasure as he bestowed featherlight kisses along the side of her neck, along her collarbone to the hollow of her throat. Yes, this was what she wanted. This man. Right now.

For once in her life, she was going to leap before she looked. For once in her life, she wasn't going to play it safe.

As if he knew she had resolved her inner conflict, he pulled her up against him, his hand sliding seductively up and down her spine.

She had to touch him. Tugging his T-shirt from his jeans, she ran her hands over his chest, felt his muscles tense at her touch.

Still holding her against him, he backed her toward the bed and then, supporting her with his arms, he lowered her to the mattress before stretching out beside her.

"Rhys . . ." Murmuring his name, she explored the width of his shoulders, the taut planes and ridges of his chest and belly.

Knowing what she wanted, he yanked his T-shirt over his head and tossed it aside, giving her access to his upper body.

Turning onto her side, she explored the width of his shoulders, the whorls of curly hair on his chest, the hard ridges of his stomach. She paused now and then to kiss him here, lick him there. Growing bolder, she pulled off his boots and his socks, and then, after a moment's hesitation, she tugged his jeans down over his slim hips. The black briefs he wore did nothing to hide the fact that he wanted her.

He let her explore his body from head to foot, and then he turned the tables on her. "My turn," he said, his voice thick, and in the time it took her to blink, she was lying naked beneath him, and he had begun a slow exploration of his own.

His hands were large yet gentle as they played over her quivering flesh. The touch of his cool skin did nothing to douse the flames that threatened to consume her from the inside out. Each stroke of his hands, each heated caress, carried her to a place where she had never been before, a place she hoped never to leave. She had made love in the past, but it had never been like this. Never before had she so desperately wanted or needed a man's touch. Never before had she known such wonder, such pleasure.

He murmured her name as he shucked his briefs, and then he rose over her, blatantly male and aroused.

With a throaty growl, she wrapped her arms around his neck, her legs around his waist, and lifted her hips to meet him.

One thrust, and she felt like she might shatter. She clung to him as the world spun out of focus. Never had she been so aware of her own body, or felt so vibrantly alive. She had heard of two bodies becoming one, but their joining went beyond that. It was as if their hearts and souls had seamlessly melded, so that she knew what he was thinking, what he was feeling. She knew where he wanted to be touched, just as he seemed to know exactly how to please her.

And please her he did, with every caress, every murmured word, until one last thrust carried her over the edge to blissful fulfillment.

Sated and complete, she murmured his name and then, with a sigh, she closed her eyes and fell into the warm abyss of slumber.

Rhys stayed at Megan's side long after she had fallen asleep. Gazing down at her, he wondered if she would have second thoughts or regrets when she woke in the morning. It had been a long time since she had been intimate with a man. What would she think if she knew her latest lover was not a man at all?

He wondered absently if she was using any kind of birth control. Not that it mattered. He carried no diseases. He could not father a child. It was the one thing that bothered him about being a vampire. Not that he would have made a good father, not that he had ever really wanted kids, but he would have liked to have had the option just the same. It was the one thing he had always envied about his friend, Delacourt. Erik had been a married man with children before he was turned. It was possible that Delacourt still had descendants living somewhere in England.

Muttering an oath, Rhys dropped a kiss on Megan's cheek, dressed, and left the house.

Filled with a sudden anger he refused to examine, he headed for his club. Even though it was late, there were still a few men and women lingering over drinks at the bar.

Rhys looked the women over, made his choice, and tapped her on the shoulder. When she started to speak, he silenced her with a look. He didn't want conversation tonight, he didn't want anything except a few minutes of forgetfulness.

The woman followed him into one of the rooms and closed the door. When she started to undress, he shook his head. He didn't want an hour of meaningless sex; he didn't want to seek comfort in the arms of a stranger. What the hell did he want?

Megan. Her name whispered in the back of his mind as he pulled the woman, none too gently, into his arms and buried his fangs in her throat. This was what he was, who he was. He would never be good enough for Megan DeLacey, never be able to give her the kind of life she deserved. He needed to remember that.

He lifted his head and stared at the woman in his embrace. And then he lowered his head and drank again. *This is what you are,* whispered a mocking voice in the back of his mind. *A monster.*

He drew back as his victim's heartbeat grew slow and erratic. If he drank any more, the girl would die. Odd that he should worry about that now. He had rarely given much thought to the fate of his prey before. In the past, he had attacked men and women without a qualm, taken what he needed without regret, and if his victims didn't survive, he had shrugged it off. Humans were prey. He was a predator. It had been as simple as that. Until the night he stepped into Shore's and gazed into Megan DeLacey's guileless brown eyes.

With an oath, he sealed the wounds in the woman's neck and lowered her onto the bed. After ordering the bartender to take care of her, he left the club without a backward glance and headed for home.

And all the while, the word *monster* echoed in the back of his mind.

Chapter 13

Tomás lifted his head, his senses drinking in the sights and sounds of the evening countryside. He had left the Ferretti behind when he left Texas. As much as he loved the yacht, there was a lot to be said for the speed and power of a fine car, and the sleek, black Lamborghini Murcielago convertible was fine indeed, able to accelerate from zero to sixty in just over three seconds.

Tomás smiled as he goosed the convertible up to ninety. As much as he had enjoyed his stay in Texas, boredom had eventually set in, urging him to seek new hunting grounds, new prey. A new method of transportation. Hence the Lamborghini, which he had purchased on the spur of the moment. He had hired someone to sail the yacht to San Diego.

He wondered idly if humans realized how long eternity could be, how monotonous life became when one had seen all there was to see, done all there was to do. For a moment, he considered settling down for a while, taking a wife, pretending to be human. How many times had he done that in the past? A hundred? Two? Inevitably, when his wife began to age and he did not, he had to move on. Occasionally, he turned those he wed, but he was too selfish, too territorial, to share his hunting grounds with anyone else, even someone he cared for. All things considered, it was better to live alone.

He grinned inwardly. Perhaps he could find the excitement he was looking for in New Mexico, the Land of Enchantment.

Chapter 14

Rhys let his glance sweep the faces of the Vampire Council. "The rogue is on the move again," he said, his voice gruff. "He's racking up killings from one end of New Mexico to the other."

"Maybe it isn't an old one," Seth Adams suggested. "Maybe he's newly turned."

"Could be," Stuart agreed. "Maybe whoever sired him neglected to show him the ropes, so to speak."

Rupert shook his head. "No, it's definitely one of the old ones. I told you, a trusted friend of mine saw one of the victims. He said the vamp responsible was definitely ancient."

"Then I guess the next step is to try to pin down where the old ones are," Rhys said. "Adrianna, New Mexico is your home base. Call around and see what you can find out. I want the rest of you to get in touch with the vampires in your areas and see if any of the old ones have moved on. Once we know who's where they should be, and who isn't, we can start to narrow the list."

"I still don't know why you're so bothered by all this," Julius said. "So what if a few humans come looking for us?"

Rhys glared at him. "What if it's more than a few?

There's already a new hunter in LA. He's probably heard about the killings. Just because we haven't heard of hunters in other cities doesn't mean they aren't there. We've had it pretty easy the last few years. Most of the human population has more important things to worry about than whether we exist or not. But if this rogue keeps killing, eventually people are going to sit up and take notice. I don't know about you, but I like things the way they are. And what if some of the young ones decide to stop being careful?" Rhys glanced around the room. He had their attention now. "I don't care what the rogue does back East, but he's heading in this direction. I like it here. I'm not ready to pack up and move on. What about you, Hastings? You ready to leave Oregon? And what about you, Winchester? You ready to give up your place in Montana? How about you, Nick? You ready to move on?"

Nick shook his head. "No. You said he's in New Mexico. How about if I go there and see what I can find out?"

"I don't need any help," Adrianna declared.

"Maybe not," Nick said, "but I'm tired of sitting around, waiting." He looked at Rhys expectantly.

"Might be a good idea to have someone there. Take Adams with you."

Adams reared back in his chair. "What? I don't want to go to New Mexico!"

"Who does?" Julius asked, laughing.

"New Mexico is my home," Adrianna said. "If you want someone to look around, I'll go."

Rhys sent her a quelling glance. He didn't like Adrianna, and he didn't trust her. Better to keep her close, where he could keep an eye on her. "We'll play it my way for now," he decided. "Nick and Seth are going to New Mexico. The rest of you get busy and check the lairs of the old ones."

"What are you going to do?" Adrianna asked.

"Check my own sources," Rhys retorted.

"You've been a little testy the last few days," Stuart observed. "Anything we need to know about? We don't usually meet this often."

"No."

Winchester looked up from his cell phone. "Must be woman trouble."

"This meeting is over," Rhys said. "Get the hell out of here, all of you."

Jaw clenched, he watched them vanish one by one, but not before Adrianna clapped Winchester on the back and said, "I think you nailed it that time."

Chapter 15

Megan was glad to be back to work on Tuesday night. She had rattled around the house all that day, trying to reassure herself that she hadn't made a big mistake the night before. She had fallen asleep in Rhys's arms, and expected to awake there, as well. But he had been gone when she awoke, almost as if he had never been there at all. She couldn't believe he would just leave without a word, not after the romantic night they had shared. She had been certain she would find a note saying he would see her again later, which just proved how wrong she could be. She had searched the house for a note that didn't exist, waited all day for a phone call that never came. Had he been stringing her along the whole time, just waiting to get her into bed? Silly question, she thought, when the answer seemed obvious. How could she have been such an idiot?

She let out a sigh as one of her least favorite customers swept into the store. In his midsixties, Richard Archibald Clark was the CEO of a major corporation based in the heart of downtown Los Angeles.

"Megan, my dear," he exclaimed, wrapping her in a bear hug. "You've had a horrible couple of weeks, haven't you? First the attempted robbery, and then the fire at the Drexel concert." He tsked softly. "Parker gave me all details. Terrible, just terrible." Holding her at arm's length, he ran his gaze over her. "Praise the Lord, you look none the worse for wear."

Disengaging herself, Megan forced a smile. "Thank you for your concern, Mr. Clark, but I'm fine now, really."

"That's my brave girl." Mr. Clark shrugged out of his coat and tossed it to his assistant, Vi. Vi was a mousy little thing somewhere in her midthirties. Megan had never heard the woman speak a word.

"I'm in need of a new suit," Mr. Clark said, all business once again. "Something dark, no stripes."

"I think we have just what you're looking for," Megan replied, moving toward the north side of the store.

"Yes, you always do," Mr. Clark said, beaming at her.

An hour and a half later, Megan breathed a sigh of relief when Mr. Clark and his assistant left the shop.

Several customers came and went over the course of the next three hours, and then, as sometimes happened, there was a lull around midnight. Force of habit had Megan looking toward the entrance every few minutes, but there was no sign of Rhys. She checked her cell phone, but there were no missed calls, no messages.

She moped all day Wednesday. By Thursday night, she was angry with Rhys, and furious with herself. How could she have been so naive? She wasn't a dewy-eyed teenager. She was a grown woman. So, she'd made a mistake. It was time to get past it. She had been attracted to the man, there was no denying it. So attracted she had slept with him, but she told herself she didn't care. It was over and done.

As the evening wore on, she convinced herself she hadn't even liked him that much. She had just been lonely, looking for a little attention, and she had gotten carried away because he was so damned good-looking. Because he had made her feel special. Because his kisses had made her go weak in the knees.

"Hah! Weak in the head is more like it!" she muttered. A few kisses, a few dances, a few compliments, and she had taken him to her bed. How could she have been so gullible? So incredibly stupid! Well, she was glad he was out of her life, the jerk. And relieved that she would never have to see him again.

Until she saw him walk through the door Friday night.

Rhys paused near the entrance, his gaze sweeping the interior of the shop; then, not caring that Mr. Parker was watching, not certain of what Megan's reaction would be, Rhys crossed to where Megan was standing and drew her into his arms.

"I'm sorry," he whispered, and kissed her long and hard, right there in front of her boss and anyone passing by who happened to look in the window.

He kissed her until she was breathless, pliant in his embrace, and then he kissed her again. "I missed you."

She blinked up at him, her lips slightly swollen from the force of his kisses.

In the distance, Mr. Parker cleared his throat as a customer entered the store.

Muttering an oath, Rhys took a step away from Megan, though he continued to hold her gaze with his own. "Can I see you later?"

"What?" She blinked several times as though to clear her head.

"Can I see you later?"

"Oh." She touched her fingertips to her lips. "Yes, of course."

"Till then," he said with a wink, and left the store, whistling softly.

* * *

He was a fool, Rhys thought, no two ways about it. But three days without seeing Megan had proved to him, once and for all, that he didn't want to live without her. No doubt he would be hurt in the end. Sooner or later, she was bound to discover what he was, and the preternatural shit would hit the fan, but until then, he planned to spend as much time with her as he could. And when it was over . . . well, he'd worry about that when it happened.

But for now, he had a date.

He was at the back door at two A.M. sharp, waiting for her. One look, and Megan wanted to throw herself into his arms. She had to remind herself that she was still mad at him for making love to her and then letting three whole days and nights go by without a word.

As though reading her mind, he drew her into his arms. "Forgive me?" he asked, and kissed her.

Megan tried to hold onto her irritation, but with his lips on hers, it was impossible. When he finally let her come up for air, she said the words she had been wanting to say, even though she feared it would be a mistake. "I love you."

Dammit, why hadn't he seen that coming? "Megan."

Shoulders slumped, she looked away. She knew it! Why hadn't she just kept her big mouth shut?

"Megan, look at me."

Still not meeting his gaze, she said, "Forget I said anything. I'm going home."

Rhys blew out a sigh, his arms tightening around her when she tried to pull away. "Dammit, Megan, you don't know how complicated this is." He knew she was attracted to him. Why hadn't he realized that a woman like Megan DeLacey wouldn't take a man to her bed unless she loved him? Maybe coming here tonight hadn't been such a good idea after all. But when he thought of leaving her again, he just couldn't do it.

She met his gaze, her eyes sparking with anger. "Let me go."

"Calm down, woman. You must know I love you, too, or I wouldn't be here now."

She stared at him, her eyes shiny with unshed tears.

"Come on," he said, slipping his arm around her shoulders. "Let's get out of here."

Megan unlocked her car, then handed him the keys, and he drove her home. She was a bundle of nerves by the time they pulled into the driveway. Rhys parked the car, then came around to open her door.

Hand in hand, they walked up the porch steps. Megan unlocked the front door, felt her heartbeat jump into double-time when he swung her into his arms and carried her across the threshold.

Like a bride, she thought, resting her head on his shoulder.

They didn't talk as he carried her up the stairs to her room. Setting her on her feet, he removed her shoes one at a time, his hand lingering on her calf, and then, ever so slowly, he undressed her, his gaze and his hands caressing each inch of exposed flesh.

When she stood naked in front of him, he sat on the edge of the bed and pulled off his boots, then started to remove his shirt, but she batted his hands away. "My turn."

A faint smile played over his lips as she peeled off his shirt and his trousers. She hesitated when only his briefs remained.

"Nothing you haven't seen before," he said, and laughed when her cheeks turned bright pink.

Spanning her waist with his hands, he fell back on the bed, drawing her down on top of him. He kissed her lightly, his hands sliding up and down her back, reveling in the feel of her bare skin beneath his fingertips, the little purr of contentment that rose in her throat.

Rolling onto his side, he drew her body up against his. He liked it that she could be bold one minute and bashful the next. He liked the way she looked at him, the way she moaned softly as he aroused her, the way her body welcomed his.

In spite of his vow not to drink from her, he couldn't resist the allure of her blood. Holding her close, he nipped lightly at the soft flesh beneath her ear and, when she didn't object, he bit a little deeper. He took only a small taste, reveling in the sweetness as her blood flowed over his tongue.

Megan moaned low in her throat. She didn't know what Rhys was doing but she hoped he would never stop. Heat sizzled through her, heightening her desire until she was lost in a hazy world of sensual pleasure, uncertain of where he ended and she began.

She cried his name aloud, her nails digging into the hard muscles of his back, as heat spiraled through her, erupting into flames that threatened to consume her. She held onto him, her body writhing restlessly beneath his, until the fire cooled and she lay sated and content in his arms.

Rhys rolled onto his side, carrying her with him, so that they lay face-to-face, their bodies still meshed. Megan felt like purring as his hand lightly stroked her back.

Murmuring his name, she closed her eyes, and fell asleep.

Rhys gazed at the vision in his arms. Warm and womanly, she carried the fragrance of flowers in her hair, the musky scent of sex—hers and his—on her skin. It pleased him that he had satisfied her as no other. He had shamelessly read her mind, knew that no other man had ever pleasured her as he had. The knowledge stroked his ego. Not that satisfying women had ever been a problem for him, before or after he became a vampire. Women had always been drawn to him. He had loved them and left them without a qualm. But Megan, ah, sweet Megan with her honey-brown eyes and tender heart, she was different. If he lived to be a thousand, he knew he would never forget her.

A familiar tingling warned of dawn's approach. He could feel the sun long before it was visible.

If only he could stay. If only he could make love to her each night, see her face upon waking. He had never regretted being a vampire. Once he had been turned, he had faced it, accepted it, and moved on. But now, for the first time in his long existence, he knew he would gladly give up immortality for the chance to spend one mortal lifetime in this woman's arms.

Slipping out of bed, he dressed quickly, then stood at her bedside, debating whether to wake her. He decided against it. It would be dawn soon, no time to stay and make love to her again as he so longed to do.

Murmuring, "I love you," he brushed a kiss across her cheek and left the house, hoping he had time for one quick errand.

Megan woke feeling wonderful until she looked to her left and saw that she was alone in bed. Again. And then she smiled. Once again, Rhys had left her after a night of lovemaking, but she couldn't be angry this time, not when the blankets were covered with vibrant red rose petals. Not when there were vases of flowers on every surface in the room. Not when she read the note he had left on his pillow:

Megan, my love.
You will be in my thoughts,
and in my heart,
until I hold you in
my arms once again.
RC

Picking up the note, she kissed it, then slid out of bed. She couldn't stop smiling, not while she showered, not while she pulled on a pair of sweats. She scooped up the loose petals and dropped them in a bowl before making the bed.

Taking a rose from one of the vases on the dresser, she plucked the petals one by one. "He loves me, he loves me not, he loves me. . . ." She knew it was foolish, but she couldn't help shouting with joy as the last petal proved that he loved her. It was nonsense, a child's game, but it reassured her just the same.

Tucking his note in the pocket of her sweatpants, she went downstairs. There were more flowers in the living room, on the tables, on the mantel. Red ones, white ones, pink and yellow ones. And still more in the kitchen, on the table, on the counter, on top of the refrigerator.

At home and later at work, it seemed the hours would never pass. Time and again she patted the note in the pocket of her dress for reassurance. He loved her. She would see him soon.

Rhys sat in his car in the parking lot at Shore's, his phone pressed to his ear. He scowled when Nicholas informed him that there had been two killings in Las Cruces, three in Albuquerque, and at least five in Santa Fe. "What else have you found out?"

"Nothing," Nick admitted. "The killer's as elusive as Jack the Ripper. So, what do you want us to do now?"

"Keep looking."

"Adams is getting on my nerves."

"Yeah? Well, if you can't handle it, I'll send Adrianna to take his place."

"That's not even funny," Nick muttered, and disconnected the call.

Rhys laughed as he slid his phone into his pants' pocket and got out of the car. No one liked Adrianna.

Entering the store, he put all thoughts of hunters and vampires out of his mind. These few hours were his. When he was with Megan, he didn't care if the rest of the world went to hell.

Chapter 16

Sitting beneath a cottonwood tree in Alamogordo, Tomás Villagrande gazed up at the vast vault of the sky. With his preternatural vision, he saw many more of the heavenly bodies than did mere mortals. Whether at sea or ashore, he had always been fascinated by the night sky, had often wondered if there was indeed life on other planets. Of course, he didn't believe in aliens—either gray or white or green. The one thing he did believe in—the one thing he feared—was the existence of a supreme being. Believing in heaven, he also believed in hell. And judgment. Should his own existence ever end, he knew he would have to account for the hundreds of lives he had taken.

With a sigh of disgust, he shook such thoughts away. He had no intention of ending his existence any time soon. And worrying about what awaited him was pointless. He couldn't change the past, couldn't resurrect the people he had killed, or the ones he had loved.

And he had loved many since he became a vampire. He grinned. "So many women," he murmured. "So much time."

He had loved a woman from Alamogordo back in the 1800s. A pretty little Navajo girl with tawny skin, long ebony hair, and bright black eyes. Alamogordo had changed a lot since those days. Once a small railroad, ranching, and farming community, it was now a thriving metropolis. Not far away stood Oliver Lee State Park. In the past, numerous battles had taken place there between the Indians and the cavalry. Today, it was a historic landmark.

Yes, he mused, the city had changed and grown. Alamogordo was also home to Holloman Air Force Base and the White Sands Missile Range. Mortals never changed, he thought with a rueful shake of his head. They were always looking for new and better ways to destroy themselves.

Rising, he strolled through the desert, enjoying the quiet, the moonlight. Animal predators gave him a wide birth, sensing a killer even more deadly than themselves.

Pausing, he stretched his arms over his head. It was time to move on. He had a score to settle with an old friend on the West Coast.

He grinned as he made his way toward his temporary lair, then began humming, "California, here I come. . . ."

Chapter 17

Rhys heaved a sigh as his gaze moved over the faces of the Vampire Council. As usual, none of the members were happy to be there. Winchester was slouched in his chair, cell phone in hand. Nicholas was paring his fingernails with a wicked-looking blade.

Adrianna smoothed a wrinkle from her skirt, then looked up, a pout on her pale lips. "Have you forgotten you're a vampire?" she asked, a whine evident in her tone. "What's with all these early meetings?"

"He's probably got a date again," Julius replied with a smirk.

"Indeed?" Rupert perked up, his dark eyes glowing. "Does she have a friend?"

"All right, that's enough!" Rhys said, scowling. "We're not here to set up a dating service."

"So, what are we here for?" Nicholas asked. "Not that I'm complaining," he added quickly. "But I'd rather be home."

Rhys nodded. One of his vampires had reported several killings in Phoenix, leading Rhys to believe that the rogue had left New Mexico. He had ordered Nicholas and Seth Adams back to LA the following night.

"It's obvious the rogue isn't staying long in any one place." Rhys leaned back in his chair, his elbows resting on the arms, fingers steepled.

"And just as obvious that he's heading in our direction," Adams remarked.

Adrianna turned her gaze on Rhys. "Maybe he's coming in *your* direction."

Ignoring her, Rhys said, "I'm getting tired of asking this question, but have any of you heard anything?"

As usual, they had nothing concrete to report. There were rumors—Morag had gone to ground; Sandoval had left Spain; a young vampire had challenged Baiba for Russia and been destroyed—but then, there were always rumors. They flew thick and fast in the vampire world.

Rhys dismissed them all out of hand. The only one that piqued his interest concerned Tomás Villagrande. One of the East Coast vampires had told Rupert that Villagrande's yacht was no longer anchored off the coast of New York.

"You don't think he's the rogue, do you?" Adrianna asked, glancing nervously around the room. "You don't think he's coming here?"

Hastings leaned forward. "You got a problem with that?"

"Of course not! Why should I?"

"I don't know," Hastings said, his brow furrowing thoughtfully. "You tell me."

"Is there something going on we need to know about?" Rhys asked. "If so, spit it out now."

Adrianna squared her shoulders. "We had a little disagreement some years ago."

"What kind of a disagreement?" Hastings asked.

"None of your business," Adrianna retorted.

Winchester looked up from his cell phone.

Adams and Hastings exchanged glances.

Rupert looked at Rhys, waiting for his reaction.

"None of our business?" Rhys repeated, his voice like

ice over steel. "In light of current events, you might want to rethink that."

"We had a squabble a long time ago, that's all. I'm sure he's forgotten all about it by now."

"Is that right?" Rhys asked. "What did you squabble about?"

When Adrianna didn't answer immediately, Julius said, "It's gotta be one of two things. Territory or prey. What else is there?"

Rhys nodded, his gaze on Adrianna's face. "Which one was it?"

"Territory," she replied sullenly. "I wanted to stay in Maine. He wouldn't let me."

Hastings shook his head. "There's got to be more to it than that."

"I think so, too," Rhys said. "What is it?" When Adrianna didn't answer, he trapped her gaze with his. "I can make you tell me," he said. "And you won't like it."

She glared at him, her expression mutinous. "I killed a woman he had marked as his."

"That wasn't very bright of you," Hastings remarked.

"Shut up!"

"All right, that's enough," Rhys said. "If Villagrande's coming here, I doubt it's to avenge something that happened years ago. If he wanted to destroy Adrianna, he'd likely have done it by now."

"Then why else would he be coming here?" Nicholas asked.

"Maybe he just wants to sail in the Pacific for a while," Rupert suggested. "Hell, don't we all like a change of scene every fifty years or so?"

"I don't give a damn where he makes port," Rhys said, "but if he starts killing in my territory . . ." He shook his head. "That's something else."

"Do you think you can take him?" Julius asked, his

close-set brown eyes glittering at the thought of two ancient vampires battling one another.

Winchester shook his head. "Villagrande's never been bested in a fight, we all know that."

"There's a first time for everything," Adams said.

"This isn't getting us anywhere," Rhys remarked, getting to his feet. "See yourselves out. I'm leaving."

Outside, Rhys slid behind the wheel of the Jag, then pulled away from the curb, his thoughts turned inward. He supposed it had only been a matter of time until trouble rolled into town again. He caught a faint scent of the hunter as he drove toward Megan's house, but he wasn't in the mood to go looking for a fight now, didn't want to go to Megan with blood on his hands. Besides, as far as he knew, the hunter wasn't doing much hunting.

He pushed all thoughts of Villagrande and the Vampire Council from his mind as he pulled into Megan's driveway. The next few hours belonged to him.

Filled with anticipation, he knocked on the door, felt his whole body spring to attention when she opened it wearing nothing but a smile.

Chapter 18

Rhys slid his arm around Megan's shoulders. It was late Saturday night, and they were sitting on the sofa in her living room. The fragrance of her hair and skin surrounded him, the scent of her blood drugged his senses.

He nuzzled the side of her neck, thinking how much his life had changed since that first night when he had walked into Shore's. Sometimes, he almost forgot who and what he was. Sometimes he felt almost human again.

Two weeks had passed since Megan had met him at the door wearing nothing but a come-hither smile. They had been the best two weeks of his existence, which was saying something, he thought, considering his longevity. He continued to meet Megan at Shore's when she got off work. On her days off, he spent his nights in her company. Sometimes they went dancing at his club; other nights they went to the movies, or spent the evening at his place, curled up in each other's arms. Last weekend, they had gone out with Shirl and her boyfriend. Rhys had been somewhat surprised that Shirl had agreed. It was obvious she didn't trust him.

But that didn't matter now. Nothing mattered but the woman in his arms. It wasn't easy, dating a mortal. She was so fragile, he had to be on guard every minute to make sure he didn't hurt her, to keep his supernatural strength carefully under wraps. But it had been worth it. He had been on his best behavior the last two weeks and had finally managed to put the last of her doubts and fears to rest. Of course, he always fed before going to her house. There was nothing more obvious than a hungry vampire. He had seen a few in his time, and it was never a pretty sight.

His existence would have been perfect, Rhys mused, if not for the new hunter in town, and the rogue vampire who was slowly making his way toward the West Coast, pint by pint, and body by body. He hadn't heard of any more vampire killings in the last week. Did that mean the rogue had finally had his fill? Or did that new hunter in town have something to do with it?

"Rhys?" Megan tapped his forehead lightly. "Hey, Rhys? You in there?"

"What? Oh, sorry. I was just thinking about some club business." He didn't like lying to her, but he could hardly tell her the truth.

"It is anything you want to talk about?" Megan asked.

"No." He stroked her cheek with his fingertips. "When we're together, I don't want to think about anything but you."

"Stop thinking," she murmured, "and kiss me."

"My pleasure, as always," he replied, and claimed her lips with his.

Megan was standing on the front porch with Rhys later that night when Shirl came home from a date with Greg.

Shirl was humming the first few notes of the wedding march as she skipped up the stairs. A nod at Rhys, a wink at Megan, and Shirl went inside and closed the door, giving Megan and Rhys some privacy.

Love was in the air, Megan thought. She hadn't seen her

roommate looking so happy in a long time. It was obvious from the glow in Shirl's eyes that she was in love with Greg. Megan grinned inwardly, wondering if people could tell just by looking at her that she, too, was in love.

Rhys waited until Shirl closed the door, then pulled Megan into his arms. "I'll see you tomorrow night," he murmured.

Megan closed her eyes as his lips touched hers in a long, slow kiss that made her knees weak and her toes curl.

Another quick kiss, a wave, and he got in his car and roared off into the darkness.

Megan was smiling when she walked into the living room.

"Things seem to be going hot and heavy between the two of you," Shirl remarked. After kicking off her shoes, she flopped down on the sofa, and looked up at Megan, one eyebrow raised.

Megan tucked a lock of hair behind her ear. Hot and heavy didn't begin to describe it, she thought, as she curled up on the other end of the sofa.

"No more doubts about him?" Shirl asked.

"Not really," Megan replied, though that wasn't exactly true. "It's just that a lot of little things bother me, like the way his eyes sometimes glow red, and the way he sometimes seems to just fade into the darkness." But none of that seemed important when she was with Rhys.

Shirl toyed with a lock of her hair, her expression thoughtful. "Doesn't it seem strange to you that you never see him during the day, and that every time we offer him something to eat, he refuses?"

Megan shook her head. Rhys had a nightclub to run; she assumed that it kept him busy during the day. As for his not having dinner with her, the few times she had invited him, he had always had a valid excuse. Still . . . "What are you getting at?"

"He wears a lot of black."

"Hello? He runs a Goth club, remember? Besides, it looks good on him." And even as she said the words, she remembered standing in Shore's parking lot and thinking that Rhys looked like the night, because he was the night. The memory sent a shiver down her spine. "Shirl, just what are you trying to say?"

"You'll laugh."

"No, I won't."

"Well, if I really believed in such things, I'd say he was a vampire."

Megan stared at her a moment. "A vampire? Are you serious?"

"No, of course not, but . . ."

"Go on."

"You said it yourself. His eyes turn red. He sort of disappears into the night." Shirl made a dismissive gesture with one hand. "You know me, I'm always looking for the real thing."

"That's what you say, but I remember how fast you dumped that guy who wanted to drink your blood."

"Isaac, yeah," Shirl said. "Well, I never told you this, but he didn't just want to drink my blood. He wanted to cut me with a razor and let the blood drip into a silver goblet. It was just too creepy." Closing her eyes, she rubbed her temples.

"Another headache?" Megan asked.

"Just a little one."

"There's no such thing as vampires, girlfriend, but those headaches are real. I wish you'd go to the doctor."

"Nag, nag, nag. You're worse than my mother. Stop worrying, will ya? And as for vampires, haven't you been listening to the news? They're finding bodies drained of blood from one end of the country to the other."

"You can't believe what you hear on the news, you know that."

"Maybe not," Shirl said. "But they showed a picture of the last victim. You might not want to believe what you read, but it's pretty hard to ignore a dead body. And on that happy note, I'm going to bed." Rising, she picked up her shoes. "I'll probably be gone when you get up in the morning. Greg's taking me fishing."

"Fishing? Since when do you like to fish?"

"Since Greg asked me to go with him."

"Have fun," Megan said, grinning as she tried to imagine Shirl baiting a hook.

"Ah, the things I do for love," Shirl exclaimed dramatically. "Night, Meggie."

"Good night."

Megan went up to bed a few minutes later. Lying there in the dark, she thought about what Shirl had said, then laughed softly. Vampires, indeed.

Sunday night, Megan convinced Rhys to go to one of the free concerts in Griffith Park. She had wanted to sit up front, near the band, but Rhys persuaded her to sit near the back. He told her it was so he could kiss her without an audience, but that was only a part of the truth. Being in the midst of hundreds of people played havoc with his self-control.

Sitting on a blanket, with Megan cradled between his thighs, his arms around her waist, he could pretend he was no different from any other man. His desire sparked to life when she shifted in his embrace. He nuzzled the back of her neck, his senses filling with her unique scent, making it easy to ignore everyone else. She moaned softly when he nipped at the smooth skin beneath her ear lobe, her soft sigh of pleasure stirring other hungers best left unfed. And yet the scent of her blood, the steady beat of her heart, all called to the beast within, urging him to drag her into the shadows and satisfy both of his hungers. His arm tightened around her waist, imprisoning her as the urge to feed grew stronger.

"Rhys?" She glanced at him over her shoulder. "Are you all right?"

"Fine," he replied, his voice rough. "Why do you ask?"

"You're hurting me."

"What?" Muttering an oath, he relaxed his hold on her and leaned back, putting some space between them. "Sorry."

Megan frowned. Why was it that, every now and then, his eyes took on that reddish hue? Was it a trick of the colored lights playing over the park? But what about when they were alone and there were no lights?

"Are you ready to go?"

"Not really," she said. "Why? Are you?"

He was more than ready to leave. So many people, all sitting close together, so many beating hearts . . . He had thought if he put some distance between himself and the crowd, it would help, but it hadn't. And then there was Megan, her body pressed close to his. A constant temptation.

He took a deep, calming breath. "We can stay if you want." Leaning forward, he brushed a kiss across her cheek. "I just need to stretch my legs. I'll be back in a few minutes."

Before she could ask any questions, he stood and melted into the shadows. The area away from the concert was dark; there were no paths, lights were few.

He had been kidding himself, he mused, as he put the crowd behind him. There was no way on earth that he and Megan could have a life together. The only reason the relationship between Delacourt and Daisy had lasted was because Daisy had accepted the Dark Gift. Rhys hadn't known Megan long, but he was pretty sure she would reject the idea of becoming a vampire out of hand.

He was about to return to the concert area when he became aware of two things simultaneously. Megan had followed him, and the hunter was right behind him. Rhys swore softly. If he met his end tonight, it would be his own damn fault. He had been so busy thinking about things that could never be, he had let his guard down.

Fangs bared, he whirled around and came face-to-face with a big bear of a man who brandished a nasty-looking pistol in one gloved hand, and a large wooden stake in the other.

Chapter 19

Megan stared, uncomprehending, at the scene before her. She looked at Rhys, but it was a Rhys she had never seen before. His body was taut and even from a distance, she could feel the power rolling off him. When he glanced her way, his eyes blazed red. She closed her eyes a moment and then looked again. His eyes were still red. It was no trick of the light this time.

The man standing across from Rhys was huge. He was dressed in black from his hat to his shoes. Megan took a step forward, her eyes narrowing. Was he holding a gun? And a wooden stake?

The man moved toward Rhys. And Rhys snarled at him, revealing . . . Megan blinked at him, and blinked again. Fangs?

She was dreaming, she thought, she had to be dreaming.

Without taking his gaze from the other man, Rhys shouted. "Megan, get the hell out of here! Now!"

Before she had time to think or respond, the man in black fired the gun. Rhys doubled over, hissing through clenched teeth as his hands pressed against his stomach.

The man in black lunged forward, the stake raised in his right hand. A low cry rose in his throat as he plunged the stake into Rhys's back. She watched in horror as Rhys slowly sank to the ground and toppled onto his side, his hands still pressed to his stomach. In the dim light, the blood leaking through his fingers looked black.

What to do, Megan thought frantically. She took a step forward, driven by her need to go to Rhys, to offer aid, comfort, something, but before she could clear her mind, the man turned toward her.

Fear for her own life sent Megan running back toward the concert area. Safety in numbers, she thought frantically, even as she tried to block the horrific scene from her mind. But the carnage played over and over again, each time more chilling than the last.

A police officer stood on the edge of the crowd. Gasping for breath, Megan hurried toward him. Her mother had always told her to look for a cop if she was in trouble. And she was definitely in trouble.

"Officer!"

He looked up as she came running toward him. "Can I help you, miss?"

"Yes! My . . . my boyfriend and I had a fight, and I don't have any way to get home and I'm afraid. . . ."

"Is he still here?" the officer asked, glancing behind Megan. "Did he hurt you? Threaten you in any way?"

"No."

"Where is he?"

"Over there." She gestured toward the deserted section of the park.

"Stay here until I get back." He pulled a flashlight from his belt and ran back the way Megan had come.

Megan stared after him. Had she done the right thing? What if the man who had killed Rhys killed the police officer, too? It would be her fault. Lordy, what if the killer came after her? She had witnessed his crime.

Grabbing her cell phone from her pocket, she punched in Shirl's number.

Shirl answered on the second ring.

"Hey, Megan, what's up?"

"Shirl, I need you to come and pick me up. Hurry, please!"

"What's wrong?"

"I can't talk now. I'm at the concert area of the park."

"I'll be there as soon as I can."

The police officer returned moments after Megan ended the call. "There's no sign of him," he said. "Do you want to file a report?"

"No, I just want to go home."

"Is there someone you can call?"

"I did, thank you. I'm sorry to have bothered you."

"No bother at all," he said with a smile.

It took twenty minutes for Shirl to get to the park. They were the longest twenty minutes of Megan's life. Why hadn't the policeman found anything, she wondered, and then answered her own question. The killer had probably taken Rhys's body away.

After climbing inside Shirl's car, Megan locked the passenger door, then huddled against the seat, her arms wrapped around her waist, shivering.

"Girl, what did that man do to you?" Shirl asked. "You're white as a ghost."

"You were right," Megan whispered. "You were right."

"Yeah? About what?" Shirl asked.

"Rhys. He's . . ." She couldn't say the word out loud. Doing so would make it real, and it couldn't be real. And yet there was no denying the proof of her own eyes.

"Meggie, you're scaring me. What did he do to you?"

"Not now. Can't you drive faster?"

It seemed to take forever to reach home. Megan glanced

out the back window before getting out of the car, racing up to the porch, and unlocking the door. "Hurry, Shirl!"

Once her friend was inside, Megan locked and bolted the door, then ran through the house, making sure the windows were locked, closing all the curtains.

Looking worried, Shirl followed her from room to room. "Megan, if you don't tell me what's going on right this instant, I'm going to . . . to . . . I don't know what!"

When she was sure the house was secure, Megan returned to the living room and curled up on the sofa. She couldn't stop shaking.

"Meggie, what's wrong? What did he do? Should I call the police?"

"You were right." Megan stared up at her friend. "You were right about him. He's . . ." She took a deep breath. "He is a vampire."

"What?"

"You heard me." She couldn't say it again.

"Why do you think he's one of the Undead? What happened?"

"We were at the concert. He said he needed to go for a walk and I . . . I followed him. I saw him and another man. They were staring at each other, almost like they were sizing each other up. The other man had a gun and a wooden stake. I must have made a noise, because Rhys turned and looked at me. His eyes, they were blood red, and he . . . he had fangs. He shouted for me to get out of there, but before I could move, the other man shot him." She shuddered with the memory. "And then the man drove the stake into Rhys's back, and . . . Rhys collapsed." Sobbing, she buried her face in her hands. "The man looked at me, and I ran away."

How could she have been so cowardly? She should have stayed. She scrubbed her hands up and down her arms, trying to get warm. What if Rhys wasn't dead? What if he had needed help? She shook her head. What if he had? What kind of help could she have given him? She didn't know anything about fighting vampires or slayers. The other man had had a gun, for crying out loud. And Rhys had . . . She swallowed hard. Fangs. Sharp white fangs that had glistened in the moonlight. And what did she have? A set of acrylic nails.

Shirl turned on the heater and lit a fire in the hearth, then sat beside Megan. "Calm down, sweetie. You're safe now."

"Am I?" What if that man had followed her home? Had she put Shirl's life in danger?

"Are you sure about this, Meggie? I mean, geez, I was kidding when I said he was a vampire. I never thought it was true. Good grief, who knew such things really existed?"

"What if he's not dead?"

"Whether he is or isn't, there's nothing you could have done."

A burst of hysterical laughter rose in Megan's throat. Of course he was dead. She didn't know much about vampires, but she had seen enough horror movies to know that a wooden stake through the heart was foolproof. She had been right to run, she thought. If she had stayed, the man might have killed her, too. After all, she was the only witness. So, why did she still feel so guilty?

Shirl looked at her, eyes wide. "Meggie, you don't think . . . I mean, if vampires are real, maybe there are werewolves and trolls and . . . and . . . who knows what else?" She pressed a hand to her heart. "I think I could use a drink! How about you?"

Megan lay in her bed, the covers pulled up to her chin. Every time she closed her eyes, she saw Rhys clutching at his stomach, falling to the ground. All the booze in the world couldn't erase that image. Or change the fact that she had made love to a vampire.

She lifted a hand to her throat. Had he fed on her?

Vampire.

It explained everything.

And nothing.

She flopped over onto her stomach. She didn't know what to think, how to feel. All she knew was that there was a hole the size of the Grand Canyon in her heart that no one else would ever fill. Vampire or not, she had loved him.

Tears stung her eyes. She had loved him, and now he was gone. It seemed odd to grieve for a man who had already died once, but she couldn't help it. Had he loved her, as well? Or had he only been using her for . . . what? Had he been planning to feed on her? He could have done that at any time. To turn her into what he was? She recoiled at the thought.

Unable to sleep, she got out of bed, pulled on her robe, and went downstairs. After turning on the light in the room they used for an office, she booted up the computer and did a Google search for vampires. There were hundreds of sites. Every civilization in the world, both ancient and modern, had its own vampire myths and legends. Transylvania had turned the Dracula legend into a lucrative business.

Hundreds, perhaps thousands, of movies had been made about vampires, everything from horror flicks to comedies and cartoons.

And then there were the Goths—men and women who emulated the vampire lifestyle. They dressed in black, wore black contact lenses, and sported fake fangs. The women wore black or blood-red lipstick, and decorated their homes in the Victorian manner. Red wine was the drink of choice, although there were some who—gag!—drank blood from willing donors.

Megan shuddered at the mere idea.

Reading on, she learned that many people were introduced to vampires by way of the role-playing game, "Vampire: the Masquerade."

Psychic vampires fed on energy—some fed during sex, others by mingling with large crowds of people, while still others fed on nature itself. Then there were psychotic vampires who were believed to have some kind of sociopathic mental illness that caused them to behave in bizarre fashion. Megan grimaced as she read about Elizabeth Bathory. Elizabeth had been a countess back in the 1500s. It was generally accepted that she had been a psychotic vampire. Beautiful and vain, Elizabeth had tortured and killed hundreds of young girls, then bathed in their blood, believing that doing so would keep her forever young.

Inevitably, one of the sites listed ways to destroy a vampire. A stake through the heart was high on the list. Reading the words made Megan's stomach churn, but she forced herself to keep reading. After all, if there was one vampire, there might be more.

Another sure way to dispatch a vampire was by beheading, or exposing the creature to sunlight. Garlic and crosses were supposed to repel them. Holy water and silver burned their flesh. A small footnote mentioned that there could be only one Master Vampire in any given territory at one time.

Megan sat back in her chair, her mind reeling, her eyes gritty from lack of sleep. She needed to go to bed, yet how could she expect to sleep now? She had no doubt that Rhys was—she blinked back her tears—had been . . . a vampire. She had seen his eyes glowing red, seen his fangs. He didn't eat; she had never seen him during the day. In all the times he had come to Shore's, he had never once looked in a mirror. Now that she thought about it, he had gone out of his way to avoid them.

Vampire. Nosferatu. Undead creature of the night.

The tears came then. Rocking back and forth, she wept for Rhys and for the burgeoning love that had died with him.

Chapter 20

Rhys pressed one hand over the ragged wound in his belly. Though his body had cast off the silver slug, it had burned like fire going in and coming out. Dark red blood dripped through his fingers as he stared at the body of the hunter sprawled facedown on the grass. He didn't know how the man had found him. Dumb luck, he supposed. Or maybe the hunter had been tracking him, although Rhys thought it unlikely. He might have been preoccupied with Megan the last few weeks, but he hadn't gone deaf, dumb, and blind.

Until tonight.

It had taken what little strength he had left to veil his presence and that of the hunter from the police officer who'd been snooping around earlier. Rhys had no doubt that Megan had sent the cop. Whether she wanted the officer to help him, or make sure he was dead, was anybody's guess. One thing he knew for sure, she had been terrified by what she'd seen, but he could hardly blame her for that.

He winced as he explored the wound in his back. This was the second time someone had staked him and missed his heart by inches, he mused. First Daisy, and now this hunter. If he wasn't careful, his luck was going to run out.

Rhys swore softly as the scent of the hunter's blood drifted on the breeze. He needed blood to heal the wounds the bastard had inflicted, but drinking from the dead, even the newly dead, was distasteful.

But there was fresh prey nearby. Moving through the shadows, he found a couple of teenaged boys sitting off by themselves, sharing a joint.

They looked up when they saw him, their expressions showing first surprise and then fear as he drew closer. Fear that turned to terror when they realized they couldn't speak, couldn't move.

Rhys took what he needed, wiped the memory of what had happened from their minds, then slipped into the shadows, enjoying a mild high from the drug in their blood.

He had to see Megan. Even knowing that she would recoil from his presence, he had to see her again. She knew him for what he was now, and the knowledge had horrified her. He had seen the revulsion in her eyes before she fled the scene. Not that he blamed her for taking off. Hadn't he told her to go? Of course, she was a smart girl, and, considering what she had seen, she likely would have run anyway.

A thought took him to her house, another to her bedside.

She slept with a light on. After what she had been through that night, he wasn't surprised. For a moment, he could only stand there, thinking how beautiful she was, her red gold hair as soft as silk, her skin the color of rich cream, her lips, pink and perfect and slightly parted.

Curious to know what she dreamed of, he let his mind brush hers.

She was dreaming that they were walking along the beach arm in arm. In her dream, he wasn't a vampire.

"Megan."

"Rhys?" Still caught up in her dream, she smiled—until she opened her eyes and saw him standing beside the bed. Suddenly wide awake, she bolted upright, the sheet clutched to her breasts as if it would protect her, the smile on her face fading, the color draining from her cheeks. "How can you be here? I thought . . . that man . . . he shot you. I saw him drive a stake into your back."

He shrugged. "As you can see, I'm fine." He clenched his hands at his sides. He could hear her heart beating wildly, taste the fear that tainted her skin. "Dammit, stop looking at me like that!"

His anger stoked her own. "I'm sorry if I'm scared, but what do you expect? It's not every day I see a man killed in front of me. Almost killed." She made a vague gesture with her hand. "Whatever! Why didn't you tell me what you were? What you are."

"Maybe because I didn't want to see that look in your eyes."

Her gaze slid away from his.

"You've nothing to fear from me," he said, his voice gruff. "I only came to make certain you were all right."

Still not looking at him, she murmured, "I'm sorry I ran away."

"What the hell do you have to be sorry about? I told you to go."

"I should have stayed."

He laughed softly. "And done what?"

She looked up at him then, her gaze meeting his. "What did you do to that man?"

"Just exactly what you think I did."

"You killed him." It wasn't a question. "Did you . . . ?"

"No."

She looked surprised. "Why not?"

"I prefer it warm." His gaze moved to the hollow of her throat. "And fresh."

If possible, her face went even paler.

"I won't bother you anymore. I just came by to make sure you got home all right. Good-bye, Megan."

He didn't wait for her to reply. Calling on his preternatural power, he vanished from her sight.

For a moment, he stood on the sidewalk below her window. She was lost to him now, that was for damn sure. He tried to comfort himself with the thought that it was just as well, and failed miserably. He had never intended to fall in love with her. Perhaps he should have told her the truth, he thought, and then shook his head. Had he done so, he would have just lost her sooner. His one regret was that she had seen him at his worst.

One regret, he thought bleakly. Hell, he had a million of them.

Muttering an oath, he went in search of prey.

Chapter 21

Megan spent Monday morning curled up on the sofa. She felt numb inside, as if her body had lost the ability to feel. She had no appetite, no desire to get dressed. No desire to do anything. Shirl had offered to stay home from work, but Megan had said thanks, but no thanks. All she wanted was to be alone with her grief. Rhys was alive, she thought, and let out a harsh laugh. Not alive, but Undead. Either way, he was lost to her.

She replayed his last visit over and over again, wishing it had ended differently, wishing . . . what? That she had asked him to stay? That she had told him his being a vampire didn't matter? If only it didn't!

She blinked back her tears. How could she have fallen in love with a vampire? Let him kiss her? Make love to her? How could she not have known what he was? Maybe she had. Maybe her initial fear and distrust had been some innate sense of self-preservation, a warning she had refused to heed. But honestly, who knew vampires were real? Sure, in the last few weeks there had been stories on the nightly news that hinted at such things, but no one took such stories seriously. You couldn't believe everything you heard on the news. Vampires terrorizing New York and Los

Angeles? Yeah, right. Who could worry about mythical creatures when there were so many real monsters roaming the streets, gunning down innocent women and children, kidnapping college kids while they were on spring break, raping children.

Heartsick and depressed, she slept most of the day away. But there was no escaping Rhys in her dreams, either . . .

He came to her, an apparition dressed all in black, his dark blond hair glowing like a halo in the darkness. His voice whispered over her skin like a caress.

"Megan." Just her name, filled with such longing it brought quick tears to her eyes.

"Rhys. I wish . . ."

He covered her mouth with his hand. "Don't say it. I can't change what I am. I can't give you the life you deserve. I only wanted to make love to you one last time."

She shook her head. "This isn't real."

His gaze burned into hers. "It's as real as you want it to be."

And because she wanted to hold him, love him, she closed her eyes and surrendered to his touch. His hands glided over her body, each stroke a symphony played by a master musician. She clung to him, wanting to be closer, closer, to believe it was more than a dream.

She shivered when his tongue slid along the tender flesh below her ear, moaned softly as his teeth grazed her skin.

He was biting her! For one endless moment of time, she gave herself up to the sensual pleasure of it. It was, after all, only a dream.

Wasn't it?

As from far away, she heard Shirl calling her name.

With a start, Megan opened her eyes, her heart pounding, her body warm and tingling from his touch.

Jumping off the sofa, she ran into the bathroom. Holding her hair away from her neck, she turned her head to the side and looked in the mirror, her stomach knotting when she saw the truth reflected in the mirror.

There, on the left side of her neck, two tiny bites and a single drop of blood.

"It had to be a dream," Shirl said.

They were sitting at the kitchen table, eating the Chinese takeout Shirl had brought home for dinner.

Megan pointed at the bites on her neck. "Do these look like a dream to you?"

"What?" Shirl leaned forward. "I don't see anything."

Megan frowned. "There were two bites there just a few minutes ago."

"Are you sure?"

"Of course I'm sure." Jumping to her feet, Megan ran into the bathroom and stood in front of the mirror. She turned her head this way and that, but her skin was smooth and unblemished.

Frowning, Megan went back into the kitchen and resumed her seat. "I was so sure. . . ." She shook her head. Maybe it had been a dream. But what if it wasn't? "Okay, so I imagined the whole thing. You're the vampire expert. How can I keep him out of the house?"

"Well, according to lore, you have to rescind your invitation."

"How do I do that?"

"You need to say that you take it back, that he's not welcome here anymore."

"Don't I have to say it to his face?"

"No, I don't think so. Just do it."

Feeling a little foolish, Megan said, "Rhys Costain, I revoke my invitation. You are no longer welcome in my home." Was it her imagination, or did the house seem to sigh? "How do we know if it worked?"

"I don't know," Shirl said, shrugging. "Wait and see, I guess."

It took all the energy Megan possessed to get up and get ready for work Tuesday night. She didn't want to go to Shore's, but she didn't want to spend another day curled up on the sofa, brooding, either.

Because it suited her mood, she wore a black sheath to work. Black was the color of mourning, after all.

And of vampires . . .

She shook the thought from her mind. She would not think of him.

She was surprised when Drexel came into the shop shortly after ten.

"Hey, babe," he said. "How are you?"

"I'm doing all right. I'm sorry about Kenny. I know how close the two of you were."

"Yeah, Ken was with me when we first started." He cleared his throat. "Best songwriter I ever knew. We're gonna miss him."

"How about you?" she asked. "No ill effects from the fire?"

He shrugged. "My throat was sore for a few days. Nothing major." He lifted his arm, which was bandaged from elbow to wrist. "The burn turned out to be worse than they first thought. Doc says I'll probably have a nasty scar." A muscle twitched in his jaw. "But it could have been worse. Anyway, I came by hoping that dude who was with you might be here. I want to thank him for getting me on that ambulance when he did."

"I'm sorry, he's not here."

"Well, give him my thanks when you see him, will you?"

"Yes, of course." She blinked away the tears scorching the backs of her eyes. "Can I show you anything tonight?"

"Just your gorgeous self," he said with a wink.

Megan shook her head. "Take care of yourself."

"You too, babe. My proposal still stands, anytime you want to say yes."

For one mad, crazy moment, she was tempted to accept. Why not? Rhys was gone, and she was tired of being alone. Drexel was cute; he was rich; he was famous. If she married him, she could have anything her heart desired—houses, luxury cars, expensive clothes and jewelry. Anything she wanted. Except the man she loved.

"We're going on tour day after tomorrow, but I'll stop in when I get back." Leaning forward, Drexel kissed her cheek. "See you soon, babe."

With a farewell wave to Mr. Parker, Drexel left the store.

Megan stared after him. She had always been fond of him, but there was a subtle difference in their relationship now, born of the fact that they had shared and survived a terrifying experience.

The rest of the night crawled by. Megan waited on several customers, but she felt as though she was moving through quicksand, as if time itself had altered somehow since that night in the park.

She was grieving for Rhys as if he had passed away, she thought, or maybe she was mourning the loss of their relationship. But she'd get over it.

"Are you all right, Megan?" Mr. Parker asked, coming up beside her.

She nodded. It wouldn't be easy, but her heart would heal, in time.

Rhys stood outside of Shore's, his presence cloaked from passersby as he gazed through the window, watching Megan move about the store.

He had tried to stay away, told himself they were both better off. In spite of the lies he had told himself, he had known from the beginning that, sooner or later, she would discover what he was and that knowledge would put an end to their relationship. He just hadn't expected it to happen so soon, or to hurt so damn bad.

He stared at her, hungering for her like a starving man deprived of food. He could smell the enticing scent of her hair and skin, hear the siren call of her heartbeat. He felt her lingering horror at discovering what he was, her feelings of confusion and betrayal. He had known she would never be able to accept the truth, yet the knowledge aroused his anger. Damn her! It wasn't his fault he had been turned into a monster. He understood her feelings, knew she had every right to be afraid of him, to be repulsed by what he was, but it did nothing to ease his anger. He could have drained her dry, turned her, killed her, but all he had done was love her. And he had thought she loved him.

She loved the man, taunted a little voice in the back of his mind. *No woman could love the monster.*

Hadn't he learned that lesson centuries ago from Josette? He would be wise to remember it in the future.

For the first time in his long existence, he hated what he was. Monster. There was no escaping it, no point in trying to be anything else.

"Vampire!" The word hissed between his teeth as he spun away from the window. Driven by a rage that would not be contained, a hunger that would not be denied, he fled into the darkness.

Chapter 22

Tomás Villagrande strolled down Hollywood Boulevard, bemused by the steady stream of humanity that hurried by, never knowing there was a killer in their midst. The scent of their blood was intoxicating. For a moment, he was tempted to throw off the thin veneer of humanity he wore and let them see him for what he was. He could terrorize the puny mortals around him like a wolf raiding a flock of sheep. He could make a game of it, see how many he could drain in, say, ten minutes.

Somewhat reluctantly, he shook the thought away. Perhaps another night. For now, he wanted to explore the city. Costain resided here. According to vampire etiquette, Tomás knew he should make his presence known to the Master of the West Coast Vampires, and perhaps he would, at some later date. But for now, he kept his presence cloaked, and he would continue to do so until he knew the lay of the land.

And so he continued to stroll along the sidewalk. How times had changed, he thought. In his day, decent women had dressed demurely and never ventured outside without a chaperone. True, women had bared a great deal of cleavage, but little more. Only the lightskirts had flashed so much skin, behaved so brazenly. A gaggle of teenage girls went by, cell phones pressed to their ears, their rounded arms and flat bellies bared to his gaze, their shorts barely covering their nicely curved bottoms. It made his mouth water just to look at them.

A couple of teenage boys cruised the boulevard in a silver convertible with the top down, music blaring from the car's speakers.

Across the street, a man dressed as a woman waited for the light to change. Farther down the street, Tomás saw a woman dressed as a man. Insanity, he thought. What was the world coming to?

With a rueful shake of his head, he continued to stroll along the city streets, enjoying the cool kiss of the night air, the faint scent of the sea carried to him by an errant breeze.

And then, as he approached a tall, glass-fronted building, he caught the distinct scent of vampire.

Chapter 23

Megan yawned behind her hand as she laid out a new shipment of Armani dress shirts. She had been miserable the last few days, and it was all because of Rhys. Even when she managed to keep him out of her head during the day, he haunted her dreams at night.

She had just finished ringing up a sale for one of her clients when Mr. Parker came out of his office, his expression grim.

"What is it?" she asked.

"Some man named Greg is on the phone for you."

"Greg?" Why on earth would he be calling her at work? "Did he say what he wanted?"

"I think you'd better talk to him."

A sudden coldness gripped Megan as she hurried into the office and picked up the phone. "Hello?"

"Megan, it's Greg. I'm at Mercy Arms Hospital with Shirl."

"The hospital! Good Lord, is she . . . ?"

"She's unconscious."

"What happened? Were you in an accident?"

"No, we went out dancing after dinner. She said she

wasn't feeling well, and we decided to come home early. I'd just turned off the freeway when she collapsed."

"I'll be there in ten minutes."

Mr. Parker appeared in the doorway when she got off the phone. "Bad news?"

"My roommate, she's in the hospital," Megan said, grabbing her coat and her handbag. "I've got to go."

He nodded. "I hope she'll be okay."

"She will be," Megan said. She refused to think otherwise.

She made it to the hospital in record time.

Shirl was in a private room on the third floor. Greg looked up when Megan entered the room. It was easy to see from the look on his face that their relationship was a lot more serious than Shirl had let on.

"How is she?" Megan asked, hurrying to Shirl's bedside.

"About the same."

"What does the doctor say?"

"Not much at the moment. We're waiting for the results of some tests."

Megan took Shirl's hand in hers. Even unconscious, her face almost as pale as the pillowcase, Shirl looked beautiful. "She's always been so healthy." Megan looked across the bed at Greg. "Except for her headaches . . ." Her breath caught in her throat. "You don't think . . ." Megan couldn't finish the sentence.

Feeling suddenly weak, she dropped into the chair beside the bed. All those headaches . . . In the movies, it always meant something awful, like cancer or a brain tumor. Fear congealed in the pit of her stomach.

She looked at Greg, seeking hope, but judging from the bleak expression on his face, he was entertaining some pretty morbid thoughts of his own.

She was surprised that no one told them to leave. Nurses came and went all through the night, their rubber-soled shoes making little or no sound as they took Shirl's vitals, her blood, changed the IV.

It was near four A.M. when Megan came awake with a start. For a moment, she forgot where she was, but only a moment. The distinct smell of disinfectant reminded her that she was in the hospital. Blinking the sleep from her eyes, she glanced around the room. Greg slept in the other chair, snoring softly.

Ignoring the ache in her back and shoulders caused by sleeping in a hard plastic chair, Megan rose. She smiled when she saw that Shirl was awake. "Hey, girl, how do you feel? Can I get you anything?"

"You can get me out of here."

"I will, as soon as the doctors say you can leave."

"No, Meggie, now, today." Shirl grabbed Megan's hand so hard Megan feared the bones might break. "Megan, please get me out of here. I don't want to die in this place, hooked up to a bunch of machines, tubes everywhere!"

"Shirl, calm down. You're not going to die." As gently as she could, she pulled her hand away, then took both of Shirl's hands in hers. "You're going to be fine."

"No." Shirl lifted a hand to her head. "I have a tumor."

"You can't know that," Megan said, forcing a note of calm into her voice that she was far from feeling. "Greg said they're waiting for the test results."

"I know, Meggie. It's been there for a long time."

"What?" Megan stared at her. "Why didn't you tell me?"

Tears welled in Shirl's eyes and dripped, unchecked, down her cheeks. "I've known for over a year. It's what's causing my headaches. I never should have gotten involved with Greg."

Megan shook her head. "I don't know what to say."

Shirl squeezed her hand again. "I'm afraid, Meggie."

"I know. I know. There must be something they can do."

"It's inoperable." Shirl quickly dried her eyes on a corner of the sheet when Greg woke with a low groan.

Rising, he kissed her cheek. "Hey, beautiful, how are you feeling?"

"Better. I'm going home."

"What? But, the tests . . . the doctor . . ."

Shirl glanced at Megan. "Could you leave us alone for a few minutes?"

"Sure." Megan looked from Shirl to Greg. "I'll be right outside."

Megan paced the hospital corridor, her mind refusing to believe that Shirl was dying. How could her friend have kept such a secret from her? It wasn't fair. Shirl was young and beautiful, at the top of her career, and in love for the first time in her life. Why had this happened to her?

When Megan reached the end of the corridor, she blinked away her tears, then started walking back toward Shirl's room. She bit down on her lower lip when Greg stalked out of the room and headed for the elevators.

Heaving a sigh, she went to offer Shirl what comfort she could.

In spite of what everyone, including her doctor had to say, Shirl insisted on checking out of the hospital.

At home, Megan tucked Shirl into bed, made sure she was comfortable, and then went to her own room. After undressing, she went into the bathroom, stepped into the shower, and turned the water on full blast so Shirl wouldn't hear her crying. Shirl was more than her roommate; she was the sister Megan had always wanted.

Megan stayed in the shower until she had no tears left. After drying off, she pulled on a pair of sweats and went downstairs to fix blueberry waffles for breakfast. She put the plates on a pretty tray and carried it upstairs, only to find that neither of them had any appetite.

Megan set her plate on top of Shirl's on the nightstand. "Do your parents know?"

"Yes."

Megan stared out the window, trying to imagine what it would be like to know your only child was dying. Was Shirl's mother remembering what Shirl had been like as a little girl, regretting the fact that she hadn't been a better mother, that they hadn't spent more time together?

"I broke it off with Greg," Shirl said, her voice barely audible. "He said it didn't matter, that he wanted to stay with me, but it's for the best."

Megan nodded. What did you say to someone whose time was running out? Everything she thought of sounded trite or silly. Instead, she found herself remembering late night pillow fights and all the times they had shared confidences over a cup of hot chocolate. She was going to miss those times, Megan thought, blinking back her tears.

Silence hung heavy in the room for several minutes before Shirl said, "Meggie, will you do something for me?"

"Of course. Anything."

"Would you get in touch with Rhys?"

"Rhys? Whatever for?" Megan asked, and then, as comprehension dawned, she shook her head. "No, Shirl, don't even think about it."

"He's the only one who can help me now."

"Shirl . . . there has to be another option. Maybe another doctor would give you a better prognosis. At least get a second opinion."

"I've gone to three different specialists, Meggie. They all say the same thing. It's inoperable."

Megan sighed. "You don't want to be what he is, Shirl. Believe me, I've seen it. It's not a pretty sight." She shook her head. "I watched him attack a man. I saw him with his mask down, his eyes red and glowing, his fangs stained with blood. . . ."

"I don't care. I don't want to die."

"Think of what you're saying, what you'll be giving up . . ." Megan bit down on her lower lip as she realized the futility of that argument.

"I'm giving up death for a new life," Shirl said. "My mind's made up, Meggie. I've been thinking about it ever since you told me Rhys is a vampire."

"I can't."

"If you won't do it, I'll just go to his club. I know what I'm doing."

"It's the reason you broke up with Greg, isn't it?"

"Yes. Living with someone who's dying is one thing. Asking him to share his life with a vampire . . . I couldn't do that."

"What are you going to tell your parents?"

"I don't know. I'll worry about it later. I wonder if it hurts—becoming a vampire, I mean."

"I don't know," Megan said. Being bitten didn't hurt. In fact, it felt wonderful, but maybe it was different when you were being . . . what was the term? Turned?

"So, will you contact him for me?"

Megan nodded. "If that's what you want."

"I do."

Even though she didn't agree with Shirl's decision, Megan couldn't still the little shiver of excitement that curled in the pit of her stomach at the thought of seeing Rhys again.

Megan called Mr. Parker that afternoon to ask for the night off. He told her not to worry about it, asked how

Shirl was feeling, said to be sure to let him know if there was anything he could do, and hung up.

Shirl slept most of the day, which left Megan with little to do except think about seeing Rhys again. She grew increasingly nervous as the hours went by, until, finally, it was time to get ready to go. She dressed with care, chiding herself for taking pains with her hair and makeup, but she couldn't help it. This would probably be the last time she saw him, and she wanted him to remember her at her best.

Shortly after sundown, she drove to Rhys's apartment, only to find that he wasn't home. Returning to her car, she sat there a moment, her fingertips tapping nervously on the steering wheel. Where else would he be? The nightclub, of course.

Her heart was pounding wildly by the time she pulled into the parking lot of *La Morte Rouge.* She sat behind the wheel a moment, willing her pulse to stop racing. Was she nervous at going into the club alone, she wondered as she opened the car door, or afraid of seeing Rhys again? Probably both, she decided as she stepped out of the car and locked the door behind her.

She glanced around as she walked toward the front of the building. The parking lot was nearly empty.

She hesitated at the entrance. From out here, the place looked closed. What if Rhys wasn't there? Only one way to find out, she thought, and knocked on the door.

It opened almost immediately, and she came face-to-face with the same man who had opened it when she'd come here with Rhys. If he recognized her, it didn't show in his expression.

"I'm sorry, miss, the club doesn't open for another hour."

"I'd like to see Mr. Costain."

He lifted one thick brow. "Is he expecting you?"

"No, but I think he'll see me."

The man looked her over a moment, then said, "Of course. Come in. Please wait here."

Standing just inside the door, Megan glanced around. The room was empty save for a red-headed woman seated at the piano, her fingers moving languidly over the keyboard.

The man returned a few minutes later. "This way, Miss DeLacey."

She wondered how he knew her name as she followed him across the floor and up a short flight of stairs. She hadn't given it, and Rhys didn't know she was coming.

Megan stared at the door in front of her, her heart pounding wildly with the sudden realization that The Red Death wasn't a Goth club at all. It was a hangout for the Undead.

She jumped when the door opened.

"Are you coming in?" Rhys asked. "Or have you changed your mind?"

"How did you know I was out here?"

"I always know where you are."

Well, that was disconcerting, to say the least.

He took a step back. "Come in."

Feeling like Daniel going into the lion's den, Megan followed him into the room, which turned out to be a large office.

He gestured at an overstuffed chair upholstered in dark red velvet. "Sit down."

She sat, her gaze darting around the room. The walls were papered in a dark red and gold stripe, giving the room the look of an old-fashioned brothel. The floors were polished hardwood. A pair of antique oak filing cabinets stood against one wall. The chair behind the desk was black leather. There were no windows in the room. She thought the state-of-the-art computer and the chrome-and-glass desk looked out of place.

He sat in his chair, watching her, his face devoid of expression. She couldn't help noticing he was wearing one of the navy-blue pinstriped shirts he had bought from her.

She clasped her hands tightly in her lap to keep them from shaking.

"So," he asked, "why are you here?"

"Shirl wants to see you."

Megan felt a little thrill of satisfaction. He hadn't seen that coming.

"Indeed? What for?"

"She wants to be a vampire."

Disbelief danced across his features, and then he laughed.

"It's true," Megan said. "She's dying."

His laughter stilled, and he leaned forward, his arms crossed on the desk. "You're serious?"

"Of course! I wouldn't make jokes about something like that."

"No, I meant the part about her wanting to be a vampire."

"She's afraid to die."

He grunted softly. "What's wrong with her?"

"She has a tumor. In her brain. It's inoperable."

He leaned back in his chair, his elbows resting on the arms, his fingers steepled beneath his chin.

Megan forced herself to look at him. Forced herself, she thought ruefully. What a lie that was. She couldn't stop staring at him, couldn't stop remembering the touch of his hands, his lips, the way his body felt against hers. Couldn't stop wishing . . . She slammed the door on her thoughts. He was what he was, and there was no changing it, no wishing away the truth. She had lost him, just as surely as she was going to lose her best friend.

"When does she want to do it?" Rhys asked.

"She didn't say. She wants to talk to you first."

"I see." He lowered his hands and leaned forward again. "What do you want?"

"What do you mean? I don't want anything."

"Why didn't Shirl come here herself?"

"Because . . . I . . . because she's . . ."

"Why did you come here?"

There was no point in lying to him, so she didn't. "Because Shirl said she'd come if I didn't, and she's sick." Megan lifted her chin. "And because I wanted to see you again."

"Ah, the truth at last."

"It doesn't change anything," Megan said, rising swiftly to her feet. "What should I tell Shirl?"

"Tell her I'll be there tomorrow night. What time is good for you?"

She shrugged. "Whenever you can make it. I'll tell her to expect you. Good night."

He was around the desk in the blink of an eye, his arm snaking around her waist, his eyes smoldering with barely suppressed desire as he drew her body up against his.

"Not so quick, my sweet, we haven't discussed my fee."

She stared up at him. "Your fee?" she exclaimed. "Are you kidding?"

"No."

"You want her to pay you?"

"No," he replied in a voice that was silky smooth. "I want *you* to pay me."

"I don't believe this!" It had never occurred to her that vampires expected compensation for making other vampires. "Isn't taking her blood and turning her into a monster payment enough?"

"No."

Megan took a deep breath. She didn't have a lot of

money saved. For that matter, neither did Shirl. "How much do you want?"

His gaze swept across her lips. "A kiss and a taste," he murmured. "One kiss, one taste, freely given."

Revulsion and anticipation warred within her as she stared into his eyes. *For Shirl,* she thought. *You can do this for Shirl.*

"Stop lying to yourself," he said, a hint of anger in his voice. "It's what *you* want."

"One kiss," she murmured. What could it hurt? Rising on her tiptoes, she pressed her lips to his.

He quickly took control of the kiss, his tongue sweeping across her lips, his mouth devouring hers as if he were a starving man and she his only hope of survival. She closed her eyes, her arms slipping around his waist, holding on for dear life as he deepened the kiss. A kiss that seemed to last forever, and ended all too soon.

For a moment, she couldn't breathe, couldn't think. She could only stand there, looking up at him, her heart aching for what was lost. And then, with a hand that trembled only a little, she pushed her hair behind her ear.

"One taste, freely given," she whispered tremulously, and closed her eyes.

He murmured her name, his tongue hot against her skin, unleashing a thrill of anticipation. She felt the gentle, teasing scrape of his fangs along the side of her neck, and then his bite, and then a rush of heat that left her gasping with sensual pleasure. Warmth spread through her whole body, settling deep in the core of her being. She pressed her body against his, driven by an almost desperate urge to be closer, to feel his skin against her own, to give him everything she had to give.

She was surprised by an unexpected spark of jealousy when she thought of Rhys's biting Shirl, giving her the same pleasure.

She couldn't stifle the soft moan that rose in her throat as he drank from her, or the soft cry of protest when he lifted his head.

Confused and on the verge of tears, she twisted out of his embrace and ran out of the office, a sharp stab of regret twisting her insides when he made no move to stop her.

Chapter 24

Shirl was asleep on the sofa, her cheek pillowed on her hand, when Megan returned home. For a moment, she stared down at her best friend, trying to imagine Shirl as a blood-sucking creature of the night, but she simply couldn't do it. Shirl hated the sight of blood, especially her own. She was afraid of the dark and slept with a night-light. Hardly vampire material.

With a sigh, Megan went upstairs to get ready for bed. In the bathroom, standing in front of the mirror, she tried to put herself in Shirl's place. What if she were dying? Would she grasp at a chance—any chance—to stay alive, no matter what it entailed? Would she do it even if it meant giving up everything she knew and loved and surviving on the blood of others? Would she be willing to take a life to save her own?

For the first time, she wondered how many lives Rhys had taken during his years of existence? How often did he have to . . . She frowned. Did he call it eating? Drinking? Where did he spend the day? Did he sleep in a coffin? How long had he been a vampire? Were there other vampires in LA? And if so, how many?

She thought about what she had read on the Web. Did

garlic really repel vampires? What about holy water and crosses? Could he turn into a bat? Why would he want to?

Feeling a headache coming on, she pressed her fingertips to her temples.

"Forget about Rhys," she muttered. "What are you going to do with a roommate who's a vampire?"

In the morning, over breakfast, Megan tried yet again to talk some sense into her friend, but to no avail. Shirl's mind was made up.

Megan took a deep breath. She had only one argument left. "Have you thought about the blood thing? Really thought about it? About what you'll have to do to get it?"

"Of course I have."

"And you don't have a problem with that? You're telling me you could kill someone for their blood?"

"Vampires don't have to kill," Shirl retorted, a sharp edge to her voice. "Give it up, Megan. I've made my decision." She paused a moment, then said, "I'm sorry, Meggie. I didn't mean to snap at you. I know you don't approve."

"It's your life," Megan said quietly. "Your decision. I just hope you don't regret it."

Megan was too nervous to go to work that night. She called Mr. Parker to let him know she needed to take another day off, and then spent the morning and early afternoon cleaning the house while Shirl slept. She mopped the floors, dusted the furniture, cleaned the bathrooms, scrubbed the toilets, did the laundry, even baked a cake she was too upset to eat.

She had hoped keeping busy would take her mind off Shirl's decision. It didn't, of course. While cleaning the mirror, she wondered how Shirl would feel when she could no longer look at her reflection and see how beautiful she was. When she took the cake out of the oven, it reminded her that Shirl's birthday was next month, but if Shirl went through with her insane plan, they wouldn't be celebrating Shirl's birthday with her favorite fudge marble cake and chocolate ice cream.

How did one become a vampire, anyway? Was being bitten the only way?

After turning off the oven, Megan sat down at the computer, went to Google, and typed in "how to become a vampire." As always, she was amazed at the number of Web pages that turned up.

According to one site, there were three ways to become a vampire: you were born that way; another vampire bit you and turned you into one of the Undead; or it happened after you died. She frowned as she read about the last way, wondering if anyone had ever really believed anything so far-fetched. For instance, in some places it was believed that if a body was buried face up, it might become a vampire. Improper burial, no burial, the wind, or a shadow falling over the corpse might cause the deceased to rise again.

According to another site, you might become a vampire if a dog or a cat jumped over your corpse. Russian folklore held that vampires had once been witches.

She didn't know much about vampires, but being bitten by another vampire seemed like the most logical way to join the ranks of the fanged and dangerous.

Shirl woke late in the afternoon. She picked at the lunch Megan prepared for her, then locked herself in the bathroom, saying she wanted her hair and makeup to look perfect when she was turned.

Feeling like she was trapped in a bad B movie, Megan went into the backyard, where she spent the next two hours pulling weeds and praying that Shirl would come to her senses before it was too late.

When she went back into the house, Shirl was in the living room doing her nails.

"Are you going out?" Megan asked, thinking what a silly question it was. Of course, Shirl wasn't going out.

"No, I'm just getting ready. I want to look my best when he turns me. Some people believe that however you look when it happens is how you'll look forever. And I want to look good."

Ignoring the knot tightening in the pit of her stomach, Megan nodded, then went upstairs to take a shower. She wanted to look good, too, and the fact that she did irritated the heck out of her. But Rhys would be there soon, and, even though it was over between them, she didn't want him to see her in a pair of worn jeans with her hair all scraggly and dirt under her fingernails.

She slipped into a pair of white pants and a blue silk shirt, brushed her hair, applied her makeup, spritzed herself with perfume, and went downstairs.

"I ordered dinner from all my favorite places," Shirl said, indicating several covered trays on the coffee table. "Filet mignon, lobster, shrimp, and all the trimmings. Pizza. And half a gallon of chocolate fudge brownie ice cream for dessert."

"Your last meal?" Megan asked, unable to keep the bitterness out of her voice.

"Meggie . . ."

"Shirl! Think about what you're doing! This isn't right. It isn't natural."

Shirl clapped her hands over her ears. "I don't want to hear it! My mind is made up. You'd do the same thing in my place."

Megan started to deny it, then dropped down onto the sofa. She had no idea what she would do in Shirl's place. She knew what she hoped she would do, but when it came right down to it, there was no way to know until it happened.

"Please, Meggie."

Megan surrendered with a nod. "I'll pour the wine."

They had just finished dinner when the doorbell rang.

Megan didn't miss the panicked look that flashed in Shirl's eyes before she blinked it away. Hope flared in Megan's heart. Maybe Shirl wasn't as sure about her decision as she thought.

Megan took a deep breath before she went to answer the door.

Rhys was dressed all in black. Fitting, Megan thought, since he was bringing death into the house.

She stared at him, struck again by the sheer beauty of the man. Unable to think of anything to say, she didn't say anything at all, just turned on her heel and walked back into the living room. When he didn't follow, she remembered she had rescinded her invitation.

She was about to invite him in when Shirl called, "Mr. Costain, please come in."

Megan felt an odd vibration in the air as he crossed the threshold. Why hadn't she felt it before?

He moved into the living room on silent feet. Watching him, Megan wondered what was different about him. And then she knew. He was no longer hiding the truth of what he was. The supernatural power that was a part of him was a palpable presence in the air. Stunned by the irrefutable truth, she sank down on the chair beside the sofa.

"Please, sit down, Mr. Costain," Shirl invited with a weak smile.

"No need to be so formal," he replied, taking a place on the sofa beside her.

She nodded. "Rhys."

"That's better. Are you sure you want this?"

"Yes."

"Do you know how it's done?"

Shirl clasped her hands in her lap. "I think so."

"Do you have any questions?"

"Have you done this before?"

Megan leaned forward, her arms wrapped tightly around her waist, as she waited for his answer. Funny, she had never wondered about that.

"Once or twice," he said.

"And were they . . ." Shirl hesitated a moment, as if searching for the right word. "Successful?"

He nodded. "Anything else?"

"Will it hurt?"

"No. It's quite pleasant, actually. I'll drink from you. You'll drink from me. When you wake tomorrow night, you'll be as I am."

"I have a question," Megan said, and felt her breath catch in her throat when Rhys turned to look at her.

"What do you want to know?"

"Is it going to be safe for me to live with a vampire, or do I need to find a new roommate?"

"Meggie!"

"I'm sorry, Shirl, but I have to know what to expect."

Rhys nodded. "It might be wise for Shirl to move in with me for a few days, until she becomes accustomed to her new lifestyle."

"I'd never hurt Megan!" Shirl exclaimed. "She's my best friend!"

"Perhaps not intentionally," Rhys said. "But it's sometimes difficult for new vampires to control their thirst." He'd had to destroy the first vampire he'd made for that very reason. She had run amok, killing everything in sight, putting his existence and the lives of everyone she knew in danger. "So, are you ready?"

When Shirl didn't answer right away, Megan felt a rush of hope. Had Shirl finally come to her senses and changed her mind? Hardly daring to breathe, Megan waited for Shirl's answer.

Rhys sat beside Shirl, unmoving, patient as only a man who isn't ruled by time can be.

"Shirl," Megan whispered. "Please don't do this."

A single tear glistened in Shirl's eyes. "I'm sorry, Meggie," she said quietly.

Megan nodded. She had done all she could. The rest was up to Shirl, but she didn't have to watch. Rising, she said, "I'll wait upstairs."

"No!" Shirl exclaimed. "I want you to be here."

Megan stared at her best friend, horrified by the mere idea. "Why?"

When Shirl seemed reluctant to answer, Rhys answered for her. "I think she wants you here in case something goes wrong."

"Wrong?" Megan echoed. "What could go wrong?"

"If her will to live isn't strong enough, she won't survive the exchange."

"Shirl, is that true? Are you telling me you're willing to do this when you might die anyway?"

"It's the best chance I have," Shirl replied, her voice barely audible. "Please stay with me."

"If you're not sure, we can do this another time," Rhys said.

"No!" Shirl said, her voice tinged with desperation. "It's got to be now!" She pressed her hands to the sides of her head. "I can't stand the pain any longer." She looked at Rhys, her eyes wild. "Do it! Do it now!"

With a nod, Rhys drew her into his embrace, then gently brushed the hair away from her neck. "Relax, child," he murmured, his voice soft, soothing. "There's nothing to be afraid of." He caught her gaze with his as he slid his knuckles down the length of her neck. "That's right, just relax."

Unable to look away, Megan stared at the two of them.

It was almost as if they were making love. As Rhys continued to speak quietly to Shirl, her eyes took on a glazed, faraway look. Her body sagged against his, her head fell back over his arm, her eyelids fluttered down.

Megan's heart slammed against her rib cage when Rhys lifted his gaze to hers. Preternatural power crawled over her skin. For a moment, she was tempted to go to him, to throw her arms around him and surrender to the longing she read in his eyes.

It took all the willpower she had to look away.

Only to feel her gaze drawn back to the scene before her.

Rhys's attention was wholly focused on Shirl now. He stroked his fingers along the length of her neck again; then, bending over her, he sank his fangs into the soft skin of her throat.

The faint, coppery scent of blood rose in the air.

Megan's hands clenched in her lap. She should stop him now, before it was too late. Could she revoke Shirl's invitation?

Shirl moaned softly, then went completely limp in Rhys's embrace.

"What's wrong?" Megan asked anxiously. "Is she . . . ?" The words stilled in her throat when he lifted his head to look at her. His eyes glowed red. She saw blood on his fangs before he licked it away.

Feeling light-headed, Megan watched as he bit into his own wrist, then held the bleeding wound to Shirl's lips.

"Drink, Shirl." His voice was low yet edged with steel.

With a soft cry, Shirl grabbed hold of his arm and pressed her mouth to the wound.

Fighting nausea, Megan lurched to her feet. She could feel Rhys's gaze on her back as she fled the room and staggered up the stairs.

Safe in her bedroom, with the door locked, she fell

across the bed and cried bitter tears for the death of her best friend.

Tomás Villagrande lifted his head, the lovely dusky-skinned woman in his arms forgotten as, somewhere in the heart of the city, Rhys Costain brought a new vampire into the fold.

Chapter 25

When she had no tears left, Megan dried her eyes. Admonishing herself to stop being a coward, she went into the bathroom and splashed cold water on her face, then went back downstairs. She had to make sure Shirl was still alive. No, not alive. Undead.

Rhys looked up when she entered the room. He hadn't moved. As far as Megan could tell, neither had Shirl. She looked even paler than before. And she didn't seem to be breathing.

Megan met Rhys's gaze. "Is she all right?" she asked anxiously. "Is she . . . ?"

"She'll be fine," Rhys replied. "She'll sleep tonight and all day tomorrow." He brushed a lock of hair from Shirl's cheek. It was an achingly tender touch. And then he looked at Megan. "When the sun goes down, she'll rise as a new vampire."

Megan swallowed hard against the bile that burned the back of her throat. *A new vampire.* Shirl had always been fascinated with the Undead. Maybe this was what she had been searching for her whole life.

Rhys studied her, one brow raised. "You don't approve." It wasn't a question.

"Of course not! You've turned my best friend into a . . ."

"Go on, say it," he challenged. "I've turned her into a monster, like me."

Megan took a step back, as if to distance herself from the truth. "I wasn't going to say that."

"But you were thinking it."

"Stay out of my head!"

"I wish I could." He eased Shirl down onto the sofa, then rose, his eyes sparking with anger.

Power rolled off him in waves. That, combined with the barely suppressed fury in his eyes, frightened Megan to the depths of her being, but she refused to let him intimidate her. Clenching her hands at her sides, she glared up at him, a sinking feeling in the pit of her stomach. What had happened to the man who had once made love to her so tenderly, she wondered, even as an annoying voice in the back of her mind whispered that Rhys Costain wasn't a man at all.

"Monster." He spat the word at her. "It's what you see when you look at me now, isn't it?"

She wanted to deny it, but she couldn't force the words past her lips.

"Damn you!" Hissing the words, he closed the distance between them quicker than her eyes could follow and pulled her body up against his. "Damn you," he repeated, but this time, it sounded like a caress.

He kissed her then, a low growl rising in his throat as his tongue plundered her mouth. There was no gentleness in him, no tenderness.

She reeled under the assault on her senses—the hard length of his body pressed intimately against hers, the heat of his tongue dueling with her own. His arm was like a band of solid steel holding her prisoner. She whimpered softly, barely able to breathe as his arm tightened around her, pulling her closer still.

She knew he wanted to hurt her, to prove, in some perverse way, that he was the monster his actions showed him to be. But, monster or not, she clung to him, her body quickly responding to the strength of his arms, the force of his kisses, the way his hand caressed her hair.

Rhys muttered something under his breath as he released her, and even though she didn't recognize the language, she knew he was swearing. Some words sounded the same no matter how you said them.

Turning away, Rhys scooped Shirl into his arms. "I'll take good care of her," he said curtly, and with his gaze riveted on Megan, he vanished from her sight.

"Show-off," Megan murmured, and burst into tears.

Rhys carried Shirl to his penthouse lair, settled her in his bed, then went out onto the balcony, his thoughts in turmoil. Why had he agreed to turn Megan's roommate? Had he hoped, in some distant part of his mind, that by saving Shirl he could regain Megan's affection?

He snorted with disgust at his own foolishness. If anything, he had caused Megan to hate him all the more. And now he had an unwanted fledgling on his hands.

The wind stirred, whispering through the trees, sending leaves and debris skittering along the sidewalk.

And on the freshening wind, Rhys caught the scent of an unfamiliar vampire. Cursing softly, he was about to vault over the railing to the street below when the vampire materialized beside him.

"What the hell!" Rhys hissed.

Looking faintly amused, the vampire bowed from the waist. "Tomás Villagrande," he said. "And you are Rhys Costain, Master of the City, are you not?"

Rhys nodded. Tomás Villagrande was tall and lean, with

dark brown hair and hooded brown eyes. He appeared to be in his late twenties.

"What brings you to my territory?" Rhys asked.

Villagrande shrugged. "I had a yearning to see the West Coast, to sail the waters of the Pacific." His eyes turned hard. "Do you have a problem with that?"

"Only if you hunt in my territory. You've left quite a trail of carnage in your wake. Don't bring it here."

Villagrande drew himself up to his full height.

Though Rhys was several inches taller than Villagrande and outweighed him by a good thirty pounds, the other vampire's preternatural power was a force to be reckoned with. Rhys felt it like a heavy hand trying to crush his own strength, a ponderous weight pushing against his mind. He brought his own power to bear, infusing it with his anger, his frustration.

Villagrande grinned impudently. "You are strong," he said, a hint of admiration in his voice. "And stubborn." He jerked his chin toward the door of the penthouse. "The woman inside, is she yours?"

"Not in the way you mean."

Villagrande grunted softly. "The young ones. You never know how they'll turn out."

"She's under my protection, as are all the vampires in my territory. I will not take it kindly if harm comes to any of them."

"I don't need you to tell me how to behave," Villagrande said with asperity. "I could destroy you with a thought."

"You could try."

"Adrianna." Villagrande spat her name. "I believe she's hiding somewhere in your territory."

Rhys nodded. There was no point in denying it. "Is she why you're here?"

"Partly."

"Still looking for retribution?"

Villagrande's eyes flickered with surprise. "She told you?"

Rhys shrugged. "I like to know what's going on with anyone who stays in my territory."

"She took something that was mine."

"It was a long time ago. Why not forget it?"

"This is between me and Adrianna. It doesn't concern you."

"Anything that happens in my territory concerns me. I don't particularly like Adrianna, but that doesn't mean you can just waltz in here and take her out."

"Do you think you can stop me?"

"I don't know. I hope I don't have to find out."

"We'll see."

"Don't leave any corpses in my city. I like it here, and I'm not looking to move any time soon."

Villagrande inclined his head. "As you wish. For now." And with that begrudging promise, he was gone.

Rhys muttered an oath. He had lost Megan. He had a fledgling sleeping in his lair. And now the most powerful vampire in the world was stalking the streets of his city. What was Villagrande really doing here? Hard to believe his only reasons for leaving the East were to avenge himself on Adrianna and sail the Pacific.

He raked his fingers through his hair. He should probably warn Adrianna that Villagrande was in town.

Pulling his cell phone from his pocket, he punched in her number.

Lingering on the sidewalk beneath Costain's lair, Villagrande listened to the conversation between the Master of the West Coast Vampires and Adrianna.

Avenging himself on Adrianna was the first order of business. He could, as Costain had suggested, forget about seeking revenge. Hell, he couldn't even remember the face or the name of the long-deceased woman who had been the cause of their feud, but if he let Adrianna's lack of respect go unchallenged, others might see it as a sign of weakness.

And then there was the West Coast. He had forgotten the beauty of the Pacific Ocean, the mild climate, the long-legged, tanned California girls. Why visit for a short time when he could just take over the territory? Of course, it might prove a difficult task. Rhys Costain was a force to be reckoned with. He was strong and more powerful than expected, but that would only make the coming battle more challenging.

As for the woman in Costain's lair, she excited him, though Tomás was at a loss to explain why. He had never seen her. Didn't know her name. But her scent, the beat of her heart, they called to him in ways he didn't understand. And since she wasn't Costain's woman, taking her shouldn't be a problem.

Chapter 26

Megan woke early after a night plagued with bad dreams. Rising, she pulled on her robe and tiptoed down the hall to Shirl's bedroom to assure herself that it had all been a nightmare. She would look in Shirl's room and find her friend asleep in her bed, the covers pulled over her head, her *Beauty and the Beast* night-light burning.

Taking a deep breath, Megan quietly opened the door. The room was dark. The bed was empty. So, it hadn't been a dream. Last night, Rhys had turned her roommate into a vampire. And now Shirl was in his lair, sleeping the sleep of the Undead, and when she woke . . .

Megan shuddered. She couldn't help wondering what her roommate would think when she woke tonight and discovered she was really and truly a vampire. Would she regret it, or would she still believe it had been the right decision? What would she think when she couldn't see her reflection in a mirror anymore? Shirl had always been a little vain about her looks, but then, who could blame her? She was gorgeous. How would she react to the reality of having to drink blood to survive? Granted, Shirl's former diet had been pretty restricted, but even celery had to be better than blood.

Megan had done a lot of research on the Undead in the last week or so. She wasn't sure how much of what she had read on the Web was fact and how much was fiction. But, thanks to Rhys, she knew the blood thing was real.

Megan shook her head. Her roommate barely weighed a hundred pounds soaking wet. Megan simply couldn't imagine her petite friend prowling around in the dead of night looking for prey.

Her mind kept coming back to the fact that Shirl was sharing Rhys's lair. Was she also sharing his bed? Rhys was an attractive man. Shirl was a beautiful woman. . . . Megan pushed the troublesome thought from her mind. It was none of her business. She had no claim on Rhys. And Shirl . . . what was she going to do about Shirl? Was it safe to live with a vampire? Especially a new vampire?

Shirl woke slowly. She felt funny. Different. Not quite herself. She lifted a hand to her head. Was she dying? Was this what death was like, this sudden clarity of sight and sound? A reminder of the perfection of life before it was snatched away? The room was dark, yet she could see everything clearly—the faint crack in the ceiling overhead; each individual thread in the silk sheet that covered her; the tiny dent on the edge of the antique dresser across from the bed.

She sat up, feeling slightly disoriented. This wasn't her room. Where was she?

She jumped when the door opened and a light came on, then let out a sigh when she saw who it was.

"Rhys." She blinked at him as everything that had happened the night before came rushing back. She frowned, and then she smiled. "It worked."

"So it would seem." He stepped farther into the room, his gaze moving over her. "How do you feel?"

She thought about it a moment, then said, "Wonderful! My head doesn't hurt anymore!" Leaping off the bed, she threw her arms around him. "Thank you!" she cried exuberantly, and kissed him.

She was beautiful, her body was pressed against his, and he did what any other man would do. He kissed her back, pretending, for a moment, that it was Megan in his arms. And then he gently pushed her away.

"No regrets?" he asked.

She laughed softly. "I don't think so, but it's a little early to tell." She pressed a hand to her stomach. "I think I'm hungry."

Rhys nodded. Her eyes had taken on a red hue. "Time for your first lesson."

"Lesson?"

"Vampire hunting 101," he explained. "Rule number one. I'm the Master of the West Coast Vampires. You're my fledgling. This is my territory. As long as you stay here, you do as I say. Got it?"

"Yes, master."

"You're learning," he said, ignoring the sarcasm in her voice. "Rule number two. I'm the only one who's allowed to hunt in this city, and I do it only rarely. Smart vampires don't hunt where they live."

Shirl nodded. That made sense.

"Number three. For as long as you exist, there will be a blood connection between us. I'll always be able to find you, and if you bring trouble into my territory, I'll destroy you. Got it?"

"Y . . . yes." She hesitated a moment, then asked, "Will you tell me something?"

"Depends on what you want to know."

"How long have you been a vampire?"

"Five hundred and twelve years."

She backed away from him and sat down on the edge of the bed. "Wow."

"Are you ready to go?"

"Go where?" She glanced around the room, noting the heavy curtains across the window, the fact that there was no mirror over the dresser, the heavy lock on the door.

"You're hungry, aren't you?"

"Yes, but I thought . . ."

"What? That I'd feed you?"

"Well, yes, sort of."

"As a rule, vampires don't feed off their own kind. A taste now and then is okay, but no more than that."

"Oh." She bit down on her lower lip. She had known she would have to drink blood, but she had assumed it would be something she could work up to gradually.

"So, are you ready?" He didn't wait for her reply.

Shirl gasped when he scooped her into his arms. A kind of dizziness engulfed her, and, when the world righted itself, they were outside a small tavern. She could hear waves in the distance, smell the salty tang of the ocean, hear the conversation coming from inside the bar. "Where are we? How did you do that?"

He shrugged as he set her on her feet. "Just another way of getting around when you're in a hurry. We're in Manhattan Beach. When we go into the bar, I want you to look around, find someone who appeals to you, and call him, or her, to you."

"What? You mean, just call them? Out loud?"

"No, mentally."

"I'm not psychic."

"You're a vampire. You can pretty much do whatever you want. Come on."

Shirl followed him into the tavern. It was nothing like what she was used to. The interior was shabby, the air was stale, heavy with the stink of smoke and sweat. Three young men were playing billiards in the far corner of the room. A woman Shirl realized was a hooker was discussing her price with a nervous-looking, middle-aged man. Several other men and women sat at the bar. A pair of young women stood in front of the jukebox, trying to decide what song to play.

Shirl pressed her hands over her ears, trying to shut out the cacophony of conversation and thoughts that bombarded her. And the smells! Perspiration, perfume, alcohol, cigarette smoke, soap, and deodorant. It was overpowering. But it was the beating of so many living hearts, the rush of blood through miles of veins, that overrode everything else. She groaned softly. She was hungry, so hungry.

She glanced at the men and women sitting at the bar. One of the men turned to look at her. He was young, in his midtwenties, with shaggy brown hair, blue eyes, and a mustache. He looked clean and didn't smell too bad. His name was Don, but people called him Sharkey.

Feeling a little foolish, she concentrated on sending him a mental summons. To her astonishment, he stood and walked toward her, his expression somewhat bemused, as if he couldn't believe what he was doing.

"Hey, beautiful," he murmured. "What's a gorgeous gal like you doing in a dump like this?"

Shirl licked her lips. "Would you come outside with me?"

"Sure, honey," Sharkey said with a wink and a smile. "What did you have in mind?"

"I want to show you something." Shirl looked at Rhys. *Am I doing this right?*

At his nod, she took Sharkey's hand and led him outside and around the corner of the building into the shadows beyond.

When Sharkey noticed Rhys following them, he tried to pull out of her grasp. Shirl didn't know which of them was more surprised when he couldn't break her grip.

"Now what?" Shirl asked, looking to Rhys for help.

"Let's see what kind of vampire you are," he said, grinning. "Just follow your instincts."

"Vampire!" Sharkey exclaimed. "What the hell?" He tried again to jerk out of Shirl's grasp. "Dammit, let me go!"

Shirl gazed deeply into his eyes. "Be quiet and hold still!" she said angrily, and when he complied, she looked over at Rhys again, waiting for his approval.

"You're doing just fine."

Shirl swallowed hard. Pain gnawed at her insides, a horrible twisting pain worse than anything she had ever known. Worse, even, than the headaches that had driven her to this. She took a deep breath, her gaze drawn to the pulse throbbing in the hollow of the man's throat. She could smell his fear. And his blood. And suddenly he wasn't a man anymore, he was prey. The hunger raged inside her. Desperate to end it, she pulled the man into her arms, felt an ache in her gums as her fangs extended.

Fangs.

Vampire.

Bending the man back over her arm, Shirl lowered her head to his neck. *You can do this.* She was surprised at how quickly and easily her fangs pierced his flesh. She had expected the act to be abhorrent, the taste disgusting. How could she have been so wrong? Nothing in all the world had ever tasted so wonderful or satisfied her so completely.

Rhys licked his lips as the scent of fresh, hot blood rose in the air. "Enough, Shirl," he said quietly.

She lifted her head, her narrowed eyes as red as the blood on her lips.

"Enough," he repeated.

Stop, now? Was he mad? She wanted more, and when she finished with this man, she wanted another. And another. She glared at Rhys, and then she lowered her head to the man's neck again.

"Enough, dammit!" Rhys said. "Any more, and you'll kill him!"

"I don't care!"

"Well, I do." Before she realized what was happening, Rhys snatched the man from her grasp, and then slapped her across the face. "I said enough!"

Stricken, she stared at Rhys, horrified by what she had almost done. She didn't want to kill anyone. And yet she wanted more. She wanted it all.

"You will listen to what I say," Rhys said angrily. "And you will do what I say, or I will destroy you. I warned you once. I'll have no killing in my territory."

"I'm sorry," she murmured contritely, and then she looked up at him. "How can you stop when they taste so good?" She licked the blood from her lips. "You didn't tell me it would taste so good."

"If you want to be a monster, that's fine with me. But not in my town."

"It won't happen again."

He grunted softly. "You can control it if you want to. It won't be easy at first, but you can do it. Now, you need to lick the wounds in his neck to seal them, then tell him to go back to the bar and get something to drink. And, most importantly, you must always remember to wipe the memory of what's happened from his mind."

"I can do that? Erase his memory? How?"

"Join your mind with his. You'll know what to do."

Rhys watched Shirl carefully. He'd had his doubts about how well she would adapt to becoming a vampire, but she seemed to be one of those who accepted the Dark Gift without a qualm. Sometimes he wondered if some people were predestined to join the ranks of the Undead.

He watched Sharkey stagger around the corner. The man would never know it, but he'd had a close encounter with death that night.

The thought had barely crossed his mind when the scent of another vampire reached his nostrils, and Tomás Villagrande strolled into view.

"You!" Rhys hissed. "What the hell are you doing here?"

"Taking in the sea air," Villagrande replied.

"Uh-huh. You followed us. Why?"

"I wanted to meet the newest member of our community," Villagrande said, smiling at Shirl. "And one of the loveliest, I might add."

Shirl smiled uncertainly before murmuring, "Thank you." She took a step closer to Rhys. She didn't know who the stranger was, but she knew instinctively that he was an old vampire. Old and dangerous. His power washed over her.

Tomás reached for her hand. Bending over it in an old-world bow, he said, "Tomás Villagrande, at your service."

Feeling totally out of her element, Shirl said, "I'm pleased to meet you, Mr. Villagrande."

"Please, my dear Shirley, call me Tomás."

"Enough of your smooth talk, Villagrande," Rhys said irritably. "I have a lot to teach her before the sun comes up."

"Indeed?" Tomás smiled at Shirl again. "If you're going to learn how to be a vampire, why not learn from the oldest of our kind? I can teach you things he does not yet know."

Shirl looked at Rhys. *What should I do?* Villagrande frightened her, yet she was drawn to him on some deep primal level that she didn't understand. Was it just the overwhelming sweep of his preternatural power? Or something more mundane, like the fact that he was quite remarkable-looking. Sort of the way she imagined a Barbary pirate might look. *Rhys, tell me what to do.*

He shook his head, the movement almost imperceptible. *This is something you'll have to decide for yourself, but I would advise you not to go with him.*

"Thank you for the offer," Shirl said, "but I think I'll stay with Rhys."

Irritation flashed in Villagrande's eyes. With an obvious effort, he reined in his anger. "I hope you don't regret it."

Shirl flinched. Had he just threatened her? In an effort to placate him, she murmured, "Perhaps another time."

But it was too late. He was already gone.

Shirl looked up at Rhys. "I think we could have handled that better," she said, her expression pensive.

"You think?"

"He's old, isn't he? Older, even, than you are."

"Yeah. No one knows just how old."

"I could feel his power. It was . . . scary." Scary, and exhilarating.

Rhys grunted softly. There wasn't much on this earth that scared him, but Tomás Villagrande was at the top of the list.

Chapter 27

Megan spent all of Saturday, Sunday, and Monday worrying about Shirl. Was her friend truly a vampire now? How was she handling it? Megan hadn't decided if having a vampire for a roommate was a good idea, but Shirl was still her best friend, and she was concerned about her welfare. Time and again, Megan picked up her cell phone and dialed her roommate's number, but there was no answer.

By Tuesday afternoon, when Shirl still hadn't called, Megan's worry for her friend bordered on anger. Shirl must know that Megan would be worrying, wondering. The least she could do was call, and if, for one reason or another, Shirl couldn't make one lousy phone call, then Rhys should have done it.

Megan arrived at Shore's early that night, glad to have an excuse to get out of the house and mingle with people who didn't have fangs, drink blood, or sleep in coffins.

At midnight, force of habit had her glancing at the front door. She shook her head, wondering how long it would take her to stop expecting Rhys to show up.

At 12:05, he strolled into the store with Shirl on his arm.

Megan stared at Shirl. Her friend had always been

beautiful but now . . . Megan shook her head. Impossible as it seemed, Shirl was even more gorgeous than ever. The changes were subtle. Anyone who hadn't known Shirl before wouldn't be aware of them, but they were there. Her skin was a little more translucent, a little paler. Her hair was thicker and more lustrous. And she possessed an almost tangible aura of seductive power that hadn't been there before.

But it was Rhys who held Megan's gaze. He wore a long-sleeved black silk shirt open over a blood-red T-shirt, and a pair of snug black jeans. He reminded her of a wild jungle cat, lean and lithe. She couldn't take her eyes off of him.

"Megan!" Shirl hurried toward her, moving with the same fluidity that Megan had noticed in Rhys.

Feeling like the ugly duckling welcoming the swan, Megan forced a smile. "Hi."

"Hi?" Shirl repeated with a frown. "Is something wrong?"

"Why should anything be wrong?" Megan tried to mask her anger behind a smile, and failed. "Why haven't you called me? I've been worried sick."

"I'm sorry," Shirl said. "I guess it was thoughtless of me, but . . ."

"It doesn't matter now." Megan glanced at Rhys, then back at Shirl, and couldn't help feeling . . . what? Jealous? That was ridiculous, and yet, like it or not, she felt like an outsider, as if they had joined an exclusive club to which she could never belong.

She was relieved when a man entered the shop, breaking the awkward silence between them. "I'm glad you're all right. Now, if you'll excuse me, I have a customer."

Relief turned to regret as she watched Rhys and Shirl leave the store.

* * *

When Megan got off work that night, Rhys was waiting for her in the parking lot. She couldn't stifle a rush of pleasure at seeing him standing beside her car.

"Megan, we need to talk."

"Where's Shirl?"

He shrugged. "I sent her back to my place."

She folded her arms and lifted her chin. "What do you want to talk about?

"You. Me. Us."

Taking a tight rein on her tumultuous emotions, she said, "There is no us."

Her heartbeat slammed into overdrive when he took a step toward her. "Isn't there?" He placed his hand on her breast. "I can feel your heart beating for me."

"Don't be ridiculous!"

"Am I? Tell me you don't want me. Say it out loud, and you'll never see me again."

"Rhys, I don't need this right now. Please, just go away."

"Say you don't want me, and I'm gone."

"All right, I want you! Are you happy? But it doesn't change anything."

He moved still closer. Too close. Memories of the times they had made love flashed across her mind. She wished she could go back in time, to the days before she knew what he was, when ignorance had, indeed, been bliss. But there was no going back. No changing what he was, or what he had done to Shirl.

Blinking back her tears, she turned her back to him and unlocked the car door. "I have to go."

"Dammit, Megan, don't do this." He put his hand on the top edge of the door so she couldn't open it. "At least give us a chance."

She shook her head. "I can't."

"When you found out what I was, I told myself it was for the best, that you were better off without me. That it would never work between us. But now . . . dammit, Megan, I'm begging you. Stay with me."

"I want to, but I can't. I'm afraid. Afraid of what I've seen. Afraid of what you are."

"I can't change that."

She glanced at him over her shoulder, her eyes brimming with tears. "But you can change me. And that's what I'm really afraid of."

Placing his hands on her shoulders, he turned her around so she was facing him again. "Would you believe me if I swore that I will never do that to you?"

"I don't know."

"Dammit!" He raked his hand through his hair. "Megan, what can I do? What can I say to change your mind?

Her tears came faster now, rolling unchecked down her cheeks. What did she want? How could she trust him? How could she let him go? He was right. She wanted him. She couldn't fight him anymore, couldn't fight the longing of her own heart. With a sigh, she rested her forehead against his chest, felt her tears start again as his arms closed lovingly around her. Right or wrong, for better or worse, this was where she wanted to be.

Placing a finger beneath her chin, he tilted her head up, then brushed her tears away. "Can I drive you home?"

With a nod, she handed him the keys to her car.

She was acutely aware of his nearness on the way home. His presence filled the car, or maybe it was her increased awareness of his power. She had always thought he was just exceptionally handsome, but after seeing the subtle changes in Shirl, she knew the flawless perfection of his face and form were a by-product of being a vampire.

When they reached her house, Rhys parked the car in the driveway, then came around to open her door.

Megan felt suddenly shy as they walked up to the porch. He unlocked the door and followed her inside. She dropped her handbag on the sofa table; he tossed her keys on top, then drew her into his arms.

"I've missed you," he said quietly. "More than you can imagine."

"I missed you, too."

"Is it okay if I kiss you?"

She laughed softly, amused that he would ask. Taking him by the hand, she led him to the sofa, pulled him down beside her, and kissed him.

His arms went around her once more, drawing her body against his. With a sigh of contentment, she closed her eyes and leaned into him, hungry for his touch, for his kisses. They could never have a normal life together and she knew it, but it didn't matter. He was here now, and she intended to savor every moment she could. And when it was over . . . She shook the thought away. She wouldn't worry about that now. It felt too good to be in his arms, to feel his body against hers, to hold him and taste him.

When they parted, Rhys leaned back against the sofa. Utterly breathless, Megan snuggled against him. She glanced at the fireplace, thinking how cozy a fire would be. She sat up, startled, when fire sprang to life in the hearth a moment later.

Beside her, Rhys laughed softly.

"Did you do that?" Megan asked. It was a silly question. Who else could have done it?

"You wanted one, didn't you?"

"Yes, but . . . You could have warned me," she said, resting her head on his shoulder. "What other tricks can you do?"

"Dogs do tricks," he said, sounding offended.

"Well, what do you call it, then?"

"It's power, my sweet. Vampire power."

"And now Shirl has it, too." It wasn't a question, but a

statement of fact. "I don't think I want her as a roommate anymore."

"She's been expecting that."

"Oh?"

"She doesn't think it's a good idea, either. She's not sure she can control herself."

"So she's going to stay with you?" Megan didn't like that arrangement in the least.

"No. She's going to find her own place."

"Oh? How's she going to pay for it?" Shirl had made good money as a model, but she had never saved any.

"She's got a job."

"How can she model now? She can't work during the day."

"She called her agent and told him she's come down with some rare disease and that her doctor advised her to stay out of the sun."

Megan frowned. "I thought vampires couldn't be photographed."

"That was true in the old days, but everything changed with the advent of digital cameras."

"I guess a lot of things have changed."

"Except the way I feel about you."

"Rhys . . . what are we doing? This can't work."

"I know, but I can't seem to stay away from you."

"Then don't."

"Ah, Megan, you tempt me in so many ways."

"Show me," she whispered. "Show me, show me, show me. . . ."

Falling back on the sofa, he drew her down on top of him, his mouth claiming hers in a kiss that was gentle and desperate at the same time. She kissed him back with the same intensity, refusing to worry about what the future might hold. They were together now, and that was all that mattered.

She moaned softly when he rolled onto his side, then sat up, drawing her with him. "What's the matter?"

"It's late. You need to get some sleep, and I need to feed."

"Oh." His words brought reality crashing down on her. Had he been an ordinary man, she could have fixed him a sandwich, but, in this case, *she* was the soup de jour.

He stood, then lifted her to her feet. "See me out?"

With a nod, she linked her arm with his and walked him to the door, then stood on tiptoe to kiss him good night. She was tempted to ask him to stay, to make love to her until dawn, but it didn't seem wise to take a hungry vampire to bed.

He grinned at her. "Smart girl."

"Will I see you tomorrow night?"

"Count on it." He kissed her again; then, whistling softly, he walked down the porch steps and vanished into the darkness.

"I guess that's just another one of his vampire tricks," she muttered, "like starting fires out of thin air and reading my mind."

In the distance, she heard the sound of his laughter.

Chapter 28

Tomás Villagrande prowled the street below Rhys Costain's lair. The vampire wasn't home, but Tomás wasn't interested in Costain at the moment. It was the woman, Shirl, who held his attention. Her scent tickled his nostrils and teased his desire. He had not made love to one of his own kind in years, and the idea of making love to a vampire as young and as beautiful as Costain's fledgling aroused him as nothing had in centuries.

Standing under the balcony, he called her name ever so softly, knowing that, with her preternatural power, she would hear him.

A moment later, she appeared at the railing.

Tomás smiled up at her. "Come, take a walk with me."

She shook her head. Moonlight danced in the soft waves of her long silver-blond hair. "I don't think so."

"Why not? It's what you want."

"I don't trust you."

His laughter filled the night. "I mean you no harm, child." In the blink of an eye, he was on the balcony, his fingers wrapped around her wrist. "And if I did, you couldn't stop me."

Shirl stared at him in astonishment. She hadn't even seen him move. "What do you want with me?"

He ran his fingers through her hair. "You're incredibly lovely. I'm rich and bored. To quote an old saying, I think we could make beautiful music together."

"Thank you, but no thanks. I'm happy where I am."

He jerked his chin toward the penthouse. "With Rhys?"

"With myself. I always work solo."

"Where's the fun in that? You're a new vampire. I'm an old vampire and rather jaded. I want to see the world fresh through your eyes."

"I'm sure there are other new vampires who would love to go out with you."

"I want you." His grip tightened on her wrist. "I can show you the world. Give you anything you want. Teach you how to use your new powers. Teach you things Rhys doesn't know. Things he may never know. Why learn from one of the Indians when you can learn from the chief?" He smiled as he released her wrist. Lifting her hand to his lips, he ran his tongue over her palm. "I can make all your dreams come true."

Shirl stared at him, a momentary tingle of fear spreading through every nerve and fiber of her being, but it quickly faded under the weight of his preternatural power, ancient power that wrapped itself around her and made her hungry for more.

A slow smile spread across Villagrande's face. "So," he said, placing her hand on his arm in gentlemanly fashion. "Shall we go?"

Chapter 29

Megan had just finished dinner and was thinking about getting ready for work when the doorbell rang. She frowned on her way to answer it, wondering who it could be. She wasn't expecting anyone. Least of all, "Greg!"

"Is Shirl here?"

"No. Would you like to come in?"

"No." He shoved his hands in his pockets. "Do you know where I can find her? I called the hospital but they said she'd checked out."

"I'm sorry, I don't know where she is," Megan said.

Greg frowned. "I thought she was sick. At death's door."

"She was, but I guess you could say she had a rather miraculous recovery."

"What happened? Did they find a cure? Is she going to be all right?"

"I really can't say, I mean . . . well . . ." Megan stared at him, wishing she could just tell him the truth. "All I know is that she isn't sick anymore, and she'll probably have a nice long life."

He frowned, then said, I guess you know she broke it off with me."

"Yes, I'm sorry."

"Yeah, me too. I was hoping to change her mind. Is there someone else?"

"Not that I know of."

"Looks like she was just stringing me along," he said, his voice bitter. "I should have known a girl like that would never stay with a lug like me."

"I'm sorry," Megan said again. She couldn't help thinking that she sounded like a parrot that only knew two words, but what else could she say? She couldn't tell Greg the truth.

He nodded. "I hope she'll be happy," he muttered. "I'm sorry I bothered you."

Megan stared after him as he turned and walked away. Poor guy. With a shake of her head, she closed the door. She stood there a moment, thinking how unfair life was.

She was about to go upstairs to take a quick shower when the doorbell rang again. Thinking Greg might have returned, she opened the door.

"Shirl!" Megan experienced a moment of fear and confusion when she saw her friend on the front porch. Clad in an off-the-shoulder white sweater and a pair of slinky black pants, Shirl looked even more exotic and exquisite than usual.

"Hi, Meggie," Shirl said, brushing past her. "I'll only be a minute. I just came by to get my things." She tossed her handbag and coat on the sofa.

"Oh?"

"Yes, I'm sure you'll be relieved to know I'm moving out."

Megan started to deny it, then decided against it. "Where are you going?" *Please,* she thought, *please don't let her be moving in with Rhys.*

"I'm going to live on a yacht."

"A yacht! You know someone with a yacht? Someone willing to share it with a vampire?"

"Yes, his name is Tomás Villagrande, and he's the most remarkable man I've ever known. I was afraid of him when I first met him, but now . . . he's simply amazing."

"That's what you said about Greg," Megan reminded her. "Have you already forgotten him? He was here a few minutes ago looking for you."

"Really?" Happiness flared in Shirl's eyes for a moment, then was quickly gone.

"I thought you loved him."

"I do. I did. But he could never have given me the kind of life I wanted." Shirl paused a moment, her expression melancholy, and then she shrugged. "And even if he could, it would never work out between us now."

"I don't know what you said to him the last time you saw him, but he looked crushed when he left here."

"You didn't tell him the truth, did you?" Shirl asked sharply.

"Of course not."

"Good," Shirl said, obviously relieved. "Come upstairs with me. We can talk while I pack."

Megan stared after Shirl, then followed her up the stairs. "So, who is this guy, Tomás? What does he do?"

"He's a vampire," Shirl said, an unmistakable note of excitement in her voice. "The oldest vampire in the world." She pulled a suitcase from the top shelf of her closet and started throwing clothes into it. "He's very powerful and very rich."

"Does he know Rhys? Are they friends?"

"They know each other." Shirl moved to the dresser, quickly taking things from one drawer after another. "I don't know if they're friends. Somehow, I don't think so." She pulled another suitcase from the closet and began filling it with shoes and handbags.

"Are you leaving L.A.?"

"No. Tomás says he wants a change of scene," Shirl replied airily. "He's thinking of staying here for a while."

Megan didn't know much about the intricacies of vampire politics, but she remembered reading online that there could be only one Master Vampire in the city, and right now, that was Rhys. If Tomás was the oldest vampire in the world, was he also a Master Vampire? Did that automatically come with age? Would Rhys have to leave LA if Tomás decided to stay? Did vampires fight over territory? The article she'd read hadn't mentioned that.

Shirl closed both suitcases with a flourish, then glanced around the room. "I guess that's everything but my cosmetics." She picked up a small bag and went into the bathroom.

Megan followed her, then stood in the doorway, watching as Shirl filled the bag with enough lipstick, rouge, powder, and eyeliner to last an ordinary woman a lifetime. "How do you put your makeup on when you can't see yourself in a mirror?"

Shirl shrugged. "That's what makeup artists are for. My agent wasn't very happy when I told him I could only work nights, but, oh, well—" She laughed softly. "I used to worry about what I'd do when I started to look older, but since I can't see my reflection anymore, that's not going to be a problem."

"They have mirrors in dressing rooms," Megan said. "What are you going to do about that?"

"I don't know. I haven't figured that out yet. But I will."

Megan grunted softly. Shirl was tall and willowy, her skin smooth and clear, her hair thick and lustrous. She would look exactly the same next year, and every year for the rest of her life. "What are you going to do when people start to notice that your appearance never changes?"

"I can always attribute my youthful appearance to good genes and Botox. Look at Dick Clark. He looked the same for years. Anyway, Tomás said I don't have to work unless I want to. He's going to show me the world."

"Well, that's wonderful, I guess, but isn't all this kind of sudden?"

"I guess so," Shirl replied with an airy wave of her hand, "but things are different now. He said he's going to make me his queen!"

"Really?" Megan tapped her fingernails on the edge of the door. If Shirl was going to be a queen, then Tomás must plan to be the king, but king of what?

"He has big plans." Shirl glanced around the room. "Do whatever you want with the rest of my stuff. Keep it, sell it, donate it to charity. Whatever."

"You're happy, then?" Megan asked. "Happy with the way things turned out? Happy being a vampire?"

"More than you can imagine."

"And it doesn't bother you . . . the blood part?"

"Not at all." She moved toward Megan. "Come give me a hug. I've got to go."

Fighting the urge to turn and run, Megan put her arms around Shirl.

"My, but you do smell good," Shirl murmured.

Megan forced herself to stay calm. She had seen enough nature films to know that running from a predator only excited them more.

"I'd better go," Shirl said.

"Let me help you with your suitcases."

"Don't be silly," Shirl said with a laugh. "I could carry all of them, and you, down the stairs with no trouble at all." She picked up her suitcases and a couple of hat boxes and glided toward the door.

Megan followed her to the head of the stairs, then stood watching as Shirl collected her handbag and coat and walked out of the house.

Only after the door had closed behind her former best friend did Megan run downstairs to turn the lock.

"He said he's going to make her a queen?" Rhys shook his head. "How the hell's he going to do that?"

Megan shrugged. "How should I know?"

Rhys had picked her up after work, and now they were sitting at the bar in his club. There were only two other people in the place—a man and a woman slow dancing in the middle of the room. She wondered if they were both vampires.

"What else did she say?"

"What? Oh, she said that I smelled good."

"She got that right," he said with a wry grin. "What else?"

"Something about living on a yacht and staying in California . . ."

"Hold on a minute. Villagrande's planning to stay here, in LA?"

"I guess so. She said he wants a change of scene," Megan replied, and then frowned. "That's not good, is it?"

"No. Dammit!" He slammed his fist on the bar top hard enough to draw the attention of the other couple, who took one look at his face and quickly went back to minding their own business.

"Shirl's changed," Megan said. "She seems more, I don't know, avaricious. She always liked nice things, but now . . . it's different."

"Sometimes becoming a vampire brings out the best in people, and sometimes the worst."

"What did it do for you?" Megan asked curiously.

"It brought out the worst in me." His knuckles glided over her cheek. "But you bring out the best."

"Flatterer."

"It's true." Leaning forward, he kissed her lightly. "Let's

go someplace where we can be alone. I want to make love to you until the sun comes up. . . ." He went suddenly still, his body tense, his eyes narrowing.

"What is it?" Megan asked. "What's wrong?"

"Come on." Taking her by the hand, he pulled her to her feet. "I need to take you home."

"Rhys, what's wrong? You're scaring me."

He shook his head. "Not now. Something's come up. I need to take care of it right away." He hurried her out to the parking lot, then thrust his keys into her hand. "Do you mind driving yourself home?"

"No, I guess not, but—"

"Good." He opened the door for her, then brushed a kiss across her lips. "I'll see you later."

"Well, that was odd," Megan muttered as she watched him walk away, noting again that he seemed to just vanish into the darkness.

It took only moments for Rhys to reach Adrianna's lair. The smell of death was strong, even from a distance. As he drew closer, he caught the scent of another vampire. Villagrande.

Rhys materialized inside Adrianna's lair, a string of curses rising in his throat when he saw what was left of her. There were only a few ways to destroy a vampire—a wooden stake through the heart, prolonged exposure to sunlight, beheading. And perhaps the worst and most excruciating of all—fire. It was the latter method Villagrande had chosen.

Rhys shuddered as he stared at the ashes scattered across the gold-veined marble floor. By sunrise, they would be gone. He had never cared for Adrianna, and she had never liked him, but even if he had wanted to destroy her, he would never have done it like this. It was a cruel thing for one vampire to do to another, he thought, and then frowned. Had Villagrande destroyed Adrianna as an act of vengeance, or was it a warning?

Rhys stood in the center of the meeting room, his gaze moving slowly from the face of one Council member to the other.

Rupert cleared his throat. "So, she's dead? You're sure?"

Rhys nodded. "I'm sure."

"Did you see the body?" Nicholas asked.

"What was left of it."

Seth Adams swore under his breath. "What do we do now?"

Rhys began to pace the floor. "I wish I knew."

Stuart Hastings glanced around the room, his expression hopeful. "Now that he's settled his score with Adrianna, maybe he'll go back where he belongs."

"It's a possibility," Rhys said. "Or maybe it's just the beginning." As succinctly as possible, he relayed what Megan had told him earlier.

"If he plans to make your fledgling a queen, he must plan on becoming a king," Julius remarked, looking pensive.

Winchester looked up from his cell phone, his brow furrowed. "King? King of what?"

Rhys came to an abrupt halt. "That's the question, isn't it? King of what? The city? The States? The whole damn planet!"

"He couldn't do that, could he?" Adams asked. "I mean, he'd have to defeat every Master Vampire in the world."

"That's not possible, is it?" Nicholas asked. "And if he did, where would that leave the rest of us?"

"I'm not paying allegiance to any king!" Julius brought his fist down on the arm of his chair so hard that the wood cracked. "Hell," he muttered with a rueful grin, "it's bad enough that I have to listen to Costain."

Nicholas laughed, then fell silent.

"I don't have any answers," Rhys said. "I called you here tonight to let you know what was going on and to warn you to be careful."

"How are we supposed to protect ourselves?" Winchester asked. "None of us are strong enough to defeat him."

Rhys shook his head. As long as humans didn't invite the Undead into their homes, they were safe behind their thresholds. Rhys didn't really understand why thresholds repelled vampires; he only knew that it worked. In a world of supernatural power, thresholds possessed a strength all their own created by the owner's sense of belonging, of love and family and shared experiences. Unfortunately, vampire thresholds had no such power. If Villagrande came calling, there was no way to keep him out.

"Safety in numbers, maybe," Adams suggested. "It worked during the war."

"It might be worth a try," Rhys said, though he didn't think the Council would go for it. Vampires were notoriously distrustful of their own kind, jealous of their hunting grounds. "You can all stay here if it'll make you feel better."

"What about you?" Winchester asked. "Are you gonna stay here with us?"

"No. If Villagrande's out to take over my territory, you guys should probably stay as far away from me as you can. Maybe you should all take a vacation to the East Coast for as long as he's here."

"You want us to leave you here alone?" Rupert asked.

Adams frowned. "I don't think that's a good idea."

"He needs to stay here," Julius said. "He's the only one who has a chance against Villagrande."

"Let's hope." Rhys slapped his hands against his thighs.

"Unless anyone has anything else to say, this meeting is over."

Rhys didn't hang around to see what the members of the Council decided. He had a sudden need to see Megan, to hold her close while he still could because, unless he was badly mistaken, the preternatural crap was about to hit the fan.

Megan woke to someone quietly calling her name. She smiled as she recognized the soft, seductive voice.

"Rhys." She murmured his name as she sat up and turned on the light. "What are you doing here at this time of the morning?" she asked, glancing at the clock on the nightstand. "It'll be dawn soon."

He sat on the edge of the bed and slipped his arm around her waist. "I needed to see you."

"Is something wrong?"

"Yeah."

She smothered a yawn behind her hand. "Is there anything I can do?"

"No."

"Is this about Shirl?"

"In a way." Leaning forward, he inhaled her scent, then kissed her cheek.

"Rhys, you're scaring me. What's going on?"

"That vampire your friend is tangled up with—Tomás? I think he's after my territory."

"You're not going to fight him for it, are you? I mean . . . are you?"

"I sure as hell hope not."

She looked up at him, her gaze searching his. "You can beat him, can't you?"

"I don't know."

"But . . . don't you have the same powers he does? I mean, aren't all vampires created equal?"

"No. There are a number of variables involved in becoming a vampire. The most important thing is who sired you. If you're made by one of the old ones, you automatically inherit some of his power. The longer you exist, the stronger you get, mentally and physically."

"Who made you?"

"I don't know. I never knew her name, or how old she was. She found me one night and took me to her home. I didn't know what she was. She said she was going to give me a gift, and that she was going to destroy herself when the sun came up." He paused, remembering. "I was young. She was beautiful. We made love all that night, and then, just before dawn, she turned me. When I woke the next night, she was gone. She left me a note telling me what I had become and what I needed to do to survive."

"Do you know who made Villagrande?"

"No. Nobody knows who made him, or how old he is."

"But he's older than you?"

Rhys nodded.

"And that makes him stronger?"

"Right."

"You never told me how old you are," Megan said, momentarily distracted by Rhys's mention of age.

"Sure I did."

"You told me you were twenty-five. Is that the truth?"

"Close to it. I was a week shy of my twenty-first birthday."

Megan groaned softy. "You're only twenty?"

"And you're twenty-nine. It doesn't bother me. Don't let it bother you."

He was right. There was no point in worrying about it, especially now. "So, you're in danger?"

He shrugged, as if it didn't concern him in the least, but

she sensed the tension in him, knew he wasn't as confident as he wanted her to believe.

"What can I do?"

"I don't want you involved in this."

Reaching up, she drew his head down and kissed him. "I'm already involved."

"Villagrande is ruthless, and he plays for keeps."

"What does he want with Shirl?"

Rhys traced the curve of her cheek with the tip of one finger. "What does any man want from a beautiful woman?"

"Don't change the subject."

"I don't know what Villagrande wants. I don't know what he's planning. I only know I've got a bad feeling about the whole thing. It might be wise for us to stay apart for a while. I don't want him finding you through me."

"No! How can you suggest that when we just got back together?"

"Megan, I'm only thinking of your safety."

With a toss of her head, she exclaimed, "I'm not afraid of him!"

That foolish declaration scared him more than anything else. "Well, I am. One more thing. I want you to change the locks on the doors first thing in the morning. If Shirl comes here again, I want you to revoke her welcome."

"What? Why? Oh! Because she's with him now."

"Right the first time."

"And she can invite him inside."

"You catch on quick, darlin'."

"You don't think she'd let him hurt me, do you?"

"I don't know, but it's better to be safe than sorry."

Megan nodded, amazed at how quickly her life had been turned upside down yet again.

Chapter 30

Upon rising the next evening, Rhys went to his club to mull things over. He nodded at several of the regulars, noted that most of the rooms were full.

Sitting at the bar, he ordered a glass of vampire wine. He sipped it slowly, his thoughts turned inward. There was no doubt that Villagrande posed a threat, but until the other vampire made a move, Rhys didn't know how big that threat was.

If Villagrande intended to take over the West Coast, then Rhys had two options. He could stay and fight, or he could surrender and move on. The first option would most likely end in his destruction; the second would destroy his pride.

And then there was Megan. He didn't want her caught up in the middle of things. He didn't know much about Tomás Villagrande except that he could be charming when it suited him. But the charm was only an act. Villagrande was a predator without equal, callous, cruel, and totally merciless. Adrianna was a prime example of Villagrande's ruthlessness. The fact that he would avenge himself on her over something so trivial only proved how brutal he could be.

Rhys dragged a hand over his jaw. Most vampires were coldhearted killers. Hell, he had done his share of killing in the past and would likely do so again. He was a predator. Hunting was second nature to his kind.

A deep breath filled his nostrils with Megan's scent. It clung to his clothes, his skin. Brave little mortal, he thought in amusement, declaring she wasn't afraid of Villagrande. If she knew just how cold and calculating his kind could be, she would run screaming from his presence.

Rhys drained his glass. Until he knew what Villagrande had in mind, he would stay close to Megan. He would guard her house while the sun was down, keep watch outside of Shore's whenever she was there, see that she made it safely home after work. Later tonight, before he sought his lair, he would return to her home and set wards around it to reinforce the power of the threshold.

He looked up when Veronique draped an arm over his shoulders. She was a comely young woman, with long blond hair and hazel eyes. Her slender figure was sheathed in a clingy black knit dress that left little to the imagination. If he'd had a favorite among the women who came to the club, it would have been Veronique.

She smiled at him, a come hither smile that few men—living or Undead—could resist.

"It's been a long time since we shared a room." She had a soft, sexy voice that conjured images of sweaty bodies entwined together. Bending down, she ran her tongue around the inside of his ear. "It's hours until dawn."

With a throaty growl, Rhys pulled her down onto his lap. He kissed her, a careless touching of his lips to hers. A kiss that meant nothing. "Not tonight, my sweet."

"Not even a taste?" she asked, pouting.

"Will that make you happy?"

"You make me happy, *mon coeur.* I've missed you."

Rhys shrugged. "I've been busy."

She knew better than to question him. Instead, she lifted her hair from her neck, then tilted her head to the side in silent invitation.

And because he was fond of her, because he was thirsty, he lowered his head and took what she so freely offered.

Chapter 31

Shirl ran alongside Tomás, thrilling to the speed and power of her new body. When he jumped over an eight-foot fence, she followed him effortlessly. When he scurried up the side of a building as agile as a spider, she did likewise. When he jumped from the roof of the building to the one across the alley, she leaped after him, laughing as she did so. There was nothing to be afraid of. She was practically indestructible. Her headaches had disappeared. She was never tired. She had the strength of twenty men. Every sense was clearer, sharper. Oh, yes, she loved being a vampire. It was like being Wonder Woman, Superwoman, and Catwoman, all rolled into one.

Of course, there were times when she missed her favorite foods, when she yearned to bask in the sun, but Tomás had assured her that her longing for such things would lessen with each passing night until they ceased to matter at all. And she believed him.

Tomás jumped from the roof to the street below and once again, Shirl followed him.

"I've worked up an appetite," he remarked. "How about you?"

She nodded, anticipation rising at the thought of hunting

the night. It was exciting, searching for prey, chasing them down, feeling their fear, listening to the frantic beating of their hearts as they pleaded for help, for mercy. Tomás was a merciless hunter. He never left his prey alive.

Shirl hadn't yet taken a life. She had been tempted, but she couldn't quite bring herself to do it. But she would, because Tomás expected it of her.

The beaches along the coast were his favorite hunting grounds, not only because he loved the sea, but because the ocean made it easy to dispose of the bodies if he was so inclined. They had hunted Manhattan Beach, Marina Del Ray, Laguna, Venice, and Santa Monica. Tonight, he took her to the Hermosa Pier. It was a popular night spot due to its many restaurants, bars, and nightclubs. There were usually long lines on the weekends. Shirl had been a frequent visitor in the past, and she hadn't been above using her celebrity to get to the head of the line.

It took only moments to get from the city to the beach. Tomás agreed to spend a few minutes walking along the shore before they went in search of prey.

After removing her shoes, Shirl waded into the water. She had always loved the beach, the feel of the warm sand between her toes, the whisper of the waves rolling in. Now, with her heightened senses, it was even better. She laughed softly as the waves lapped at her ankles. The air was filled with the bouquet of sand and salt and seaweed. The evening breeze caressed her cheeks and danced in her hair.

She paused as a whiff of prey chased everything else from her mind.

Tomás had smelled it, too. A man and a woman were stretched out on a blanket just a few yards away, so wrapped up in each other they were unaware that they were no longer alone on the beach.

"I'll race you!" Shirl cried, and took off running.

In spite of her head start, Tomás beat her. He was

already bent over the woman's neck when Shirl reached the blanket.

She smiled down at the man, who was looking on in horror. Mesmerized by Tomás, the man was unable to move.

His eyes grew wide with fear when Shirl lifted him to his feet as though he weighed no more than a child.

"Don't be afraid," she cooed. "I'm not going to hurt you." And so saying, she gathered him into her arms, the hunger pounding through every fiber of her being in time to the frantic beat of his heart.

Looking over the man's head, she smiled at Tomás.

"Take him," Tomás said. "You'll never know what it's truly like to be a vampire until you've made your first kill."

Shirl licked her lips. The urge to drain her victims dry was always there when she fed, but so far, she hadn't succumbed to it. She wasn't sure why, but it was a line she was reluctant to cross.

"Are you a vampire or not?" Tomás challenged. "Sooner or later, you have to let go of your old notions of right and wrong. You're a predator now. He's prey. Take him!"

Shirl gazed into the frightened eyes of the man caught in the web of her embrace. She knew Tomás was watching her. How could she disappoint him again?

Experiencing a moment of regret, she smoothed the man's hair from his brow, then glanced at the woman on the blanket. Was she his girlfriend? His wife? Did they have children waiting for them at home? Feeling the weight of Tomás's gaze, she thrust the troubling questions from her mind.

After a murmured, "I'm sorry," she lowered her head, sank her fangs into the man's neck, and drank.

It was intoxicating, the taste of his blood, the thrill of power that moved through her as she subdued his struggles with her superior strength.

Chapter 32

Rhys didn't have to wait long to discover Villagrande's intentions. He had spent the evening with Megan, kissed her good night, and tucked her into bed a little after 1 A.M. He was outside, taking a turn around the house, when his cell phone rang.

"Costain? It's Nicholas. Winchester has been destroyed."

"How do you know?"

"Winchester wanted to watch the football game tonight, so the two of us went to his place. We were playing poker later when Villagrande showed up. He destroyed Winchester before I realized what was happening."

"Why not you?"

"He needed a messenger boy. He told me to tell you he's taking over the West Coast. He said you can either swear allegiance to him or he's going to destroy the rest of us, one by one. And then you."

"Where's the rest of the Council?"

"Here, at the meeting house. We're all here. What are you going to do about Villagrande?"

"I wish I knew."

"None of us are strong enough to take him."

"I know. Have you told the others what happened?"

"Not yet. I called you first."

"What did you do with the body?"

"I left it where it was."

"Okay, I'll take care of it."

"What do you want me to do?"

"Stay there until you hear from me. No one's to leave the house, understood?"

"Yeah."

"And don't say anything until I get there." Muttering an oath, Rhys ended the call. He lingered on the porch for several minutes, his brow furrowed. He needed to dispose of Winchester's body, and then he should probably meet with the Council members and let them know what was going on.

"Dammit!" Rhys dragged a hand through his hair. He had to decide what he was going to do. Villagrande had laid down an unmistakable challenge, and it was up to Rhys to answer it.

"So, what's it gonna be?" he muttered. "Stay and fight? Or tuck your tail between your legs and run like a damn dog?"

He grunted softly. Why hadn't he thought of it before? There was a third option, and one he might have to use if things got any worse.

Chapter 33

Erik Delacourt frowned when his cell phone rang. When he read the time, he knew it couldn't be good news.

Daisy looked up from the book she was reading, a question in her eyes.

"It's Rhys." Erik mouthed the words before he answered the phone. "What's wrong?"

"I'm having a little trouble with Villagrande," Rhys said. "I could use some backup from someone I can trust."

"Villagrande!" Erik exclaimed. "What's going on?"

"He's after the West Coast."

Erik uttered a short, pithy curse. "What makes you think that?"

"He said so."

"The killings across the country?" Erik asked. "Were they . . . ?

"Yeah. You're lucky he didn't get hungry in Boston. He made his way here one body at a time. Earlier tonight, he killed a Council member." Rhys didn't mention Adrianna. That feud had been between her and Villagrande, and Villagrande had the right to settle it as he saw fit, even if Rhys disagreed with his methods.

Erik swore again. "What do you want me to do?"

"Right now I'm only concerned about one thing."

"And that would be?"

"A woman."

Erik stared at the phone, wondering if he'd heard right. "A woman? You mean, a mortal woman?"

"Yeah."

"Is she in danger?"

"I don't know, but I don't want to take any chances."

"She means a lot to you."

It wasn't a question. And Rhys didn't answer. "I was wondering if you'd come and work some of your black magick on her house. I'm not sure a threshold, even one I've warded, is strong enough to keep Villagrande out."

"Do you think it'll come to a fight?"

"I sure as hell hope not. I don't think I could take him."

"We'll be there first thing tomorrow night."

"Thanks. I'll owe you one."

"Right," Erik said, chuckling. "Let's just hope you're around to pay up."

"What was that all about?" Daisy asked after he ended the call.

"Do you remember Tomás Villagrande?"

"How could I forget him?"

Erik grunted softly. Not so long ago, Villagrande had kidnapped Daisy's father and brother. He remembered it as if it had happened yesterday. He had tracked Daisy's father and brother to Villagrande's yacht. . . .

Going below, Erik followed the vampire's scent into a stateroom where he found the two O'Donnell men lying on the floor, bound and apparently under some kind of preternatural enchantment. He was moving toward them when he realized he was no longer alone.

Erik whirled around, fangs extended, and came face-to-face with one of his kind. Clad in a pair of black trousers and a loose-fitting white shirt, the vampire was tall and lean and looked to be in his late twenties, though his aura was much older.

"What are you doing here?" the vampire asked. His voice was mild, though his eyes blazed red.

"I know these two," Erik said, gesturing at Daisy's father and brother. "They're not to be harmed."

The other vampire lifted one brow. "Indeed?"

Erik nodded.

"They violated my lair. They tried to destroy me. I am within my rights to do with them as it pleases me. And it pleases me to kill them."

"I'm afraid I can't allow you to do that."

"No? Who are you?"

"Erik Delacourt."

"Ah."

"You know me?" Erik asked.

"I have heard of you. It is said you are a close friend of Costain's."

Erik nodded, wondering if that was good or bad. "Who the hell are you?"

"Tomás Villagrande."

Erik swore under his breath. Villagrande was the Master of the East Coast Vampires, and was even older than Rhys. It was rumored among the ranks of the Undead that Villagrande had been one of the first of their kind, that it was Villagrande who had bequeathed the Dark Gift to Dracula himself. Erik didn't know if that was true, but Villagrande's preternatural power was unmistakable.

Villagrande folded his arms over his chest. "Why do you care if these two live or die?"

"They're related to someone I hold dear."

"That does change things, does it not?" Villagrande mused aloud. "And yet the fact remains that they are mine."

Tension thrummed through Erik as he summoned his power. If the other vampire wanted a fight, so be it, although pitting his strength against that of a much older vampire seemed like suicide.

"This someone you hold dear, is it a woman?"

"Yes."

"Ah. And is she young and beautiful beyond compare?"

Erik nodded even as he wondered what game Villagrande was playing.

"You are in love with her?"

"Yes."

"An overrated emotion to be sure," Villagrande remarked, his voice melancholy. "Yet I confess that I, too, have been caught in that snare from time to time. Tell me, are you willing to challenge me in combat to save these two?"

Erik swore inwardly. He had hoped it wouldn't come to that, but he couldn't go back to Daisy and tell her he had failed. Better not to return at all. "If I have to."

Villagrande stroked his chin as he contemplated Erik's decision. "She means that much to you, this woman?"

"And more."

Villagrande laughed softly. "I do not wish to kill you. You have trouble enough. Take them and go."

"Just like that?"

"Just like that." Villagrande smiled, showing a hint of fang. "Never let it be said that Tomás Villagrande stood in the way of true love. As for your inept friends here, I am surprised they have survived as long as they have. They should wake in half an hour or so. You might tell them to be more careful in the future," he said, and with a wave of his hand, he vanished.

"So, what did Rhys have to say?" Daisy asked.

"It seems Villagrande is planning a takeover of the West Coast," Erik replied, and quickly relayed what Rhys had told him over the phone.

"What was that about a woman?"

"I think our Mr. Costain has fallen in love," Erik said with a grin.

"No way!"

Erik nodded. "I think he's in love big-time."

"So, we're going to California?" Daisy remarked.

"Looks that way."

"I can't wait. I'm anxious to meet the woman who finally captured his heart. And maybe," she said, her eyes twinkling, "we'll even find time for a midnight stroll on the beach."

Chapter 34

"Rhys!" Megan pressed a hand to her heart. She hadn't anticipated finding him waiting for her in the garage. "What are you doing here? I didn't expect to see you until later."

"I thought I'd drive you to work tonight."

"Oh?"

"We'll have to take your car. I left mine at home."

She looked at him curiously. He wore a black long-sleeved shirt over a white T-shirt, black jeans, and boots. His hair gleamed like dark gold in the glow of the overhead light. Dark and dangerous, she thought, no doubt about it. "What aren't you telling me?"

"Villagrande's on the rampage again. He killed one of my vampires earlier tonight. It isn't safe for you to be alone outside of your house." He paused a moment, then decided she needed to know it all. "And maybe not inside."

Megan felt a cold chill at the mention of Villagrande's name. She had told Rhys she wasn't afraid of the other vampire, but it had been nothing but bravado.

Rhys opened the passenger door for her, and she got into the car. She had once thought her life completely boring. And then she met Rhys.

He slid behind the wheel, switched on the engine and the lights, hit the garage door opener, and backed out of the driveway. "Have you heard from Shirl?"

"No. Do you think she knows what Villagrande is planning?"

"Probably." He pulled onto the street.

"Maybe I should just stay home tonight," Megan suggested, and hated how cowardly that sounded. And yet, she didn't have the physical strength to fight off a vampire, even if she knew how. She didn't have any super powers. And she was pretty sure a can of pepper spray wouldn't be much of a deterrent.

Rhys slowed the car. "Do you want to go back home?"

"Yes. No. I don't know."

"It's up to you."

Megan tapped her foot on the floorboard, then blew out a sigh. "Mr. Parker's expecting me."

"That's my brave girl," Rhys murmured, and hoped neither of them would regret it.

Things were quiet at the store that night. Megan was ever aware that Rhys was just outside, watching her every move. She assured herself she was perfectly safe, that Rhys wouldn't let any harm come to her, and yet she felt herself tensing every time a man she didn't recognize entered the shop.

She was relieved when quitting time came.

"So," she asked when they were in the car on the way home, "what are you going to do about Villagrande?"

"I've called in some outside help."

"Really? Who?"

"Erik Delacourt and his wife, Daisy."

"Are they vampires, too?"

"Yeah. Delacourt and I go back a long way. His wife's

only been a vampire a short time." He grunted softly. "She used to steal vampire blood and sell it on the Net. Her brothers were hunters. The younger one was killed by a vampire."

"And she still wanted to be one?"

"Not exactly. I destroyed the last vampire who wanted to take over the city. Mariah wasn't nearly as strong as Villagrande, or as up front about it. She offered a reward for my head. I took hers instead. Delacourt, Daisy, and her brother, Alex, all had a hand in it. Apparently Mariah had a boyfriend. He went after Daisy and almost killed her. Delacourt brought her across to save her life."

"It isn't really life," Megan murmured, then bit her tongue, hoping she hadn't hurt his feelings.

"Maybe not, but she seems damn happy with the way things turned out. I think you'll like her."

Megan shook her head. Not long ago, she hadn't believed vampires existed. How times had changed. Her former roommate was a vampire. She was in love with a vampire. And now she was going to meet two more, and possibly one that wanted to kill her.

Suddenly, her old, boring life didn't seem half so bad.

And when Rhys showed up at her door the next night with two vampires in tow, Megan began to wonder if her life would ever be normal again.

Erik Delacourt was long-legged and broad-shouldered. He could have been the poster boy for vampires, she mused, with his thick black hair and striking black eyes. He appeared to be in his thirties, but with vampires, you never knew how old they really were. His wife, Daisy, looked like she was in her midtwenties. She had heavily lashed green eyes and long, reddish-brown hair. Megan thought she looked more like a country girl than a former Blood Thief turned vampire.

Megan invited the newcomers into the house. After

Rhys made the introductions, Erik and Daisy sat on the love seat, holding hands, while Megan and Rhys shared the sofa.

One thing about vampire guests, Megan thought as she tried to relax, she didn't have to worry about offering them refreshments. And then she grimaced because, among less friendly vampires, she would have been considered the snack.

"Perhaps we should have had this meeting somewhere else," Daisy said quietly. "I don't think Megan's very comfortable, having us here."

At Daisy's remark, Rhys ran his knuckles lightly over Megan's cheek. "Do you want us to leave?"

"No, of course not," she said quickly.

"You've nothing to fear from us," Erik assured her.

"I'm not worried," Megan said, surprised to find that it was true.

"Rhys has asked me to come here and use my witchcraft to add a protective spell to your house."

"You're a witch, too?" Megan asked, unable to hide her astonishment. Mortals and vampires and witches. Oh, my.

Erik nodded, his eyes twinkling with amusement.

"What kind of spell?" Megan asked.

"Nothing too complicated. It will repel any unwelcome visitors from entering your house. And since I don't know how powerful Villagrande is, it will also keep him from materializing inside, uninvited."

"You're sure it will work?" she asked.

"Guaranteed. Of course, I won't do it without your permission."

"You've got it."

Erik smiled at her. "I'll take care of it later tonight."

Megan nodded. At this point, she would take all the protection she could get. Since vampires were real, who knew what other mythological creatures might be stalking the shadows?

"So," Erik said to Rhys, "do you have any plans for besting this interloper?"

"Not really. You've met him. Do you think I've got a chance against him?"

"I don't know. I've felt his power, and it's stronger than anything I've ever come up against. I guess it all depends on how badly you want to remain Master of the City."

"Yeah," Rhys muttered. "That's the real question, isn't it?"

"Why don't you just leave?" Daisy asked. "What's so special about LA?"

Erik and Rhys exchanged glances.

"It's more than that," Rhys said. "If I leave, it's like admitting I'm afraid."

"What's wrong with being afraid?" Megan asked.

Erik and Rhys exchanged glances again.

Megan looked at Daisy. "Men," she said. "They're all the same."

"Tell me about it," Daisy said, grinning. "Man or vampire, it doesn't matter. You should meet my brother, Alex. He's Mr. Macho personified."

"It's not just about male pride," Rhys said irritably. "In the human world, it doesn't make much of a difference if you're a coward. In my world, it's a sign of weakness, and like the song says, only the strong survive."

"I guess that settles it, then," Erik said. "If he wants a fight, we'll give it to him."

"There is no 'we,'" Rhys said emphatically. "I only asked you here to help fortify Megan's house." He took Megan's hand in his. "And to look after her, if anything happens to me."

"Don't say that!" Megan exclaimed. "Nothing's going to happen to you."

Rhys squeezed her hand. "I hope not, but I have to know you'll be okay, just in case."

"I've got a spell that might protect her," Erik remarked.

"Are you talking about the same one you used against me?" Rhys asked. It had been the first time since he'd become a vampire that his powers had failed him. He didn't know what kind of spell Erik had concocted, but it had seemed as if an invisible barrier had surrounded him, trapping him inside. If Erik had wanted to take his life, Rhys wouldn't have been able to stop him.

"It's the same type of spell, but instead of rendering Megan helpless and immobile, it would repel Villagrande's power."

"If it will protect me, you should use it on Rhys, too," Megan said.

"Probably wouldn't hurt," Erik said. "Of course, I'd have to beef it up for it to work against Villagrande."

Rhys shook his head. "You're not using it on me."

"Why not?" Megan asked.

"The odds of beating Villagrande in a fair fight are pretty slim," Erik remarked. "But you know that."

"Of course I know it! Dammit!" Rhys raked his fingers through his hair.

"Honor among vampires? Is that it?" Megan asked in disbelief. "Villagrande wants to kill you. You said yourself he's stronger than you are. What have you got against leveling the playing field, so to speak?"

"Because it's cheating. No one on the Council is going to respect me if they find out I used black magick to immobilize my enemy so I could destroy him." He shook his head. "It's like shooting him in the back."

"Sounds like a good idea to me," Daisy muttered.

"I guess it would, to a former hunter," Erik said good-naturedly.

"Hold on a minute!" Megan said. "I don't mind your

working your hocus pocus on my house, but I don't think I want anybody working black magick on me."

"It isn't black magick," Erik said. "Just a little witchcraft."

She shook her head emphatically. "No way."

"Megan, my love," Rhys said, "don't be stubborn."

"Why not?" she retorted. "You are."

Rhys blew out an exasperated sigh. "It's different with me."

"All right, you two," Erik said. "This isn't getting us anywhere. We can take the matter up again tomorrow. I'll go out and put the wards on the house, and then I need to find a place where Daisy and I can spend the day."

"You can stay in my penthouse, if you like," Rhys offered. "I'll be staying here."

Megan looked at him, obviously surprised by this bit of news, but she didn't object.

Erik nodded. "Thanks."

Rising, Rhys pulled Megan to her feet. "I'm going to go let them in, and then I'll be back."

"Be careful."

"Don't worry."

"Right."

Rhys drew her into his arms and kissed her soundly, then kissed her again, more tenderly. "I won't be gone long."

He followed Erik and Daisy outside, stood with Daisy while Erik cast a protective spell around the house. Supernatural power electrified the air. Rhys swore softly as it danced over his skin like thousands of tiny shocks, raising the short hairs along his arms and the back of his neck.

"That spell we talked about for Megan," Rhys said when Erik finished casting the protective wards on Megan's house. "Can you work it on her without her knowing?"

"Sure, that won't be a problem. The only thing is, I don't know if I can make it strong enough to repel Villagrande."

"Just do your best."

"But Megan said . . ."

"Never mind what she said. Just do it."

"All right. I'll come back and take care of it later tonight."

"Thanks. Guess I owe you another one."

It took only minutes for the three of them to transport themselves to Rhys's penthouse. Rhys let Erik and Daisy in, invited them to make themselves at home, then quickly returned to Megan's. She opened the door before he rang the bell.

"What the hell are you doing?" he demanded angrily. "Why didn't you . . . ?"

"Blood bond," she reminded him with a saucy grin. "I knew it was you."

"Think you're pretty smart, don't you?" he muttered as he closed and locked the door.

She stood on her tiptoes, pulled his head down, and kissed him. "It's going to be morning soon," she said, nipping at his lower lip. "Do you want to stand here and argue until dawn?"

"What do you think?" Swinging her into his arms, he carried her swiftly up the stairs and down the hall to her bedroom. "I think I can find a better way to pass the time."

Chapter 35

"What about Megan?" Shirl asked as she slid under the covers beside Tomás. "What's going to happen to her?"

He shrugged negligently. "I have no quarrel with her."

"But she's in love with Rhys."

"That's unfortunate."

"I don't understand why you want to rule the West Coast," Shirl said, frowning. "I'd be perfectly happy to live in New York."

"You'll understand, in time." Villagrande stroked her hair, a faraway look in his eyes. "When you live for hundreds of years, you can't help becoming bored now and then. I've grown weary of the East, so I've decided to stay here a while."

"But why does Rhys have to leave?"

"Master Vampires don't share their territory."

She considered that a moment before asking, "What if he won't leave?"

The sudden narrowing of Villagrande's eyes gave her all the answer she needed.

Shirl rested her head on his shoulder. She was intrigued by Tomás, awed by his power, addicted to his lovemaking. He had taught her much about being a vampire in the last few days, had regaled her with stories of his past. He had traveled the world many times, seen everything there was to see. It was almost impossible to comprehend just how old he was. He wasn't sure exactly when he was born, but he had known ancient kings and queens, fought in many battles in many countries, both on land and sea, visited America before the white man came.

Living with him was exhilarating, fascinating. And a little frightening. He had been a vampire for so long, he seemed to have forgotten that he had once been human. After eons of being a vampire, he viewed mankind as nothing more than prey, to do with as he wished. He drank from the males. Dallied with the females. Sometimes he toyed with them before taking them. But he always killed them in the end.

She had disappointed him the other night. He had urged her to make her first kill, and even though she had wanted to please him, she hadn't been able to do it. The fact that he killed indiscriminately frightened her. Would she one day be as cold and callous as he was? He had no friends that she knew of. He had lived alone on his fancy yacht for decades before she met him. Thinking of friends brought Megan to mind again. Though she refused to admit it, she missed Megan's friendship more than she would have thought possible.

Thoughts of Megan faded into the distance when Tomás reached for her. Shirl had been intimate with only two men in her lifetime, but they both paled beside him. She wondered how many other women he had loved.

She had asked him once, and he had laughed. It was the first time she had heard him laugh with such open amusement. When she had insisted on knowing what was so funny, he had patted her on the head as if she were a little girl who had asked a silly question.

"Ah, my sweet innocent," he had replied, still grinning. "Do you really expect me to remember after so many years?"

Now, as his hands moved masterfully over her body, she didn't care if he had made love to one woman or a million. It didn't matter. Nothing mattered but the touch of his hands deftly arousing her, the painful pleasure of his fangs against her skin, the unequaled delight of his flesh melding with hers.

She clung to him, never more vitally alive than when Tomás made love to her. With her enhanced senses, she was acutely aware of everything around her—the tangy scent of the salt air, the gentle rocking of the boat, the sound of waves lapping against the hull. But, most of all, she was aware of the man who brought her to fulfillment again and again before the rising sun chased the moon and stars from the sky.

Chapter 36

When Megan woke in the morning, she was alone in bed. She frowned, wondering when Rhys had left, and where he had gone. After inviting Daisy and Erik to stay at his penthouse, Rhys had indicated he would be spending the day at her place. Had he changed his mind and decided to go home?

Sitting up, she hugged Rhys's pillow to her chest, then buried her face in its softness, inhaling his unique scent. He had never stayed over. Why not, she wondered, then shook her head. How could she be so obtuse? He obviously didn't want her to see him while he was at rest. She wondered if there was some kind of vampire law that prohibited vampires from spending the daylight hours with mortals? She shook her head. That sounded preposterous, even to her. So, what reason could there be? Was it because he looked dead when he slept?

The thought made her shudder. She hadn't given much thought to that part of being a vampire. She knew they took their rest during the day, but she had assumed they slept like everyone else. Did he dream?

Did he wear pajamas? Somehow, she didn't think so,

but if he did, she was certain it would be bottoms only. Black silk.

Did he sleep in a coffin? She had been to his penthouse, seen his bedroom. No sign of a coffin there, but that didn't mean he didn't have one stashed away somewhere else.

Shaking off her morbid thoughts, she went into the bathroom to shower and get dressed.

Megan had just finished breakfast when a delivery man arrived with a single, perfect red rose in a smoked crystal bud vase. She didn't have to read the card to know it was from Rhys, but of course, she read it anyway. It said simply, "I love you. RC."

An hour later, another delivery man showed up on her doorstep bearing two red roses in a blown glass vase with a card that said, "I'm counting the hours until I can see you again. RC."

She received four red roses and a heart-shaped balloon an hour later. The note said, "I'm thinking of you. RC."

She was waiting at the door when the next delivery arrived. Eight perfect red roses in an elegant silver vase, and a heart-shaped box of Belgian dark chocolates. The note said, "I can't wait to kiss the chocolate off your lips. RC."

An hour later, she received sixteen long-stemmed blood red roses in a Waterford crystal vase. The card read, "See you soon, my love. RC."

Whether she was changing the sheets on her bed or mopping the kitchen floor, Megan couldn't stop smiling. He loved her. She laughed softly as she stuffed a load of towels into the dryer. Sure, he was a vampire, but no relationship was perfect. They still had a lot of issues to discuss and decide, but she was confident they could work things out. And if they couldn't . . . ? She shook her doubts aside, determined to ignore the negative and focus on the positive.

Megan had just finished clearing the dinner dishes when

the doorbell rang. She glanced around the living room as she went to answer the door, thinking the room looked like a florist shop that specialized in exquisite red roses.

She smiled as she started to open the door and then, without knowing why, she hesitated, her hand on the latch. "Who is it?"

"It's me, Shirl. Why won't my key work?"

"I changed the lock," Megan said, and then, taking a deep breath, she added, "You're not welcome here."

"Meggie, what are you saying?"

"I'm sorry, but you can't come in." Megan closed her eyes against a sudden rush of tears. Shirl had been her best friend for years. And then she frowned, certain that Shirl wasn't alone. She could almost taste the preternatural power coming from the other side of the door, power far too strong to belong to a fledgling vampire.

"Meggie, I can't believe you're doing this."

"Are you alone?"

There was a brief pause before Shirl said, "Of course I'm alone."

A peek through the peephole showed that Shirl was lying. A tall man clad in a dark green shirt, brown pants, and boots stood off to the side.

"Villagrande." The name whispered past Megan's lips. According to Rhys, Villagrande was the oldest vampire in the world. What was he doing here?

"Indeed." His voice was deep, tinged with an accent Megan didn't recognize

She took a step backward, discomfited by the knowledge that he had heard her murmur his name. Taking a deep breath, she looked through the peephole again, watched as he reached for the door handle. What was he doing? He couldn't enter without an invitation. Could he? Maybe the rules no longer applied when a vampire was as old as he was.

She waited, hardly daring to breathe, as his hand curled around the doorknob.

There was a flash of bright white light, a crackle like static electricity, followed by a sharp curse from Villagrande.

Megan recoiled. And then she grinned. It was obvious that whatever magical whammy Erik Delacourt had placed around her house was working perfectly.

Her grin faded as quickly as it had come. Rhys would be arriving soon to take her to work. What would happen if he showed up while Villagrande was still there? Would they battle it out on her front porch?

When she looked through the peephole again, Shirl and Villagrande were nowhere to be seen.

Rhys swore softly when Megan told him what had happened with Shirl earlier that evening.

"Why do you think he came here?" It was a question she was reluctant to ask because she was sure she wouldn't like the answer.

"Could be a lot of reasons," Rhys said. "Maybe he just wanted to see where you live. Maybe he was looking for me."

"You left out the most logical reason," Megan said. "That he wanted to use me to get to you."

Rhys nodded. He hadn't wanted to suggest that, but he should have known Megan was smart enough to reach that conclusion on her own. Just as surely as there was crap and corruption in Washington, he was sure that had been Villagrande's motive.

"At least Erik's magick spell worked," Megan said, looking on the bright side. "You should have seen the way Villagrande jumped when he tried to open the door. It was almost comical."

"Yeah. Sorry I missed that."

"Where did you spend the day?" she asked, unable to stay her curiosity any longer.

"At my club."

"Why didn't you stay here?"

The wary look in his eyes warned her not to pursue the subject, making her think she had guessed right earlier. He didn't want her to see him when he was at rest. But why?

"So," she asked, going back to their original conversation, "what do we do now?" She tried to keep her voice even, but she wasn't completely successful.

Rhys was tempted to take Megan to his lair, but in the long run, he thought she would be safer here. He was about to tell her so when his cell rang. He answered it with a curt, "What?"

"It's me," Rupert said, his voice equally curt. "The meeting house is on fire. I'm afraid Adams didn't make it out. I think he was the only casualty."

"Where are you now?"

"We scattered. I'm in Phoenix. I don't know where the others have gone."

Rhys swore softly. He had told the Council to stay together, thinking there would be safety in numbers. He didn't often make mistakes, but he'd miscalculated badly this time.

"I want you to get in touch with the others," Rhys said. "Tell them to head for the Midwest. When you get there, get in touch with Volger. Tell him I'm calling in the favor he owes me."

"Volger, right. What are you going to do?"

"I don't know. Just do as I say. I'll be in touch." Rhys disconnected the call without waiting for a reply.

"What is it?" Megan asked. "What's happened?"

"Villagrande burned down a house I own. One of my vampires was destroyed in the blaze."

"I'm so sorry." Shivering, Megan wrapped her arms

around her waist. Being burned alive had to be the most horrible way to die. Thinking about the vampire who had perished in the fire brought back the horror of the inferno at Drexel's concert and reminded her of how lucky she was to still be alive.

"I need to go check out the house," Rhys said. "Make sure Adams was the only casualty."

Megan looked up at him, her gaze searching his face. "Do you think that's a good idea?"

"Probably not, but I'm going anyway. You stay here. Keep the door locked. Don't talk to anyone. Don't let anyone but me inside."

"Be careful."

He kissed her, hard and quick, and then he was gone amidst a flurry of sparkling silver motes.

Megan shook her head. Just when she thought she had seen all his spooky tricks, he did something totally unexpected.

Rhys materialized at the end of the street. The fire department was still at the scene. The acrid stink of burnt wood and smoke hung heavy in the air, along with a smell that Rhys recognized as vampire remains.

He made his way closer to the house, mingling with a handful of curious neighbors. Standing there, he listened to the conversations around him.

"We never saw anybody in the house," a man remarked to one of the firemen. "And we never saw any lights. . . ."

"Yes, we did," the woman said. "But it flickered, you know, like candlelight."

"Yeah, that's right," the man agreed, as if it wasn't very important. "We never saw anybody around during the day, though. If it wasn't for the cars we saw parked in the driveway now and then, and the fact that a gardener came to mow the lawn, we would have thought the house was haunted. . . ."

"Wonder how it started . . ."

"I never saw a house go up so fast," muttered a tall, dark-haired man clad in gray sweatpants. "You'd have thought it was made out of flash paper. Strangest thing I've ever seen."

A woman holding a baby nodded. "Whoosh!" she said. "Just like that, it was gone."

"I heard a scream," said an elderly woman in a bright pink bathrobe. "It was horrible. Gave me the shivers, it did."

When the firemen started packing up, Rhys went around to the back of the house. Closing his eyes, he opened his senses. Adams had died in the hallway. There was no way to tell if Adams had been destroyed by Villagrande or by the flames, but he was the only casualty. Villagrande's scent was strong here in the backyard. And Shirl's, too. Had she participated in starting the fire, or had she merely been an observer? Not that it mattered. As far as Rhys was concerned, she was equally culpable in Adams's destruction.

Sifting through the ashes, he found himself wondering what type of incendiary material Villagrande had used to start the fire. It was obvious that the blaze had burned hot and fast. The only thing left intact was a small portion of the brick fireplace. Rhys muttered an oath as he dusted off his hands. Either someone had stolen the sword he had kept over the fireplace, or it, too, had perished in the blaze.

"What happened?"

Rhys slid a glance at the vampire who had materialized beside him. "Villagrande happened."

Erik's gaze swept over what was left of the house. "He's not fooling around, is he?"

"How'd you know I was here?"

"We went by Megan's. She wouldn't let us in, and she

wouldn't talk to us. I left Daisy there to keep watch while I followed your scent here."

"One of my vampires perished in the fire. That's three of mine he's destroyed."

"He's going to keep pushing until you quit the field or you agree to meet with him."

"He was at Megan's earlier tonight. Shirl tried to get her to open the door."

"He plays dirty, Rhys. You know that."

Rhys nodded. Foolish as it seemed, he had expected better from the oldest vampire in the world. Then again, maybe playing dirty was how you survived long enough to become the oldest vampire in the world.

"You know you can't beat him on your own," Erik said quietly.

"We've already had this discussion," Rhys said curtly. "There's nothing more to be done here. I'm going back to Megan's."

Without waiting for a reply, he dissolved into mist.

Erik was right behind him.

Daisy was waiting for them on the front porch of Megan's house. Erik kissed his wife on the cheek while Rhys knocked on the door.

When there was no reply, Rhys called, "Megan, it's me. Open up."

"How do I know it's you?"

Hearing the teasing tone of her voice, he said, "I could tell you how many times we made love last night."

Soft laughter rose in the air as she unlocked the door. "Is nothing sacred?"

"Not much." Rhys stepped into the entryway, followed by Daisy and Delacourt. Erik locked the door behind them.

Rhys took Megan in his arms. "Are you okay?"

She nodded. "Did you find any more . . . anyone else?"

"No. Adams was the only fatality."

"What are we going to do now?"

Rhys kissed the tip of her nose. "*We* aren't going to do anything. This is between me and Villagrande and no one else."

"How can you say that?" Megan exclaimed. "Shirl and Villagrande were both here, trying to get in. I'm pretty sure they weren't just stopping by for a cup of coffee. I mean, Shirl lied to me!"

"She's got a point," Erik said.

"A darn good one, I'd say," Daisy added.

With a shake of his head, Rhys pulled Megan into his arms. "All right, you foolish woman. What do you think we ought to do?"

"Leave town," Megan said quickly.

Rhys looked at Daisy. "What do you think?"

"I agree with Megan. There's a whole world out there. Why shed blood over a few acres?"

Erik laughed at her quick reply.

Rhys snorted softly. "For the last time, I'm not slinking out of town like some whipped cur."

Megan exhaled sharply. "You and your silly pride."

"Sometimes it's all a man's got to call his own," Rhys said quietly.

Erik nodded. "Better to go out with a bang than a whimper, right?"

"Exactly," Rhys said.

And that, Megan thought glumly, was that.

Chapter 37

On Monday night, Rhys thanked Erik and Daisy for their help. Megan had expected them to be anxious to return to Boston, so she was surprised when Daisy said she wanted to stay for another week or so.

"I haven't been to Beverly Hills yet," she explained with a sidelong glance at Erik.

"I'll be broke by the time I get her out of those shops," Erik complained, but he was smiling when he said it.

Daisy just grinned. "Let's go find a nice hotel," she suggested. She gave Megan a hug and Rhys a kiss on the cheek, then with a final wave, she and Erik left the house.

The next few days passed peacefully enough. Rhys continued to drive Megan back and forth to work. He kept watch from outside while she was at Shore's, and slept by her side until dawn.

Megan hadn't heard anything more from Shirl. In spite of everything, Megan missed her roommate. Good friends were hard to find. She wondered if they could ever be friends again now that Shirl had been turned and she was living with Villagrande. She still had a faint hope that it might be possible once Shirl learned to control her thirst.

After all, Megan thought, who was she to judge Shirl's choice of men when she, herself, had a vampire lover?

As far as Megan knew, Rhys hadn't heard from Villagrande. She couldn't decide if that was good or bad.

"Maybe he changed his mind," Megan suggested when Rhys drove her to work on Saturday night.

"No, he's still here. He's up to something, I just don't know what." Rhys drummed his fingertips on the steering wheel. Villagrande had threatened to destroy the members of the Vampire Council one by one and then come for Rhys. But he seemed to have backed off since destroying Adams. Maybe it was only a reprieve while Villagrande dallied with Shirl. Or maybe Megan was right and Villagrande had indeed had a change of heart.

When they reached Shore's, Rhys parked the car, then walked Megan across the parking lot to the back entrance.

"Do you really think it's necessary for you to stay here every night?" she asked. "I mean, it must be terribly boring, watching me all night long."

"Not at all." He slipped his hands around her waist and kissed the tip of her nose. "I can't think of anything else I'd rather do."

"Right."

"Time doesn't have the same meaning for me that it does for you," he reminded her.

She supposed that was true. What were a few wasted hours when he had centuries ahead of him?

He kissed her again, then opened the back door. "Send a smile my way now and then."

It was near the end of her shift when Mr. Parker poked his head out of the office, a sour expression on his face. "Phone for you."

Megan nodded. Mr. Parker was a sweetheart about most things, but the one thing he frowned on was personal calls at work, so Megan always kept her cell phone off.

Mr. Parker left the office, giving Megan her privacy.

"Hello?"

"Megan, it's Shirl."

"Shirl, this is a surprise. Is everything all right?"

"Of course."

"So, do you still like being . . ." Megan paused and peered out the door to make sure no one could overhear her conversation. "A vampire."

"It's wonderful, Meggie. I wish you'd think about it."

"Are you kidding? No way!"

"Well, I'll keep hoping. Think how much fun we could have. We could room together again."

And hunt together. Megan frowned. Had Shirl spoken those words aloud?

"There's so much to do," Shirl was saying. "So much to see. Everything is new and exciting. Megan, you can't believe how wonderful it is. I have so much energy, and I'm never tired, and—"

"I'm glad you're happy. Are you still with Villagrande?"

"Yes, but he scares me a little. He can be really intense at times."

"Is he still planning to take over Rhys's territory?"

"I don't know. He's out of town right now."

"Oh? Where did he go?"

"He told me but I don't remember," Shirl said. "He said he had some kind of vampire business to take care of. I don't suppose you'd consider getting together tomorrow night, maybe go see a movie."

"I don't know."

"I guess you still don't trust me."

Megan stared into the distance. Neither one of them had family nearby and so, in good times or bad, they had always turned to each other. She remembered the fun times, the silly times, all the laughs they had shared. And the sad times, when they had comforted one another. Once, she would have trusted Shirl with her life. But now . . . how could she, when her roommate was so changed?

"Megan?"

"How can I trust you when you lied to me the other night?"

Shirl was quiet for a long moment, so long that Megan wondered if she was still on the line.

"I couldn't help it," Shirl said. "Tomás told me to."

"Do you do everything he says?"

"No, but—"

"I can't talk anymore. I have to get back to work. Why don't you call me tomorrow night?"

"All right," Shirl agreed.

Megan felt a twinge of guilt when she heard the disappointment in Shirl's voice.

"I miss you, girlfriend," Shirl said quietly.

"I miss you, too. Good night."

Megan hung up the receiver, then stood there, replaying the conversation in her mind, until Mr. Parker knocked on the door.

"You through in here?" he asked. "Clark's out front waiting for you."

With a nod, Megan pasted a smile on her face and went out to wait on her least favorite client.

Later that night, on the way home from work, Megan told Rhys about her conversation with Shirl. "I told her to call me tomorrow night." She looked at Rhys and shook her head. "I don't know what to do."

"She said Villagrande's out of town?"

"Yes. Is that important?"

"I don't know. Did she say how long he's going to be gone or where he was going?"

"No. So, do you think I should see her?"

Rhys pulled into the driveway and killed the engine. "What does your gut tell you?"

"I don't know. I miss my friend, but I don't know if I trust the vampire. What should I do?"

"It's up to you."

"You don't trust her, do you?"

"Right now, I don't trust anyone."

Megan heaved a sigh. "I think I have to see her."

Rhys nodded. He wanted to see Shirl, too. He was beginning to think bringing her across had been a mistake. "Whatever you decide, I'll be there with you. Wait here."

As he had every night, Rhys got out of the car, his senses probing the night. Only when he was certain that Villagrande hadn't been there did he pull into the garage.

Inside the house, Megan turned on the lights, dropped down on the sofa, and kicked off her shoes.

Seeing the look on her face, Rhys sat beside her. "Give me your foot."

She turned sideways on the sofa and obligingly placed her left foot in his hand. She sighed as he began to massage her ankle. "That feels wonderful." She closed her eyes, reveling in the soothing touch of his hands.

A few minutes later, he lifted her other foot.

"You're in the wrong business," she murmured. "You should be a masseur."

"Is that right?" His hand moved up, his fingers kneading her calf.

"I'll give you an hour to stop that."

"Only an hour?"

"I'm easy," she said. "Take two."

His hand slid farther up her leg, stroking the tender flesh of her inner thigh. "Two hours should be just about right." And so saying, he swung her into his arms and carried her swiftly up the stairs to her room.

The light came on, seemingly of its own accord, as he

laid her on the bed. His clothing disappeared as if by magic, and then he stretched out beside her, his hands and lips teasing, touching, tasting, as he undressed her.

She clung to him, every nerve humming with anticipation, her heart beating in time with his, her hands restless as she caressed him in return.

"Open to me, Megan." His voice washed over her, softly entreating. He was asking for more than her physical surrender. Wanting to please him, she lowered every inhibition, letting their minds merge so that each caress was shared. She knew his thoughts, sensed his pleasure when she rained kisses on his cheeks, his neck, his chest. She experienced his desire, so different from her own, and yet the perfect complement to hers.

She writhed beneath him, lost in his touch, yearning for more, more. She cried his name as he rose over her, his eyes dark, glowing with need, with a craving she would never understand or share.

"Let me." His voice was ragged with longing, with a need she couldn't begin to imagine.

And because she loved him, because she wanted to please him, she turned her head to the side, giving him access to her throat. She moaned softly when he bit her, the faint sting swallowed up in the sensual pleasure that exploded through her as his body melded with hers. The sheer wonder of it was almost more than she could bear as she experienced his climax as well as her own.

Drifting, floating somewhere between worlds, she ran her hands over his shoulders and down his arms, marveling at the latent strength that flexed beneath her questing fingertips. His hair, soft and silky, brushed her cheek as he lowered his head to kiss her, a long, slow kiss that had her wanting him again.

"So soon?" He nuzzled her neck, his tongue hot against her cooling flesh.

"Only if you want to."

"Silly question," he murmured, and then he was moving inside her again, carrying her away to heights only he could climb, evoking sensations only he could arouse.

He was gone in the morning, but she was used to that by now. At loose ends, nervous at the thought of seeing Shirl later, Megan did something she hadn't done in months. She went to church.

Not wanting to talk to anyone, she arrived a few minutes late. Slipping into the back row, she closed her eyes and listened to the choir. They were singing "Come, Thou Fount of Every Blessing," which was one of her favorite hymns. The words soothed her.

When the hymn ended, the reverend began to preach. He spoke of the resurrection, when the soul and the body would be reunited, never to be separated again. Did vampires have souls? Or did the soul leave the body when a person was turned? But that didn't seem right. Wasn't it the soul that kept the body alive? What happened to vampires when they were destroyed? She knew Rhys had killed to survive. Would he find forgiveness in the next life? And what about hunters? If vampires didn't have souls, was killing them a sin?

Megan pressed her hands to her temples. Maybe coming to church hadn't been such a good idea after all.

When the service was over, she went for a walk in the park across the street from the church. Here, with the touch of the sun on her face and a gentle breeze stirring the leaves on the trees, it was hard to believe that vampires were real, or that anyone would choose to become one. And yet, Shirl didn't seem to have any regrets. Was it that easy to go from human to vampire? To exchange warm sunny days for endless night? To give up strawberry sundaes and bread fresh from the oven for a warm liquid diet? To give up the chance to marry and have children and grandchildren and instead, live long enough to watch everyone you knew and loved pass on?

Driving home from the park, she thought about Rhys. He had lived alone for centuries. When you had no family, no one to share your life with, what was the point in living at all?

Overcome by a sudden longing to hear her mother's voice, Megan called her parents when she reached home. She felt better as soon as she heard her mother's "hello."

"Hi, Mom, it's me."

"Megan! Is something wrong?"

"No, of course not. I know I haven't called in a while. I'm sorry. I just wanted to say hi and see how you are."

"We're fine," her mother said, relief evident in her tone. "Your dad's been very busy with the Boy's Club. It's fund-raising time, you know. We've hardly been home at all this last month or so." Megan's father was Ways and Means Chairman of a local organization that supported a homeless shelter for teenage boys. "So, how are you doing, Meg?"

"I'm good. Busy at work, as usual."

"How's Shirl?"

Megan hesitated before saying, "She's fine."

"Tell her hello for me. Listen, sweetie, I hate to cut this short, but your dad's waiting for me out in the car. We were just leaving."

"That's okay, Mom. I didn't want anything special. I just wanted to say hi. Give my love to Dad."

"I will. Come see us when you can. We miss you."

"I miss you, too. Love you."

"Love you more, sweetie. Bye."

Megan sighed as she closed her phone. She really needed to call home more often. It grounded her in a way nothing else could, reminded her that, no matter what other craziness was going on in her life, there were two people in the world who loved her unconditionally.

It was near dusk when Megan's cell phone rang. Caller ID showed it was Shirl. After taking a deep breath, Megan answered.

"So," Shirl asked, getting right to the point. "What have you decided?"

Memories of good times, shared times, flashed through Megan's mind. "Why don't you come over later? Say around seven thirty?"

"Sounds good! I'll see you then."

Doubts assailed Megan as soon as she ended the call. Was she making a mistake? How could she trust Shirl as long as Villagrande was in the picture? Still, she felt she owed it to Shirl and the friendship they had once shared to give her friend one more chance.

She managed to shake off her melancholy mood before Rhys arrived that evening. As always, when she knew he was coming, she dressed with care. Tonight, she wore a pair of slinky black pants and a hot pink, off-the-shoulder blouse.

Rhys whistled softly when he saw her. "If you're trying to seduce me, babe, you wore the right thing."

"Maybe later," Megan said. "Shirl's coming over in a few minutes."

"I can wait," he said with a wicked grin. "Just don't make me wait too long."

The gleam in his eyes sent a rush of heat to every nerve ending in her body, then the fire pooled low in her belly. She went willingly into his arms, lifting her face for his kiss, a long, slow kiss that left her senses reeling.

He kissed her again, then jerked his chin toward the stairs. "I'll be up there."

"You don't have to hide. I mean, Shirl will know you're here, won't she? Can't you sense each other?"

Rhys shook his head. "I can shield my presence from her."

"More vampire magick?" Megan muttered.

With a grin, he chucked her under the chin. "She's here." Rhys kissed Megan on the cheek, then went up the stairs, moving so fast he was little more than a blur.

A moment later, the doorbell rang.

Megan took a deep breath. When she had talked to Shirl on the phone earlier, inviting her over had seemed like a good idea.

Now, she wasn't so sure.

Chapter 38

Forcing a smile she was far from feeling, Megan invited Shirl inside.

As she followed Megan into the living room, Shirl asked, "Is Rhys here?"

"Why do you ask?"

Shirl made a vague gesture with her hand. "His scent . . . I can smell it."

"I'm not surprised." Megan sat on the sofa and crossed her legs. "He's here every night. He'll probably come by later."

Shirl dropped into the chair across from the sofa. Megan fought off a twinge of envy. Shirl looked radiant. She wore a strapless white sundress and three-inch heels. Her pale complexion made her blue eyes and pink lips seem more pronounced; her luxurious silver-blond hair fell over her shoulders in a riot of waves.

Amazing what vampire blood could do, Megan thought. Too bad you had to become one of the Undead to enjoy the benefits.

Shirl smoothed a nonexistent wrinkle from her skirt with one pale hand. "Has Rhys said anything about my being with Tomás?"

"Why should he?"

"Well, it's customary for fledglings to stay with their makers, so . . ." She shrugged. "I just wondered how he felt about my leaving." Shirl leaned forward, her gaze intense. "I really wish you'd join us, Meggie. I would have done this years ago if I could have," she said exuberantly, and then laughed softly. "Of course, I didn't know vampires really existed back then. It's so amazing! It's a high unlike anything you can imagine. I can have any man I want."

"I guess you don't want Greg anymore."

"Mortals and vampires don't mix. You'll never understand Rhys, or truly be his, until you're one of us. Greg was nice, and we had fun together, but now I can have as many men as I like."

"Nothing new about that," Megan remarked. Men had always flocked around Shirl. What man over puberty and still breathing could resist a gorgeous cover model?

"It's different now. It's part of being a vampire. We all have it. It's some kind of supernatural glamour that makes us irresistible to mortals. When I see a man I want, all I have to do is call him, and he comes running."

Part of being a vampire, Megan thought. *They all have it.* Was that why she was so attracted to Rhys? Had he worked some kind of vampire mojo on her? Was she really in love with him, or was he manipulating her emotions for his own amusement? And how would she ever truly know?

"You're not thinking of turning Greg, are you?" Megan asked.

Shirl's brow narrowed in a frown, and then she shook her head. "No, I don't think he'd make a good vampire. He's too . . . oh, I don't know, too moral. Too rigid. Maybe you and Rhys and me and Tomás could get together some time," she said, brightening.

"Shirl, you do know that Tomás is planning to take over

the West Coast, don't you? I hardly think Rhys is in the mood to socialize with him."

Shirl leaned forward, her gaze focused on Megan's face. "Is Rhys going to give Tomás what he wants?"

"Is that why you came here? To find out if Rhys is going to surrender?"

Shirl's eyes grew wide. "Of course not, Meggie. How could you even think that?"

"I think it's time for you to go. Rhys will be here soon."

Shirl rose elegantly, effortlessly. "I'm sorry you can't see things our way, Meggie, truly I am."

"I am, too," Megan said. Rising, she pointed at the door. "Please leave now. Your invitation is rescinded."

Megan watched in astonishment as Shirl left the house; it was almost as if a giant hand had pushed her out the door.

Megan was trying to process what had happened when she sensed Rhys behind her.

"She didn't come here because she missed me," Megan said without turning around. "She just came to find out what you were going to do."

Rhys slid his arms around Megan's waist and pulled her back against him. "I'm sorry, love."

"She said I'd never understand you unless I became a vampire. She said she can have any man she wants, that she can manipulate them." Megan paused and then, before she could change her mind, she asked the question that was bothering her. "Is that what you're doing with me? Are you playing with my emotions?"

Rhys grasped her shoulders and turned her to face him. "No."

"How can I be sure that what I feel is real?"

"I guess you'll just have to trust me."

"That's easy for you to say."

"Megan, do you seriously think I'd be happy making love to a woman who was little more than a robot?"

"But, when we make love, I feel what you feel. . . ."

"It's because I've taken your blood, not because I'm deliberately influencing you." He smiled down at her. "You like it, don't you?"

She felt a rush of heat flood her cheeks. "Yes, it's wonderful."

"I told you once I'd never do anything you didn't want me to do. It was a promise I didn't make lightly. And one I intend to keep."

How could she doubt him when he looked at her like that, his gaze open and honest? "I believe you."

"Maybe we could go upstairs, and I could prove it to you."

"Oh, I'd like that." Megan was reaching for his hand when the doorbell rang. Frowning, she glanced over her shoulder. "You don't think Shirl's come back, do you?"

"No, it's Erik and Daisy."

"What are they doing here?"

"Only one way to find out."

With Rhys at her heels, Megan went to invite his friends inside.

"Sorry to bother you," Erik said when they were all seated in the living room, "but we found the body of a young woman not far from here."

"Recently drained," Daisy added with a grimace.

"It has Villagrande's stink all over it," Erik added.

"I guess that means he's back in town," Rhys muttered. "Dammit."

"We didn't mean to spoil your evening," Daisy said, "but we thought you ought to know."

"Yeah," Rhys said. "Thanks."

"We're leaving for home tonight," Erik said. "Daisy's dad called earlier. Her mother is in the hospital."

"I hope it's nothing serious," Megan said.

"She took a tumble down the porch stairs and broke a few ribs and her left leg," Daisy said. "My dad assured me that she isn't seriously hurt, but . . ." Daisy shrugged. "I'm sure she'll be all right, but I need to be there."

"Of course," Megan said.

"Be careful, you two," Erik said. He slipped his arm around Daisy's shoulders. "If you need us, all you have to do is call."

Rhys nodded. A moment later, Erik and Daisy took their leave.

"What are you looking so pensive about?" Rhys asked when they were again seated on the sofa and alone.

"I was thinking about what Daisy said, about being sure her mother will be all right."

"Go on."

"Do you think Daisy would turn her mother into a vampire if her injuries were life-threatening?"

"I don't know, but I doubt it. It's my understanding that, except for her own daughter, Irene O'Donnell doesn't have much love for vampires. I guess you can't blame her, since vampires turned her daughter and killed her youngest son. Last I heard, Daisy's surviving brother, Alex, was on an extended vacation, one he paid for with my money," Rhys added.

"Your money?" Megan exclaimed.

"Yeah. It's a long story, but he had a hand in finding a traitor who had put a two-hundred-thousand-dollar reward on my head."

"Two hundred grand! Wow. He must have wanted you dead awfully bad."

"She," Rhys said.

"What happened to her?" Megan asked. Then, seeing the merciless look in his eyes, she said, "Never mind, I don't want to know."

"So," Rhys said, his voice suddenly low and seductive, "where were we?"

"I think you were about to prove that my feelings for you are my own," she said, and then murmured, "although I don't know how you can do that."

"It's easy. We'll go upstairs and get undressed. I'll lie on your bed, with my eyes closed. And anything that happens after that will be all your idea."

"Really?" She slid her hand under his shirt and raked her nails over his chest. "So, if I don't want you to touch me, you won't?"

"That seems unlikely," he said dryly.

"Never mind." Her fingers curled in the hair on his chest. "If I say I just want to go to sleep, then that's what we'll do, right?"

He cleared his throat. "If that's what you want."

Her fingers trailed downward, sneaking beneath the waistband of his jeans. "And if I want you to spend the night *and* the day in my bed, will you?"

"Megan . . ."

"Having you spend the day with me is the one thing I *know* is my own idea."

"Fine," he said gruffly. "I'll spend the day here if that's what it takes to convince you."

"Then that's what I want," Megan said, even as fresh doubts assailed her. Did she really want to see him when he was at rest? What if he looked gross? What if he turned into some shriveled-up, disgusting, gray-skinned corpse?

The thought had barely crossed her mind when Rhys burst out laughing. "Shriveled-up, disgusting, gray-skinned corpse?" He spoke through gales of laughter. "Is that what you think?"

She started to yank her hand from inside his jeans, but he was too fast for her. When his hand covered hers, she looked up at him. "I take it you don't look like that."

"Recently made vampires look dead when they're at rest. I merely look like I'm asleep."

"Then why haven't you ever stayed the day?"

"It's just a quirk of mine, a holdover from when I was first made. It's a matter of trust. New vampires are vulnerable when they're at rest, so I never spent the day anywhere but in my own lair."

"Well, you're not a new vampire anymore, so I guess you don't trust me."

Releasing her hand, he kissed her cheek, then swung her into his arms and carried her swiftly up the stairs. "Didn't I already say I'd spend the day here? If that's not trust, honey, I don't know what is."

When she would have spoken again, he silenced her with a kiss that burned every other thought from her mind. His mouth was still fused with hers as he lowered her to the bed and undressed her, though how he managed to remove her clothing and kiss her at the same time, she could never remember.

Moments later, he stretched out beside her, as naked as she, the length of his body pressed intimately against her own. His skin was cool against hers but she hardly noticed. She was on fire for him, desperate for his touch, for that moment when their bodies melded together, two halves now whole, two hearts beating as one.

She closed her eyes as he whispered love words in her ear. The warmth of his voice washed over her, arousing her still further. She raked her nails down his back, her hips lifting to receive him.

"Megan." His voice near her ear was filled with silent entreaty.

A low moan rose in her throat as she turned her head to the side, giving him access to her throat, not caring whether he took a taste or took it all if he would just satisfy the ache that burned through her with every breath.

She sobbed his name at the touch of his fangs, moaned with indescribable pleasure as he moved deep inside her, carrying her away to that place where nothing existed but the two of them.

Megan slept until almost noon the next day and woke with a smile on her face as she recalled the night past. She flung one arm out to the side, and nearly jumped out of bed when she realized she wasn't alone. Her momentary panic disappeared when she saw Rhys lying beside her, his body covered by the sheet from his waist down. How could she have forgotten his promise to spend the day in her bed?

Propped up on one elbow, she stared at the vampire sleeping only inches away. Would he know if she touched him? She stared at him for several seconds, then ran her forefinger, ever so lightly, over his chest. "Such a nice chest," she murmured, and then grinned. "Thank goodness he isn't gray and shriveled-up."

"You forgot disgusting."

"Oh!" Startled, she reared backward. "You're awake!" she exclaimed, and then frowned. "How can you be awake?"

"Hush, woman. I need my rest."

"But you're awake!" Sort of, she thought, since his eyes were still closed.

"Old ones, like myself, can move about during the day, if necessary."

"Then why haven't I ever seen you when the sun's up?"

"I'm a vampire," he replied, his voice thick with sleep. "I prefer the night. And being in the sun for more than a short time is . . . unpleasant."

"Will it bother you if I take a shower?"

"No," he said with a faint smile, "but if you wait until later, I'll wash your back."

"That's an offer I can't refuse," Megan said with a

grin. Kissing him lightly on the cheek, she slid out of bed, slipped into a pair of sweats and a T-shirt, and went downstairs.

Going into the kitchen, she stood there a minute, trying to decide if she was in the mood for breakfast or lunch. In the end, she decided on a fried egg sandwich and a glass of grapefruit juice.

After breakfast, she tidied up the kitchen, then stood at the sink, staring out the window. The day stretched before her. She didn't feel like shopping or cleaning house. And with Villagrande prowling around, it probably wasn't safe to stray too far from home, anyway. She mulled over what Rhys had told her. If he could be active during the day, Villagrande probably could, too.

After a moment's indecision, she fixed a tall glass of iced tea, grabbed her sunglasses, plucked the latest Dean Koontz from the coffee table, and went outside to read. Of course, with her head filled with images of the sexy vampire in her bed, and that same sexy vampire washing her back—and perhaps the rest of her, as well—she couldn't really concentrate on the story.

With a sigh, she put the book aside and seriously contemplated her future. Should she stay with Rhys? Or end their relationship before it went any further? Did she want to spend her life with a man who would never grow old? A man who couldn't give her children? Did she want to live without him? Should she try? What were the chances that she could find a man she would love as much as she loved Rhys?

She sipped her iced tea as she tried to imagine finding a man who could take Rhys's place. Of course, it would be impossible. No mortal man could ever compete with a vampire's supernatural abilities or paranormal charisma. Rhys was like a rare vintage wine, unique and unforgettable. Compared to him, any other man would seem like cheap ale.

Of course, she could be taking a lot for granted. Maybe Rhys didn't want to spend the next thirty or forty years with her. And why would he? Why would any young man want to stay with a wrinkled old woman? Sure, he might stay with her for ten or fifteen years, but after that, he would surely want a younger woman, one who could make love all night long.

Megan shook her head. Why was she doing this to herself? There could be no happy ending for the two of them. Pairing a vampire and a mortal was like pairing a lion and a lamb. Sooner or later, the lamb was going to get hurt.

Shaking off her troubling thoughts, she spent the next couple of hours working in the yard, which had been badly neglected lately. She pulled weeds, trimmed the rose bushes, watered the grass.

Deciding she needed a break, she went into the house and fixed another glass of tea, then returned to the backyard. Standing in the shade, she sipped her drink, her thoughts again drawn to the man sleeping in her bed.

Her gaze followed her thoughts, and she glanced up at her bedroom window. Impulsively, she set her glass on the patio table and went inside. She hesitated at the bottom of the staircase, took a deep breath, and slowly climbed the stairs. She had seen him earlier, but he hadn't really been asleep.

She paused outside the door, her hand on the knob. Another deep breath, and she opened the door as quietly as she could and peeked inside.

Rhys lay on his back, one arm folded behind his head, the other resting on his chest. She stared at him for several moments. Was he breathing?

Curious, she tiptoed into the room and stood beside the bed. The phrase *as still as death* whispered through the back of her mind.

She was about to turn away when his hand clamped around her wrist.

Megan gasped. She hadn't even seen him move, but he was awake now, staring up at her, his eyes narrowed.

Muttering "sorry," he released her, then sat up. "Is anything wrong?"

"No. No, I was just . . ." she shrugged, "curious."

"Ah." His gaze probed hers. "Were you repulsed by what you saw?"

Megan shook her head. "No, but you weren't breathing." She stared at his chest. He was breathing now.

"I don't have to breathe," he said. "I do it when I'm awake because it makes me less conspicuous. But when I sleep there's no need."

"Oh." Just when she thought she knew it all, there was more creepy stuff to learn. It made her wonder once again if they could make things work between them. "I'm sorry I disturbed you."

"I'm not." He held out his hand in invitation. "As you can see, I'm wide awake now."

"What?" She frowned, and then she saw the evidence of his desire beneath the sheet. "Oh! Now? In the daytime?"

He arched one brow. "With you, anytime."

Laughing, Megan peeled off her clothes and crawled under the sheet. Doubts be damned, Rhys was here now, and she wanted him. And if he broke her heart later, then, so be it. Maybe it was time to live in the moment, to grab happiness with both hands while she could and stop worrying about the future. After all, she reminded herself, life was uncertain, and no relationship was perfect.

But he was, she thought, from the top of his head to the soles of his feet. Wrapped in his arms, she kissed and caressed him with an abandon she had never felt before, no doubt because now, for better or worse, she had tied her future to his. He must have sensed the change within her because his kisses grew longer, deeper, as his hands stroked her flesh.

She whispered, "I love you," when he rose over her.

"And I love you," he said, his voice a throaty growl in her ear. "Be mine forever, Megan, my love. Say you'll marry me."

"I will."

He reared back, a look of surprise on his face.

She grinned at him. "Didn't expect me to say yes, did you?"

"Well, not without taking a few days to think it over."

"Did you mean it?"

"Of course, but—are you sure?"

"Very sure," she murmured, and pulled him closer, linking her arms around his neck as his body merged with hers, his movements strong and slow, arousing her until she writhed beneath him, her mind empty of everything but her need for Rhys.

She felt his fangs at her throat. Her body arched upward, the pleasure of his bite sweeping her over the edge. She sobbed his name, her nails digging into his back as wave after wave of sensual heat flowed through her.

Sated, she closed her eyes, felt herself smiling as she curled up against him. He loved her. They were going to be married.

She was on the brink of sleep when Rhys jackknifed into a sitting position. "Dammit! He's struck again."

"What?" Megan blinked up at him.

"That bastard, Villagrande. He's killed another of my people."

Suddenly wide awake, she sat up, clutching the sheet to her breasts. "How do you know?"

He raked his fingers through his hair, then gained his feet. "I know."

"How?"

"I just know." There was no way to explain it, but he knew Hastings had been destroyed, his existence snuffed out at Villagrande's hand only moments ago. Pacing the floor, he muttered, "That makes four." Dammit! Why hadn't Hastings stayed with the others?

"What are you going to do now?"

Rhys paused in front of the window. Drawing the curtains aside, he stared out into the gathering darkness. "I'm going to give him what he wants."

Chapter 39

It was nearing nine o'clock that night when Megan got out of the shower. Glancing at the clock, she decided there was no point in getting dressed. Instead, she pulled on her bathrobe, then went downstairs. Since she was too hungry to cook anything that took more than a few minutes, she settled for scrambled eggs, toast, and orange juice.

It had been an exhausting day, what with working in the yard and then making love to Rhys, not once but three times. Tugging her bathrobe around her, she smiled at the memory, then yawned behind her hand. He might be inexhaustible, but she wasn't! Not only that, but she hurt in places that had never hurt before. And in some places she hadn't even known she had, she thought, amused. But it was a pleasurable kind of pain, a reminder of the most wildly erotic, passionate afternoon of her life.

A day she would never forget because Rhys had proposed to her and she had said yes. She smiled as she recalled how she had said yes without a second thought, and how surprised he had been when she accepted. She was getting married. All she had to do was name the day and decide whether she wanted a big church wedding with all the trimmings. Or a small, intimate ceremony. Or if they should just elope.

Her smile faded as she recalled Rhys's anger and distress when he sensed that another of his vampires had been destroyed by Villagrande. Had Rhys meant it when he said he was going to give Villagrande what he wanted? And what, exactly, did that mean? She was sorely afraid there might be more to it than just leaving the city.

With a sigh, she rinsed her dishes and put them in the dishwasher, then stood at the sink staring out into the darkness.

Rhys had gone out, but he would be back soon. She was thinking about slipping into a sexy black nightgown she had bought on a whim and never worn when the doorbell rang. Wondering who it could be, she drew her robe around her and went to the door.

Looking through the peephole, she saw her former best friend standing alone on the front porch. But it wasn't surprise that had Megan gasping. It was the blood dripping down Shirl's face and neck, the complete lack of color in her face.

Without thinking of the consequences, Megan opened the door and reached for her friend. Shirl staggered forward, then came to an abrupt halt at the threshold.

Megan tugged on her arm, frowning, and then, after muttering "Shirl, come in," she helped her friend inside and guided her to the sofa. "Shirl, what happened to you?"

"Tomás . . . he got angry with me because I refused to try to trick you into coming to the boat. He beat me and drank from me and . . ."

"Are you going to be all right? What can I do?"

"I could use a glass of wine."

"Of course."

Megan hurried into the kitchen, her thoughts tripping one over the other as she opened a bottle of wine and pulled a glass from the cupboard. Shirl needed to get away from Tomás, she thought as she filled the glass. But that wasn't all. Shirl needed fresh blood to heal her wounds and a place to stay. Maybe Rhys would know what to do.

Megan was still weighing possibilities when she returned to the living room, only to come to an abrupt halt when she saw Tomás Villagrande standing in front of the hearth, a smirk on his face.

Feeling betrayed, Megan looked at Shirl, who had miraculously recovered. "How could you?"

"We've no time for this," Villagrande said.

Before Megan could respond, he was at her side, his arm snaking around her waist. She stared up at him, a hard, cold knot of fear forming in her stomach as his gaze trapped hers.

His eyes grew darker, more intense. He whispered one word. "Sleep."

And the world went black.

Megan woke slowly. Her first thought was to wonder why the room was rocking back and forth. Were they having an earthquake? She took a deep breath, and her nostrils filled with the scent of the ocean. It took her a moment to realize she was on a boat.

A boat? Frowning, she tried to sit up, only then realizing that her hands were tied behind her back. A quick glance showed she was lying on a narrow bunk. In the dim light of a hanging lamp, she could see that the floor was highly polished. A patch of sky sprinkled with stars was visible through the porthole across from the bunk. How long had she been unconscious? How had she gotten here?

Fear hit her then, hard and quick, in the pit of her stomach. Feeling as though she was going to be sick, she rolled onto her side as the memory of what had happened came rushing back. Shirl had come to the house with some phony story, and Megan had swallowed it hook, line, and sinker. And then Shirl had invited Villagrande inside, and he had hypnotized her or something.

Where was he now? And what was he going to do with her? Nothing good, she was sure of that. She told herself there was nothing to worry about. Rhys would find her.

And then she gasped. Of course, that's why Villagrande had kidnapped her. Because he knew Rhys would come after her.

But maybe she was worrying for nothing. Rhys had said he was going to give Villagrande what he wanted, so maybe there was nothing to fear. If Rhys wasn't going to fight Villagrande for control of the city, then the conflict should be over.

So why didn't that make her feel any better?

Her heart skipped a beat when the cabin door opened. A moment later, Shirl came into view looking as long-legged and gorgeous as always. Tonight, she wore a pair of skintight white pants and an emerald green silk shirt.

Megan glared at her. It was hard to remember that Shirl had once been her best friend. They had shared a home, laughter and tears, their secret hopes and dreams. Looking at Shirl now, all Megan saw was a stranger. Rhys had told her that becoming a vampire brought out the best or the worst in people. It had definitely brought out the worst in her former best friend.

Shirl moved closer to the bunk. "Would you believe me if I said I was sorry?"

Megan struggled into a sitting position. "What do you think?"

"I can't help it, Meggie. I have to do what he says."

"I don't believe that either."

"He promised not to hurt you."

"And you believed him?" Megan asked incredulously.

"Meggie, you're my best friend."

"Then untie me and let me go. There's no need for any of this. Rhys isn't going to fight your lover for the city. He's going to leave."

"Did Rhys tell you that?"

"Yes. Where's Villagrande?"

"He went hunting." A dreamy smile played over Shirl's lips. "He loves to hunt when the moon is full. I don't know why."

"Why didn't you go with him?"

"I went earlier. Sometimes he likes to hunt alone." Shirl lifted one shoulder and let it fall, as if it was of no concern whether he hunted alone or not, but she couldn't disguise the petulant tone in her voice.

Megan shook her head. "I look at you and I hear you, and I can't believe what I'm hearing. You talk about hunting as if it's nothing at all. Have you forgotten that you were once human? That all you wanted was to live a normal life? And now you're no better than he is."

"I'm sorry you feel that way," Shirl murmured.

"Then let me go! If there's any humanity left in you, let me go before it's too late."

"He'll only find you again," Shirl murmured, sounding both resigned and proud at the same time. "No matter where you go, he'll find you. You can't hide from him. You can't fight him. He's not only immortal, Meggie. He's invincible. And some day, I'll be just like him."

Megan closed her eyes as Shirl's words crushed her only hope of escape. She didn't know what Villagrande had done to Shirl, but it was obvious he owned her, body and soul. Megan had a terrible suspicion that Shirl would kill her without a qualm if Villagrande said the word. And that was the scariest thought of all.

* * *

Rhys whistled softly as he made his way back to Megan's house. If he had known what spending the day in Megan's bed would lead to, he would have done it a hell of a lot sooner, he thought, and then swore softly. He would have to be more considerate of Megan in the future. He had behaved like a rutting bull. She hadn't complained, but in the future, he needed to remember that she didn't have the same strength and stamina that he did. Had it been up to him, they would still be in bed, but she had needed rest and nourishment, and so he had told her he needed to feed and left the house.

He had contacted Nicholas earlier and learned that the three remaining Council members were staying in one of Volger's lairs in Blue Grass, Iowa, and that several of Volger's vampires, along with a few trusted humans, were also on the premises to keep an eye out for Villagrande. Rhys had snorted when he heard the name of the town. Blue Grass had a population of just over a thousand; twenty-five percent of the residents were under the age of eighteen. And then he had grinned inwardly. Julius had always had a taste for young blood.

As for Hastings, no one knew where'd he gone. According to Nicholas, Hastings had been there one night and the next he was gone. The general consensus was that he'd headed back to Medford and Villagrande had found him there.

"Stupid," Rhys had muttered. If Hastings had just stayed put, he'd still be alive.

Nicholas had added that they were all getting antsy and wanted to know when they could return to their own lairs.

Rhys had assured Nicholas it would be soon, and hoped that was the truth. As for himself, he hated to leave LA, but what the hell, the world was a big place. He hadn't been to Italy in a while. He wondered if Megan had ever been to Naples or Sicily, and then frowned. He was taking a lot for granted. True, she had said she would marry him, but that didn't mean she wanted to quit her job or leave the country. For that matter, they hadn't set a date for the wedding, either. He didn't know if she wanted a big wedding or if she would be content with something more intimate, say just the two of them. One thing he did know—she was going to make a beautiful bride.

A glance at the sky showed it was almost eleven. Smiling, he quickened his step, eager to see her again.

He knew, before he opened the front door, that she was gone. A single, indrawn breath told him what had transpired. Oh, not the details, but Shirl's scent was strong in the air, as was Villagrande's. Rhys didn't know how the other two vampires had managed to penetrate the protective wards and spells that had been placed on Megan's house, but that didn't matter. All that was important now was that Villagrande had Megan.

Rhys swore a vile oath as he stepped back and slammed the door. Dammit! So much for Erik's protective magick! Why the hell hadn't it worked? And where was Megan?

He followed her scent until it disappeared and then, closing his eyes, he took several slow deep breaths and opened his senses, homing in on the blood bond that connected them.

It drew him unerringly down the coast toward San Diego.

Speeding through the night faster than the human eye could follow, he prayed he wasn't too late.

Chapter 40

Megan didn't hear him coming, but she knew when Villagrande boarded the ship. It was as if a dark shroud settled over the craft. Evil slid along her skin and crawled inside her like some loathsome insect. She knew, somehow, that when she had seen him before, he had been masking his true self, and that what she sensed now was the real Tomás Villagrande. Had he been masking his true nature from Shirl? Or was she so infatuated with his supernatural power and his promises that she had turned a blind eye to the truth of what he was?

He appeared beside the bunk between one heartbeat and the next. Eyes red, fangs bared, he was a nightmare come to life.

"So." Moving closer to the bunk, he swept his gaze over her. It made her feel dirty, defiled. "It's time for dinner."

Megan stared up at him. Heart pounding, body trembling uncontrollably, she couldn't think, couldn't speak. Like a fox helplessly caught in the jaws of a trap, she could only stare up at him while a voice in the back of her mind whispered that this was what death looked like.

Thoughts flew through her mind like leaves in a wind storm. She would never see her parents again. Never see

Rhys. Never be a bride. Darkness swirled at the edge of her consciousness, and she prayed she would pass out before Villagrande sank his fangs into her throat. What if he didn't intend to kill her? What if he turned her into a vampire? For a fleeting moment, she thought she would rather be a vampire than die so horribly, but then Villagrande grinned at her and she knew she'd rather be dead than become what he was.

His fangs lengthened. Gleaming. Bright white. She took a deep breath as fear coiled deep in the pit of her stomach. She tried to look away from his hellish gaze, but like a rabbit mesmerized by a snake, she could only lie there, waiting for death to strike.

Megan tensed when Villagrande lowered his head to her neck, but then a curious thing happened. As soon as his fangs touched her skin, a shower of bright golden yellow sparks exploded between them. Villagrande reared back, a vile curse issuing from his lips.

Startled, Megan cried out, her whole body tensing in fearful anticipation as the fiery embers rained down on her face and neck, but there was no pain. The bright yellow sparks vanished when they touched her skin.

Villagrande wasn't so fortunate. The embers burned his skin wherever they touched, leaving raw, red patches.

He reeled backward as Shirl burst into the cabin. "Tomás, what's going on . . . ?"

She had scarcely uttered the words when Rhys appeared behind her in the doorway. His eyes took on a warm red glow when he saw Villagrande, and, before Megan could move or speak, Villagrande and Rhys were on each other.

With her hands still bound behind her back, Megan struggled to sit up as the two vampires battled each other. The smell of blood and scorched flesh mingled with the scent of sea and salt, making her stomach churn.

Villagrande hurled Rhys against the wall with such

force, Megan was surprised the wood didn't crack from the impact. With a feral cry, Rhys sprang to his feet and lunged at Villagrande, his hands like claws, his fangs dripping blood.

It was a battle unlike anything she had ever seen. Like two superheroes, they flung each other to and fro, fangs and claws rending preternatural flesh that healed almost instantly. Blood splattered on the walls, the ceiling, the deck.

As blood sprayed over her face and robe, Megan cowered against the bed, praying that Rhys would be the victor even as she wondered how much more punishment he could take.

She let out a cry as Shirl struck Rhys from behind, opening a gash in the back of his head and knocking him off balance. Springing forward, Villagrande seized Rhys by the nape and slammed him to the floor, facedown; then, straddling his back, Villagrande grasped a handful of Rhys's hair, jerked his head backward and buried his fangs in the side of Rhys's neck.

Megan glanced at Shirl, but one look at Shirl's face, contorted with bloodlust, banished all thought of asking for help. Her former friend's eyes burned with excitement as the scent of Rhys's blood filled the air.

Megan swallowed the bile rising in her throat. Rhys had told her that vampires rarely fed on other vampires, but Villagrande drank for what seemed like forever, then rose gracefully to his feet.

Moving toward a small desk, Villagrande picked up a long wooden letter opener and tossed it to Shirl. "Finish him and throw him overboard."

Shifting his focus to Megan, Villagrande lifted a hand to his face, his fingers gingerly probing his scorched flesh. He glared at her for a long moment; then, muttering, "This isn't over," he stalked out of the cabin.

Shirl stared after Tomás and then, to Megan's astonishment,

Shirl laid the stake aside and sank her fangs into Rhys's throat.

Megan stared at Rhys. She had to do something, but what? Clinging to the faint hope that the blood bond she shared with Rhys would somehow give her the strength she needed, she struggled against the rope that bound her wrists.

She didn't know whether it was the adrenaline coursing through her body, the power of her connection to Rhys, or if the ropes hadn't been as tight as she'd thought, but one last desperate tug, and her hands slipped free.

Moving as silently as she could, she tiptoed toward Shirl. Sending a quick prayer winging toward heaven, Megan grabbed the letter opener and plunged it into Shirl's back, aiming for her treacherous heart.

The wood slid through skin and flesh and muscle as easily as a needle through cloth.

Shirl toppled onto the cabin floor without a sound.

Megan didn't waste time wondering if Shirl was dead. Surprisingly, she didn't care one way or the other.

Kneeling beside Rhys, she shook his shoulder, gently at first, and then more vigorously. "Rhys! Dammit, Rhys, I need you to get us out of here. Now!" When he didn't speak, didn't even twitch, she shook him again, harder. "Rhys! Don't you dare be dead!"

"I'm already dead," he muttered.

Relief washed through her when he rolled onto his back, but only for a moment. He was badly hurt. His face was swollen and discolored; blood seeped from the gash in the back of his head, staining the floor beneath him.

"Rhys, we need to go, now." Knowing that Villagrande could return at any moment, she glanced warily at the door.

"I need . . . blood."

She blinked at him, then sighed in resignation. She was

the only game in town. Rolling up her sleeve, she offered him her wrist.

His gaze met hers for stretched seconds, and in his eyes she saw regret for what he was asking of her, and gratitude for her willingness to give it to him.

She turned her head away as he drew her arm to his mouth. He drank greedily, the pull of his mouth on her skin both repellant and oddly sensual. He had tasted her before, but this was different. This wasn't an act of love but survival.

A growl rose in his throat and then, abruptly, he pushed her away.

Megan watched the red fade from his eyes, the bruises vanish from his face. Moments later, he was standing over her, as silent and still as a statue. The hair raised on her arms as he drew on his preternatural power.

"Hang on," he said, and lifted her into his arms.

Weak from the loss of blood, she rested her head on his shoulder and closed her eyes, her stomach roiling as the world spun out of focus. There was a dizzying sensation of movement, as if she were on an out-of-control roller coaster, a rush of wind in her ears, an overwhelming sense of disorientation, and then nothing.

When her stomach and the world stopped spinning, she opened her eyes. And frowned. "Where are we?"

"Boston."

"Boston!" She sagged against him. "What are we doing here?"

Rhys jerked his chin toward the house behind them. "This is Erik's place."

The house was small and square, with a red brick chimney, bright yellow shutters, a white picket fence, a security screen door, and white bars over the windows, upstairs and down.

The front door opened before Rhys knocked, and Erik

peered out at them, a comical look of surprise on his face. "What the hell! What are you doing here?"

"Looking for a place to spend the day," Rhys muttered. "Can you put us up?"

Rhys could almost see the wheels turning in the other vampire's head as Erik glanced from Rhys to Megan and back again. Megan looked weak and pale, and he knew Delacourt was wondering if Rhys had started to bring Megan across and then changed his mind.

"Sure, come on in." Erik stepped aside, then closed and locked the door before following Rhys and Megan into the living room. "Sit down and tell us what happened. Daisy, why don't you get Megan a glass of wine?"

With a nod, Daisy disappeared into the kitchen.

Rhys eased Megan down on the sofa, then slipped his arm around her shoulders. Her head fell back, and her eyelids fluttered down. It worried him that she looked so pale. Had he taken too much?

Erik lifted one brow. "So?"

"Villagrande kidnapped Megan. I almost got there too late. I owe you a big one. If it wasn't for that spell you worked on Megan, I think he would have killed her."

"She looks half-dead now."

"I needed blood. Villagrande beat the crap out of me."

"Ah."

Rhys ran his knuckles lightly over Megan's cheek. "I was going to let the bastard have the city," he said quietly, "but I never got a chance to tell him so."

Daisy glanced at the glass in her hand, then looked at Rhys. "Should we wake her up?"

Rhys shrugged. "I don't know."

"I think you should let her rest," Erik remarked. "She looks exhausted."

Megan stirred in Rhys's embrace. "I'm thirsty."

Rhys took the glass from Daisy and held it to Megan's lips. "Here you go, love."

Megan looked up at him, a half smile on her face as she murmured, "Wine is supposed to be good for the blood."

Rhys shook his head, amazed that she could find humor in the situation, then muttered, "Just drink it."

Megan drained the glass, then curled up against his side and closed her eyes.

"I think she'll be all right once she's had some sleep." Daisy took the glass from Rhys and set it on a side table.

Rhys nodded.

"I'll make up the bed in the guest room," Daisy said. "She'll be comfortable there. You're welcome to share our lair in the basement."

"No, I'm staying with her."

"Do you think that's wise, all things considered?" Erik asked.

"Probably not, but I'm not leaving her alone again. If Villagrande finds us, he'll have to go through me to get to her."

"Looks like he already did that once," Erik remarked with a wry grin. "Are you planning to give him a second chance?"

Rhys glared at Delacourt.

Daisy placed her hand on her husband's arm. "I'm not sure you're helping." She looked at Rhys. "You don't think Villagrande will come here, do you?"

"I hope not."

"Well, if he does, it'll be three against one. Four, when Alex gets home."

"Is he still spending my money?" Rhys had paid Alex O'Donnell two hundred thousand dollars for his help in locating Mariah. He had learned later that Alex had split the money with Daisy.

"Just as fast as he can," Daisy said with a grin. "Or he was. He'll he home from his honeymoon tomorrow night."

"He got married?"

"Last month. They've been touring Spain but they'll be home soon. I'll have Megan's bed made up in two shakes."

A short time later, Rhys carried Megan up the stairs. He waved Daisy away when she offered to help get Megan into bed. "Thanks, but I can do it."

Megan muttered something incoherent as Rhys eased her out of her bathrobe, noticing for the first time that it was stained with blood. Not all of it was his. He could smell Villagrande on her. "What'd you say?"

"I need a shower. I feel dirty."

He nodded. If she hadn't suggested it, he would have. The sooner they washed Villagrande's stink off of her, the better. "Wait here, I'll turn the water on."

Grunting softly, he went into the bathroom and turned on the taps. Standing there, waiting for the water to get hot, he tried to understand how she must feel, but couldn't. He had killed when necessary and never lost any sleep over it. He knew he had a reputation for being a hard-ass, and sometimes he was, although since Megan had entered his life, he seemed to have lost a little of his edge.

"Nothing like the love of a good woman," he muttered as he tested the water.

When it was warm enough, he walked Megan to the shower, closed the door after her, then turned his back, giving her some privacy. He probably should have left the room, but he wasn't leaving her alone as long as Villagrande was a threat.

It took him a minute to realize she was standing under the spray, crying. Well, who could blame her? She'd been through hell tonight.

Undressing, he opened the shower door, stepped inside, and gathered her into his arms. He held her until the water started to cool, then took the soap and scrubbed her from head to foot. When he was done, he turned off the water, then wrapped her in a towel and carried her into the bedroom.

"I'm sorry," she murmured.

"Nothing for you to be sorry for." He cursed his body's instant reaction to hers as he dried her off. It was all he could do to keep from seducing her. Like the lust for blood, battle often aroused his baser instincts. Reining in his desire, he slipped the nightgown Daisy had provided over Megan's head, then tucked her into bed.

"You could have been killed," she murmured.

"Get some sleep, darlin'."

"I don't think I can."

"You need the rest."

"You won't leave me?"

"No." He wiped a lock of damp hair from her brow. "You'll feel better in the morning."

She looked doubtful, but obediently closed her eyes.

In minutes, the slow, steady beat of her heart told him she was asleep.

He switched off the bedside light, then sat beside her, staring into the darkness. Dawn was only a few hours away.

He was leaning against the headboard, his eyes closed, when Megan bolted upright. "Rhys! Rhys!"

"I'm here."

She stared at him, her eyes wild, then slumped back on the pillow. "I was having a nightmare."

"I'm not surprised."

"Shirl's really dead, isn't she?"

Rhys nodded. Guilt was an emotion he rarely suffered, but it flayed him now. Because of him, Megan had killed her best friend. "I'm sorry." He blew out a breath. "Are you all right?"

"I will be. I couldn't let her destroy you, and . . ." Her fingers worried the edge of the blanket. "It wasn't really

Shirl that I . . ." She couldn't bring herself to say the word *killed* out loud. "Villagrande twisted her thinking somehow. Or maybe it was just what you said before, that being a vampire brings out the best or the worst in people. I guess in her case it brought out the worst. And being with Villagrande didn't help."

"You should hate me."

Her eyes widened. "Why? It wasn't your fault. It was mine. I'm the one who asked you to turn her. Or maybe it was Shirl's fault. She begged me to ask you. None of us knew it would end like this."

"I put too much faith in Erik's magick," Rhys muttered. "I never should have left you alone."

"It wasn't your fault. Erik's magick worked just fine."

"Then how . . . ?" Rhys looked at her, his eyes narrowed. "Tell me you didn't invite Villagrande inside."

"Of course not!" Megan said, scowling at him. "Shirl tricked me. She came to the house, all bloody and pale, and told me Villagrande had beat her up—"

"And she invited him in," Rhys finished for her. He brushed a lock of hair from her brow. "It's over now." Sitting on the edge of the bed, he drew the covers over Megan, then kissed her cheek. She was too good for him by half, her heart too pure, too forgiving.

"Stay with me and keep the nightmares away?" she asked sleepily.

Nodding, he took her hand in his, his heart aching with tenderness. Foolish girl, didn't she know he was the biggest nightmare in her life?

He sat beside her, watching as sleep claimed her again. He had come close to losing her tonight. Too damn close.

In spite of the fact that she was human and he wasn't, he had hoped they could have a life together. He should have known better. Relationships between vampires and mortals never ended well. Every minute he spent with

Megan put her life in danger. Even if he managed to destroy Villagrande, which seemed doubtful, he had other enemies who wouldn't hesitate to use her to get to him.

If he had never turned Shirl, Megan's life might not be in danger now. But Megan had found the courage to destroy Shirl and save his life, and Villagrande wasn't one to forgive and forget.

Adrianna was proof of that.

He dragged a hand through his hair. He didn't know how he would be able to leave her when this was over, didn't know if he wanted to go on existing without her. But he couldn't go on putting her future at risk. She deserved to live a long and happy life surrounded by people who loved her. Getting out of her life was the best thing he could do for her.

But first, he had to destroy Villagrande. It was the only way to protect Megan.

And when it was done, he would tell her good-bye.

Chapter 41

Megan woke slowly, certain that something was wrong. And then, between one breath and the next, memory came flooding back. She had killed her best friend last night. She remembered it all now, the horrible encounter with Villagrande on the boat, then traveling, vampire-style, to the Delacourt house in Boston.

But all of that was swallowed up in a wave of guilt and grief. Shirl was dead. The words repeated in her mind over and over again. Shirl was dead. It hadn't been a nightmare. She had plunged a wooden stake into her friend's back and pierced her heart.

Megan bit down on her lower lip as hot tears stung her eyes and cascaded down her cheeks. Conscious of Rhys sleeping beside her, she tried to muffle her sobs, but it was no use. Memories of the fun she and Shirl had once had swam to the surface of her mind. She remembered all the good times they'd had visiting their favorite day spa, going to the movies and shopping, the shared confidences, the foolish hopes and dreams they had confessed to each other late at night in front of the fire, Shirl's excitement when she was accepted by the top modeling agency in the city.

"I'm sorry," she murmured. "Oh, Shirl, I'm so sorry."

She glanced at Rhys. If she had never met him, Shirl might still be alive. Yet, even as the thought crossed Megan's mind, she knew it wasn't true. As cliche as it sounded, Shirl had had a date with death. Becoming a vampire had just postponed it a few weeks. Maybe you couldn't cheat death. Maybe, when it was your time to go, the Grim Reaper would find you one way or another. . . .

Megan shook the morbid thoughts from her mind, then used a corner of the sheet to wipe away her tears. What was done was done, and there was no going back. Shirl had changed once she became a vampire, and not for the better. Megan had been forced to make a choice last night. She hadn't had time to think it over or to weigh the consequences. Her best friend had been about to kill Rhys, and Megan's heart had made the decision.

Trying to ignore the guilt that still gnawed at her, Megan slid out of bed, turned on the bedside lamp, and glanced at her surroundings. The curtains, a pale sage green, matched the walls. The ceiling was white, the floor was polished hardwood. The furniture looked like antique mahogany. The bathrobe and gown she had worn the night before were nowhere to be seen.

Feeling the need to relieve herself, she went into the bathroom and closed the door. Clean towels had been laid out, as well as two bathrobes, a pink one for her, a black one for Rhys. A pair of toothbrushes, still in the packages, and a new tube of toothpaste sat on top of the towels. Megan couldn't help grinning. It had never occurred to her that vampires brushed their fangs.

After brushing her teeth, she wrapped up in the fluffy pink bathrobe and tiptoed down the hall toward the stairs.

She passed two doors, both closed. Were Erik and Daisy sleeping in twin coffins behind one of them?

Belting the robe tighter, Megan made her way down the stairs. She wandered through the house—living room, family room, dining room, bathroom, laundry room. Daisy's taste ran to bright colors. There was nothing out of the ordinary, nothing to indicate that a pair of vampires lived in the house and yet, even though Megan was sure it was only her imagination, the rooms seemed eerily silent.

"Like a tomb," she muttered. Which she supposed it was, since there were three of the Undead resting here.

She paused in the kitchen doorway, wondering what the odds were of finding anything to eat in the refrigerator. Moving across the floor, she reached for the handle, then hesitated, hoping it wasn't filled with bottles of blood. After taking a breath, she opened the door, and breathed a sigh of relief. Inside, she found bacon, a dozen eggs, a carton of butter, a package of Swiss cheese, another of ham, and a quart of milk. She found small jars of mayonnaise, ketchup, and mustard on the counter, along with a loaf of bread, a small frying pan, and a spatula.

Daisy was indeed a good hostess. She had obviously gone to the store late last night so Megan would have the fixings for breakfast this morning and lunch later in the day.

Concentrating on the task at hand, Megan fried bacon and scrambled eggs for breakfast. She ate in the living room. In an effort to keep her grief at bay, she focused her thoughts on Daisy Delacourt, wondering how long she had been a vampire and whether she missed being mortal. If it wasn't for the blood thing and not being able to be outside during the day, being one of the Undead might not be so bad. Not so bad? What was she thinking? Vampires killed people. Being Undead made formerly normal, fun-loving young women like Shirl into monsters. . . .

Megan set her plate on the coffee table as fresh tears scalded her eyes. She cried for what she had done, for what Shirl had become, and for Shirl's parents, who would never know what had happened to their daughter. She cried because she loved Rhys with all her heart, because she wanted to be with him for the rest of her life, and because she was sorely afraid she was going to lose him.

Gradually, her tears subsided. Depressed and lethargic, she curled up on the sofa and fell asleep.

When she woke, the sun was going down. Feeling stiff, she sat up and stretched her arms over her head. She heard the faint sound of hushed voices from the next room. Her ears perked up when someone—Daisy?—mentioned her name. Megan frowned. Why were they talking about her?

Rising, she tiptoed toward the door. She didn't approve of eavesdropping, as a rule, but desperate times called for desperate measures.

"What makes you think she'll be safe without you?" Daisy's voice, her tone slightly impatient.

"He could have killed her," Rhys said. "He damn near got me."

"Listen," Erik spoke up. "Between us, we can look after her. We'll get Alex to come and stay here during the day. Daisy's dad, too, if necessary. With all five of us guarding her, she should be okay."

"And what if she isn't? How am I supposed to live with myself if she gets killed because of me?"

"It's that serious, huh?" Erik asked, a note of wry amusement in his voice.

"I asked her to marry me."

"Really?" Daisy exclaimed. "Did she say yes?"

Megan had had enough. Before Rhys could reply, she stepped into the room. "Why don't you ask the prospective bride?"

They all turned to look at her.

"Eavesdropping, were you?" Rhys asked.

"How else am I going to find out what's going on around here?" She marched toward him. "Just going to walk out on me, were you?" She stabbed a finger at his chest. "Don't I have anything to say about it?"

"Megan . . ."

"I know you're worried about me. I'm worried, too. And scared to death. But I don't think your leaving will make me any safer. Villagrande has a score to settle with me, too, remember? His last words were 'this isn't over.' Sure sounds like a threat to me."

"I agree with Megan," Erik said.

Rhys swore softly. "I was going to give him the city," he muttered. "None of this was necessary."

"Well, it doesn't matter now," Daisy said. "Sounds like Villagrande's after both of you."

"So, it's settled then." Erik took Daisy by the hand. "If you'll excuse us, we need to go out for a while."

"We won't be long," Daisy called over her shoulder.

After Delacourt and Daisy left the house, Rhys pulled Megan into his arms. "I'm sorry I got you involved in all this."

"It's not your fault."

"Isn't it?"

"Rhys, stop blaming yourself. I'm with you because I want to be. Every relationship has its problems."

He snorted softly. "Is that what you call Villagrande? A problem?"

"Well, a mighty big one, and . . . oh! I need to call Mr. Parker and tell him I won't be in tonight."

"Or any night, as long as you're in danger," Rhys said, reaching into his pocket. "Here, use my phone."

Megan stared at the BlackBerry in her hand, noting, absently, that it was top of the line. But that was immaterial at the moment. Once again, her life had been turned upside down because of Rhys Costain. This time, it could cost her her job. Being a glorified saleswoman wasn't the greatest job in the world, but she enjoyed working at Shore's, and she got along well with Mr. Parker. Still, business was business. How much time could she take off before he decided to let her go?

"Megan?"

She looked up at Rhys, nodded, and punched in Mr. Parker's private number.

Chapter 42

Shoulders hunched, Tomás Villagrande sat atop the Hollywood sign, letting the cool air soothe the burns scattered over his face, hands, chest, and shoulders. His clothing had been no protection against the hellish embers that had burned through cloth and skin alike. He hadn't hurt so badly in centuries, and it was all that red-haired tart's fault. Once his initial pain and anger had subsided, Tomás realized his power had been kept at bay by some supernatural spell. The woman wasn't a witch, which begged the question: Who had worked the enchantment? And the only logical answer was Erik Delacourt.

Tomás swore softly. Not long ago, he had done Delacourt a favor by sparing his life. And then, in an uncommon burst of charity, he had spared the lives of Daisy's father and brother, as well.

"Just goes to show you," Tomás muttered. "Sooner or later, every good deed comes back to bite you in the ass."

He lifted a hand to his face, grimacing as his fingers encountered puckered flesh. What foul curse had Delacourt conjured, Tomás wondered, that prevented his injuries from healing overnight?

Yes, Delacourt had much to answer for.

And then there was the matter of Shirl's destruction. It surprised him to realize that he missed her. He had been drawn to her from the first moment he saw her, captivated by her ethereal beauty. She had enjoyed being a vampire, reveled in her preternatural power. He had been charmed by her exuberance when she was on the hunt, puzzled by her reluctance to take a life.

And now the lovely Shirl was gone, her existence snuffed out before he had fully savored her. Before he had tired of her. The tart would pay for that, too, he mused, though he wasn't sure what form his vengeance would take. A life for a life? Perhaps.

Or perhaps he would destroy Costain and make the whore his slave, subject to his every whim. He would humble her, degrade her, until she had no will of her own, and then, when she no longer amused him, he would drain her dry and toss her aside, an empty husk.

But first, he had to find her.

Chapter 43

Mr. Parker assured Megan that her job would be waiting for her when she returned to LA. She had told him a crisis had arisen in her family and that she hadn't had time to call him before she left town. She had been grateful when he didn't ask for details.

She'd no sooner ended the call than a booming male voice yelled, "Hey, Daisy Mae, we're back!" and a tall, athletic young man with dark brown hair and brown eyes strolled into the living room, his arms filled with gaily wrapped packages. "Wait until you see what I brought you from Spain. . . ."

His voice trailed off, and he came to an abrupt halt when he saw Megan and Rhys. Exclaiming, "What the hell?" he glanced around the room; then, eyes narrowed, he glared at Rhys. "Where's my sister, vampire?"

Rhys grinned at the other man. "How's it hanging, hunter?"

Megan studied the man. It could only be Daisy's brother, Alex.

He dropped the packages on the sofa. "Ex-hunter. I'm a married man now. Just got home from my honeymoon, as a matter of fact." He glanced at Megan, then looked back at Rhys. “So, are you going to introduce me to this pretty woman?”

“Megan, this is Daisy’s brother. Alex, this is Megan DeLacey.”

Stepping forward, Alex shook Megan’s hand. “Pleased to meet you. Why don’t we sit down? So,” Alex said when they were all seated, “what brings the two of you to Boston?”

As succinctly as possible, Rhys told Alex about Villagrande.

“Damn!” Alex leaned back in his chair. “Did you have to antagonize the baddest badass vamp of them all?”

“It wasn’t my idea.” Rhys lifted his head, his nostrils flaring. “Your sister’s home.”

Rhys had no sooner spoken the words than Daisy and Erik materialized in the living room.

“Alex!” Daisy cried, and threw herself into her brother’s arms. “Welcome home. Where’s Paula?”

“I dropped her off at her parents’ house. She couldn’t wait to tell them the good news. She’s pregnant!”

Megan had expected Daisy to look happy; instead, a sudden sadness flitted through her eyes.

“That’s wonderful,” Daisy murmured. “It’ll be nice to have a baby in the family.”

Megan frowned, puzzled by Daisy’s reaction. And then she understood. Daisy was a vampire. She would never have a child of her own.

When the awkward moment passed, Rhys, Erik, Daisy, and Alex tossed around ideas on how best to protect Megan and destroy Villagrande.

“Does he know you’re here?” Alex asked.

Rhys shook his head. “I don’t know. But he’s tasted my blood. He shouldn’t have any troubling finding us.”

Alex grunted softly. “I’d like to have seen that spell you mentioned in action.” He looked at Erik. “Where’d you find it?”

"In an ancient grimoire."

"How'd you know it would work?"

"I didn't. I layered it into another spell, just in case. I think it was the combination of the two that caused the damage Megan told us about."

Alex chuckled. "I'm all in favor of anything that'll repel vampires. Present company excepted, of course," he added with a wry grin.

"Of course," Rhys muttered.

"So, Erik," Alex said, "maybe if you ramped up that hellfire spell, it would destroy Villagrande."

"Maybe," Erik replied. "And maybe it would destroy Rhys, as well."

"I'd like to avoid that, if possible," Rhys said.

Alex yawned behind his hand. "This isn't getting us anywhere. I'm gonna go get my wife, take her home, and make love to her all night long. My wife," he repeated with a grin. "I like the sound of that." Rising, he kissed Daisy on the cheek, cuffed Erik on the shoulder. "I'll talk to you guys tomorrow night. If I come up with anything before that, I'll give Megan a call."

Rhys sat on the foot of the bed, watching Megan sleep. She seemed to grow more beautiful with every passing day, or maybe it was just that he loved her more every time he saw her. And she loved him. That was the most remarkable part. In spite of the fact that he had not only complicated her life but put her in danger, she still wanted to be with him.

"Rhys?"

"I thought you were asleep."

"I was. Come to bed. It's lonesome without you." She turned the light on when he started to undress.

He paused in the act of removing his shirt, one brow arched as he looked at her. "What are you doing?"

"Watching you."

"You've seen me undress before."

"So, sue me. I like to watch."

With a shake of his head, he shrugged out of his shirt and tossed it on a chair and then, ever so slowly, he unbuckled his belt and let it fall to the floor. With his gaze locked on hers, he toed off his boots and kicked them aside.

Megan sat up, grinning, as he pulled off his socks and threw them at her, one by one.

"Are you watching?" he asked, his voice dripping with sexual innuendo.

She nodded, her grin fading as he unfastened his jeans, then made a production of slowly lowering the zipper, sliding the jeans down over his hips, kicking them out of the way.

Clad in nothing but a pair of black silk briefs, he moved toward the bed. His feet made no sound on the hardwood floor as he stalked toward her, lithe and dangerous as a jungle cat.

She laughed when he growled low in his throat.

"Jungle cat, eh?" he mused.

"Stop reading my mind. It isn't fair!"

He slid under the covers beside her and drew her into his arms. "Are you sure you want me to stop? If I did, I wouldn't know how much you like it when I touch you here . . ." His hand caressed the sensitive skin of her inner thigh. "Or kiss you there . . ." Bending his head, he brushed his lips across her breast.

Megan sighed as the heat of his mouth warmed her skin.

"You're overdressed," he murmured, and in a blur of movement, he removed her nightgown and tossed it on the floor. "That's better."

She looked up at him, marveling anew at how remarkable

he was. He was a man like no other she had ever known, a creature of myth and legend, and she loved him more than life itself. Wanted him beyond words. Locking her arms around his neck, she whispered, "What am I thinking now?"

"Shall I tell you?" He nuzzled her breast. "Or show you?"

"Haven't you heard?" She slid her hand down his hard, flat belly, her fingertips tracing the narrow line of hair that disappeared beneath his briefs. "Actions speak louder than words."

Chuckling softly, he wrapped his arms around her. "Ah, fair lady, my only purpose in life is to fulfill your every wish, your every desire."

"I wish you'd stop talking and kiss me."

The words had scarcely left her lips when his mouth covered hers. He kissed her slow and deep and then, with a low growl, he rained kisses along her neck and the valley between her breasts before returning to her mouth. His tongue sought hers, an intimate caress that spread through her like lightning.

He kissed her until she could hardly catch her breath and then he drew back, a wicked grin curving his lips. "You're not going to faint on me, are you?"

"Don't be silly," she retorted, and then she frowned. "Don't tell me you've actually made women swoon?"

"Shall I show you?"

"No, thank you," she said primly.

"We're not going to stop now, are we?"

"I hope not." She tugged at the waistband of his briefs. "Who's overdressed now?"

He was out of them in an instant, boldly displaying the evidence of his desire. "What now, my lady?"

"Do I have to tell you everything?" With an exaggerated sigh, she flung her arms out to her sides, a smile playing over her lips. "Just do what you do best."

His gaze moved quickly to the pulse throbbing in the hollow of her throat.

"I give you leave to taste," she said, her voice a whisper. "But only a taste."

"Aye, my lady. I will do my best to obey." Gathering her into his arms, he kissed her again, his mouth hot against her skin as he caressed her, his hands and lips arousing her until her whole body thrummed with need.

Megan murmured his name, her pleasure increasing when she felt the prick of his fangs at her throat, and then she was lost, floating in a world without time, without boundaries, where nothing existed except the two of them. It was a sensation like no other, and, for that one moment, when her desire melded with his, she didn't care if he took one sip or if he took it all, as long as they were bound together, body and soul. As long as she was a part of him.

Rhys made love to her all night long, every kiss, every caress branded in his mind, memories he would carry with him for the rest of his existence when, at last, he told her good-bye.

Chapter 44

As so often happened after a marathon night of love-making, Megan woke with a smile on her face. She was getting good at judging the time, she mused as she sat up, stretching. Without checking her watch, she knew it was late afternoon. A rush of tenderness engulfed her when she looked at Rhys, lying peacefully beside her. Was there ever such a lover as he? Tireless, inventive, always careful to see to her pleasure before his own.

Leaning down, she kissed his cheek ever so lightly, then slid out of bed. He didn't stir, but she wasn't surprised. Surely even a vampire needed his rest after a night such as they had shared.

She was wishing for a change of clothes when she glanced toward the closet. The door was open, and when she looked inside, she found some of her own clothes hanging there. Bless the man. Sometime in the wee small hours of the morning he had gone to her house and raided her closet.

Humming softly, she pulled a sweater and a pair of jeans from the hangers. Wondering if he had thought to bring her clean underwear, she opened one of the dresser drawers and found a week's worth of bras and panties. Carrying her clothing into the bathroom, she closed the door and turned on the shower.

Sometime later, her hair freshly washed and her teeth brushed, she dressed and went downstairs. All that loving had left her famished, and she raided the refrigerator, munching on a handful of blueberries while she debated what to have for breakfast. In the end, she cooked a waffle and two strips of bacon, and washed it all down with a glass of orange juice. After cleaning up the kitchen, she poured herself a cup of coffee and carried it into the living room.

Curling up on the sofa, she sipped the coffee, wondering how long it would be until she could go home again. She refused to think that Rhys might lose the battle with Villagrande. Instead, she skipped ahead to the time when the fight was over and Rhys was the victor. He had asked her to marry him, and she had said yes. Sitting there, a cup of coffee in her hand and the sun shining brightly, she let herself think about the kind of wedding she wanted. Something simple yet elegant. Of course, it would have to be in the evening. Refreshments would be light, since the groom and his guests wouldn't be eating.

Better to just elope. They could go to Vegas and get married there. Erik and Daisy could stand up with them, and when it was done, Megan could call her parents and tell them the good news. Her mother would be hurt, perhaps angry, that her only daughter had eloped, but in the long run, it would be easier than trying to explain why she wasn't having a big wedding with six bridesmaids, an orchestra, and a sit-down dinner.

Megan blew out a sigh. She should call her parents. Still, she hesitated as she imagined telling them she was getting married. What could she say? *Hi, Mom. Dad. Guess what? I'm in love with a vampire and as soon as he destroys the bad guy, we're getting married.*

Megan chewed on her thumbnail. How could she explain why Rhys never went out in the sun or why he didn't eat? How long could she make excuses for his odd behavior before her parents got suspicious?

When the trouble with Villagrande was over, she would have to go up to Redding and spend a few days with her folks. After all, news like this really should be related in person, at least the part about getting married. The vampire part would have to wait.

A subtle shift in the atmosphere told her that the sun was going down, and the vampires were rising. She knew Rhys would be the first to appear. She could sense his presence in her very bones, and even as she tried to understand how that could be, he was there, striding toward her. And she was smiling, her heart lifting at the sight of him.

She went into his arms gladly, a warm sense of contentment and belonging sweeping over her as he drew her close. His lips moved in her hair, his breath warm as he whispered that he loved her.

"I knew you were coming," she said, her voice muffled against his chest. "Even before I saw you, I knew you were nearby. How is that possible?"

"It's the blood link we share. It grows stronger every time you share your blood with me."

She looked up at him. "Am I going to turn into a vampire?"

"No, love. Not unless you want to."

"Would you love me more if I was like you?"

Hope sparked in the depths of his eyes. "Megan!"

"Don't get any ideas!" she said, pushing him away. "I didn't say I wanted to be a vampire. I just wondered if you'd love me more if I was."

"I love you more every day." He drew her into his embrace once more. "Mortal or vampire, it doesn't matter to me."

"But I'll grow old . . ."

Rhys covered her mouth with his hand. "It doesn't matter." At any rate, he wouldn't be there to see it. If he were an honorable man, he would tell her now that he intended to leave her as soon as Villagrande had been taken care of, but he didn't want to face the consequences. He knew she would object, perhaps strenuously. She might insist on going home, and he couldn't allow that. Better to say nothing, he decided, and enjoy whatever time together they had left.

"Oh, sorry," Daisy said, entering the room, "we didn't mean to interrupt."

"There's a bed upstairs, you know," Erik said, his voice tinged with amusement.

"Yeah, yeah," Rhys retorted good-naturedly. "Like you never kissed Daisy in the living room."

"Well, not when we had company," Erik said, winking at Daisy. "We're going out for"—he glanced at Megan and grinned—"a bite, you should excuse the expression. We won't be gone long."

"Do you want anything from the store?" Daisy asked.

"Maybe some chocolate ice cream," Megan said. "And a box of brownie mix."

"How could I have forgotten chocolate!" Daisy exclaimed with a grin. "It's a staple in every woman's diet."

"Behave yourselves while we're gone," Erik said. Taking Daisy by the hand, they vanished from sight.

"I wish I could just disappear like that," Megan exclaimed.

"I can arrange it. Just say the word."

"Are you going to nag me about becoming a vampire?"

"Would it help?"

"No. I'm happy just as I am, thank you very much." And so saying, she flounced into the kitchen and poured herself a glass of grapefruit juice.

Rhys followed, of course. Standing in the doorway,

he couldn't help admiring her softly rounded buttocks, the curve of her breasts, the way her hair framed her face. The flowery scent of her perfume mingled with her own unique scent, teasing his senses. How was he ever going to let her go?

Seeing him, Megan lifted the glass in a silent toast. "I like eating and drinking too much to give it up. And even though you won't admit it, you must miss it. How could you not?"

He snorted softly. "After five centuries, I don't remember what any of it tastes like."

She leaned back against the counter. "Did you miss it after you were first turned?"

"No. The scent of cooked meat was nauseating. Fruits and vegetables held no appeal."

"But you drink wine. Red, of course."

He chuckled softly. "Yes, the redder the better. It's the only thing I can drink." Seeing her look of wry amusement, he added, "Other than the obvious, of course."

"Of course." Turning toward the sink, she rinsed out the glass and put it in the dishwasher. The machine must have come with the house, she mused, since she couldn't think of any reason why vampires would need a dishwasher or any other appliances, for that matter. Facing Rhys again, she said, "I wonder why you can drink wine."

He shrugged. "I have no idea." He didn't tell her that, among vampires, it was a common practice to add a little fresh blood to the fruit of the vine.

"Are you going out later?"

"No." Closing the distance between them, he drew her into his arms. "I fed earlier." Before Megan came into his life, he had only fed once a week or so, sometimes less. The hunger, insatiable and irresistible in new vampires, burned less hot with each passing year, though there were circumstances that sparked that primal need. Lovemaking was one of them. Unwilling to put Megan's life at risk, afraid of losing control when they made love, he was careful to feed each night.

Megan locked her hands around his neck; then, rising on her tiptoes, she kissed him because he was so close, because she couldn't be near him and not want him. Because she loved him.

She was startled when, with a low growl, he crushed her body against his. His tongue plundered her mouth, hot and wild, as he backed her up against the wall, sending waves of sensual heat to her very core. Suddenly desperate to have him, she wrapped her legs around his waist, a groan rising in her throat.

"Now, Rhys," she said, gasping. "Now!"

Muttering an oath, he dragged his mouth from hers and set her on her feet just as Erik walked through the back door carrying a sack of groceries. Daisy and Alex were right behind him.

A rush of embarrassment heated Megan's cheeks when Erik said, ever so dryly, "I knew we should have knocked."

Megan kept her back to the others. How was she ever going to face these people again?

"Nothing to be embarrassed about, Megan," Erik said cheerfully as he set the bag on the counter. "Sex is a fact of life, you know. We all do it."

"Yes," she replied, her voice muffled against Rhys's chest, "but not in someone else's kitchen." Not in front of two vampires and a man she had only met once before.

Glancing over Megan's shoulder, Rhys said, "You wanna give us a few minutes?"

"Of course," Daisy said, and followed her husband out of the room.

"You might want to put that ice cream away before it

melts," Alex said as he sauntered toward the door. "There's enough sexual heat in here to melt iron."

"Well, that was humiliating," Megan remarked as she put the ice cream in the freezer. Delving into the sack again, she saw that Daisy had thoughtfully included a can of whipped cream and a jar of hot fudge.

"It could have been worse," Rhys said with a grin.

Tossing a bag of cookies into the cupboard, she muttered, "I suppose." Five minutes later, and they would have been caught in the act.

Laughing softly, he took her by the hand. "Come on, darlin', you can't hide in the kitchen forever."

"Wanna bet?" Reluctantly, she accompanied him into the living room.

Erik, Daisy, and Alex were sitting on the sofa. Avoiding their eyes, Megan sat on the love seat. Rhys sat beside her.

"So," he said, "what's going on?"

"We ran into Alex at the market. I think you should hear what he has to say." The seriousness in Daisy's tone told Megan it could only be bad news.

Rhys leaned forward. "Spit it out."

"We haven't had any vampire trouble since you left town," Alex said. "Until last night. I met a friend of mine who's a hunter. He said an entire family was found drained of blood out on Centre Street." Alex took a deep breath. "The youngest victim was only six months old."

"That's awful!" Daisy exclaimed.

"Damn right," Erik said.

Megan stared at Rhys. A muscle worked in his jaw, his hands were clenched. "Do you know who did it?" he asked, his voice grim.

Alex shook his head. "I don't know. But it was clearly a vampire. He didn't bother to make it look like anything else."

Rhys stood. "I need the address."

Megan sprang to her feet. "You're not thinking of going there!"

"I have to know if it's Villagrande."

"How could it be?" she asked. "How could he know where we are?"

"I should have known leaving LA would be a waste of time," Rhys said quietly, almost as if he was talking to himself. "Villagrande's the oldest of our kind. We've been kidding ourselves, thinking we could hide from him. I have a feeling he's there, waiting for me."

Megan grasped his arm. "You can't go. I won't let you!"

"Maybe I can talk to him, tell him to keep LA."

"And what if that's not enough anymore?" Erik glanced at Megan.

She knew what he was thinking. It wasn't just about territory now. Villagrande was angry because she had destroyed Shirl.

"If he wants a life for a life," Rhys said, "I'll give him mine."

"No!" Fear for Rhys, fear for her own life, leeched the strength from Megan's legs, and she dropped down on the love seat. "I'm the one who killed Shirl."

"This isn't open to discussion, Megan," Rhys said, his voice gruff. "I told you before, this is between Villagrande and me. No one else."

"You know you can't face him alone," Erik said. "Hell, I'm not sure the five of us together can beat him."

"He's so old," Daisy remarked, a note of awe in her voice. "Who knows, maybe he is indestructible." With a shake of her head, she murmured, "Maybe he really is immortal."

"Only one way to find out," Alex said with a cocky grin.

"The address," Rhys said, his voice sharp. "I want it now."

With an apologetic glance at Megan, Alex gave Rhys the street address.

Before she could beg him not to go, Rhys was gone. Springing to her feet, she cried, "Erik, you've got to go with him! Please! You said it yourself, he doesn't stand a chance alone."

"She's right," Alex said, pumping his arm in the air. "Erik, let's you and me go kick some vampire ass."

Megan sighed and glanced at her watch. It seemed like Rhys, Erik, and Alex had been gone for hours.

She was about to ask Daisy how she could appear so calm when her husband might be fighting Villagrande at that very moment, when Daisy suddenly rose to her feet.

"What's wrong?" Megan asked, her mind filling with horrible possibilities.

"I thought I heard Erik calling me."

"Why would he do that?"

"I don't know. Maybe something's gone wrong." Daisy moved toward the front door. "Erik?"

Rising, Megan walked up behind Daisy. "I don't hear anything."

"He's calling me," Daisy said, her brow furrowing.

"Why doesn't he come inside?"

"He's badly hurt. He . . . oh, no!"

"What is it?" Megan asked anxiously. "What's happened?"

"Megan, I'm so sorry. He said Alex is badly hurt and . . . and Rhys is dead."

Megan pressed her hand to her chest as the room began to spin. Rhys was dead . . . dead . . . dead. "No." She shook her head. "I don't believe it. . . ."

A high-pitched cry came from outside. Shouting Erik's name, Daisy opened the door and dashed out into the night.

Megan started after her, only to come to an abrupt halt as a dark shape filled the doorway.

Before her mind could register what she was seeing, pain exploded through her head and everything went black.

Chapter 45

Rhys stood in the shadows on Centre Street, his senses reaching out toward the brown-and-beige, two-story Colonial house. The yard was well kept, the lawn green, with a few shrubs in front. Five steps climbed to the front porch. Rose bushes grew on either side of the stairs.

The stink of death shrouded the place. Under the stench of fear and blood, the unmistakable smell of vampire lingered in the air. A distant part of his mind wondered how Villagrande had gained entrance to the house.

A thought carried Rhys into the living room. He wouldn't have been able to enter the house uninvited if the family had still been alive, but murder had been done here, destroying the threshold's basic protection. He had no need of an invitation. And no need to wonder further how Villagrande had gained entrance. The blood splattered on the floor inside the entryway told the tale. Someone had unwittingly invited Villagrande inside. And died because of it.

Rhys moved silently through the dark rooms, following Villagrande's trail. The vampire had struck the four other members of the family while they slept, as evidenced by the blood-stained sheets and blankets carelessly tossed over the bodies.

Rhys lingered in the nursery where the last murder had occurred. The room was decorated with fairy wallpaper and pictures of Tinker Bell. The baby had died last. A Tinker Bell quilt, bright with blood, covered the dead infant. A Peter Pan lamp stood on the dresser beside a framed photo of a woman holding a baby. The mother and child? The woman was young and pretty, with dark brown hair and hazel eyes. The baby was rosy-cheeked and blue-eyed.

Rhys swore softly. He had done some pretty despicable things in the course of his existence, but he had never killed an infant. Would he do such a thing if he existed as long as Villagrande? Would he view mortals as nothing but prey, his to do with as he pleased? The thought brought him up short and with it came the realization that he was close to feeling that way now. Or he had been, until Megan had come into his life. She had reminded him of how frail mortals were, how tenuous and precious their hold on life.

Megan. Needing to know she was all right, he closed his eyes, concentrating on the bond between them, and felt nothing. Only two things could prevent him from linking with her; she was either unconscious, or dead.

Before he could determine which, he sensed Villagrande's approach. An instant later, the vampire materialized in the room. Preternatural power radiated from him, enhanced by the fresh blood he had recently consumed.

"So," Tomás said. "We end it, now."

"What have you done with Megan?"

A smile that was pure evil spread across Villagrande's face. "You'll never know."

"Dammit, where is she? What have you done to her?" He couldn't ask the question uppermost in his mind. Couldn't ask if she was dead, afraid that saying it aloud might make it so.

"Me?" Villagrande spread one hand over his heart. "I've done nothing."

"Don't play games with me, you bastard. Where is she?"

Villagrande rocked back on his heels. "She killed Shirl. She wounded me. I will have my revenge."

"No! Dammit, if you want a life, take mine."

"I intend to."

Rhys glared at the other vampire, his mind racing. How had Villagrande managed to bypass the safeguards on Delacourt's house? And having done so, what had he done to Erik, Daisy, and Alex? Had he destroyed them all?

The thought had scarcely crossed his mind when Erik and Alex appeared in the room.

Villagrande looked at them and laughed. "Three against one, Costain? Hardly sporting."

"I don't want to have to fight you," Rhys said. "Take the West Coast. Take my life. Just spare Megan."

"It's too late to make deals." Villagrande's gaze swept over the three of them. "You have all defied me," he declared imperiously. "And the penalty is death." And with that ultimatum, he sprang toward Rhys, fangs bared, hands transforming into lethal claws.

Baring his own fangs, Erik leaped onto Villagrande's back, but Villagrande shook him off, like a pit bull shaking off a rat. Erik slammed into Alex, and the two of them sailed through the air, a tangle of arms and legs as they hit the wall, hard.

Rhys charged toward Villagrande, the only thought in his mind to destroy the vampire who threatened Megan's life. They came together in a furious rush. Villagrande's power lashed out at Rhys with the force of a tornado.

Rhys was hardly aware of the pain as Villagrande's teeth and claws savaged his neck and chest. The physical pain was as nothing compared to the ache in his heart at the thought that Megan might be dead. If she was dead, it was all his fault. He never should have drawn her into his life.

He knew a moment of respite when Erik leaped into the fray again, momentarily drawing Villagrande away.

Alex crawled toward Rhys, his left arm dangling uselessly at his side. Holding out his good arm, he said, "Drink."

Rhys didn't argue. With a low growl, he buried his fangs in the other man's wrist. He didn't have time to take much, but even a little helped. He spared hardly a glance for Delacourt, who lay facedown on the floor. There was no time to worry about Delacourt, no time to think of anything but his own survival. He refused to believe Megan was dead. She was out there, somewhere, and she needed him. It was that thought that gave him the strength to meet Villagrande's next attack.

They battled in silence, fangs and claws shredding cloth and flesh alike. The air was thick with preternatural power and the coppery scent of blood.

Breathing hard, Rhys fell back. Blood flowed freely from numerous bites and gashes on his face, neck, chest, and back.

With his heightened senses came an increased ability to feel pain and he felt it now with every movement he made, felt his strength ebbing. Wounds that should have healed quickly continued to bleed; the more blood he lost, the weaker he would become. His whole body screamed in protest when he moved.

Villagrande stared at him, a smug smile on his face. He had won, and he knew it.

Rhys took a deep breath. He couldn't lose. If he did, it was like signing a death warrant for Delacourt and Alex, although he wasn't sure if Delacourt was even still alive. Alex lay slumped in the corner, his pale face streaked with blood.

Dammit, he couldn't quit now. Summoning Megan's

image, Rhys gathered what strength he had left. He was about to charge Villagrande when Daisy and Megan materialized in the room.

Rhys swore, his overwhelming relief at seeing Megan alive warring with his anger at Daisy for bringing her here.

Villagrande looked at the two women, then threw back his head and laughed. "Costain and Delacourt for dinner," he crowed. "And two plump females for dessert."

"Is that right?" Megan exclaimed. "Well, eat this!" Pulling a stake from the folds of her skirt, she sprang forward, the stake aimed at Villagrande's chest.

Daisy was moving, too. Taking a bottle from her pocket, she threw the contents in Villagrande's face.

Rhys knew a moment of hope. Was it possible that Daisy and Megan had accomplished what he couldn't? But no. With a roar of pain and outrage, Villagrande backhanded Daisy, sending her flying across the room. Her head struck a corner of the dresser, and she crumpled to the floor beside her brother.

In a move faster than the eye could follow, Villagrande grabbed the stake from Megan's hand. He tossed it aside; then, grabbing Megan by the throat, he lifted her off her feet. "Perhaps I'll have dessert first," he said with a growl.

There was a sudden rush of movement as Erik regained consciousness. A wild cry rose in his throat when he saw Daisy sprawled on the floor, her hair stained with blood from a gash on the back of her head.

Villagrande dropped Megan and spun around to face Delacourt.

And in that one instant, when Villagrande was distracted, Rhys snatched the hawthorn stake from the floor and drove it into the vampire's back. It sliced through Tomás Villagrande's ancient preternatural flesh like a hot knife through butter, piercing his black heart. Blood fountained from the wound in a crimson arc, spraying over the room's inhabitants, as well as the walls, the ceiling, and the floor.

Villagrande turned on Rhys with a scream of rage, his eyes as wide and red as the depths of hell. And then, as if someone had jerked his legs out from under him, he toppled to the floor and lay still.

Megan ran toward Rhys, her face fish-belly white. "Is he dead?"

"Oh, yeah," Rhys murmured.

And even as he spoke the words, Villagrande's body began to shrink in on itself, the flesh melting away, the bones disintegrating, until there was nothing left but dust.

"Holy crap!" Cradling his broken arm, Alex limped over to stand beside Rhys. "I've never seen anything like that."

"Ashes to ashes, dust to dust," Megan whispered, and buried her face against Rhys's shoulder.

He ran his hand up and down her back. "Are you all right?"

"Yes. Are you?"

"I will be." Rhys glanced over his shoulder to where Delacourt was kneeling beside Daisy. "How is she?"

"I'm fine," Daisy said. "Alex, are you okay?"

"Well, other than my wounded pride, my sprained ankle, and my broken arm, yeah, I'm okay." He looked at his sister, at Erik, and at Rhys, then looked at Megan. "I'm thinking, as the only two humans in the room, that we should make ourselves scarce for a while."

"Why?" she asked, frowning, and then, suddenly aware that all three vampires needed blood, she said, "Oh."

Rhys glared at Alex. "Do you really think we'd feed off you?"

Alex snorted. "Delacourt's done it before. And I seem to remember you gnawing on my arm just a few minutes ago."

"That wasn't feeding," Rhys said, scowling.

"All right, that's enough," Daisy said, pushing herself

to her feet. "This is what we're going to do. We'll transport Megan and Alex to the nearest hospital. Megan will stay with him while the rest of us go and, uh, get cleaned up. And then we'll meet back at the hospital. All right?"

"Who put you in charge, Daisy Mae?" Alex asked.

"Have you got a better idea?"

"No, I guess not."

"It's settled then," Daisy said. "Let's go."

Megan looked up at Rhys. "You can drink from me if you want."

Rhys shook his head. "I need more than you can spare." He ran his knuckles over her cheek. "What happened? I couldn't sense you anywhere. I thought . . ." He took a deep breath. "I thought you were dead."

"We're fine," Daisy said, smiling. "It's the zombies that are dead. I think Villagrande sent them after us, maybe just to keep us out of the way, or maybe . . ." She shrugged. "Who knows?"

"What happened to the zombies?" Megan asked.

Daisy looked at her as if she wasn't very bright.

"Oh."

"As soon as they were out of the way, I grabbed you and transported us here and that, as they say, is that."

Alex cleared his throat. "Do you think you two could reminisce about that later? I'm in a bit of pain here."

"Sorry," Rhys muttered. He glanced at Erik and Daisy. "Let's go," he said, and wrapping his arms around Megan, he transported the two of them to the hospital.

Moments later, Erik, Alex, and Daisy materialized beside them.

Daisy smiled at her brother. "Make up a good story," she said. "You used to be aces at that when we were kids."

"Yeah," he muttered. "Catch ya later."

Megan looked up at Rhys. "Be careful."

"Don't worry about me. Ask the doctor to check you over while you're in there."

She rubbed her hand over his cheek. "I'm fine. Come on, Alex," she said, slipping her arm around his waist, "let's go get you patched up."

Rhys shook his head as he watched Megan help Alex up the driveway toward the emergency room entrance. She was quite a woman.

"Costain?"

He answered Erik without taking his gaze from Megan. "Not now."

Erik took Daisy's hand in his and gave it a squeeze. "We'll meet you back here in, oh, say, half an hour, all right?"

Rhys nodded, his attention still on Megan. No matter how long he lived, he knew he would never see her like again. She was everything a man could want in a woman—kind, caring, with a loving heart and a generous nature, and he knew that, from this night on, his existence would never be the same. Leaving her would be the hardest thing he had ever done, but it was best for both of them. When he was gone, her life would go back to normal and so, he thought glumly, would his.

He watched her until she was out of sight, and then he melted into the darkness, where he belonged.

Chapter 46

Feeling chilly, Megan wrapped her arms around her middle. It had been a heck of a night. Alex hadn't wanted to stay in the hospital, but the doctor had insisted. In addition to his broken arm and sprained ankle, Alex had two broken ribs and a possible concussion.

Rhys had told her to have the doctor check her over, too, but there had been no need for that as far as she was concerned. She didn't have any broken bones, and there was no cure for the nightmares she was likely to have.

Tapping her foot, she glanced up and down the street. Where was Rhys? Hadn't he and the others agreed to meet back here in half an hour? Had she been mistaken? Or maybe it had just taken them longer to get cleaned up. Cleaned up, indeed. She knew what that meant. They had all gone to feed. Good grief, she was hanging out with vampires. Megan shook her head. After all she had seen and heard, did Daisy really think she was such a nervous Nelly that she couldn't handle the truth?

Megan scrubbed her hands up and down her arms as a chill wind blew down the street. Of all the times to be without a cell phone, she thought impatiently, and then lifted a hand to her head. She had a bump the size of a goose egg where the zombie had hit her. She was, she thought, lucky to be alive.

She almost jumped out of her skin when Daisy and Erik appeared seemingly from out of nowhere. Even in the faint glow of the lights that lined the driveway, Megan could see that they had both fed and fed well.

"Where's Rhys?" Daisy asked, glancing around. "I thought he'd be back by now."

A horrible sense of foreboding settled over Megan. Closing her eyes, she tried to find the bond she shared with Rhys, but there was nothing there. Only emptiness.

When she opened her eyes, the look on Erik's face, the pity in his eyes, turned her stomach cold.

"Come on," he said, putting his arm around her. "We'll take you home."

Before Megan realized what was happening, she was standing in her own living room.

"Why don't you sit down?" Erik suggested. "Daisy, would you bring her a glass of water?"

"I don't want a glass of water or anything else," Megan said, her voice brittle. "I just want to know what's going on."

"Why don't you sit down?" Erik repeated.

Megan sat on the edge of the sofa, her hands tightly folded in her lap. "He's left me, hasn't he?"

Erik nodded. "I'm afraid so."

"But why? It's over. Villagrande's not a threat anymore."

"He's afraid for you," Erik explained. "Afraid of what might happen in the future."

"So, just like that, it's over?"

Erik's gaze slid away from hers.

"Why didn't he come and tell me all this himself?"

Erik shrugged. "That should be obvious."

"I never took him for a coward," Megan said.

"I'm sure he was only thinking of you," Daisy said. "You'll always be in danger as long as your life is tied up with his. It's one of the reasons vampires rarely get involved with mortals."

"Is that right?" Megan asked, her anger rising. "Then how do you explain the two of you?"

"I said rarely, not never. It happens from time to time. But such pairings aren't usually successful unless . . ." Daisy looked at Erik and smiled.

"Unless the mortal becomes a vampire," Megan said. "Is that what you're trying to say?" Rhys had left her. She couldn't think about it anymore, not now, when the hurt was so fresh. And so she changed the subject. "Why did Villagrande send zombies after us tonight?" *Zombies.* Megan shook her head. Even now, it was hard to comprehend.

"For no good reason, I'm sure." Erik smiled at his wife. "Whatever his reasons, I guess he underestimated your powers."

Daisy made a face at him. "I can't believe I was so stupid. As soon as I went outside, I knew I'd made a mistake. While I was dispatching one of the zombies, the other one got inside and knocked Megan unconscious. By the time I got back in the house, the zombie had Megan slung over his shoulder and was heading for the back door."

"I can't believe such creatures exist," Megan said.

"Oh, they exist all right," Erik said. "But they're not too bright."

"How do you . . . ? Never mind," Megan decided. "I don't want to know." Zombies had once been human. Did they return to normal when whoever held them in thrall released them? Or did they remain mindless creatures with no will of their own?

"It's late," Daisy said, patting Megan's hand. "You should get some sleep."

Sleep? After the last few days, she didn't think she

would ever get another peaceful night's sleep. And even as the thought crossed her mind, she was yawning.

"We'll stay until morning, if you don't want to be alone," Erik offered.

The idea was appealing. But rather than seem cowardly, Megan shook her head. "I'll be all right, but thank you, both of you."

"You've got our number," Daisy said, giving Megan a hug. "Call if you need us."

Megan nodded. She started to rise, intending to walk Daisy and Erik to the door, but they were gone in a swirl of twinkling blue and dove gray motes before she gained her feet.

"A neat trick," she murmured, and burst into tears.

Thursday morning dawned cold, gray, and gloomy, the perfect setting for Megan's misery. She had cried most of the night, hadn't slept more than an hour or two at most, which explained why she woke with a headache and eyes that felt like they were filled with sand.

It seemed strange to wake in her own bed in her own room. Strange to know she was alone in the house. The nightmare was over. Tomás Villagrande had been destroyed. Erik and Daisy had returned to Boston. And Rhys . . . ? Where was he? Knowing it was useless, she tried to open the link between them, but it was like trying to call a number that had been disconnected. No one was there.

Rising, she stepped into her slippers and plodded downstairs to make a pot of coffee. When it was done, she sat at the table staring into her favorite Grumpy coffee cup and wishing she could just disappear. How was she supposed to go back to her old, boring life after having known Rhys? Yes, he was dangerous. Yes, being around him was risky.

But as scary as it had sometimes been, being with him had made her feel vibrant and alive. And she loved him as she would never love anyone else.

She carried her coffee cup into the living room and switched on the TV. Talk about a vast wasteland. Did anyone even watch TV in the morning? There was nothing on but black-robed judges trying to look important while they ruled on mundane cases, cheerful talk show hosts who discussed even more mundane topics, ubiquitous soap operas, and mindless cartoons. Where had all the good shows gone?

She refilled her cup twice and then, deciding she couldn't just sit around in her pj's and mope all day, she called Mr. Parker and told him she was back in town and that she would be at work that night. Early.

It turned out to be the best decision she could have made. Mr. Parker was genuinely happy to see her again. Being back at work, talking to people who didn't drink blood or disappear in the blink of an eye helped to ground her in the real world again.

Shore's was having its once-a-year sale, which meant they were even busier than usual, for which Megan was grateful. She didn't have any time to think of anything—or anyone—else.

It was after eleven when Drexel swaggered into Shore's. Clad in a fluorescent pink shirt, black velvet vest, and skintight black pants, he was a sight to behold. His face lit up brighter than his shirt when he saw Megan.

"Babe!" he exclaimed as he wrapped her in a bear hug. "I'm so glad to see you!"

"Thanks, Drexel. I missed you, too," she said, and meant it. "Hey, I thought you were going on tour?"

"We cut it short."

Extricating herself from his embrace, she asked, "Is something wrong?"

"Just my head. Ever since the fire, I've been having trouble performing on a stage unless it's outside. My shrink says it'll pass, in time. He says I should take a vacation, so that's what I'm gonna do. So, I need some new threads, something hip but subdued, you know?"

"I'm sure we can find something that will work."

Ninety minutes and nine thousand dollars later, Drexel pulled her into another exuberant hug. "Thanks, babe. Just seeing you makes me feel better." He smiled at her, though it didn't quite reach his eyes. "So, babe, have you decided to marry me yet?"

"Drexel . . ."

"I know you think I'm too young and that I'm just kiddin' around, and that I don't really mean it, but if you say yes, I'll make you the happiest woman in the world."

"You're sweet, really, but I wouldn't be good for you or anyone else right now."

"What happened, Megan? Some guy hurt you?"

"In a way." Lifting a hand, Megan caressed his cheek. "If I was going to marry anyone, it would be you."

He laughed at that. "I'll hold you to it," he said, and kissed her on the cheek. "See you soon."

Megan stared after him as he left the shop. Maybe she should marry Drexel. He wouldn't ask much of her, and it would be nice to share her life with someone so uncomplicated, someone who adored her. . . .

Good grief, what was she thinking? Drexel was nineteen years old. Did she have some kind of perverse weakness for younger men? Rhys might be an old vampire, but physically he was still on the shy side of twenty-one.

Pain stabbed at her heart when she thought of him. Young or old, right or wrong, she missed him more than she would have thought possible. Why was it, when she had finally met the perfect man, it turned out he wasn't really a man at all?

She blinked away her tears as a new customer stepped into the shop. Grateful for the distraction, she hurried toward him.

The first two weeks without Rhys were the hardest. She went to work early. She offered to come in on her nights off and help Mr. Parker take inventory. She decided to paint her kitchen, and spent a day looking at color swatches before choosing a pale yellow. When that was done, she threw herself into redecorating her bedroom. She painted the walls a pale, pale lavender. Painted the trim and the ceiling white. She bought a new white quilt and a lavender dust ruffle for her bed, then added several throw pillows in varying shades of lavender and purple. She bought new white curtains, and ordered new carpeting, recovered the seat cushion on the desk chair to match the dust ruffle. And when she was finished, she hated it because she couldn't imagine Rhys being comfortable with all that lavender.

The next day, she painted the room sky blue, traded the lavender dust ruffle for a white one, exchanged the lavender and purple pillows for blue, and threw her paint roller away.

Later, standing in the doorway admiring her handiwork, she decided she was going insane.

"Definitely insane," she muttered, "when you worry that a man you're never going to see again might not like lavender."

With a shake of her head, she went in to shower and get ready for work.

Rhys stood outside Shore's, avidly watching Megan's every move. He was jealous of every man who entered the store and talked with her, heard her voice, shared her laughter. It was all he could do to keep from charging in and breaking the neck of the handsome young man she was currently assisting.

Hands clenched, he took several deep breaths. He had known it would be hard to stay away from her, known he would miss her, but the reality was far worse than anything he had imagined. Standing there, cloaked in the shadows of the night, he decided he was a damn fool; worse, he was a glutton for punishment. He had shared her bed, tasted her blood, asked her to marry him, all the while knowing that they could never have a life together.

He swore softly. Even with walls and windows separating them, he could detect the flowery perfume of her hair, the warm, womanly scent that was uniquely hers. And her blood . . . Damn! The vibrant, coppery scent aroused vivid images in his mind—images of the two of them in bed, her body writhing beneath his, her voice crying his name. He licked his lips, remembering the sweet taste of her life's blood on his tongue, the way it had flowed into him, warming all the cold places in his body as her loving acceptance had warmed the dark, empty hollows of his soul.

"Megan." Her name slipped past his lips, as soft and fervent as a prayer.

Megan glanced at the clock. Almost midnight. Most people called it the witching hour, but at one time, it had been the vampire hour. Unable to help herself, she glanced toward the door, but there was no sign of her vampire. *Her vampire.* If only that were still true.

"Miss?"

She turned, forcing a smile as a tall, good-looking man came toward her. "Do you have this in a size forty-four?" he asked. "I couldn't find one on the rack."

"I think we might have one in the back. Just let me . . ."

Whatever she had been about to say fled her mind with the overwhelming feeling that she was being watched. Pivoting on her heel, Megan stared at the front window, but could see nothing more than a few cars parked at the curb and the lights from the restaurant across the street. But that sense of being watched persisted.

"Miss?"

"What?" She glanced at her customer, her mind blank. "I'm sorry, I . . . What were you looking for?"

He held up the navy blazer. "You were going to see if you had this in my size."

"Oh, right." With a last glance at the front window, Megan went to check the back room.

The rest of the night went by quickly. Megan couldn't stifle a sense of disappointment when Mr. Parker locked up after their last client departed. Knowing it was foolish, she still found herself hoping that Rhys would be waiting for her when she went out to her car. She should be used to it by now, but she hated going home to an empty house.

Thoughts of going home brought Shirl to mind. Thinking of her former best friend brought the sting of tears to her eyes. She quickly wiped them away before Mr. Parker could see them. The last thing she wanted to do was explain why she was crying. She could hardly tell Mr. Parker the truth, and she wasn't in the mood to think up a plausible lie.

"Well," Mr. Parker said, coming up behind her. "If we do this well tomorrow night, I guess Mary Lou will get that cabin in Big Bear after all."

Mary Lou was Mr. Parker's wife. She was fifteen years younger than he was. They had been married for twelve years, had two sets of twins, and seemed very happy together. Megan couldn't help envying them.

"Come on," Mr. Parker said, as he did most every night. "I'll walk you out."

With a nod, Megan grabbed her coat and handbag.

"I don't think I ever realized just how valuable you are to the business," Mr. Parker remarked as he unlocked the back door. "Two of our best customers said they wouldn't be back until you were. I'd hate to think what would happen if you quit."

"Well, I don't see that happening anytime soon," Megan said. "I'll see you tomorrow."

"Take care."

Megan waved at him; then, with a sigh, she unlocked her car and slid behind the wheel.

A scream clawed its way out of her throat when she realized she wasn't alone. "Rhys!" She pressed a hand to her thundering heart. "Good Lord, are you trying to scare me to death?"

She took several slow, deep breaths, her fear quickly replaced by the sheer joy of seeing him again. Her heart did a little somersault when she saw that he was wearing clothes she had sold him. He was as breathtakingly handsome as always, and she reveled in the sight of him.

After the first rush of happiness, anger reared its ugly head. "What are you doing here?"

"I'd think that would be obvious."

"Oh?" She clasped her hands in her lap to keep from reaching for him. "Why is that?"

"I know you're upset with me."

"Upset? Why on earth would I be upset?" She could hear her voice rising, but she couldn't help it. What right did he have to leave her without so much as a word of good-bye and then just reappear as if nothing had happened?

"Megan . . ."

"Would you please get out of my car?" When he didn't

move, she wondered if cars were like houses. Could she rescind her invitation?

His gaze moved over her face, as warm and tangible as a caress. "That's not what you want."

She glared at him. "Quit. Reading. My. Mind."

"Listen, I'm sorry, okay? I shouldn't have taken off the way I did. I know that." He raked his fingers through his hair. "Dammit, Megan, I couldn't look in your eyes and tell you good-bye. Leaving you was hard enough as it was."

"Daisy told me you left because my life would be in danger as long as you and I were together. So, what's changed? You're still a vampire, and I'm still human, and unless you've figured out a way to become human again . . ." Her voice trailed off. "Please, Rhys, just go away. I can't do this again."

"Megan." He caressed her cheek, ever so lightly. "I don't want to go on without you. I was alone for a long time and content to be so, until I met you. I'm in love with you. That hasn't changed, and it never will. I know you love me. I know it's risky for you to stay with me, but maybe if we leave LA, go to a small town where there aren't any other vampires . . ." He shrugged. "Maybe we could start over, pretend we're like any other couple."

It was tempting, so tempting. But what if it didn't work out? Did she want to try again? Risk her heart again? What if some other maniac vampire showed up? "I don't know."

"I promise I won't ever leave you again, unless you tell me to go."

And still she hesitated.

"Megan."

She bit down on her lower lip. How could she resist the love she heard in his voice, the longing in his eyes? She had agreed, perhaps rashly, to marry him not long ago. Did she still want that? Did she really want to spend her life with a man she would never understand? Did she want to give up the chance to have a family and live a normal life?

He was reading her mind again. She could see it in the clenching of his hands, the tightening of his jaw.

"I'm sorry I bothered you," he said, his voice tight. "It won't happen again."

She stared at him, her heart pounding. He was leaving. What if she never saw him again? Did she want to spend the rest of her life without him?

Preternatural power filled the air, and she knew that in moments he would vanish from her sight.

"Good-bye, Megan."

"No!" She grabbed his arm, realizing in that moment, when he was about to leave her, perhaps forever, that she couldn't live without him. "Don't go!"

She frowned as a slow smile spread across his face. Pulling her hand away from his arm, she glared at him. "That's so unfair!"

"What?"

"Oh, I hate you! You were reading my mind again, weren't you? You knew I wouldn't let you go!"

Chuckling softly, he reached for her, but she pulled away. "No, not until you promise to stop reading my mind."

"I'll do better than that," he said, still grinning. "I'll teach you how to block me."

"There's a way to do that?" she exclaimed. "Why didn't you tell me that before?"

He shrugged. "Because I like reading your mind," he admitted. "I like knowing what you're thinking about me."

"So, can you read everybody's mind?"

"Pretty much. In the beginning, it took a lot of concentration to block them all out."

"Can all vampires do it?"

"As far as I know."

"So, how do I block you?"

"You have to erect a barrier around your mind. Visualize it as a brick wall, or a dam, or some other structure that's solid."

"And that works?" she asked skeptically.

"It takes a lot of practice, but that's the only way I know." Seeing the look of concentration on her face, he took her hands in his and gave them a gentle shake. "Do you have to try it now?"

"I guess not."

"So, what do you say we go to your place? I'll grovel at your feet until you forgive me, and then we can indulge in some hot make-up sex."

Megan laughed as she fumbled with her keys. "You're incorrigible."

"I know." His hand curled over hers. "Leave your car here. I've got a lot of groveling to do, and I want to get to the huggin' and kissin' before dawn."

Before she had time to say ah, yes, or no, they were in her bedroom. Rhys was sitting on the foot of the bed, and she was on his lap.

"Vampires," she muttered.

Rhys fell back on the mattress, carrying her with him. When they landed, they were lying face-to-face. "Be honest, would you have me any other way?"

"No." She might wish for him to be human, but if he was, he wouldn't be the Rhys she had fallen in love with.

"You promised to marry me, remember?" His hand slid slowly up and down her back, a gentle caress.

"Hmm, I'm not sure that promise is still valid, since you went off and left me."

"No?"

"No."

He pulled her body closer to his. "I want you."

She could feel the hard evidence of that want against her belly.

"And you want me." His voice was a low purr in her ear.

"Are you reading my mind again?"

"No. I can smell it on you."

"You cannot."

"It's a sweet, musky scent, guaranteed to drive a man wild."

She grinned. "Are you wild?"

"Baby, you'd better believe it." He bared his fangs. "Want me to show you?"

"Oh, Grandma, what big teeth you have."

He leered at her. "That ain't all that's big."

"Are you gonna show me that, too?"

"You bet."

"Will I like it?"

"I've never had any complaints." Rhys swore softly when she went suddenly quiet. Damn. He didn't have to read her mind to know she was wondering how many women he had known, how many he had loved. He hoped she wouldn't ask, but since she was a female, it was inevitable.

"Rhys?"

He blew out a sigh. Here it comes.

"Can I ask you something? You don't have to answer if you don't want to."

"You can ask me anything." He was only surprised she hadn't asked before.

"Have there been a lot of . . . Never mind. I don't think I want to know."

"There's only been one other woman who ever meant anything, Megan."

"Did you love her very much?"

"I thought I did. I was a young man, a young vampire

back then. I'm not sure how much of what I felt for her was love, and how much was lust, but it was nothing compared to what I feel for you. So, are you still willing to marry me, pretty Megan?"

Cupping his face in her hands, she closed her eyes and whispered, "Read my mind."

Chapter 47

Megan turned slowly in front of the triple mirror. The dress, long and off-white with fitted sleeves and a square neck edged with lace, made her feel like a fairy-tale princess. What would Rhys think of it?

They hadn't talked about when or where they would get married. Hadn't decided whether to run away to Vegas or stay in town and have a judge perform the ceremony. Either way, she was going to be ridiculously overdressed. Still, a girl only got married for the first time once, and she had always dreamed of a dress exactly like this.

It was a little after four when she left the bridal shop, the wedding gown in hand. After laying the dress in the backseat of her car, she walked across the street to 31 Flavors and ordered a hot fudge sundae with extra whipped cream and a cherry. Tonight, she and Rhys had a lot to talk about. When and where to get married. Who, if anyone, to invite to the ceremony. Where they would live. As for what would happen when the difference in their ages became impossible to ignore, she refused to think about it. She loved Rhys, and he loved her, and that was all that mattered.

Megan was smiling when she left 31 Flavors. Humming softly, she started across the street toward her car.

A loud screech of brakes was her only warning. She screamed once. And then everything went black.

Rhys jackknifed into a sitting position, Megan's scream still ringing in his ears, but when he tried to link his mind to hers, he found only emptiness.

Stone-faced, Evelyn DeLacy stood at her daughter's bedside, one of Megan's hands held tightly in her own. George stood on the other side of the bed, tears streaming down his cheeks. Evelyn tried not to look at her husband, tried not to hear his sobs. She had to keep her emotions under control. If she didn't, she knew she would shatter into a million pieces and, like Humpty Dumpty, they would never be able to put her back together again.

A drunk sixteen-year-old boy driving a stolen car had hit Megan as she crossed the street. Megan had been in surgery for seven hours. The doctors had told Evelyn and George that if Megan survived the next twenty-four hours, there was a chance that she would recover, though it was unlikely she would ever walk or use her left arm again.

Evelyn didn't care about that or anything else. All she wanted was for Megan to wake up. Tears stung the backs of her eyes as she gazed at her daughter's battered face, at the casts on her legs and arm, at the bandages that covered numerous wounds, at the tubes and wires that hooked her to beeping machines.

As she brushed a lock of hair from Megan's brow, Evelyn murmured a silent prayer, asking, begging, for a miracle.

She looked up, startled, as a tall man with dark blond hair and impenetrable dark brown eyes appeared in the doorway. Something about him made her take several steps forward, putting herself between the stranger and her daughter's bed. "May I help you?" she asked.

Rhys paused in the doorway when he realized Megan wasn't alone. He had been so intent on getting to her, he hadn't bothered to scan the room for anyone else. There was no doubt that the stranger was Megan's mother. She was a pretty woman with reddish-brown hair and blue eyes. The man was tall with brown hair just going gray at the temples. His eyes were the same shade of brown as Megan's.

Rhys inclined his head slightly in the woman's direction. A quick search of her mind told him her name was Evelyn. The tearful man standing across from her was Megan's father, George.

Rhys stepped farther into the room. "I've come to see Megan."

"Are you a friend of hers?" Evelyn asked.

"You could say that."

George DeLacey wiped his eyes, his narrow gaze assessing as he looked Rhys up and down. "Who are you?"

"Rhys Costain."

George shook his head. "She never mentioned you."

Rhys looked past Megan's parents to where she lay, a slim, pale-faced figure swathed in bandages. He had followed the scent of her blood to this place. Try as he might, he had been unable to link with her mind. The thought that she might never regain consciousness frightened him in ways nothing else ever had.

He took a deep breath. "I just want to see her," he said quietly. Nothing they said or did would stop him, but he would try to get their permission first.

Evelyn and George exchanged glances, then George nodded almost imperceptibly.

"Alone," Rhys said.

George shook his head. "No way."

Swallowing his irritation, Rhys moved toward the bed. "What do the doctors say?"

"Nothing very hopeful," George replied, his voice thick. "Even if she wakes up, she won't walk again."

Rhys took one of Megan's hands in his. "What happened?"

"She was out shopping for a wedding dress. A drunk driver hit her when she was crossing the street."

"Where is he?"

"In jail."

Rhys nodded. If Megan died, all the cops in the world wouldn't be able to protect the kid who had done this to her.

"How do you know our daughter?" Evelyn asked.

"We met at Shore's. We've been dating for several months." Rhys swallowed hard. "I asked her to marry me, and she said yes."

George and Evelyn exchanged glances again. George looked incredulous.

"She never told us," Evelyn murmured. She looked at her husband. "Why didn't she tell us?" she asked, and burst into tears.

George put his arm around his wife's shoulders and guided her, gently, toward a chair. When she was seated, he knelt beside her.

Rhys moved swiftly to Megan's side. Taking her hand in his, he tried once again to join his mind with hers. It hadn't worked from a distance; he prayed it would work now. *Megan?* He squeezed her hand, silently willing her to respond. *Megan, can you hear me?*

"Dammit, Megan," he whispered urgently. "You've got to hear me!"

But silence was his only answer.

* * *

Rhys wandered the dark streets, heedless of where his feet carried him. Nothing mattered now but Megan. Four days had passed since the accident, and she was still lost to him, locked in a coma. He had gone to see her every night. Her parents no longer questioned his right to be there. Not wanting Megan to be left alone, her mother and father were taking turns staying at her bedside. Evelyn stayed during the day, George at night. Rhys arrived at the hospital late at night, after exhaustion and worry had taken their toll and her father finally succumbed to sleep.

And now Rhys again stood at her bedside. Unmindful of her father, asleep in a chair, Rhys held Megan's hand, speaking softly of his love for her, of the life they would have together if she would only awaken. Even though he wasn't sure she heard him, he went on, reminiscing about the nights they had spent together, the times they had made love.

"Megan, my sweet." His fingertips brushed her cheek, traced the curve of her lips. Her face was as pale as the pillowcase beneath her head, her skin as cool as his, her breathing shallow. How much longer would she lie there, unmoving and unaware, before he lost her for good?

His gaze moved to her throat, to the pulse slowly beating there. If he brought her across, would it restore her to good health?

Or condemn her to spending an eternity in the horrible state she was now in?

And how was he to know?

Three long weeks passed. Fear and concern for Megan drew Rhys and her parents together. Rhys found himself genuinely liking George and Evelyn. They were good, honest people, openly expressing their gratitude to the doctors and nurses caring for their daughter. Rhys knew they were naturally curious about the man who claimed to be engaged to Megan, but their questions were tactful, and they didn't pursue subjects he was reluctant to discuss.

He knew they wondered why he always arrived after dark, even on the weekends, why he never went for coffee with George or accepted any of the donuts or homemade treats Evelyn sometimes brought to the hospital to share with the staff. He considered telling them what he was but, in the end, years of discretion kept him silent. It was one thing for Megan's parents to think of him as somewhat mysterious, another entirely for them to know the truth.

George and Evelyn spent hours talking to Megan or reading to her. A radio played constantly in the background in the belief that it might stimulate a response.

Rhys continued to speak to her as well, sometimes vocally, sometimes mentally, but there was no response. She didn't speak, didn't open her eyes, didn't move. Some of the bandages had been removed, revealing ugly bruises on one side of her face and along her right arm.

Earlier that night, the doctor had called Megan's parents into his office. Curious to hear what the physician had to say, Rhys had dissolved into mist and followed them. The news hadn't been good. As gently as possible, the doctor had explained that, with every passing day, it became more unlikely that Megan would regain consciousness. He also advised them that there was a possibility she would regain consciousness but be in a vegetative state, meaning she would have lost all cognitive neurological function. She could be awake and appear normal, but if the cognitive part of her brain ceased to function, she would be unable to respond to her surroundings.

Distraught, Evelyn had sobbed, "It would be better if she died! She wouldn't want to live like that."

"There's always a chance she'll wake and regain all

her faculties," the doctor said. "But I thought you should be prepared for the worst as well."

With a nod, George led Evelyn out of the doctor's office.

Rhys had been back at Megan's bedside when they entered her room.

He was there now, his hand lightly stroking her brow. It was almost two in the morning, and the hospital was quiet save for the soft shushing of rubber-soled shoes as the night nurses checked on their patients, and the ever-present wheezing and beeping of life-support machines. Megan's father slept in one of the chairs, his brow furrowed with worry even in sleep.

As he had every night, Rhys tried to connect with Megan's mind. Tonight, fear and a sense of doom caused by the doctor's gloomy prognosis drove him to persist longer than usual. Intent on the task at hand, he did not notice as the minutes and hours passed, until he felt the warning tingle that signaled the rising of the sun.

He was about to kiss her good-bye when her voice sounded in his mind.

Rhys?

Megan! Hope flared in his heart and soul. *Megan, can you hear me?*

Where am I? Where are you? It's dark, so dark.

Heat from the rising sun prickled along his skin. Moving quietly, he went to the window and closed the blinds. *Open your eyes for me, Megan.*

I can't. What's wrong with me? Am I dying?

No, love, you're in a coma.

Then how can we be talking?

I don't know. I want to try something.

What?

I'm going to give you some of my blood.

He smiled faintly as he sensed her revulsion. *It might help heal you.*

Afraid she would object, he didn't wait for a reply. He bit into his wrist, and, after gently parting her lips, he held his arm over her mouth and let a few drops of his blood trickle onto the back of her tongue, hoping they would slide down her throat.

He would have given her more, but a nurse chose that moment to pause outside the door.

Turning his back to the nurse, Rhys closed the wound in his wrist, bid the nurse good night, and left the room.

Outside, he took a quick moment to admire the sunrise before willing himself to his penthouse.

He was back at the hospital at sundown the following night. Earlier that day, he had touched Megan's mind. Even though she hadn't answered, he had assured her that he loved her, missed her, would see her soon. He was whistling softly when he arrived at the hospital, unable to contain the hope that his blood had worked a miracle, that he would walk into Megan's room and find her sitting up in bed, smiling and happy.

But such was not to be. Even though she was now breathing on her own, Megan lay as before, pale and unmoving. George and Evelyn stood together at her bedside. The weeks had taken their toll on Megan's parents. Her father's hair had turned completely gray; deep lines of worry bracketed his mouth. Her mother, too, had aged in the last month. Evelyn never smiled now; the dark shadows under her eyes were evidence of sleepless nights and anxious days.

Two to four weeks, the doctor had said. If Megan didn't come out of the coma in that time, the odds were she would lapse into a vegetative state and never recover.

Taking her uninjured hand in his, Rhys bent down, his lips brushing her cheek, her eyelids, the pulse beating in the hollow of her throat.

"Fear not, my love," he whispered. "I won't let that happen to you." She didn't respond, of course, and because he wanted her to know he was there, he reached for the link between them; he found only emptiness.

In that moment, he made up his mind. No more waiting. No more hoping and praying for a miracle that might never come. Tonight, he would bring her across. But not here. If it worked, she would wake with a ravenous thirst. It wasn't something doctors or nurses were equipped to handle, nor was it something he wanted her parents to see.

He glanced at George and Evelyn. It would be cruel to take Megan away without warning them beforehand. They had suffered enough.

His decision made, he closed the door to Megan's room. "George, Evelyn, why don't you sit down? I have something to tell you."

They exchanged glances, then sat side by side, holding hands. Evelyn's cheeks were damp with tears. George looked mildly curious.

Rhys dragged his fingers through his hair. "I'm not sure how to say this except to say it straight out. I'm a vampire."

Evelyn blinked at him.

"This is no time for jokes," George said angrily. "My daughter is dying."

"Do I look like I'm joking?"

Clenching his fists, George started to rise. There was no doubt in Rhys's mind that the man was looking for any excuse to hit something. He had been through hell in the last month, and, up to now, he had managed to hold it all together.

Drawing on his preternatural power, Rhys forced the man back into his chair.

"What the hell!" George exclaimed. "Who are you?"

"I told you, I'm a vampire. Do you need more proof?" And so saying, Rhys bared his fangs and unleashed the monster within him. He knew what they saw. He had seen enough of the Undead to know that his face took on a hardness no human's ever wore, that his eyes were blood red.

Evelyn opened her mouth to scream, but no sound emerged.

George stared at him. "Why are you telling us this? Are you going to . . ." His face paled.

With a shake of his head, Rhys retracted his fangs and willed the beast back inside. "I'm telling you because I'm going to take Megan to my place. I'm going to bring her across. I think it's the only way to save her."

"You want to turn my daughter into a vampire?" George shook his head emphatically. "I won't hear of it."

"George, let him do it."

"Are you out of your mind, woman?" George exclaimed. "He wants to make her into a monster!"

"I don't want to lose Megan." Evelyn turned pleading eyes on Rhys. "Do it. If it will bring Megan back to us, do it."

George brought his fist down on the arm of the chair. "Dammit, Evie, you don't know what you're saying!"

But Evelyn wasn't listening to her husband. Her gaze was focused on Rhys. "Please," she said, "save her for me."

"I'll do my best, but there are no guarantees."

Evelyn bit down on her lower lip, obviously disturbed by the implication that something might go wrong. And then she squared her shoulders. "You're our only hope."

"Megan wouldn't want this," George said. "And if she knew what you were, she wouldn't want you, either."

"She knows."

George stared at him, all the fight gone out of him.

"I'm taking her out of here tonight," Rhys said quietly.

"I want you to go talk to her doctor and tell them you've decided to take her home to die. I'm sure they'll try to talk you out of it. Just stand firm. Sign whatever papers you have to."

George nodded, though it was clear from the look on his face that he was against it.

"When that's done, I think the two of you should go home. There's nothing else you can do here."

Evelyn clutched her husband's arm, her expression growing even more anxious. "But you'll bring her to us, after? You swear it?"

Rhys nodded. "When she's ready to see you, I'll bring her home. You have my word on it."

Chapter 48

After the necessary papers were signed, Megan was wheeled out to the curb to a waiting ambulance. Once the nurse who had accompanied Megan returned to the hospital, George dismissed the ambulance. Evelyn sobbed quietly as she kissed Megan's cheek.

Rhys lifted Megan from the gurney. "We need to go."

"Remember your promise," Evelyn said. Sobbing now, she kissed Megan's cheek.

George stared at Rhys. "I don't care who you are. I don't care what you are." His voice broke." If anything happens to my daughter . . ."

Rhys nodded. "I hear you."

Since George and Evelyn knew what he was, there was no need for subterfuge. Rhys removed the casts from Megan's legs, then willed the two of them to his penthouse.

Doubts plagued him as soon as he laid her on his bed. What if it didn't work? What if he took too much and killed her? What if his blood brought her out of the coma but left her body unable to move, her mind unable to function?

Sitting on the edge of the bed, he ran his knuckles along her check. She was cold. Cold and unresponsive.

Guilt burned through him. No matter how you sliced it,

this was all his fault. If he had stayed out of her life, she wouldn't have been looking for a wedding dress on that fateful day, wouldn't have been crossing the street at just that moment. Wouldn't be lying here, more dead than alive.

His fingertips slid down the side of her neck to rest in the hollow of her throat. He could feel the faint beat of her heart, hear the sluggish flow of blood wending its way through her veins, the labored sound of her breathing.

"If you're gonna do it," he muttered, "you'd damn well better do it before it's too late."

Murmuring, "Forgive me for breaking my promise, my love, but I can't let you go," he drew her into his lap and brushed the hair away from her neck.

He didn't realize he was crying until the red of his tears dripped onto her cheeks.

"Forgive me," he said again, and lowered his head to her throat.

She didn't respond when his fangs pierced her skin.

He drank, and her blood was warm and sweet and more satisfying than anything he had ever known.

He drank until the spark of life within her guttered and then, biting into his own wrist, he held it over her mouth, lightly stroking her throat in an effort to make her swallow.

"Drink, my love," he pleaded. "You've got to drink."

Nothing. No movement, no fluttering of her eyelids, no change in her breathing or heartbeat.

"Megan!"

His blood dripped into her mouth, slid down her throat.

Slowly, so slowly that at first he thought he was imagining it, her skin grew warmer, color returned to her cheeks, her heartbeat grew stronger, steadier.

"That's it! Come on, darlin', fight!"

When she swallowed, he placed his wrist closer to her mouth. Relief poured through him when her hand came up, grasping his wrist to hold his arm closer.

"Megan." Murmuring her name, he caressed her cheek with his free hand. "Drink, Megan. Take as much as you want," he said fervently. "As much as you need."

Megan reached upward. It was like rising from the bottom of a deep, dark pit with nothing to guide her. She had no recollection of how she had fallen, no explanation for the pain that engulfed her, no memory of anything but a shadowy figure with blazing red eyes. . . .

"Rhys?"

"I'm here."

She tried to open her eyes, tried to follow the sound of his voice, but the smothering darkness dragged her down again.

"Fight, Megan! Come on, love. Come to me."

His voice rang in her mind. Rhys. If she could find him, if she could just touch him, everything would be all right.

She struggled through the thick blackness, clawing her way toward his voice, and slowly, ever so slowly, the inky blackness faded to a dark gray that gradually grew lighter even as her body felt lighter, almost weightless.

"Yes, that's it. Come to me, Megan, my love. I'm here, waiting for you."

"Rhys!" She fought her way toward him until, with a final burst of energy, she opened her eyes. "Rhys!" she cried. "Oh, Rhys, I had the worst nightmare! I tried and tried to wake up, and I couldn't."

Gathering her into his arms, he murmured, "I know, love." He rained featherlight kisses on her cheeks, her chin, the tip of her nose.

"Why is my arm in a cast? What are all these bandages? Why am I wearing a hospital gown?"

"Don't you remember what happened?"

"No, I . . ." She stared at him as if seeing him for the

first time, then frowned. "You look different somehow." Turning her head slowly, she scanned the room. "Everything looks different." She wrinkled her nose. "Smells different."

"Megan—"

"What's happened to me? Why is everything so strange? Why do I feel so funny?"

"One thing at a time, love. You were hit by a car. You've been in a coma for almost a month."

"A coma!" She stared at him, disbelief in her eyes, and then shook her head in denial. "No, it was just a bad dream."

"Then how do you explain the cast and the bandages?"

Confusion flickered in the depths of her eyes. "I don't know."

"Like I said, you've been in a coma. The doctors weren't hopeful that you'd recover. They said there was a good chance you'd be in a vegetative state for the rest of your life, and if you recovered, you'd never walk again."

She stared at him. "If I was as bad off as all that, why aren't I still in the hospital?"

"Megan, wiggle your toes."

"My parents must be worried to death. Good Lord, what must they think?"

"They know everything. I spent the last few weeks at the hospital with them."

"You did?"

Rhys nodded. "When we realized you weren't going to recover, I told them what I was—"

Megan's eyes widened. "I don't believe you!"

"I told them I was going to take you out of the hospital and bring you here."

"And they agreed?" she asked skeptically.

"Megan, wiggle your toes."

With an exasperated sigh, she stretched her legs out and wiggled her toes. "Happy now?"

Uttering a wordless cry, he cradled her to his chest, a silent prayer of thanks rising in his heart.

It took him a moment to realize she had gone rigid in his embrace.

"You turned me, didn't you?" she asked, her voice brittle as memories of Shirl and how her friend had changed after being turned jumped to the forefront of her mind. "That's why I feel so funny, isn't it! How could you do such a thing without asking me?" She pushed off his lap, then stood staring down at him. "How could you?" she repeated, her voice sharp with accusation and anger. "You promised . . ."

"Would you rather be back in the hospital, unconscious?"

"No, of course not, but . . ." She glanced around the room, only then realizing she could see everything clearly even though the lights were off. She could smell the oil and gasoline from a passing truck, the scent of garbage from somewhere down the street, the hint of rain in the air.

Maybe she wasn't a vampire. There were all kinds of stories about people waking from comas with abilities they hadn't had before.

Turning on her heel, she walked out onto the balcony. She couldn't be a vampire, didn't want to believe it was true. But why would Rhys lie?

"Vampire." She grimaced as she murmured the word. Was that why she felt so strange, so unsettled? So empty inside?

"You're hungry," Rhys said, coming up behind her. "You need to feed."

Feed? Visions of a cheeseburger and a chocolate malt rose in her mind, and with it the knowledge that she would never again enjoy any of her favorite foods. She was a vampire now. No more onion rings. No more spaghetti and meatballs. No more hot, fresh bread from the bakery. No more lemon meringue pie. And even as the thought crossed her mind, she realized she had no desire for any of the foods she had once loved.

Vampire. She repeated the word in her mind. *Vampire. Vampire.*

She was hungry, and she was a vampire.

Hungry vampires didn't eat hamburgers and French fries.

They drank blood.

"Megan?"

She turned, ever so slowly, to face him. "I'm a vampire."

He nodded. "Hate me if you like. Destroy me if it will make you happy. But I can't be sorry for what I've done." He smiled faintly. "I couldn't bear to think of the world without you in it."

"You said my parents know everything. Does that mean they knew what you were planning to do?"

He nodded again.

"And they didn't care?" she exclaimed incredulously.

"They believed it was the only way to save you."

"I'll never see them again."

"Of course you will. I promised to take you home when you were ready, but there are a few things you need to learn first."

"Like how to . . . to hunt?"

"Exactly."

She shook her head. "I don't think I want to learn. I don't think I want to be a vampire."

"I'm afraid there's no going back."

She stared at him, trying to determine how she felt. She should be angry or sad or curious or something. But she didn't feel anything. Only a strange kind of numbness. Maybe it wasn't surprising, since she was no longer human. "I don't want this."

"I know, but why don't you give it a try before you make up your mind?"

"It's not like buying a new dress," she said bitterly. "I can't take it back if it doesn't fit."

"Being a vampire isn't all bad. I know you're worried about the blood part. You're probably thinking it'll be repulsive and you won't be able to do it. But trust me, it won't be as bad as you think."

"Was it that easy for you to accept being a vampire? One day you were human, and the next you weren't?"

"Exactly. I wasn't particularly happy with it at first, but I knew it couldn't be undone and so I decided to make the best of it. And I've never been sorry."

"You've never wanted to be human again? Not once in five hundred years?"

"No." It wasn't entirely true. Not long ago, he had thought he would gladly give up being a vampire to spend one mortal lifetime with this woman. But now that she was nosferatu, they could have many lifetimes together, if she would accept what had happened and move on. He held out his hand. "Come hunting with me."

"What if being a vampire brings out the worst in me?"

"It won't."

"How do you know? I don't want to be like Shirl!" Her eyes grew wide as a new thought occurred to her. "She was like Villagrande's slave. He told her to kill you, and she would have done it. She would have killed me if he'd told her to. It was like he was her master and she didn't have any will of her own."

"He was a strong vampire," Rhys said quietly. "And she was new. It was easy for him to influence her."

"You're a strong vampire," Megan retorted. "And I'm new."

"That's true. The difference is, I love and respect you. I'm not looking for a sex slave or a sycophant. I just want to make this as easy for you as I can." Once she had accepted being a vampire, he would take her to meet what was left of the Council so they would know she was under his protection. He had contacted them soon after Villagrande had been destroyed and informed Rupert, Nicholas, and Julius that he was staying on the West Coast. Odd, that the three who had been with him the longest had survived the latest conflict.

"So, what do you say?" he asked. "Are you ready to go out and face the world?"

"No, but let's get it over with." She wouldn't admit it to Rhys, but she couldn't deny that she was curious. Of course, Rhys being Rhys, he was probably reading her mind even now.

If she decided to stay with him, she was going to have to practice blocking him or she would never have any privacy, she thought irritably, and then frowned.

If she stayed with him.

That was the sixty-four-thousand-dollar question, wasn't it?

After removing the cast from Megan's arm and the last of the bandages, they made a quick trip to Megan's house. There, she changed into something a little more appropriate than an open-in-the-back hospital gown, and then Rhys took her hunting down by the beach.

Megan felt surprisingly calm as they strolled along the boardwalk, perhaps because none of it seemed real. This had to be a continuation of her nightmare, some sort of extended fever dream, and she would soon wake up in her own room, in her own bed.

She followed Rhys into a small tavern, stood near the entrance as he studied the men and women inside. When he asked her which patron she fancied, she pointed at a young man with black hair and dark blue eyes. Moments later, Rhys left the tavern, and the young man followed him down the street into the shadows. Megan trailed behind them. Rhys hadn't spoken to the man or signaled to him in any way that she had seen; nevertheless, the man followed at his heels like a well-trained puppy. When Rhys came to a stop, the young man stopped, too.

Rhys looked at her over the man's head; then, slowly and deliberately, he bit the man's neck.

The coppery scent of fresh blood wafted through the air, warm and fragrant. The smell teased Megan's nostrils, bringing the world around her into sharp focus, and her hunger with it. The numbness that had gripped her, the odd sense of unreality, all faded away, and she wanted nothing more than to take the young man in her arms.

She looked askance at Rhys, who nodded once.

And Megan took the dark-haired man into her embrace, lowered her head to his neck, and drank his life's blood as if she had been doing it for years.

"Will I be able to be awake during the day, the way you are?" Megan asked.

"Not at first," Rhys replied, "but soon." He had been surprised at how quickly and efficiently she had fed the first time. Now, walking back to his penthouse, he wondered at the wisdom of bringing her across. The thought of losing her had been more than he could bear, but now, with his head clearer, he couldn't help thinking about Shirl. He hadn't made many mistakes in his life as a vampire, but turning Shirl was right up there in the top two.

They walked in silence for several moments before Megan declared, "I'm going back to my place."

A number of responses chased themselves across his mind, and then he shrugged. "If that's what you want."

"Aren't you going to try to talk me out of it?"

"No. I'm through making decisions for you."

Megan blinked at him, not at all sure she liked this new side of him. At best, she had expected an argument; at worst, she had thought he would tell her outright that she was staying with him, like it or not.

"A few things you need to remember," he said, his voice cool. "You need to be inside before the sun comes up. Your preternatural instincts will tell you when you're in danger. You'll need to feed every night for the first year or so. If you kill anyone—"

"I'm not going to do that!"

He shrugged. "It happens sometimes, especially with the newly turned. They can't always control their hunger. So, like I was saying, if you kill anyone in my territory, be sure to dispose of the body."

His territory. How had she forgotten that Rhys was the Master of the City? Among the West Coast vampires, his word was law.

"You need to meet the members of the Vampire Council," Rhys said. "I'll arrange it for tomorrow night."

When he came to a stop, she realized they were in front of her house. She had been so stunned by what he was saying, she hadn't paid any attention to where they were. In a distant part of her mind, she was amazed that they had covered so much ground in such a short time, and that, in spite of the long walk, she wasn't the least bit tired.

"I've rented a house near the beach," he said, and rattled off the address. "Be there tomorrow around midnight."

Megan crossed her arms, her chin jutting out defiantly. "What if I don't want to meet the Council?"

"Be there, or I'll come and get you."

Forcing as much sarcasm as she could into her voice, she muttered, "Yes, Master."

"Exactly," he said. "And don't you forget it."

With a huff, she turned on her heel and walked up the driveway.

Rhys stifled the urge to call her back. She had every right to be angry with him. Dammit! He could compel her to return, force her to stay with him, but that wasn't what he wanted. He loved her, and although she might not want to admit it now, she loved him.

Whether they spent their future together or not was up to her.

Chapter 49

Aware of Rhys's gaze on her back, Megan went up the stairs and into the house, then slammed the door behind her. She knew it was childish, but she felt better for it. Then, unable to help herself, she hurried to the front window and peered out at the sidewalk. There was no one there. She couldn't help feeling hurt that he had let her go so easily. Oh, she knew she had made him angry, but what had he expected? One day she was trying on wedding dresses and the next thing she knew, she was a vampire.

Vampire.

Undead.

Creature of the night.

She licked her lips, remembering how enjoyable it had been to feed off the dark-haired man, amazed by how natural it had seemed, how good he had tasted. She should have been repulsed by what she had done; instead, she was eager to go out and do it again. What if she went to visit her parents and all she wanted to do was snack on them? What would they think when they saw her, when they knew what she was? Would they be horrified? Or overcome with guilt for agreeing to let Rhys turn her into a monster?

But she didn't feel like a monster. She felt the same as always, only better.

What was she going to do about Rhys? He had asked her to marry him, but she had been mortal at the time. Was his proposal still valid now that she was dead?

Not dead. Undead.

She blew out an impatient sigh. Whatever she was, she felt more vital and alive than ever before. Stronger mentally and physically. More sure of herself.

She lifted a hand to her face. Did she look the same? Shirl had looked the same, and yet not. Her hair had been more lustrous, her eyes more intense, her skin almost luminous. None of the changes had been blatant, but they had been there.

Just her luck, Megan thought ruefully. She probably looked better than she ever had but, being a vampire, she would never be able to see for herself.

Filled with a sudden nervous energy, she dived into a frenzy of housework, vacuuming the rugs, changing the sheets on her bed. Moving into the kitchen, she stared at the refrigerator for a moment and then, taking a deep breath, she opened the door.

Megan had expected to find a gallon of sour milk and a crisper filled with spoiled produce; instead, the refrigerator was empty. That was odd, she thought, then realized that while she had been in a coma, her parents had probably stayed here. Her mother must have cleaned out the fridge and watered the plants.

Murmuring, "Oh, Mom," she sat on one of the kitchen chairs and burst into tears. How was she ever going to face her parents? How could she ever trust herself to be with them? What if she went to see them and they were repulsed by what she was, or, worse, afraid of her? But they hadn't been afraid of Rhys, not if what he said was true.

Her sobs came harder, faster. She cried for her lost

humanity, for the children she would never have, the suntan she wouldn't get next summer, all the chocolates she would never eat.

She grabbed a towel and wiped her face, stared at the faint streaks of red on the towel, then, with her finger, she wiped a tear from her eye. It was red. But of course it was. She was a vampire now. Fighting a rush of hysteria, she went to the sink and splashed cold water on her face. So, she was a vampire. Time to stop feeling sorry for herself and look on the bright side. She would never get sick. She would never have to worry about getting old and wrinkled and helpless. But even that had its drawbacks. All the people she knew would age and die—her parents, Mr. Parker, Drexel, all of her other clients. Sooner or later, they would all be gone.

All but Rhys . . .

He loved her.

She loved him.

He was a vampire.

She was a vampire.

There was no reason for them to be apart now. Whatever danger she might have faced as his mortal companion no longer existed.

She sat there, thinking about her future, until a rather unpleasant tingle skittered down her spine. She knew instinctively that it was almost dawn.

She checked all the doors and windows to make sure they were locked, closed the curtains in her bedroom, then changed into her nightgown and climbed into bed, her heart pounding.

Lying on her back, she stared up at the ceiling. What would it be like when she was compelled to sleep during the day? Was it like death? A cold knot of fear formed in the pit of her stomach. What if she didn't wake up again?

Megan, close your eyes and relax.

The sound of Rhys's voice calmed her immediately. His thoughtfulness made her love him all the more. In spite of everything, he hadn't left her to face her first day as a vampire alone.

Megan came awake as the sun went down. For a moment, she lingered under the covers. The Dark Sleep really was like death, she thought. Judging from the unrumpled blankets on her bed, she hadn't moved at all once she closed her eyes. Nor had she dreamed.

Throwing the covers aside, she went into the bathroom to shower. Emerging some fifteen minutes later, she pulled on her bathrobe, then sat on the edge of the bed. What did vampires do to pass the time?

Feeling at loose ends, she found her cell phone, took a deep breath, and called her parents. As soon as she heard her mother's voice, she knew everything would be all right. Vampire or not, her parents loved her. Nothing would change that. She talked to her mom and then her dad, and then her mom again. After assuring her mother that she was fine and promising to see them soon, Megan ended the call, had another good cry, and went out to try hunting solo.

At eleven thirty, Megan stood in front of her closet, her foot tapping impatiently as she went through her clothes. Nothing suited her mood. And then, on impulse, she reached into the back and pulled out a dress she had bought on a whim but never worn. Removing the plastic, she held it up. It was perfect. A pair of three-inch black heels and her grandmother's antique pearl necklace completed the outfit.

"You can't go wrong with basic black and pearls," she muttered, and left the house.

She arrived at the address Rhys had given her ten minutes late, on purpose. It was a small act of defiance, but it made her feel better.

The house was small, the wood siding weathered and gray. A white picket fence surrounded the yard. Lights glowed from behind the curtains in the front window. The scent of sea and sand was strong, accented by the sound of waves endlessly rushing to the shore.

An inhaled breath told her Rhys was inside the house, and that he wasn't alone.

Gathering her courage, she stepped through the gate and walked along the crushed shell path to the front door.

It opened before she knocked, and Rhys stood there, his dark blond hair gleaming in the lamplight.

Taking a step back, he said, "Come in."

She followed him into the living room. Two black leather sofas faced each other in the middle of the room. There was no other furniture. A tall man with wispy gray hair and blue eyes stood next to the fireplace. A man who appeared to be in his twenties slouched on one of the sofas, regarding her through slitted brown eyes. A red-and-black snake tattoo adorned his left arm. A third man, with black, slicked-back hair and a thin mustache, reminded her of an old-time matinee idol. He sat on the other sofa, his ankles crossed, a faint smile on his handsome face.

Rhys gestured at the gray-haired man. "Megan, this is Nicholas. The man who looks like Valentino is Rupert . . ."

"And I'm Julius." The tattooed man eyed her as if she was a bowl of cream and he was a hungry cat.

Rhys glared at Julius before returning his attention to Megan. "I've told them that you're mine and as such, you're under my protection, and by my law, theirs as well."

She hesitated, unsure of what to say, then murmured, "Pleased to meet you."

"My dear, the pleasure is all mine," Nicholas said. Coming forward, he bowed over her hand.

Rupert and Julius exchanged glances; then, as if pulled by the same string, they rose and offered her their hands.

"Nice to have a pretty woman on the Council," Julius remarked with a smile just short of a leer.

"Yes, indeed," Rupert agreed.

Megan looked at Rhys askance. He hadn't said anything about her being a member of the Council. Good grief, she had only been a vampire for one day.

Rhys shrugged, then turned his attention to the others. "That's all. I just wanted you to meet Megan."

"My pleasure," Nicholas said, and vanished.

"Ciao, baby," Julius murmured, and he, too, disappeared from sight.

"It was nice to meet you, Megan, my dear," Rupert said. "I'm sure we'll meet again soon."

Megan nodded, but before she could think of anything to say, Rupert was out the door, leaving her alone with Rhys. Suddenly nervous, she rubbed her hands up and down her arms. Why had she worn this come-and-get-me dress? Tight and black, it outlined her every curve.

"You look lovely," Rhys said quietly.

"Thank you." She cleared her throat. "I'm . . . I . . ." She looked up at him. He had always known what she was thinking, why wasn't he reading her mind now?

"The meeting is over," he said formally. "Thank you for coming."

She stared at him, mute. If she didn't say something, do something, she had the feeling she might never see him again.

She cleared her throat. Squared her shoulders. And blurted, "You promised to marry me not long ago, Mr. Costain. Do you intend to renege on that promise?"

"Megan . . ."

"I love you." She spoke quickly, before her courage could desert her. "And I know you love me."

He regarded her silently, one brow raised, for several moments.

Megan resisted the urge to wring her hands as she waited for him to say something, anything, to break the tension between them.

And then the corner of his mouth twitched. "Reading my mind, are you, Miss DeLacey?"

"I believe turnabout is fair play, Mr. Costain."

"Indeed? What am I thinking now?"

"Nothing I would dare repeat," she replied with mock horror.

Laughing, he pulled her body against his and kissed her, long and hard. "If you think that's bad, just wait until I get you home."

Home, she thought, as he swept her into his embrace and kissed her again. Home wasn't a house with a roof and four walls; it was here and now, in the arms of the man she loved.

Epilogue

Megan glanced over her shoulder. "How do I look?"

Evelyn DeLacey blinked back a tear as her daughter pirouetted in front of her. "Beautiful," she murmured. "Like a fairy-tale princess." The dress looked as if it had been made for her, simple yet elegant with its fitted sleeves and square neckline edged with delicate lace. "How do you feel?"

"Wonderful!" Megan exclaimed, and then, seeing the tears in her mother's eyes, she whispered, "Mom, please don't cry. I'm happy, truly I am."

Evelyn forced a smile as she blinked back her tears. Her daughter, her only child, was a vampire, and in a few minutes, she would be married to a vampire. But, vampire or not, Megan was here, as loving and happy as always, and for that Evelyn would be forever indebted to her future son-in-law. And even though it certainly wasn't the kind of life she would have wished for Megan, Evelyn couldn't deny the proof of her own eyes. Megan had never looked happier. And Rhys adored her, anyone could see that.

There was a knock on the door, and then George peeked inside. "Everybody ready?"

"Yes, dear," Evelyn said. She hugged Megan, then left the room to take a seat in the living room with the others.

"So," George said, his voice gruff with emotion, "this is it, the big day."

Megan nodded, suddenly too choked up to speak as she recalled a night a year or so ago when she and Shirl had talked about weddings and promised to stand up for each other when the time came.

George cleared his throat. "You look beautiful, princess."

"Thank you, Daddy, so do you." Standing on tiptoe, Megan kissed her father's cheek. "I love you."

George blinked back a tear as he placed her hand on his arm. "Okay, sweet pea, here we go. I hope that man of yours knows how lucky he is."

Megan's heart fluttered with excitement as they walked down the short hallway that led into her parents' living room. They had decided on a small wedding, just the immediate family and a few close friends. She winked at Daisy and Erik, who were sitting beside Alex and Paula, nodded at Mr. and Mrs. Parker, smiled at Drexel, who made a sad face in return. And then she saw Rhys. Clad in a black tux from Shore's, he stood next to the minister in front of the flagstone fireplace.

As she moved toward him, Megan overheard several of her friends remarking on what a hunk Rhys was, whispering how lucky she was to have him. She couldn't have agreed more.

He smiled at her then, a slow, sexy smile that released a million happy butterflies in her stomach. Her heart swelled with love, and she knew, deep inside, that choosing to stay with Rhys had been the right decision.

When the minister asked if she would have Rhys Costain as her husband for the rest of her life, Megan smiled inwardly, thinking that the minister had no idea just how long that might be.

Moments later, her husband swept her into his arms and claimed her lips with his in a long, slow kiss that turned her legs to jelly and set her blood on fire, and she knew without a doubt that no matter what the future held, she would face it unafraid as long as Rhys stood beside her.

Smiling, she looked up into his eyes. "And just like in the fairy tales," she murmured, "they lived happily ever after."

If you liked this Amanda Ashley book,
check out some of her other titles currently
available from Zebra . . .

NIGHT'S TOUCH

One Kiss Can Seal Your Fate . . .

Cara DeLongpre wandered into the mysterious Nocturne club looking for a fleeting diversion from her sheltered life. Instead she found a dark, seductive stranger whose touch entices her beyond the safety she's always known and into a heady carnal bliss . . .

A year ago, Vincent Cordova believed that vampires existed only in bad movies and bogeyman stories. That was before a chance encounter left him with unimaginable powers, a hellish thirst, and an aching loneliness he's sure will never end . . . until the night he meets Cara DeLongpre. Cara's beauty and bewitching innocence call to his mind, his heart . . . his blood. For Vincent senses the Dark Gift shared by Cara's parents, and the lurking threat from an ancient and powerful foe. And he knows that the only thing more dangerous than the enemy waiting to seek its vengeance is the secret carried by those Cara trusts the most . . .

NIGHT'S KISS

He Has Found His Soul's Desire . . .

The Dark Gift has brought Roshan DeLongpre a lifetime of bitter loneliness—until, by chance, he comes across a picture of Brenna Flanagan. There is something hauntingly familiar about her, something that compels him to travel into the past, save the beautiful witch from the stake, and bring her safely to his own time. Now, in the modern world, Brenna's seductive innocence and sense of wonder are utterly bewitching the once-weary vampire, blinding him to a growing danger. For there is one whose dark magick is strong . . . one who knows who they both are and won't stop till their powers are his . . . and they are nothing more than shadows through time . . .

NIGHT'S MASTER

Passion Has a Darker Side . . .

Kathy McKenna was sure that the little Midwestern town of Oak Hollow would be isolated enough for safety, but the moment the black-clad stranger walked into her bookstore, she knew she was wrong. Raphael Cordova exudes smoldering power, and his sensual touch draws Kathy into a world of limitless pleasure and unimaginable dangers.

Oak Hollow was supposed to be neutral territory for supernatural beings. Instead it has become home to an evil force determined to destroy them—and kill any mortal who gets in the way. As leader of the North American vampires, Raphael has always put duty first, but then, no woman ever enthralled him the way Kathy does. And as the enemy's terrifying plan is revealed, Raphael's desire could be a fatal distraction for all his kind, and for the woman he has sworn to love forever . . .

NIGHT'S PLEASURE

Desire Casts a Dark Spell . . .

Savanah Gentry's life was so much simpler when she was a reporter for the local newspaper. That was before her father's sudden death drew her into a mysterious new world she was just beginning to understand. A vampire hunter by birth, Savanah has been entrusted with a legacy that puts everyone she cares for in danger—including the seductive, sensual vampire who unleashes her most primal desires . . .

Rane Cordova has always been alone, half-hating himself for his dark gift even as he relishes its extraordinary power. But one look at Savanah fills him with the need to take everything she has to give and carry her to heights of unimagined ecstasy. And though he never intended their relationship to go this far, now Savanah is in more danger than she knows—and facing a relentless enemy determined to eliminate Rane and all his kind . . .

IMMORTAL SINS

Desire Is the Darkest Magic of All . . .

Three centuries ago, vampire Jason Rourke succumbed to temptation with a wizard's lovely daughter—and that brief taste of pleasure earned him a powerful curse. Trapped within a painting, unable to quench the hellish thirst that torments him, Jason has given up hope of escape until Karinna Adams purchases the painting and unwittingly frees him.

At first, Jason plans only to enlist Kari's help in navigating this strange new world so he can find and punish the wizard who entrapped him. But Kari's enticing sensuality and innocence incite a growing need in Jason to touch and taste her, to possess her utterly. For the gulf between them—and the danger that awaits—is nothing compared to a potent, primal hunger that will last for all eternity . . .

EVERLASTING KISS

Desire Never Dies . . .

Daisy O'Donnell doesn't get the attraction some women feel for vampires. She likes her men with a heartbeat. And she's just met one who's full of life: Erik Delacourt, the unreasonably sexy man she keeps meeting at a popular L.A. nightclub called the Crypt. She barely knows him, but there's no resisting the connection she feels . . .

There's one important detail Erik hasn't gotten around to telling her yet. He's a powerful vampire out to hunt the Blood Thief who is draining young vampires all over the city—and who has just raised the stakes by destroying one of Erik's friends. To Erik, Daisy is a bright spot of innocence in a world of darkness and menace. He'll do anything—even lie to her—to keep her safe and pure.

If only he knew that Daisy has something of her own to hide . . .

And here's a sneak peek
at the latest from Amanda,
coming in September 2011!

When Skylynn O'Brien McNamara came home to bury her grandfather and settle his estate, she was surprised to see that the house across the street was still vacant. The big, old, three-story house, surrounded by a high wrought-iron fence, sat on a half-acre lot. A covered porch spanned the front of the house. The place put her in mind of a giant among midgets, surrounded as it was by newer, smaller, more modern homes. Granda had once told her that Kaiden Thorne's grandfather had refused to sell the place to real estate developers, and so they had built around him.

Kaiden Thorne had moved away shortly before Skylynn left for college. She thought it odd that he hadn't sold the house when he moved. As far as she knew, the house had been vacant ever since.

He had been a strange one, Mr. Thorne. For years, he had collected his mail and his newspaper after dark and always mowed his front yard after the sun went down. He had gone to the high school football games, but only the ones held at night.

Sky had been five or six the first time she had seen Kaiden Thorne. She remembered it as if it had happened yesterday. She had been sitting on the front porch that summer evening, playing with her favorite Barbie dolls, when a moving van pulled into the driveway of the house across the street. Curious, she had watched two men in gray overalls jump out of the cab and begin unloading the truck. There hadn't been much in the way of furniture, just a black leather sofa and a matching chair, a couple of glass-topped end tables, a dresser and chest of drawers, and a big-screen TV. The last thing the movers had unloaded had been a large oblong box.

Skylynn had frowned when she saw it. What on earth was in there? Her interest in the new neighbor soon waned when she realized there would be no playmates her age moving into the house, only a tall man with thick black hair. At five, she had thought of Kaiden Thorne as an old man. Looking back, she realized he had probably been in his late twenties or early thirties.

Her second distinct memory of Kaiden Thorne occurred on Halloween, Sky's favorite holiday, except for Christmas, of course. Back then, everyone in the neighborhood decorated their houses, each family trying to outdo the other, but none of them could hold a candle to Mr. Thorne. His yard looked like something out of a Hammer horror movie. There had been a coffin that looked as if it was a hundred years old, a skeleton that looked so real, it had given Sky the creeps. Ancient torture devices had lined his driveway. A scary-looking clock that would have looked at home in a Vincent Price movie chimed the hours as assorted ghouls and monsters popped up out of old pirate chests and from behind weathered headstones.

Sky had been seven when her brother, Sam, took her trick-or-treating at the Thorne house. Sam had been ten at the time, and even though her brother could be a major pain, she had idolized him. He had told her, straight-faced, that Mr. Thorne was a vampire, but Skylynn hadn't believed him because Granda had told her there were no such things as vampires, witches, ghosts, ghouls, or skeletons that walked and talked. But when Mr. Thorne opened the door, Sky had taken one look at his blood-red eyes, his gleaming fangs and long black cape, and screamed bloody murder. Her brother had teased her for months about the way she had turned tail and run back home just as fast as her legs would carry her. She'd had nightmares for weeks afterward, even though her grandfather had persuaded Mr. Thorne to come over and explain that he had been wearing an elaborate costume.

As time passed, Granda and Mr. Thorne spent more and more time together. They made an odd couple—her short, gray-haired grandfather and the tall, dark-haired Mr. Thorne. As far as Sky could tell, they'd had nothing in common. Granda was a retired doctor who dabbled in chemistry and alchemy in his lab down in the basement. He had often kidded her that he was looking for the secret of eternal life. As for Mr. Thorne, she didn't know what he did for a living. For all she knew, he, too, had been retired. The two men had spent many a night locked up in Granda's lab.

More than once, she had snuck down to the basement. With her ear pressed to the door, she had caught snatches of conversation, but Granda's talk of plasma and platelets and transfusions meant nothing to her.

Occasionally, a strange man came to visit Granda. Sky never saw his face, never heard his name, but there was something about him that, even back then, had made her skin crawl.

The summer Sky turned twelve, she started spying on Mr. Thorne. She wasn't sure why. Curiosity? Boredom? Who could say? She bought a notebook and made copious notes about his habits, the cars he drove, the clothes he wore. He rarely had visitors, but when he did, she wrote down the color and make of the car and the license number and descriptions of the people who came and went so infrequently. Sam thought he was a drug dealer or a hit man.

Sky had always had a flare for art and she drew numerous pictures and portraits of the elusive Mr. Thorne. A faint white scar bisected his right cheek. He had another scar on his back near his left shoulder blade. She had seen it one night during a scavenger hunt. The last item on her list had been to find an old newspaper and she had gone knocking on Mr. Thorne's door in hopes that he could help. He had answered the door wearing a pair of swim trunks and nothing else. He had invited her to step inside while he went to fetch the paper, and she had glimpsed the scar when he turned away. As she grew older, she began to wonder how he had gotten those scars.

By the time she was thirteen, she had a full-blown crush on the mysterious Mr. Thorne. And then, when she was fifteen or sixteen, an odd thing happened. For no apparent reason, he stopped staying inside during the day.

She would never forget the Friday afternoon she had come home from school and seen him outside, mowing his lawn. Wearing only a pair of cut-off blue jeans and sunglasses, he looked sexier than any man his age had a right to.

But that had been eight years ago, and she was no longer the wide-eyed innocent child she had once been.